OF FATE & FURY

A DEADLY SIN ANTHOLOGY

LINA C. AMAREGO   CASSIDY CLARKE   CASS MAREN

C. M. MCCANN   MADDIE JENSEN   L. E. REINER

KAYLA WHITTLE

SILVER WHEEL PRESS

TO THE CYCLE-BREAKERS, MAGIC-MAKERS, & EARTH-SHAKERS.
TO THE FURIES OF HEALING & CHANGE.
WE SEE YOU.
WE ACCEPT YOU.
WE ARE YOU.

CONTENT WARNING

This book is intended for adult audiences and contains themes of abuse, addiction, death, homophobia, manipulation, mental illness, murder, panic attacks, PTSD, self-harm, suicide, and violence. Please be advised and read at your own discretion.

TABLE OF CONTENTS

Prologue

The Master of Nothing BY L.E. REINER

The Temptation of Magic BY C.M. MCCANN

Bittersweet BY MADDIE JENSEN

Lovesick BY KAYLA WHITTLE

A Million Dreams BY CASSIDY CLARKE

Refuse Thy Name BY LINA C. AMAREGO

Forget Me Not BY CASS MAREN

Sin of the Father BY LINA C. AMAREGO

PROLOGUE

We start our tale in *a* beginning.

A beginning, set in the place between nowhere and everywhere. A village, nestled gently at the boundary where the sea kissed the sky. Both a meeting of worlds and a world removed.

A beginning, written by three Fates; the keepers of eternal tomes. Neither good nor evil–they just *were*. The creators of the threads of life, they wove the stories of both men and gods.

A beginning, executed by the powers of the Four Horsemen. The tools of the cosmos—Plague, War, Famine, and Death—strode through the realms of man with purpose in their saddles. The hands of the gods, these Furies, made fast work of the divine.

In *this* beginning, there was a Fury astride a pale horse. His name was *Thanatos*, born of sorrow and woe. A man shrouded in chaos, the favorite son of the gods. With his immense power, he wandered the lands of men, the kiss of Death on his lips.

In this beginning, there was a woman. *Chara*, they called her, a mortal made from sunlight and abundance. A girl bathed in joy, an ordinary daughter of humankind. With her beauty, she stole the heart of a Fury, and turned the shadows bright.

Thanatos presented Chara with his kiss of Death, her stilled heart meant as an offering to the gods of old and the siblings he served. But Chara warmed the frozen parts of the Fury's battered soul. A union both blessed and cursed. For once the first taste of love touched Thanatos's tongue, there was no return to darkness.

In this beginning, there was a family. Chara bore Thanatos seven heirs, each endowed with their father's blood and their mother's human heart. Anointed with power and the gift of its responsibility.

The eldest, *Mnemosyne*, a young woman who could trap memories in her fingertips.

The second born, *Balshasar*, a son who turned everything he touched to golden luck.

The third child, *Erisichthon,* named by his mother's tongue, who could swallow dreams.

The fourth, *Edana*, a girl who could stir passion from the depths of any soul.

The fifth child, *Athene*, a girl who could forge illusions from the mind's eye.

The sixth, *Talitha*, a daughter who could amplify the gifts of others with a thought.

And the last, *Caedmon*, a little boy who saw people as they could be, not as they were.

And for a time, they all lived with their cups poured high, their bellies stuffed full, and their hearts blanketed in joy.

But the gods of old were dissatisfied with their fallen angel, as they had need yet for his kiss of Death. So they sent his siblings after him to collect the offering they were owed.

Erra came first with an empty regret. Famine's sharp hunger pangs stung every hollow belly until they all doubled over, clutching their middle for relief from the sister's scythe.

Resheph struck second, washing the village in a blight. The Fury of Plague held no grudge against their brother, but did not discriminate as they laid waste to his family's lungs, chests aching with coughs that never cleared.

Against his siblings' power, Thanatos held on to his family, to his wife, through the pain and suffering. The angel of Death did not let go—come Fate or Fury—of the life he'd built from the bones of the one he had before. Of the hope he'd found in his wife's eyes.

But it was *Tyr* that delivered the killing blow, the king of conflict feeding greedily from the spoils of War. A war that made enemies of head and heart. Of brothers and sisters. Of husband and wife.

When Chara took her own life, she stole the sun from the sky and cast the world in darkness once more. She killed the man that Thanatos had become, too, the ghost of the angel of Death rising from his ashes.

In this beginning, there was a tragedy. Chara abandoned Thanatos and her seven heirs, each cursed with their father's broken heart and their mother's tarnished legacy. Saddled with power and the burden to repeat their fates over and over again as penance for their sins.

Mnemosyne, the girl who could not forget. Who trapped secrets behind her smiles, hoarding them for rainy days.

Balshasar, the boy with the gilded touch. Who turned his own tender heart to stone.

Erisichthon, the son without a dream. Who swallowed his own feelings like medicine.

Edana, the girl without a companion of her own. Who stirred herself dizzy with worry.

Athene, the girl who deceived the mind. Who forged herself into a weapon to shield her own.

Talitha, the daughter made of mirrors. Who amplified her own darkest insecurities.

Caedmon, the boy that could see potential. Who saw himself in black and white, blind to the color of his own heart.

And *Thanatos,* the Fury with the kiss of Death. Who sheathed the scythe of sorrow and buried it deep in his own wounded soul.

We start our tale in *a* beginning.

A beginning, set in the place between nowhere and everywhere. A world, scattered across time and space, told through the eyes of many lifetimes and reincarnations.

A beginning, written by three Fates; the keepers of eternal tomes. Neither good nor evil–they just *were*. Creators of threads of life, they wove the stories of both men and gods.

In *this* beginning, there are seven sons and daughters of Fate and Fury. Their names are ever-changing, but they are always born of the same original sorrow and woe. A family fractured by catastrophe, the forsaken children of the cosmos. With their oppressive powers, they wander the lands of men, the stain of sin on their lips.

CHAPTER I

THE MASTER OF NOTHING

L.E. REINER

LONDON, 1846, WESTMINSTER

The walls were poison, but it would take some time before the people of London learned the truth. It was the only way to capture such a vibrant shade of green and make it last. I could not see it for myself—I hadn't seen color in over a hundred years. *Scheele's Green*, they called it, after the bastard who thought to use copper arsenite to manufacture it—the key ingredient being *arsenic*.

I ran my index finger along the floral paper of my drawing room walls, filtering through all the remembered shades of green from my past. *Which one are you?*

"Lovely wallpaper, Lord Ackerman."

I cringed at the sound of my...*guest's* mousy voice, but forced a smile, feigning pleasure. "Indeed."

No one knew I couldn't see it, so I pretended. As I pretended with most things in my life. I traced the lines of the gray ivy and avoided the blackened depths of the spaces in between—the green, which my eyes registered as charcoal.

"This colorless world gives way to loneliness," I murmured. Despite never touching the black, the void grew inside of me, threatening to devour me as it had so many times before.

No, not the void. The oblivion.

"You were saying, My Lord?"

And then, it was gone. I whipped around to my guest, replacing distress with delight. "Just a passing thought. I can't even remember what it was."

She beamed and dipped her head as her teeth sank into her bottom lip. Despite not being able to see the color of her cheeks, I knew they flushed. I knew that simpering expression all too well. It was the same look they all gave me when they suspected the rumors were true—that I was a living, breathing muse. And what else could they have expected? A visit with me often resulted in artists creating their greatest masterpieces.

I cleared my throat. "You had something you wished to show me?"

She perked up, as if she'd forgotten the reason for the visit. "Of course."

I slinked into the black abyss of my velvet sofa. Or rather, crimson, from what I'd been told. My body settled into the crevice frequent lounging created, and I started spinning my Thaumatrope —a paper disk that created an illusion from pictures on either side when it was spun. Like a man riding a horse. Or a fish in a bowl.

I was partial to the bird and the cage.

Finally, my guest lifted a canvas, breaking my concentration and striking horror within me.

"What do you think? It's you!"

"I..." Words evaded me, at least socially acceptable ones. I set my Thaumatrope aside and cleared my throat. Her elation started to settle. "Forgive me, I just...you mentioned a fondness for landscapes last we spoke."

"Yes, well...inspiration had other plans for me." That ingratiating stare reemerged, and my skin crawled.

I never said I inspired fantastic work. Only work within that individual's skill set, and many so-called *artists* had wasted their time and money in my company. As a small consolation in those moments —where the outcome was abysmal—I reminded myself of the works I had inspired that moved me. Beethoven's last five piano sonatas, composed after his hearing failed him, for example. Dante Alighieri's Divine Comedy. Primavera by Sandro Botticelli, commissioned by the Medici after word traveled that he'd been in my company for a short time.

They didn't know the truth behind my curse. A curse disguised as a gift.

"You hate it," she said.

"No. You flatter me."

I groaned while swinging my legs from their perch on one of my throw pillows and stood with all my effort. My guest drained more from me than most others. Whether she needed more inspiration or she simply bored me to no end, I didn't care to speculate.

I dragged my sluggish legs across the Axminster carpet, which I'd been told was cream and gold with aubergine flourishes. I lifted the canvas high, hiding my face and the distaste that spread like a sickness.

The painting was varying shades of gray, though black dominated the canvas. Somehow I knew it was not from my inability to see color, but simply the chosen color palette.

My appearance—much like my vision—was just a blend of black, gray, and white. Colorless, meaningless. I wished I could say that true beauty was found within, but the oblivion forming inside of me contradicted that belief.

I lowered the canvas. "Is this for me to keep?"

"If you'd like it," she said through a grin.

"I would." *Mostly so that no other person should ever see it*, I thought while sinking back into the perfect crevice of my sofa. "I shall hang it in my library."

"Now you flatter me, My Lord."

Do shut up.

I did not say those words, but instead hummed in mock delight. As a bell from the foyer rang, I dropped my head back—fighting an audible groan until my butler, Albert, appeared in the doorway with a young woman beside him.

My head whipped up again, ready to start Act II.

"Master Ackerman, Miss Scarlet Everly."

Despite my propensity for acting, I couldn't keep at the charade. "I'm afraid I don't know who you are."

"She's my cousin, here to escort me home," my guest announced while standing, and I was torn equally between clapping my hands in victory and reprimanding the unwelcome intrusion.

"Dearest cousin," I drawled while exhausting my remaining efforts in standing once more. *Up and down, up and down—round and round we go in this indomitable circus we hold for the crows.*

The young woman cowered as I approached and dipped her head. "I didn't mean to intrude. My cousin and I are needed elsewhere—"

I waved my hand. "No harm done." My shaking fingers reached for my guest's elbow to escort her and quicken their departure. With my legs heavy like lead and my heart rapidly hammering in my chest, I'd clearly reached my limit. "I do not wish to keep you ladies from your pressing schedule."

My guest looped her arm through mine. "Lord Ackerman, will you be attending the exhibition at the Royal Academy of Arts this weekend?"

"Will you be presenting?" I asked, nearly cringing at the honey dripping from my tongue.

She giggled. "More flattery." *No.* "I'm afraid I've yet to reach that level of distinction." *Nor will you ever, I'm afraid.* "My cousin and I will be there, should you make an appearance..." My eyes met with the cousin's, and any remaining shred of resolve I had drained from me.

The gray ivy ripped from its tomb in the walls, ensnaring me wholly—wrapping around my limbs to drag me back into the oblivion.

Please, no.

They did not see it coil around me. Only when they turned to leave did my body fight the paralytic that surged through me, and I snatched the cousin's wrist—as one grabs a branch from the shore before being drowned by the tides.

They gasped. But there it was, clear as day and hanging from the lobe of her ear like a teardrop.

Her earring—the first color I'd seen in over one hundred years.

I almost didn't recognize it, and I held my breath as the words filtered through my mind. Blue.

No, not just blue. *Cerulean.*

"You're hurting me," she gasped.

"Where did you get that earring?"

"Let go of me!" She ripped her wrist from my grasp as my guest intervened, grabbing her cousin's arm and escorting her from my drawing room. "What sort of company do you keep?"

My guest craned her neck to me and offered a whispered apology before disappearing from sight. Perhaps my position as a viscount encouraged her to do so.

Had I been hallucinating? Or had I really seen color for the first time in a century?

"Master?"

I stiffened at the weary, croaky voice from the doorway. "Albert."

"Shall I turn down your bed, sir?"

My frantic eyes darted across the gray and black—*the green*—wallpaper, then regarded my perfectly pitted black—*crimson*—sofa. The comfort that I'd sought throughout my afternoon calls had fled with the cerulean earring, and only despair remained.

I grimaced. "Yes. I cannot sleep here tonight." I brushed past him, my stride a bit lighter and quicker than before, but my head grew heavy—foggy from the events of the day. And from all those who I *inspired.*

~

I SLEPT FITFULLY for three days. Were it not for my dreams of cerulean, I may have sunk deep into darkness and lost myself to nightmares—inky black visions of monsters and shadows, of sickness and death.

I remembered everything—every gruesome detail of my life save for my childhood. I'd been Caedmon back then, changing my name to Cardan when I cut ties with my past.

My six siblings had grown to be nothing more than tiny little scratches in the foundations of my mind—scratches that when acknowledged irked me to no end. Like the crevices engrained in hardwood when scuffed without care, splintered and ever present. My brother, Eris, grated my mind more than the others. His very existence made a mockery of me. Because all good things I collected throughout my life, I gave as sources of inspiration to others, leaving me hollow. Yet he only took them away.

But this little bit of light—the little bit of good I found in the form of a cerulean teardrop— that I could not give up to anyone. Because the last time I saw color was the last time I saw *Them*.

It was in France in 1720. I'd spent a harrowing few decades within the confines of the Bastille at the order of the sovereign himself, Louis XIV. Perhaps I grew too chummy with the bastard, inspired one too many grand ideas for the palace of Versailles. One moment I was sipping champagne, and the next, I had a mask slapped over my face. Which, contrary to popular belief, was not iron. Nor did I have to wear it all the time. The mask was merely to keep my *identity* hidden. For my own benefit, he'd said, but I knew the truth. He feared the wrong person might discover my *talents* and exploit them—inspiring an uprising against the monarchy.

Though it wasn't all bad. I spent my days lazing about, playing chess with approved visitors, reading, drawing, writing. For decades, I enjoyed peace.

Until someone from my past decided to step in.

"Do you plan on pouting in solitude to get what you want?

Hiding away in confinement to avoid what's destined to be, dear nephew?"

I dropped my head back onto the stone wall of my cell, bathing my metal shield in the moonlight breaking through the bars.

"Love the mask," the voice of my visitor added.

"I think it suits me." Finally, I turned my gaze. "Resheph." Heterochromatic eyes stared back at me. It never mattered that I couldn't see color–my father's sibling always had colored, glowing eyes. One green and one blue. Preferring androgyny—as gender was a construct of the human mind, Resheph used to say—they presented as the perfect blend of all things. Caring, nurturing, yet somehow without room for question or doubt–there was an intense sort of calm within them.

Like one would see before a brutal storm.

"Indeed, it does suit you," they said, their voice genial.

I swallowed the lump growing in my throat. And they watched every movement I made, like a hawk watching their prey. I knew better than to spew venom at one of the Furies despite our close familial relations. But the pain caused by their existence often splintered any resolve I managed to find.

I forced a laugh to hide my grief. "I assume that since you're here, Resheph, France is about to be stricken by a terrible plague."

"You cannot stay here."

"I know." *But I want to.*

They extended their hand and clenched my shoulder, and I turned my head away from the extension of affection–body tensing beneath the comfort of it.

"I will take care of this."

It was not long after Resheph disappeared with the shadows, chased away by the sun's rays, that word of the sovereign falling ill began to travel. The great King himself succumbed to gangrene not long after.

After my release, I kept myself in a perpetual state of drunken foolery and in the company of French idealists along the way.

Rumors had traveled that a muse lived in Paris, inspiring artists and architects—musicians, writers, and the like.

"Monsieur Deveraux," a young mistress cooed as I traipsed through the corridors of the Château de Saint-Cloud.

Chandeliers lined the hall, hung from ornate carvings of what I assumed to be gold—as were most embellishments of the era. Separating each ornate fixture that dangled from the ceiling by a thick strand of velvet fabric were murals of clouds.

How I longed to see color.

Already drunk on champagne, my eyes struggled to make out details of my monochromatic world through the firelight of the Château when a deep, velvety voice called to me from the darkness, "You're the one they call Muse."

"And you're the one lurking in the shadows."

He stepped forward, and my muscles tensed when he emerged. Though devoid of color like all things, there was no mistaking his features for anything but striking.

My person changed with every life cycle—every rebirth they encountered. They were my tether. My heart was bound to their soul —it didn't matter the physical manifestation.

"Why do I feel like I've met you already?" he asked.

"We've met many times before."

He stopped only inches away from me. In that incarnation, he towered over me, and I could tell by the lighter shades of gray that his long, unkempt curly hair was blonde.

His eyes narrowed. "Your dialect is—"

"Strange, I'm sure. I am English." A mischievous grin disturbed his pensive expression, and I noted, "Your dialect is not Parisian at all."

"I am from a small commune called Saint-Émilion." I was taken with his words—enamored with the way his lips moved as he spoke them. His voice, guttural yet listless in his pronunciation—a perfection I could never attain in speaking his native tongue no matter the effort.

From the corner of my eye, movement grasped my attention. A drapery of gossamer blew with the warm evening wind, and I could not bite back a smile when I noticed it was no longer deep gray but rose pink. "Tell me," I drawled to my tether, "what is it you want from this life?"

"I do not know all that I want. But I do know what I desire at any given moment."

My breath hitched as he dipped his face closer to mine. "And what do you desire now?" I crooned.

"Right now?" I didn't dare speak with his lips so close, hovering over mine. I only nodded. "I desire to know all your secrets. Sing in me, Muse. And through me..."

"Tell a story," I hummed, delighted.

His arm snaked around my waist and pulled me into the warmth of his firm body—the very feeling igniting my flesh. "Show me all the ways you can inspire me." His eyes pulsed—glowed like fiery emeralds.

"Your eyes are green."

His mouth enveloped mine, and I inhaled a sharp breath of him —needing him like a drowning man needed oxygen.

His name was Manon. We didn't speak much the rest of the night—words were inconsequential between us.

I awoke the following morning surrounded by an array of sumptuous colors—glorious hues I'd been denied for so long. There were so many that I could not identify all the boudoir had to offer. It left me breathless, the way they merged and melted together—so saturated and rich, full of something I knew nothing about. The whorls of pink and gold met with white clouds and blue skies. Through the cream gossamer draperies, even more colors funneled through my vision, dizzying me.

I thought I wanted to see them again—all the colors of the world and the beauty they had to offer. But my heart hammered in my chest, making it difficult to catch my breath.

It was an ambush, an onslaught of variety overwhelming my

senses. It burned my very eyes. As if I'd been living underground for so long, and I'd finally caught a glimpse of the sun.

My breath hitched. Manon rested beside me—the perfect curves of his body displayed, painted in the sun with not a hint of black or gray in sight.

And yet...it grew within me. The oblivion, forming in the very depths of me and coiling around my heart—the one thing that tethered me to Manon's soul. I'd lost him before, so many times.

In the previous life, he'd been Maria.

Before that, Elantine.

Cassian.

Adele.

Maxson.

Felix, Sophia, Rosalie, Julian.

And before all of them, Samara.

I threw the fawn-colored linens from my body and sat at the edge of the chaise. Despite all the color Manon brought back into my life, I left him there.

He died in Marseille from the plague a month later.

I STRAIGHTENED my tailcoat in the mirror with a grimace so distinct my muscles went sore. It was dirty, dingy, and wrinkled beyond salvation. Having avoided most social gatherings for close to five years, my evening wear left something to be admired.

"Master Ackerman, I...*oh.*"

I turned my gaze over my shoulder to my faithful butler, who hung his head to avoid my eye. "Oh, out with it. It's terrible."

"No, sir."

"Don't lie to me," I stormed past him. It *was* terrible, but it was too short a notice to do anything about it—not that I cared enough to put forth the effort even if I could.

I hurried down the steps and snatched my walking stick as Albert kept on my heels. "I won't be out late."

He placed my hat on my head, and I whipped my scarf over my face as I left.

The Royal Academy of Arts was not a long carriage ride, though I debated even entering once we arrived. Members of high society donned in their finest evening wear sauntered about—some coming and going, others dilly-dallying and making my exit from the carriage even more daunting.

"Right." I thrust my back into my seat. "Take me home." I tapped the brass handle of my walking stick into the carriage wall. As it lurched forward, my heart stilled and dropped into the pit of my core.

I did all I could to keep my gaze from the Academy, but the further the carriage traveled, the faster my heart drummed. And my soul cried out in a manner that ignited a panic and clawed its way out from my throat in the form of the word, "Stop!"

I relied heavily on my walking stick while approaching the Academy. Despite wearing composure like a mask, my body trembled with every heavy step I took. Leaving incited anxiety because I knew what could happen as a result. But approaching inspired dread.

Public places always took a toll on me, physically as well as emotionally, thanks to what others demanded of me. In previous periods of my life, I'd used alcohol to dull the senses, but I'd discovered that it negatively impacted the people around me, inspiring them to recklessness. I then decided to try opium, but found myself in the company of inspired individuals too dizzied to do anything with their talents.

My presence persuaded good and bad behavior alike. As if I needed any other reason to *loathe* myself.

I declined giving up my hat and coat; without them, I'd be easier to identify. The fewer people who noticed me, the less energy I'd need to expend. Instead of offering greetings and gestures of friendship to any of the aristocrats fluttering about, I wove in between them—moved through them like a phantom.

In the main viewing hall, paintings covered the walls from floor to ceiling with the same monochromatic palette I'd grown accustomed to observing. Meanwhile, those present admired and discussed various works while others lounged in the seating area, drinking and laughing boisterously.

It was a place to socialize and be merry. But, mostly, it was a bunch of wealthy people bolstering their own egos and debating who was the wealthiest among them.

My eyes cut through the crowd in search of cerulean—the tiniest glimmer of hope hidden amongst the greediest parasites London had to offer, though I doubted it'd be easy to find.

Across the hall, I caught sight of my mousy guest from days prior. I debated even approaching with other ladies in her company, but she was my only lifeline. The only source I had to find my tether.

I sauntered through the crowd again, keeping my head down and my top hat tipped low on my brow. I brushed through bushels of crinoline and maneuvered around gentlemen carrying glasses of brandy. It was not proper for a single man to approach a group of women uninvited, so instead, I positioned myself at a painting directly beside them.

It was a portrait of a woman. From the looks of it, a member of the royal family. I regarded the painting with *great interest*, as if oblivious to the chattering group of ladies in fits of giggles from gossip when I heard a gasp.

"Lord Ackerman?"

The show begins. I craned my head, my eyes widening in mock surprise. "Oh. Hello." I faltered. "Lovely to see all of you." The words were strained, meager—as if I were but a mouse in a den of vipers.

"I'll admit, I'm surprised to see you here! You didn't seem so interested last we spoke."

"I am always interested in discussing art with artists such as yourself." I bowed my head; they swooned. The act continued despite my moment of weakness, though it could not go on for long. Already, I felt vitality leaving my body—as if their batting lashes and quickened breaths beckoned more from me than usual. "And, uh... where might your cousin be? You did say she'd be here."

Too direct, too desperate. I couldn't think clearly with my head fogging.

Her eyes flitted over the crowd. "Oh, she's here somewhere."

"I really must apologize for my behavior—I was quite rude at our first meeting."

One of them giggled. "You, Lord Ackerman? I simply can't imagine."

"It's true, I admit. I was not myself."

"Oh, there she is!"

My heartbeat in my ears muted all other sounds. Through the mesh of gray and white gowns and black suits, a breathtaking sight emerged—shredding through the insipid exhibition.

Yellow.

No, not just yellow. Canary. The gown had a sweeping sort of majesty to it—whether it was because it was the only color I saw or because *she* wore it, I wasn't sure. My eyes traced upwards to a neckline festooned with flowers. She wore her hair up in curls, accentuating a slender neck bedecked with amber jewels. I wondered if there was a way to restore color to her completely.

I'd live in a world so drab if only I could see *her* in full color.

"What was her name?" I asked.

"Scarlet."

The Fates had a sick sense of humor—that I already knew. "Ladies, do enjoy your evening." I brushed past them before they could say a word.

I met with more obstacles trying to reach Scarlet. The crowd seemed to flourish, making it more difficult to pass through unnoticed and with ease.

"Lord Ackerman, how do you do?"

"Very well, and you?" I managed. But despite having trained as an understudy at the Globe Theater during the original production of Romeo and Juliet, even I could not feign interest in discussion.

Though, memories of my acting days forced me to grin.

"Why must I fill the role of Juliet?"

The great William Shakespeare leered. *"Because you're so pretty."*

I was sad when he died. One of the few friends I'd lost that actually troubled me.

My eyes fixated on the yellow, even when Scarlet started moving away from me—it only motivated me to push harder through the exuberant crowd.

"Excuse me, you're blocking my—" A violent thrust to my side cut off my words. The exhibition had taken a drastic turn—the patrons' discussions of art and politics escalating to drunken buffoonery and obnoxious laughter. "Watch where you're going," I snapped at the offender.

"Apologies, My Lord."

But Scarlet was getting away. I saw only the faintest glimmer of canary silk disappear through a doorway across the hall. If I lost sight of her, I might never be able to find her through the chaos. The crowd devoured me. They laughed, as if mocking me. Teasing me for my failed efforts to reach her.

Desperate times called for desperate measures. It wasn't just about finding Scarlet now, but getting away from the leeches that sucked and pulled every ounce of ambition from my bones.

I whipped my walking stick into the kneecap of a particularly unruly guest—Lord Caraway—known for his lascivious and vulgar nature. He crumbled, shouting expletives to the ceiling.

I feigned concern. "Oh dear, is there a doctor in the house?"

The crowd parted around us, giving me a clear route of escape. No one suspected me, at least not outwardly.

I emerged from the viewing hall into a corridor, taking heavy breaths to remedy the haze muddying my mind. There were far fewer parties funneling through the passageways between smaller viewing rooms. I hurried past them in search of complete solitude to recuperate when I crashed into a figure turning the corner.

Color flooded my vision. Canary silk and amber pendants. I'd found her—collided with her. As pristine as I'd ever seen her and emblazoned with gold—fitting for the pedestal on which she belonged.

Her eyes narrowed. "You."

And then, all the romanticism fled on swift wings. The sharpness of her tongue enraged me. "Ah," I spat back. "*You.*" As if I hadn't been chasing her glorious shades of yellow through a horde of madness and debauchery.

"What are you doing here?"

The words jumbled at the base of my tongue. I swung my cane swiftly into the frame of a painting to our left. "Admiring the art. What else?"

"You're not following me, are you?"

The audacity! "Madam, you flatter yourself."

"Well, seeing as how you never offered an apology for your behavior the other night, I just assumed you might attempt at some point." I stiffened, fighting every impulse inside of me to retort with equal amounts of venom. "I don't forgive you, by the way."

"You *don't*," I reiterated, astounded.

"No, of course not. Why should I?"

"I...because it was an accident!"

She laughed. Confusion eclipsed my anger. "Bumping into someone is an accident. Spilling your drink is an accident. Grabbing them—"

"An act taken out of context—"

"Then enlighten me. In what circumstance, what...*context* is it acceptable to put your hands on a woman?"

I gritted my teeth. "I'm sorry."

"You mustn't tell lies, My Lord. It's unbecoming of a gentleman." My mouth unhinged. Before I could think of anything to say, she turned away from me and proceeded down the hall, leaving me in awe.

Just leave her be. "I can't, I—" Once more, words stilled on my tongue. The painting I had just assaulted demanded all my attention.

For a moment, I forgot how to breathe when color blossomed like flowers at the dawn of spring. Various shades of purple and pink —lilac, lavender, coral, and peach overtook the painting of a garden, and my breath shook.

"Wait!"

THE EVENING HAD GROWN CHILLIER—THE cold air stinging my throat and lungs with every heavy breath I took to catch up to her.

"Did you not bring a coat?" I called to her.

"You *are* following me!" she barked over her shoulder.

"Only to right this misunderstanding!"

"Oh, just leave me be—I don't care enough to discuss the matter any further!"

Aristocrats in passing craned their necks to us, disapproving of the spectacle. In those moments I grew to miss the effects of drugs and alcohol—sobriety brought an onslaught of negative emotions with it. Shame and humiliation, for example.

"Scarlet—"

She stopped so abruptly that I nearly crashed into her. Her thin lips and narrowed eyes made me recoil. "That is *Miss Everly* to you, Mister...Mister..." She searched for the memory of my name.

"*Lord*—"

"No, I don't care what your name is," she stammered, throwing her hands outward in indignation. "You're rude. You are coarse, and you are conceited, and I bid you good night, *sir*." Her tone willed me into silence. As she spun away from me, I remained rooted in place.

Once more, confusion eclipsed all other emotions. Color had

started to return, yes, but our interactions were forced and volatile, leaving me questioning every little thing, every thought.

Could I be wrong again? Could it be...like it was with Maria?

Shouts and cries coming from up the street disrupted my intrusive thoughts. Horse hooves cantering on cobblestone beckoned my attention to a mob of aristocrats darting out of the way as two horses rounded the corner, dragging behind them a carriage with no coachman.

The vessel tilted from the sharp turn—balancing precariously on the right side's wheels as the horses charged down the street. I dragged my gaze to where Scarlet hurried across—only finding her through the mass of frenzied people because of the canary silk.

She can't see. "Scarlet!" I shouted. *She won't make it across!*

As the crowd hurried from the road to make way for the incoming carriage, I felt more drawn to her than ever before—even the presence of color didn't beckon me so much as the moment where I pictured horses trampling her, stamping out the fire burning within her and covering her color with the black and gray filth of the London streets.

"Fates be damned!"

Pain shot through the soles of my feet and into my legs with every quickened, heavy step I took. The frigid air burned my lungs, and my heart hammered so fiercely in protest to the exertion that my body trembled the closer I came.

The horses approached with the same horrifying presence as so many tragic accidents and incidents from previous lives—a vengeful Plague, an enraged fire, a perilous river, Famine, War, killing after killing, death after death—all at the hands of my very own kin.

My body went cold—all senses numb as I tore my eyes from the horse-drawn carriage barreling toward us.

I was not yet strong enough to face the oblivion, but I somehow managed to find the strength to pull her out of its way when I wrapped my arms around her waist and tackled her to the other side of the street.

The horses passed, and I shielded her from the aftermath as death licked my spine and continued on its path of destruction.

Scarlet's heavy breaths warmed my neck. I picked up my head and stared down at her wide eyes. Globs of black and gray coated the canary silk—mud from the streets. But before I pulled away, her hand clenched my arm.

"Why bother...risking your life for me?"

Because I love you. "To prove that I was right. There are circumstances in which it's acceptable to put your hands on a woman. Such as this."

Her eyes narrowed. "Why do I feel like I've met you before?"

The words weakened me, disarmed me of any remaining wit I had. With just those words, certainty chased my doubt like light chases a ghost. She was my person. My tether. She was *Them*.

I FELL in love with a painter in 1507. It was the sort of love that broke me apart and put me back together again—one that magnetized yet repelled me at the same time. The village was Anghiari, and the Tuscan sun warmed me in ways I never experienced—burning the frigid nothingness from my bones.

I smelled the wisteria before I saw its purpled majesty spilling from a drab wicker basket. I chased the vibrancy through the shadowed alleys created by the steep, stone buildings that once made up a military stronghold. The cobblestone streets, now favoring artists over strategists, caught the toe of my boot, yanking me to the ground.

My head whipped upward; my eyes fixed on the insipid passerby devouring the vitality of the flowers. "Wait!" I shouted in my atrocious Florentine dialect, but all inspiration evaded me when I lost sight of my beacon.

The beauty of Anghiari enraptured me—the sights, the smells, the sounds. But now was the dawn of dreamers—of poets and painters, musicians and inventors. Their very spirit drained me of everything I had—any shred of vigor pumping through my veins and powering my heart, I gave it all to them begrudgingly.

Exhausted, I hung my head and touched my forehead to the cool cobblestone beneath me. Defeated, uninspired—I convinced myself I was not yet ready to experience my tether in this life.

But...visions of purple polluted my mind. My understanding of color was basic—rudimentary at best, as I'd lost the ability to see color many centuries before and only caught glimpses since. The wisteria was not just purple, though.

Just as I knew the sky was not just blue.

The woman carrying the wisteria had arrived just before me. I stood in the doorway and watched as she offered the basket to a dainty yet determined set of hands reaching down from a stepstool. I followed the trail of purple to delicate lips that curled upward from the flowers' scent. But as beautiful as the creature was, my breath caught in my throat as select portions of a fresco behind her sprang to life.

I gasped. *"Signora!"* My voice startled her, echoing throughout the studio and forcing a gasp from both of them. I pointed to the fresco. "What color is that?"

"Are you blind?" she replied in a smoky voice, deep and velvety, similar to a glass of chianti. "It is green."

"That is not just green," I countered, "but something much more significant."

A smirk quirked on her perfect lips, and she pulled a paintbrush from behind her ear. "Terra verte." She climbed down from her step stool, and it was only then I noticed her curly black hair flowed freely past her shoulders. She only wore a corset and skirt that fell to her ankles. I watched her delicate bare feet as she padded toward me. "It's also known as verona." The very same green I grew curious about streaked her arms.

She stopped inches away from me. Though she remained in

varied shades of gray, black, and white, she held my attention over the lively wisteria and paint. *"Bellissima."*

∾

I DRAGGED my finger along the gray ivy imbued in the wallpaper of my drawing room, focused on trying to remember every shade of green I ever bore witness to in my life.

"Terra verte."

"You say something, My Lord?"

I dropped my hand and whipped around to my butler in the doorway. "Albert. Has anyone come to call?"

A moment of hesitation—perhaps even confusion. "Uh...no, sir."

I sucked in a sharp breath of air through my nose. It had been two days since the incident at the Royal Academy, and *Miss Everly* had yet to extend her gratitude in a suitable manner.

"No calls, then?"

He shook his head. "No, sir."

Ungrateful! I brushed past him while exiting the drawing room. "I'm going to bed."

"At this hour, sir?"

I halted on the stairs, my eyes darting to the tall-case clock in my foyer. Three in the afternoon. I drummed my fingers on the wooden banister, contemplating. "Now's as good a time as any." Before ascending any further, I whipped around to him—pointing a stiff finger at the door. "If anyone comes to call, send them away. I don't wish to receive guests for the remainder of the day."

"Yes, sir."

"Especially a *Miss Scarlet Everly*, do you understand?" He nodded, and I perhaps lingered a bit longer than necessary to test his resolve. "No matter what she says—"

"I will send her away, sir."

"Very good."

. . .

I SLEPT FITFULLY THAT AFTERNOON, which angered me. Sleep was the one thing I found solace in—a sliver of peace in the madness and calamity of the world and a talent I spent centuries perfecting. I mastered the art of passing unwanted time with fantastical dreams, yet since my first encounter with Scarlet, anxiety plagued me while lounging in my bed. Hours passed before I resigned myself to insomnia.

With wrinkled clothes and disheveled hair, I padded down the creaking hardwood stairs to retreat to my sofa instead.

"Good evening, My Lord."

I ground my palm into my eye. "Albert. Did anyone come to call while I slept?"

"Yes, sir."

My heart shuddered. "Who?"

"A Miss Scarlet Everly," he said with a proud smile, and I stiffened.

"She did?"

"Yes, sir."

"And you...?"

He beamed with pride. "Sent her away, just as you asked."

"I see." I rocked back on my heels, my gaze dragging to the bay windows of my drawing room. The thick draperies shielded any view of the street outside, but I knew they bustled with evening foot traffic. "When did she leave?"

He contemplated, then shrugged. "Not five minutes ago—" He'd hardly spoken before I was in the hall with my evening coat and top hat in hand. He hurried behind me, the picture of harried confusion. "Your walking stick, sir!"

I snatched it from him.

My eyes flitted every which way as I started in the direction of Lambeth—unsure of what drew me to that particular borough. But with only intuition guiding me, the further I walked, the more disillusioned I became, until a woman in passing grazed my shoulder with hers.

My initial reaction was to recoil at the unwelcome contact, but then I noticed the emerald green feather protruding from her hat. Like me, she headed in the direction of Lambeth, and so I soldiered on. As I walked, I noticed more flourishes of color—small nuances I might otherwise have missed if not so desperate for a sign. Crimson roses from a nearby vendor, the lush, earthy green hedges of the gardens—only vaguely illuminated by street lamps scattered along the sidewalks.

And then, *her*. In a periwinkle gown with a robin's egg coat and bonnet. And for the first time, the color of her hair came to life.

Gold, like the sun.

"Miss Everly?"

She slinked away from the street vendor, her weary eyes meeting with mine, and for a moment, it seemed as if she brightened at the sight of me.

She straightened. "Lord Ackerman."

"I see you remembered my name."

"Yes, my cousin has aided my memory."

I contemplated asking why she came to call or pretending our meeting was a happy coincidence. But as I opened my mouth to speak, she continued.

"I came to call on you not long ago. I...wanted to thank you for what you did for me at the Royal Academy the other night."

"It was nothing."

"It was everything," she countered, and it was only then I noticed the distress in her eyes. "When I think of what could have happened if you hadn't been paying attention—"

"Best not to think about such things." Still, she seemed troubled. "Is everything all right?"

"I, uh...seem to have...gotten lost. The streets look so different at night."

"I'd be happy to help you find your way. I know London's streets better than anyone."

"I'd hate to be an imposition."

I tossed my walking stick into the other hand and offered her my elbow. "It would be much more imposing wondering if you made it home safely." She smiled before looping her arm in mine.

Foot traffic decreased once we crossed over into Lambeth, but in exchange we were met with darker roadways and the abysmal dwelling spaces of London's proletariat.

"You say you were lost. I take it you're not from London, then?"

"I'm from Gloucester, but I'm here visiting family and staying with my uncle. He works long hours—a business owner—so he's asked me to tend to things while he's away."

"Your stay is temporary, then?"

"I'd like to stay in London. There's so much to see and do. Though, I suppose if my uncle grows tired of my company, I shall have to return." We walked in silence for a long while, the news of her impending departure weighing on me like poverty weighed on Whitechapel. "Are you from London, My Lord?"

I inhaled a sharp breath. "You may call me Cardan. And my life is...a bit complicated. I was not born in London, but I've lived here for a very long time."

"Where were you born?"

I hummed through a forced smile. "I don't even remember the name of the village, if I'm being honest." We fell into silence once more, and I felt foolish for bringing the conversation to a screeching halt. Talking about my past always proved difficult.

"I heard that you once denied a visit with the Queen."

I did a double take. "Where did you hear that?"

"My cousin told me. I thought it was just a rumor, but..." Her eyes widened. "You did, didn't you? Only *you* would."

"I've had less than desirable encounters with royals."

She snorted. "She is the Queen of England."

"And a wonderful pen pal, I might add." Once more, she laughed. It was a sound I could listen to all night. "What is it that you want from this life?"

"What?"

"Your life? What do you plan to accomplish?"

A moment of contemplation passed. "You have to promise you won't think me foolish."

"I can't promise something like that; I haven't the faintest idea what you're going to say." Her eyes sliced into me like a dagger into my heart, and I certainly knew the feeling from my time spent in Rome. Such a violent era. "I'm sorry."

"You're incorrigible."

"I'll admit, I've been called worse."

"Such as?"

"A charlatan."

"Are you not?"

I twisted my neck to her, regarding her momentarily while biting back a cheeky remark. Instead, I chose to refocus our conversation. "You were saying?"

Whimsy replaced skepticism. "I want to fall madly in love."

How dreadful. "And get married, no doubt."

"Of course I want to get married. I do want children."

"Love is strenuous—taxing on the heart and soul. Wouldn't it be wiser in this day and age to marry for money?"

"I don't care about money."

"Then it's clear you've never been without."

She scoffed. "That's rich coming from a viscount."

But it wasn't always so, yet I had no way to defend my stance. How could I tell her I had spent centuries in poverty before choosing to exploit my curse for profit, when she still believed the basis was rooted in superstition?

She stopped at a set of steps leading to a townhouse and removed her arm from mine. I did not wish to discuss the matter any further, but she wore a smug smile, waiting for my retort.

"Love is brutal."

"It's beautiful—"

"It is unkind."

"Have you ever been in love?" she asked.

I hesitated. My mind raced with possible responses; in the end, I had nothing to offer but a bewildered laugh. Then it hit me, and I furrowed my brow. "Have you?" I asked, more accusatory than curious.

"No," she began. "But I dream about it quite frequently. In my dreams, there's someone I love very much. I don't know who he is—I can never see his face, but...I know him, and I know that I love him."

Intrigued, I closed the gap between us. "How do you know it's love if you've never loved before?"

"I don't know. Just a feeling, I suppose." I lost her to a daydream. "But, when I find him, then he shall be the one I marry."

She turned away from me and ascended the steps. I almost followed her before catching myself, saying instead, "So you suspect this phantom is real?"

"He has to be. I believe it to be true."

"And what if he's me?"

She dipped her head. Yet even in the darkness of the night, I detected a slight grin before she met my gaze again. "If you want me to marry *you*, perhaps consider making me fall in love. Good night, My Lord."

But I wasn't ready to let her leave. I gripped the wrought iron fence around the flower bed and pulled myself closer. "Call on me tomorrow."

She frowned. "Lord Ackerman. If you wish to see me tomorrow, then it is you who must call on me." She tipped her head before disappearing inside, leaving words hanging on my lips.

I HARDLY NOTICED the shadows devouring every last bit of firelight from the streets on my venture home—having lost myself to fantasies of my tether. It was only when the head of my walking stick started to reverberate against my gloved palm that my senses flooded back to me in an onslaught of dread.

Darkness surrounded me, but it wasn't the oblivion. The scent of evergreens and freshly damp soil invaded my nostrils—the intrusion so potent I tasted the dirt on my tongue.

I halted my stride as the sweet aroma of freshly bloomed roses flourished beneath my nose. It was not pleasure I found while planting both my hands firmly upon the head of my walking stick, but annoyance.

"I suppose it was only a matter of time."

A low, velvety chuckle from behind. "You don't sound very happy to hear from me, Cardan."

"Should I be?" Like a breeze at the dawn of spring, the Fate closed in on me—beckoning my reach for warmth. I met with his glowing verdant eyes—that same impish grin he always wore when intruding upon my peace.

Just like all of our encounters before, he dressed according to the times—always at the height of fashion as well. Practically peacocking in his evening attire, the Fate tipped his hat with his gloved hand. "Hello, little one. It's been some time."

"Ninety-seven years, to be exact. Danome."

He gleamed. "You remembered."

"It is my curse. I remember everything." I soldiered onward, challenging him to follow, and I knew he would.

"All this time, and it saddens me to say that you still don't know what your curse truly is. Have you learned nothing over the lifetimes you've lived? Gathered no further knowledge of what it is you are?"

I spun to him. "And what, pray tell, am I?"

Danome lifted his glass-head walking stick to my chin—encouraging me to *look up*, as always. "A god amongst men."

"I don't feel very divine."

"Not yet, but you will!" he insisted while bringing his hand to my shoulder, either to stop me from leaving or to create a bond. "You're very close this time—I can feel it."

For as long as I *could* remember, I remembered him—wiping my tears after my mother died and my family fell apart. I was so little, but he always made sure I had food and water, shelter. And yet, I still grew to hate him. I shucked off his hand.

"A trick, no doubt. To keep me in this cursed loop you *Fates* gain so much pleasure from."

"Has everything I've ever said to you been trickery?" I snorted, mostly to perturb him, but the truth was, I wasn't sure. I didn't know anything anymore after what happened with *Maria*. At the very thought of her, the oblivion eclipsed my heart. "Cardan?" he called after me. "Please pay attention to the world around you. You spend far too much time in your head. A life in your mind does not equate to a life fully lived out here," he said while motioning around him—as if showing me the world for the first time. "You cannot resign yourself to inaction in all things."

Danome's warning crawled up my spine like a spider, raising the hair along my body. I did not cower before him, only continued my stride to Westminster, and when far enough away from the smell of a fresh spring morning and soggy woodlands, I sharply inhaled the putrid stench of London's streets.

It was only then the street lights illuminated once more, this time pulsing in an unmistakable tangerine glow.

I'd rented a room in Anghiari but only frequented it out of necessity —in moments where my energy had been depleted so excessively by my artist, I could no longer keep my eyes open.

I called her *Tesoro*—my darling.

She demanded much from me, and I gave her everything I had—though her assistant was kind enough to replenish me with food and wine most evenings. Despite that, if my Tesoro asked me to slit my throat because she needed more red paint, I probably would have.

Just as lively as her paintings, she matched their spirit and vigor without fail. The most beautiful addict I'd ever encountered was an artist addicted to their craft—an addict who only needed a canvas and paint, or a parchment and ink, a marble slab and a pick—the latter having a sort of carnal violence that always excited and terrified me.

I fell in love with her, yes. But in just one sentence, she collapsed the foundation I built for her when she said the words, "I've never met anyone like you before." And I realized I had made an egregious error.

I started at the sound of rapping at my door. Blackness blanketed the sky, and my heart jolted in my throat at the sight—the thought of the oblivion. Disoriented, I hurried out of bed and to the window, only to find stars dappling the night. I had not lost color yet.

"Cardan, I know you're in there!"

"One moment." I did not hurry to dress—I dreaded another evening in the studio. I pulled the door open, revealing her small stature—a masterpiece of black and gray. "Hello, *Tesoro*—"

"Where have you been? Sleeping this whole time?" Despite the shadows of the night devouring any detail in her expression, I heard the tremble in her voice.

I peeled a piece of hair from her wet face. "Don't cry, *mi amore*. Everything is—"

She swatted my hand away. "I'm not crying for you."

She pulled me into the shadows of the night and dragged me along at a hurried pace back to the studio, and I wondered if I could find the strength within myself to tell the truth.

Or if it'd be easier to just disappear.

A priest exiting the building broke me free of contemplation. We hurried inside and to a corridor leading to the back of the workshop

—an area I'd never frequented. At the end of the corridor, a door stood ajar, and within, a pulsing tangerine glow.

"Where are you taking me?"

She pushed the door open, and we entered a quaint bedroom with only a wash basin, a water-stained mirror above it, and a solitary stained-glass window depicting an archaic rendition of Madonna and Child by Duccio.

In the bed beneath it, my artist's assistant rested. Though devoid of color, even I could see the blackened crescents beneath her eyes—the sweat slicked pallor of her skin.

"What's the matter with her?"

"She's ill. She does not have long," she whispered and then took the chair beside the bed, gripping her assistant's hand to offer comfort.

I did not wish to intrude on the moment, but after a few more hushed words, the assistant's dark eyes flitted to me. "*Signore*," she spoke, and the attention she awarded me felt undeserved.

I stood upright. "Ye...yes?"

"Why...do I get the feeling that we've met before? Before all of this?"

"What?"

Her throat bobbed. "I feel like I've met you before. But perhaps you just have that kind of face." My heart stilled, triggering the all-too familiar pitfall in my stomach, sickening me. All things in existence seemed to cease in those agonizing moments when my mind raced, searching for the meaning in her words.

"I'm sorry, I—" I hadn't noticed. From the moment I followed her to the studio on that fateful day, all my attention had become consumed with my *Tesoro*—with wisteria and terra verte. With, who I thought, had brought color back to my eyes.

"Maybe...it was nothing," she said.

No words had ever cut so deep.

But I'd fallen in love with another woman right in front of her. The betrayal was severe—visceral. After catching a glimpse of myself in the water-stained mirror, bile clawed at my throat. My own reflection disgusted me.

My *Tesoro* sobbed from beside the bed. "Maria?"

I inhaled a sharp breath and wiped my face. But I couldn't look at her—at either of them. "Would you excuse me for a moment? I need some fresh air."

"You're not leaving, are you?"

I halted my stride in the doorway, split between the cool, fresh air of freedom—and the stifled, sickening miasma of betrayal from within the room. "No, I'm not...I'm not leaving." Finally, I forced the only bit of comfort I could pull from within myself to offer to her. A faint smile. "I wouldn't do that to you, *Tesoro*."

IT RAINED for eight days after my walk with Scarlet, denying me the satisfaction of seeing the tangerine sun chasing the gray from the sky. I lamented the loss of a beautiful sunrise, but after my encounter with the fate, I welcomed the excuse to brood.

His warning unsettled me, reminding me that I was not yet in the clear. And while I didn't doubt he meant it as a motivating factor, my blood went cold at all the possibilities of what could go wrong.

But even when I convinced myself that doing nothing had more severe repercussions, I spent another three days delving into the depths of my own self to try and pull my emotions from within—to write them on the page in a legible manner—a manner which might inspire feelings of love and gratitude in Scarlet. Inspiring others may have been my strong suit, but my tether was immune to my charms —at least in that regard.

And with our tumultuous start, it was no wonder I continually slashed my words out so fiercely the pages on my desk tore. Again and again with ink-stained fingers, I pored over the letter I wrote— torn equally between bouts of passion and terror. The words of romance always evaded me.

I should have listened closer to Voltaire's drunken ramblings about love.

My Dearest Scarlet,

I am writing to say all the things my lips have grown too weary to speak. My tongue stills in my mouth at the very thought of expressing my feelings for you so openly. I can't even begin to articulate the extent of my affections as your gaze holds mine. I crumble beneath the weight of those eyes. So, instead, I shall write them down. That way, you have these words forever.

I love you

No, that's too sudden—too much, and she'd never believe me.

I adore you. Since we met, thoughts of you have ~~polluted~~ my mind, and I cannot think clearly. ~~Lost in the haze of you, I~~

I balled the paper in my fist and chucked it across my drawing room into the blazing inferno of my hearth. Polluted? Haze? *How insulting.* How could I expect to romance anyone with such discordant words? *Positive emotions, that's what she's meant to inspire!* But how could she? When every encounter through my life had brought nothing but pain, sorrow, regret?

Despite the rancor, my heart swelled with affection when I thought of Them through every life. And Scarlet was a combination of all. It was only then I realized that with every incarnation of my tether, I loved them more and more.

My dearest Scarlet,
     I dreamed of you too.

I considered sending a messenger, but my stomach twisted in knots at the thought of not having an immediate answer; yet with every step I took toward Lambeth, dread clawed its way from my belly up my throat, burning my inside flesh.

The brass head of my cane upon her door resounded a hollow yet brazen cry for attention. I tucked it behind my back, waiting for acknowledgement as my mind raced with worst possible scenarios. A slammed door in my face, or perhaps laughter at the words I scribbled on a page for her.

Why did I even write a letter? I'm here now, I could very well have just told her—

The door creaked as it swung open, but it was not the beauty of my tether I came face to face with. Instead, my eyes pored over the puffy face of her cousin—her cheeks wet with tears.

I collapsed inward. "Good morning—"

"Lord Ackerman," she nipped, and I'd never heard such angst behind my name—not from her. Finally, she stepped aside, swinging the door open further to allow me to enter. It was strange, stepping beyond that threshold—entering Scarlet's home, or the place she *called* home for the time being.

It did not befit her. The loose, splintered floorboards creaked beneath my scuffed shoes, as if protesting my presence. A bitter draft blew through the entry hall, and I shuddered to think it was colder than outdoors.

The scent of mildew mixed with oil from lamps fused together in a sickening perfume that polluted the air and nearly choked me.

"Scarlet's in the parlor," her cousin sighed as she brushed past.

"I didn't realize you lived here as well."

"I don't." It was all she said to me. She wiped her face and disappeared into a room at the end of the hallway.

I knew the parlor because it was the same in every household. A room to host guests, located off of the entry hall—a way to maintain the privacy of the household.

The only warmth came from that room.

I stood in the doorway and regarded a meager fire in the hearth, nearly reduced to a glowing pile of ash that was so potent I tasted it on my tongue.

"I'll admit, I did not expect to see you again."

A voice once full of silk and honey rasped at me from the chaise in the corner of the room. But even the grate from her throat didn't prepare me for the weight of her appearance.

I'd never seen her in color before, but her varied shades of gray, black, and white painted a clear enough picture of the medley that made her so enchanting. Her skin had been a cloud, but her cheeks were pewter—pink, I decided, had color ever returned. Her lips had been stone—mauve to all other eyes. So I imagined.

But now, all those varied shades gave way to blanch, insipid, ghost-white skin that invaded every inch. Even her golden hair was now slick with oil and sweat, dulling its magnificence to brass.

And then black beneath her eyes.

"You're ill," I choked.

"It happened so sudden—"

"Have they sent for a doctor?" Her cracked lips curled upward. "How can you smile at a time like this?"

"I didn't think you cared so much." Her throat bobbed. "The doctor has come and gone."

"And what is the prognosis?"

Her teeth bit into her lip, and her eyes squinted—as if she had trouble seeing me clearly. "Why are you here?"

I crossed the room and sat beside her, taking her cold, stiff fingers in mine. "I..." My breath quivered—all inspiration fled on swift wings when her sunken eyes met with mine, brow furrowed in what appeared to be intrigue. "I wrote you a letter." I pulled it from my pocket and held it out to her.

Her strained voice said, "Read it to me."

"I cannot."

"Why?"

Because I'm afraid. "Because I took the care to write it, so I want you to read it."

She clasped it, but her hand fell to the chaise. As if that small exertion exhausted her. "I'll read it when everything stops being so... fuzzy." A faint smile spread across her face. "I had hoped I would see you again."

"You hoped...to see me?"

She nodded, and a faint smile appeared. "Yes. It seems that despite my greatest efforts to detest you, I ended up...falling for you instead."

My eyes burned, and my lips stuttered. I whipped my head away, terrified of her seeing the mask I wore slipping away with her very words. I scoffed. "I...*you've* fallen for *me*?"

"There's just...something about you." Her words beckoned my wide eyes. "I don't know how to describe it, but since the day we met, you've been the only thing on my mind. Such an imposition, you are. It's very rude of you to intrude upon my peace of mind."

When her lips curled upward, a laugh shot from my mouth unwarranted. "Yes, well, you haven't been the most welcomed guest in my thoughts, either."

She snickered. "Oh?"

"Like a parasite gnawing at my heart."

"You're wicked."

"You're impossible."

"Tempestuous is a word that best describes you."

I brushed her hair aside and ran my thumb along her face. My heart thrummed, creating an ache deep within me that threatened to collapse me at any moment. "Exasperating is what you are."

She laughed again. It hurt more than anything because it lacked vigor. It was all the inspiration I needed to lean over her and press my lips onto hers. It had been difficult not to—I'd wanted to feel the press of her lips to mine, the softness, the warmth. I felt none of those things. Her lips were coarse, rough, and cold. And yet, I never wanted to stop.

When our mouths parted, her weary eyes gazed up at mine, freezing my heart momentarily when I saw it. The deepest, most breathtaking shade of blue and green—turquoise with a gold sunburst around the iris. My heart wrenched. And unbidden, warm tears streamed down my cold cheeks.

"Your eyes are blue."

"You've only just noticed?"

I laughed through the pain. My thumb caressed her blanched pallor—somehow even in her sickly state still so beautiful.

But that's when I noticed not only her eyes gave way to animation and color. The walls around us, a bright, vibrant green that commanded my attention. My head whipped around in every direction, the same green from floor to ceiling. A death trap disguised as a home.

"We have to get you out of here—" My tongue stilled at the tip of my teeth when I saw the vacancy behind those once-bright eyes. In only a matter of seconds, the golden sunbursts dimmed to nothing.

The walls were poison. But it would take some time before the people knew.

THE FIRE BURNING in the hearth cut out the barest sliver of illumination from the darkness that devoured my drawing room. Slouched deep within my armchair and facing the orange flames head on, I twisted my Thaumatrope wildly—losing myself in the image of a caged bird.

The absence of Scarlet disintegrated the barest remnants of whatever heart I had left. No matter how far I reached for the catharsis, the memory of her, lying on the chaise as her life slipped through my very fingers, did not force the sickness of grief outward. It continued to surge through me, poisoning me.

How many years had passed since I'd actually cried? Shedding tears here and there would not rid me of this illness. And yet, my recovery felt stunted with every loss–buried beneath the culmination of all my sorrow.

A draft carried with it the smell of the forest—of evergreens, soil, and rainfall—a sort of freshness and vitality that only spring knew so well.

"I regret the part I played in this," Danome said as he stepped into the firelight. "Perhaps you would have succeeded by now had your sister and I not meddled so much."

"What are you talking about?" I drawled, twisting my Thaumatrope between my fingers.

"Memory is not your curse, Cardan. Just as your ability to inspire is not a curse. A colorless world is not your curse, but is the result of self-inflicted pain."

I stopped twisting, awarding him my full attention. "What do you mean?"

"You were so young when it all happened. We thought we were helping you."

Dread gnawed at my stomach, threatening to climb up my throat in either bile or venom at his obscurity. "Tell me."

"I cannot tell you." As he stepped toward me, he brought on his coattails a biting cold that only the dead were acquainted with. "I must show you." Before I uttered a single syllable, he pressed his index and middle finger onto my forehead.

And the oblivion devoured me.

PAIN EXPLODED through my side and coursed through my body, allowing the winter's cold to enter into my bloodstream. I'd been attacked—my first *mortal* wound. "Come with me," she said, "and rest your head in my bed. I have a fire within, and food and water to replenish you."

A world in color surrounded me—I hadn't lost the ability to see it yet. But the biting at my side overshadowed my senses, and I threw my head back into the bed and howled.

"You're hurt. Not to worry; I have just the thing."

I'd been stabbed for thievery. It would not be the last time. The mysterious woman spread a sour-smelling viscous concoction over my side, and it invaded every inch of me—burning me like hellfire. My vision pulsed and then faded to nothing.

I awoke the following morning with little to no pain. The intoxicating scent of lavender and a blend of earthly yet sweet aromas greeted me just as the sun might, were it not for the cottage's shutters.

I lifted the blanket to observe my wound, but it was covered with a cloth and sealed with some kind of sticky paste.

"Don't touch that."

A young woman, with long, curly tendrils the darkest shade of ebony. Her russet eyes danced with fire—the sort that drew unsuspecting moths like me in for a closer look. But even more breathtaking, her skin. So smooth, unmarred and shimmering like umber silk in the sunlight.

I didn't want to leave her side after that day. Her name was Samara, and loving her came as instinctively as breathing air.

She lived alone and miles away from the nearest town but often visited to help those in need—the sick, the injured—using the tinctures and ointments she made in her cottage.

But one day, she returned sullen and with a defeated look in her eyes.

She grabbed my hands and pressed her forehead into mine—something she often did to calm me. "Sit with me," she murmured, and we kneeled in the garden with our fingers interlocked.

"Did something happen?"

She smiled. "Would you like to see a trick?" I nodded. She pulled from her satchel a disk made from thick parchment with two strings attached to the edges. On one side, she pointed to a sketch of a birdcage. And on the other, a bird. Intrigued, I watched as she took the strings between her fingers and twirled them. Through some sort of magic, the images combined in the motion—displaying the bird within the cage. "How did you do that?"

"It is an illusion."

They came for her the following morning. I closed my eyes as they dragged her from the cottage. "I don't want to see this."

"*You must,*" Danome said.

My vision came to again in the village square. The townspeople booed and threw things at a pyre, and my heart faltered when I saw Samara with ropes binding her in place.

"Witch! Burn the witch!"

I pushed through the crowd.

"She killed my son!" a woman cried.

At the base of Samara's feet, they lit a fire. I opened my mouth but no words came—I could think of nothing to say in her defense, not while the flames devoured the hem of her dress.

"Caedmon!" she called for me.

Say something. But I could not. Fear dominated me, keeping me firmly in place and muting my voice. *Do something to stop this!*

She screamed as the thick white smoke enveloped her, and by then, I knew it was too late. Through the calamity, I could no longer hear her—a mixture of white smoke and tangerine flames swallowed her whole.

As the crowd cheered, I staggered back through them—putting distance between myself and the pyre. Ash wafted throughout the square on the wings of a violent wind. Ash that covered all things... the people, the ground, and even blanketed the sky. Until gray shrouded all of the colors.

I gasped for breath and fell to my knees before the crackling flames of my hearth. My heart bounded and grew heavy with the weight of my memories returning to me.

Danome stood over me, and for the first time ever, I felt beneath him—less than and not worthy of mercy. "Your eldest sister, Mnemosyne, agreed to take your memory of what really happened that day. All she left you with was your return to the cottage. You came to believe that Samara just disappeared."

My eldest sister. I clenched my teeth at the fading memory of her —of my father. All my brothers and sisters.

"How come I remember everything else? I believed remembering was my curse—"

"Your mind is trying to fill the gaps that were stolen—desperately clinging to every memory to make sense of something it never could. We wanted to protect you. We feared what losing your mother at such a young age might do, but we only made things worse."

The returning memories—though having taken place centuries before—felt as new and fresh as the memories from just yesterday. Her name rested on my tongue, and though I grew desperate to call out for her, I was not worthy to speak her name.

Samara.

"This is your fault!" I shouted instead, pointing a stiff finger to the Fate. "You, my sister...my father—all the suffering, all the pain. It's all your fault!" But no amount of shouting could convince even myself that those words were true. Because ultimately, it was all me.

I did nothing to save her.

I did nothing to save *them.*

I did nothing.

～

OXFORD, ENGLAND; HEADINGTON BOARDING SCHOOL;
PRESENT DAY

The girls under my tutelage all gasped and giggled as I whipped my
chalk across the blackboard. I bit my tongue to hide an audible
groan, though no amount of self-inflicted pain could keep me from
snorting when I faced them—their mouths agape with stars in their
eyes.

I hesitated and pointed to the board. "Romeo and Juliet—"

They erupted in excited squeals and whispers.

"Girls," I warned.

"We're just excited, Professor. It is so romantic."

"Romeo and Juliet is not a romance, Sophia. It's—"

A tragedy," another of my students finished.

"Very good, Emilia. Romeo and Juliet is, indeed, one of the
greatest tragedies ever written and is regarded as one of William
Shakespeare's most notable works." I grabbed the stack of
playscripts and handed them to a student nearby to pass them
along.

"He must have been such a tormented soul."

"I can assure you, he wasn't. He was rather boastful, actually.
Never took anything seriously, either." They fell silent. I whipped my
head up from the pages on my desk to see their questioning gazes,
waiting for an explanation. "At least, that's what they say." As the
bell rang, my students shuffled from their desks, gathering their
belongings and slinging their messengers over their shoulders. "You
have the weekend to become acquainted with the play. We'll discuss
through act two on Monday."

Thunder rumbled in the distance. The sky was grayer than usual
as raindrops pattered the arched windows of the classroom. My
head, dizzy and fogged, fell to my shoulder, and I gripped the edges
of my desk for support. It was my penance for all I'd done—or hadn't
done. Giving every bit of myself to the eager and thirsty minds of the
next generation of writers, editors, publishers—

"Professor?"

I lifted my head to the arched doorway. "Can I help you?"

A young man—no older than twenty-five—closed the gap with a wide smile, accentuating the perfection of his teeth and a dimple on his left cheek. He clung to a leather messenger slung over his shoulder. With his index finger, he pushed his square framed glasses further up his nose, then extended his hand to me.

"Idris Foxx. I'm the new English Composition instructor."

"Cardan—"

"Evers. Yes, Professor. I know just who you are."

I regarded him momentarily, wondering if our paths had crossed before.

He hesitated. "I read your article in *The Critical Review.* About the social influence of aestheticism in the Victorian era as depicted in—"

"The Picture of Dorian Gray." I forced a smile. "I'm familiar with it."

"Yes. Of course you are."

I circled the desk as a wave of heat passed through my body. Classes usually drained me so thoroughly, I often left the school with lead in my Oxfords and sweat pooling beneath my wool pullovers.

I pressed my forehead into the blackboard to cool myself. "Did you have a question, Mr. Foxx?"

"Just that...in your article, you described the Victorian era in such a descriptive manner—almost like you'd been there yourself. Or perhaps you're just a big fan of Oscar Wilde." I snorted. "Though, you disputed his take on morality."

"The morbid constituents we refer to as Victorians lived through a very bleak and dreary time. Desperate for progress, they were the guinea pigs for innovation and industrialism. Sacrificing their morality for art and culture was not a conscious nor a malicious decision."

"They were doing the best they could with what they had."

I picked my head up from the board. "Precisely. Art—beauty is what makes life worth living. We've gone to war over less profound endeavors."

"Like politics."

"Or religion."

Once more, a smirk spread across his face. He pulled a handkerchief from his tweed blazer and handed it to me. "Don't worry, it's clean." He pointed to his forehead. "You've got chalk on you."

I accepted it grudgingly. "Thank you." After slinking into my desk chair, I wiped my forehead lazily with the handkerchief. "I will clean this before returning it to you."

"No worries. I don't wish to disturb you—I know you must be busy. I just wanted to come by and introduce myself."

"And?"

"Sorry?"

"Come now, that's not all you came for." I met his stare again, his smile fading. Though he remained in varied shades of black and gray, I did my best to decipher his true colors. Ebony hair—lush curls on top that faded on the sides. Behind his square framed glasses, I imagined honey eyes stared back at me. And then the glow of rich mahogany in his skin.

"I did come to...ask your thoughts on a paper I'm working on. I felt your opinions would be vital."

"Let me guess. You want to be a writer."

"No, I...quite enjoy reading, sure. But my calling is in higher education." He shrugged and lifted his bag higher on his shoulder— modest, meager. Caving in on himself, he managed to pull a bit of guilt out of me when he forced a chuckle. "Have to be published in a few journals before that can happen."

I was very familiar with the whole song and dance—acquiring a PhD took a lot of unnecessary work, but it was work people like us were forced to do to prove our true fortitude. I had no interest in writing as an art form, just as Idris claimed he had none as well. I simply grew to love writers above all others because they showed me a world could be beautiful in black and white.

Unlike him, though, I had no interest in *higher education*. I hated the politics.

I waved my hand. "Leave it on the desk."

He pulled the papers from his messenger and slid them on the edge, but before leaving, he ran his fingers over the rose petals of the bouquet delivered just that afternoon. "Lovely flowers."

"They're from my father."

I buried my face in my hand, unsure if I might even make the walk home to my apartment—I debated catching a few winks at my desk while the storm soldiered on outside. The sound of rain pattering on my window did soothe me, as did the thunder.

"Have a good evening, Professor."

"You as well." I wasn't entirely sure how much time passed when I lifted my head again to see the vacant archway leading into the corridor. The students were gone already—faculty members no doubt ducking out with them to enjoy the coming weekend, but I remained—too weary and dazed to even cross campus.

It was only when I dropped my hand from my face that I saw it—something so foreign yet long desired, and it paralyzed me. So stark against the black and gray world, my father's roses came to life in a vibrant yellow. No, not just yellow.

Saffron.

The hairs along my body stood upright as the oblivion reached outward from the blackboard, threatening to devour me whole. There I sat in the maw of darkness and felt the bitter chill of its death call on my spine—a sinister promise of torment whispered onto the nape of my neck.

Lightning struck outside the window. And deep within me, a wild beast fought to claw its way free.

"Wait!"

I staggered into the corridor, head whipping in either direction to find the barest sliver of him. The quickest way out of the school was to the left. Despite the anchor of exhaustion weighing me down, I sprinted through the corridor—past large arched windows that displayed the ferocity of the downpour outside when I noticed students in passing, no longer wearing black pullovers but navy blue.

My Oxfords slipped on the wet stone of the courtyard. Within seconds of being outside, the rain drenched my clothes—soaking me through to my core, but pink roses and green vines climbing the stone walls distracted me instead. I trembled—whether from the cold, the colors, or the exertion, I couldn't be sure. But all I could think of was the rain...the lightning—I had to find him before it was too late.

The main entrance of the school stood in my way, and I swung open the wrought iron gate. The bus stop was not far—perhaps I might find him there. Once more, my Oxfords threatened to take me out as I rushed down the stone steps to reach the main roadway where various shades of motor vehicles muddled the path.

Mint, aegean, mulberry, rust!

Just across the street, Idris stood beneath a vermilion umbrella at the bus stop, and I exhaled a sigh in relief.

I lifted my hand to wave to him. "Idris!"

We locked eyes as I crossed. And for a moment, everything around us seemed to stop—the rain, the traffic, the people without umbrellas running for cover. I only saw him, and there he stood, only seeing me. With a look of horror on his face.

The deep, guttural howl of a bus's horn cut through the tranquility of our reunion and reverberated my chest. I had not a moment to stop or retreat. Only to stare the oblivion directly in the face as it barreled toward me in the form of headlights that blinded me.

It did not hurt as much as I imagined.

Though I soon realized, from the gasps and screams of those around me, 'twas not the bus that hit me.

"Have you gone completely mad?" Idris shouted, and I took a moment to observe my surroundings. Flat on my back with him beside me and others standing over us, I lifted my head to see the bus stopped in the street. "Didn't your mother ever tell you to look both ways before crossing the street?" Idris shouted again, and it was only then I noticed the throbbing pain in my side.

"Ugh," I groaned while falling back on the wet sidewalk. "Did you play rugby as a boy?"

"No." He wiped his face that dripped with rain. "I played my *whole* life."

"I think you ruptured my spleen."

"Well, it serves you right! Better than being splattered all over the street." It was as if *They'd* been waiting centuries to deliver that blow. He grabbed my arm and yanked me from the wet cement with so much force, I thought he might dislocate my shoulder.

"Thank you." The small crowd around us started to disperse, and traffic continued as he gathered his belongings. "I was, uh..." His eyes ripped the words right from my tongue, and instinctively, my hand shot to my messy wet hair to slick it back. My heart hammered away with so much vigor I thought I might collapse, so I turned my back to him.

I should ask him to dinner. But that seems so sudden—even though he did just save my life. Perhaps coffee might be more suitable? But who, OTHER THAN YOU, drinks coffee in the evening? He could just have tea? Everyone likes tea.

I straightened my blazer. *Right. Take two.*

But when I faced him, he was already walking away, and my heart plummeted. "Hang on!"

His damned eyes stole my words again. "Everything all right, Professor?"

"There's...a coffee shop just around the corner." *IT'S TOO LATE FOR COFFEE!* "They have tea as well. And pastries. Little sandwiches, too," I said while pinching my fingers together, as if to show him the size.

His brow furrowed. "Are you asking me for coffee?"

"I..." hesitated. "Or, if you prefer tea—"

"We look a mess."

I observed his soaked attire—rumpled from my rescue—then pulled my blazer apart to regard my own disheveled appearance. Though not the worst I had ever looked, the times demanded a more groomed state in most establishments. My cheeks burned from the rejection—I'm sure he noticed the redness swelling my face.

I turned away, wanting to disappear into a cave for the next century or two—I couldn't move fast enough as his eyes burned into my back.

"There is a pub!" he shouted, and I nearly skidded on the pavement from my abrupt stop. When I peered over my shoulder, he grinned. "Just a few blocks away, but I'm willing to share my umbrella." A laugh escaped me—the damage from the rain had already been done. "They probably won't mind how we look."

"I..." *Don't hesitate. Don't think—not even for a moment.* "Yes, all right."

He extended his umbrella to me, and I hurried to join him. He held the vermilion shield above our heads, and by his side I no longer cared to note the colors springing to life around us. I waited for his eyes and his eyes alone to animate.

Perhaps I was wandering deep into the oblivion once more, my own eyes shut tight in ignorance or bliss. Or perhaps, I was becoming a bird in a cage no more.

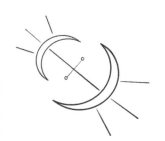

The
Temptation
Of
Magic

G.M. McGann

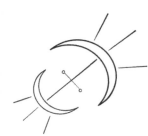
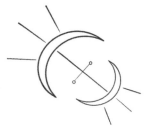

CHAPTER 2

TEMPTATION OF MAGIC

C.M. MCCANN

The grimoire thudded closed as I inhaled power, shaking. The sour scent of lemon assaulted my nostrils. Enhanced senses—nothing particularly special. Blinking past the bright red aura that momentarily blinded me, I shoved to my feet, the new magic murmuring through my veins.

Ugh. If I was lucky, this new power might last a day, two at most. Nowhere near what I needed. With such a weak power, hopefully whatever I lost was equally insignificant. Like being able to see the color orange. I hated orange.

I glanced at the man laid across from me—if not for his bindings, he would actually look peaceful. It was enough to make me want to take everything on him. Although, that consisted of little more than a worn watch and a tarnished ring.

Dragging a hand through my ash-blonde curls, I extinguished each candle in the corners before dumping the liquid wax in a tin and throwing it all in my bag. I should've known his bragging was nothing but lies. *I can see further than a hawk*, he had claimed. *Hear better than a bat.* I closed my eyes and tapped into his power, my nose wrinkling at the lemon persisting with the attempt. Sweet whisperings and soft moans flooded my ears from the next room, and I quickly dropped the power with a huff. I could've heard the same thing pressing my ear against the wall. *Useless.* At this rate, I'd never find something more powerful than what Alyra held. How was I ever supposed to compare to my sister if I couldn't find the right magic?

I collected the rest of my belongings and scowled at the empty potion bottles rattling at the bottom of my bag. A visit to Resheph was in order. Maybe they would have something stronger this time —something was lacking in the ritual, I was sure. No power I took lasted more than a week, and they were always mere whispers compared to any Magi I had ever seen. Except once.

I shuddered as cold, empty eyes flashed across my mind. Tamping the memory down, I took a pillowcase and stuffed it in the bag, hoping to dampen the noise. I refused to think about that first attempt.

Maybe you just don't know how to use their magic properly.

I pursed my lips at the harsh voice in my mind. Using magic was simple. I felt people use their magic any time I touched them and amplified their magic whether I wanted to or not. It created a tether, a bond I never asked for, and while I could not take from them, I *could* sense as they pulled power from their core and exuded it through their fingers, eyes, or mind.

I just hadn't found the right power yet. Whatever my tendency was, obviously I hadn't tried to take it.

I need to make a list.

It would have to wait. With the deep black lifting to sunken gray beyond the frosted window, I had maybe an hour before my parents would ask too many questions. Maybe I should've accepted Marek's suggestion to move in with him. I could come home at breakfast and he'd never think twice.

I dismissed the thought as quickly as it came. Every crown I earned went directly back into the cost of these rituals. And a few guilty pleasures. Since I had no plans to give up either...

The man let out a low groan, and I jumped. He should've been knocked out cold for hours yet. Panic climbing into my throat, I crept behind him, fingers inching towards the dagger at my thigh.

I counted to thirty, waiting.

He didn't move again, didn't make another sound, and I let out a breath of relief. My hand relaxed at my side. Safe, for now at least. Dropping my sack to the ground, I rolled my sleeves to my elbows. This was the hardest part, but I knew better than to leave behind any evidence of my work.

Dragging him by the ankles, I maneuvered him as close to the bed as possible before shifting to his head and hooking my arms under his pits. A guttural groan escaped me as my muscles strained trying to get him onto the bed. They had seen us come in together, so this couldn't look like some drunken bender with him haphazard on the floor surrounded by empty bottles. Next time. Sneaking in and incapacitating was harder, especially with ritual supplies, but the cleanup was simpler.

With sweat sliding down my spine and dampening every crevice, I left him there, pants unbuckled and shirt yanked up, one bottle empty on the ground near his hand. When he woke in the morning, he should be left with nothing but a forgotten night and a wicked hangover. He'd likely question why he couldn't access his magic, but who would listen to a poor man's concern?

The man at the front desk smirked at me as I passed and I ignored him, shoving out the door into the brisk autumn night. A shiver rushed through me. I ducked into the closest alley, sidestepping a puddle of piss, and quickly shucked the shirt I wore into the dark. Stolen from the wealthiest Madam past Kaster Street, I could always get another.

I unhooked my thigh sheath and tucked it into my bag before pulling out a shawl and wrapping it over my shoulders to hide my spilling cleavage. Not that there was much, but the bustier emphasized the little I did have. Pinning the fabric in place with a plain silver brooch, I sighed. Not warm, but presentable, should I run into my parents coming in. Thankfully, Alyra wouldn't be home for another week or so. She took too much interest in my comings and goings.

With a sharp tug, I pulled the bone pins from my hair and gathered them between my fingers before stepping out of the alley. I squared my shoulders and set my jaw. My figure was far too small to be considered intimidating, but acting large would make me less of a target. And the bone pins would buy me enough time to reach the dagger I still had in my boot.

I strode through the city, peripheral vision catching every shifting shadow. The moon, fat and full, lit the night even better than the flickering orange lampposts. In a different part of Enssa, it might have been considered peaceful. In a different part of Enssa, I risked being caught. No one cared what happened here on the outskirts, tucked away in a pocket of grime, as far away from the city gates as you could get. From Kaster Street to the wall, everyone looked the other way. Guards gambled, nobles lined the pockets of prostitutes, and even Duchess Farrow, ruler of our humble city, could be spotted ducking into opium dens. The only people you never saw were Magi. At least, not in their robes.

I crinkled my nose. *Magi.* Anyone could have magic. But rarely would anyone from the slums make their way to that title, no matter how powerful they might be. I had inhaled plenty of power that laced far deeper than the man today, power I truly thought could rival Alyra's, and I found most of my prey on these streets.

I would likely have to start looking further out, closer to the gates. It would prove a challenge. Men I could get to follow me anywhere, even past Kaster Street, but women...they would be trickier. And not being able to dump the unconscious bodies in a place where no one would ask questions...

A problem for another day, Alessa.

I didn't relax until I crossed Kaster Street into Vant Market. The stalls stood empty, most of them covered in dilapidated, dull cloth. A drunkard leaned against a stall and swung a bottle haphazardly, singing out of tune.

"—named Mary, but her back was so hairy. I got out of there, and then I did swear, I'd rather marry her big brother Larry."

I skirted the back of the stalls, putting as much distance in between us as I could. As happy as he seemed, that mood could change in an instant, and I had no interest in fending off more drunk men tonight.

Once his caterwauling faded into the distance, I loosened my grip on the pins and tucked them into my bag. A guard rounded the corner, and I nodded to him. He stared a moment too long. I forced myself to keep moving, my fingers clutching the brooch at my sternum. With every step past him, I waited for him to call out, accuse me of not belonging, *something*.

It never came. The further I went into the heart of the city, the busier the streets got, despite the hour. People flowed from one tavern to the next, meandered in front of inns, and lounged on balconies like the night chill didn't threaten to take their bare fingers. I shuddered and tucked my hands into the pits of my arms. If I had another choice, I'd be bundled in a coat, gloves, and probably even a hat. Maybe I needed to consider a safe house. Marek would probably let me stash things with him, but if I wanted to do that, I should've just said yes to living with him.

Too many questions. At least with Alyra gone, my parents didn't care enough to question me.

I finally turned onto my street with my nose and toes aching. A fire would have been better, but after the third ritual, I could no longer feel its heat, the flames nothing more than crackling wisps. They could still burn—my finger twitched at the memory—but they were lukewarm at best.

I would settle for a hot water bottle and a warm cup of tea. Bergamot tea. The thought curled a memory from the recesses of my mind...rough, dark hands around a chipped mug. A luxury I couldn't afford then, but splurged on anyway. I didn't even think about the cost now. Another cup was just a fenced jewel away.

Tucking thoughts of a different life away, I eased open the back door to our house—I still couldn't think of it as *home*—and slipped inside.

And froze.

"—good to have you home, dear."

"Alessa!"

What is she *doing here?*

I barely managed to hide my shock when Alyra threw her arms around me. My bones refused to listen to my brain, which urged me to respond so she wouldn't ask even more questions. Finally, my arms snaked around her, and I pressed my face into her perfect golden-blonde hair.

"How are you home so soon?" Sense managed to dictate my harsh thoughts.

My sister extracted herself and stepped back, grasping my hands in hers. "Magi Barakat has business here, and I was asked to assist him." She beamed bright enough to blind the sun. Once, we were considered twins in appearance. Now I was the dull to her shine: barely blonde frizz to perfect golden curls, splotchy tanned skin to glowing porcelain complexion, stick-straight to soft curves. Even her eyes shone bluer than normal in the dim firelight. Life in the Magi Tower suited her.

Of course. Everything suited her.

"Alessa?"

I blinked. "Sorry?"

Alyra smiled, gracious as always. "Aren't you cold like that?"

I shrugged and forced back a shiver. Alyra's own fur-lined coat was draped across the back of the dining room chair, luggage nowhere in sight. Not like she needed it. My sister's tendency was conjuration. I knew nothing stronger. New dress? Conjured. Fully cooked meal? Conjured. Anything she had seen or touched or tasted before, she could conjure. It was no wonder that a full-blown Magi wanted her, even as a Novitiate.

"I hadn't planned on staying out so late. How long do you get to stay?" I asked.

Get to, as if my sister being here wasn't entirely a burden. I could only hope whatever business she was assisting with would keep her busy.

"Through Caralin's Festival, at the very least. I may be here later, depending on how things go with Magi Barakat. Even if we finish early, he doesn't see the point in making me return only to come back again in a few days. Too much magic expended for needless back and forth."

I nodded lamely as our parents lit up like Yule came early. My jaw clenched. They would never react to me the same way. And despite their behavior being the same for the past ten years, it still stung.

I chose my next words carefully. "I'm sorry, Alyra, can we continue this tomorrow? It's been a long day."

"Don't you think she's had a long day traveling? If she can be up, so can you, Alessa," our father scolded. Our mother dipped her chin, her mouth pressed into a thin line. Of course. How dare I act weak while my sister was so strong?

"It's fine, Papa." Alyra turned to me. "Go on, we'll chat later."

I nodded, not meeting my parents' eyes as I ducked past to go upstairs to my room. Anger built slowly in my veins, tiny embers flaring into full flames. I slammed my door shut and immediately regretted it. My fury quickly stomped out the regret, though, tumbling over my thoughts. I only got brief glimpses into my previous lives, tiny snippets of memories, but I knew every iteration had a younger sibling. And not one of them seemed as flawless as my current sister. Not even the original, Caedmon.

I glared at the floor. There went all plans of a hot water bottle and bergamot tea. I couldn't go back down there, not for a few hours at least, and I'd be asleep by then.

Ripping off the shawl, I stomped over to my wardrobe, tucked my sack carefully into the back, and yanked out something warmer: a loose tunic and thick leggings and wool socks. My fingers made quick work of the bustier, undoing the laces and sighing as it dropped to the floor. Red lines marked my ribcage from the boning. I rubbed at them as I pulled off my boots.

"Alessa…"

I jumped, throwing an arm across my chest and whirling towards the door. "What the queens, Alyra!"

"I thought you might want these." She shouldered open the door, a laden tray in her hands. Bright bergamot wove through the air over buttery crust and sweet blackberries. I hated that my mouth watered.

Turning my back on her, I tossed on my shirt before finishing changing and plopping onto my bed, arms outstretched expectantly. My sister's knowing smile dug under my skin as I accepted the tray and placed it carefully on my lap. Aching hands wrapped around the warmth of a hand pie and a clay mug. As my hands came back to life, I looked at Alyra.

"Go on."

She frowned. "'Go on,' what?"

"Do your nagging or ask your questions or whatever it is you're doing here." I took a long sip of tea and stifled a moan. Beguiling bergamot rolled over my tongue, pulling at the edges of a memory. A coal-haired woman with sage-and-sea eyes pressed a mug into my small, young hands, the warmth in her gaze tugging at my heart. I shoved it aside, knowing it would return in my dreams. If it came over me now, Alyra would only ask more questions. Memories had a way of removing me from reality, leaving gaping moments in my life the longer I remembered another. Like a waking sleep.

Alyra had the nerve to look put out. She bit her lip. "Can't I just want to catch up?"

I shrugged, not wanting to argue. "Sure." Wiping my hand across my mouth, I shifted on the bed, making room. She perched beside me before helping herself to one of the pies. I was tempted to slap her hand away but took a long gulp of tea instead, scorching my insides.

"So, any prospects?"

I choked, spluttering around the edge of the mug. Alyra patted my back in what she likely thought was a reassuring gesture, but it only made me stiffen. As a future Magi, Alyra wasn't even allowed to consider prospects. Magi could only marry once they made rank, not that I could fathom *why*, or how she was okay with that. Before she came into her power, it was all she talked about, like her future partner would be some prince to whisk her away to a dream world.

"No one," I muttered, thanking the gods that after the fifth failed suitor over the past two years—since my twenty-first birthday—my parents had stopped trying to push a new one on me. They already considered me a failure in most aspects of life; what was one more?

Alyra quirked a brow. "What about that friend of yours? What's his name...Marek?"

I wrinkled my nose before shaking my head and taking a long gulp of tea. "Absolutely not." He was just a friend. Always had been. Alyra had seen him once and immediately made assumptions. Ridiculous, fanciful assumptions.

"You could do a lot worse."

I tilted my head. I probably could, but I had no interest in tying myself to someone that wanted to control any and every aspect of my life. Marek wasn't like that now, but who knew how marriage might change him? I didn't want to owe anyone anything.

"And if I don't want to marry?" I eventually ventured.

Alyra considered me, then dropped her gaze to her hands. She picked under her nail despite her beds being perfectly clean half-moons. I glanced at my own dirty fingers, itching to hide them under my thighs. Hopefully Alyra wouldn't notice the rusty color lining them.

Letting her think, I grabbed a hand pie and nibbled along the edge.

And immediately spat it out.

I tuned out my sister's noise of concern as I stared at the pie in dismay. *No no no no no.* I took another bite. The flaky pastry crumbled like ash in my mouth. *No, please no.* I bit deeper, the blackberry filling oozing out the sides. Relief rushed through me as the tart berries burst over the ash of the crust. I hadn't lost the blackberries. Butter, if I had to guess. Just the taste, though, since it still smelled normal.

Letting out a groan, I set the pie down and wiped my mouth. Losing the taste of butter was unfortunate, though much better than losing the spice of hot peppers, which disappeared after the second ritual.

"Are you okay?"

I looked over to my sister. "Yeah, fine, sorry. Wasn't as hungry as I thought."

After a beat, Alyra shrugged. "Fine, just drink the tea, yeah? You look drawn." I sipped obediently. "As for the marriage..." She sighed. "If you don't get married, what will you do?"

"Think the Magi would employ an amplifier?" I half-joked.

"I can ask."

I lowered the mug from my lips. Never in a millennium did I think Alyra would actually consider that as a possibility. *It'll give you more access to magic.* It would also put me under a much more watchful eye. The Magi would notice if they suddenly lost access to their magic for any length of time. Maybe a Novitiate or Apprentice wouldn't?

But if I went to the tower, I would need every possible potion and accessory for the rituals with me. Who knew if I could easily stock up once there?

I would have a much better chance of finding the right magic, though.

And a much better chance of being caught, my mind reasoned. Who knew what kind of precautions they had in place?

"You would do that?"

Alyra smiled. "Why not? There are already a few amplifiers working within the tower, so I don't see why they wouldn't take you too. I can ask Magi Barakat when I see him tomorrow, if you're serious."

Was I serious? I drained my tea. I couldn't be a thief my whole life, and I certainly couldn't live with my parents that long, but the Magi Tower wasn't a good idea in the long run. Once I found my true tendency, the one that wouldn't abandon me after a few days or weeks, I wouldn't be an amplifier anymore. And if the Magi Tower found me suddenly able to do magic, I didn't think it would go over well.

Yet now that I suggested it, I had a hard time backtracking. "Let me think about it? I honestly don't know if that's what I want or not."

Alyra nodded. "That's fair. You have plenty of time. It would be easier to ask Magi Barakat while he is here, so before the festival?"

"Is he coming too?" The festival lasted three days. If I couldn't find the right magic by then, I could go to the Tower.

"Yes—most in the Tower are allowed to return home to celebrate for any of the Queens' Festivals, and Yule of course."

I bit down hard on the smile that threatened to spread on my mouth. If those in the Magi Tower were able to come back for the festival, it meant I had a much wider pool to choose from. I wouldn't need the tower at all, assuming the right magic came around.

"Deal." I only had a couple of weeks to prepare. The festival had celebrations across Enssa, but the Magi would likely be concentrated in the Main Square, which would make things harder. More wealth meant more guards, less abandoned buildings, and little anonymity. I'd need that safe house after all.

Alyra stood, plucking the tray from my lap. "Do you have plans tomorrow?"

I narrowed my eyes. "Why?"

"I should have a few hours around lunch. Did you want to go to Aveis Market with me?"

Going around with Alyra would be less suspicious than shopping on my own, so I ventured a nod. She smiled and balanced the tray in one hand before reaching out and touching my shoulder. I inhaled sharply as honey filled the air and pale gray light filtered over my vision. A moment later, she dropped her hand and the world returned to normal.

Beside me on the bed was a pile of deep green and slate fabrics. I frowned at it.

"I saw one of the prettiest dresses at the Tower. I thought it would suit you. There's a coat there as well, and some gloves. You should wear them tomorrow. The color will bring out your eyes."

Before I could respond, she flitted out the door with a quick, "Goodnight."

I stared at the gift for a moment and finally lifted up the green—the dress. The fabric shifted over my fingers like water. Tiny gold buttons dotted the spine, subtle gilded embroidery belting the waist. Not particularly fancy, yet still nicer than anything I owned. I shook out the coat with interest. Coat, not cloak, which was unusual in its own right—men generally wore coats while women wore cloaks. Thick slate wool tapered at the waist and flared just slightly, ending at the hips. The sharp *V* of the neck would show off the front of the dress, or a scarf if I chose to wear one. I plucked the gloves off the bed last, what should have been supple leather melding to my hands. I shucked them immediately.

Another magical side effect. While I could avoid the unfortunately rough, scratchy sensation of my boots with socks, there was no way I could wear these. They matched the coat in color, and were finer than anything I'd ever worn.

How would I explain to Alyra why I didn't wear them tomorrow?

I carefully moved it all to my wardrobe. Such fine things, and my sister hadn't thought twice about creating them and giving them to me. They were beautiful, and I hated it.

Shaking my head, I crawled into bed, the scent of honey lingering on my quilt. Having magic let you do anything, yet my sister's was highly coveted amongst them. To create something from just an image...

I wish.

Darker thoughts swirled in my mind. *Take hers. She's right there.*

Take her magic. She's your sister, she's powerful, her magic should be yours. It would last forever.

It wasn't the first time the thoughts had tempted me. Her magic *was* likely more compatible as my sister. Yet the thought of taking that from her, no matter how much she irritated me, never sat right.

Her magic should be yours... The thought echoed in my mind, more insistent this time, the hint of honey wrapping around me.

If I wanted to even consider taking my sister's magic, I had to be sure my ritual was sound. No matter how powerful the magic, it needed to last longer than a few days. Maybe my ingredients were wrong. The wrong color candles, the wrong runes, the wrong potions... The grimoire had the answers, surely, but maybe I had interpreted them wrong.

I rolled out of bed, the pull of seizing her magic too strong for me to quiet my mind. Flipping open the grimoire, I found a blank page and started listing the powers I had already taken. Seeing through animals—which smelled oddly of tobacco and left everything tinged gray-brown. Truthreading—sharp cinnamon with a haze of lavender. Manipulating clouds—fresh rain in pale blue-gray. Controlling plants, enhanced physique, bending sunshine, telekinesis, and finally my newest, enhanced senses.

Truthreading had lasted the longest, the first power I managed to wrangle after getting my hands on the grimoire. I had walked around sensing lies for over a month. But was that because I had the right ingredients for the ritual, or because that person had particularly strong magic?

I tucked my head between my knees with a groan of frustration. There were no easy answers, and the only person who might understand—Resheph—was likely to run me around in riddles rather than answering anything outright. And even if they did have answers, they specialized in potions, not the full ritual.

I rubbed at my temples. I didn't have time to experiment with more than a few different options. And I didn't want to risk doing too many rituals too close together. I was careful, but there was always the risk that someone would notice, especially if I showed my face too frequently in the same area. I had maybe two chances to get this ritual right before the festival. It would have to be enough.

~

As my sister dragged me through Aveis Market—named for one of the first queens—my gaze swept the area, mapping it out in my mind. Most "alleys" in this part of the city cut all the way through the block, a narrow passage rather than a dead-end. The market itself differed from the one near Kaster Street, too. Stalls stood as branches of the shops themselves, beckoning customers inside with a small taste. Benches and circular tables sat scattered across the center of the market to allow people to enjoy their sweets or tea or meat pies out in the open.

I shuddered as the wind nipped at my bare neck. Few shoppers utilized the seating today, most choosing the safety and warmth of the shops instead. I didn't blame them. Even with the wool coat and my hands double-gloved—the only solution I could think of—the autumn chill still had a bite.

Alyra kept her arm linked with mine as she wandered stall to stall, examining the jewels and scarves and trinkets with a discerning eye. As we left yet another stall, I wondered if she actually planned on buying something, or if she just planned on committing the items to memory to conjure for herself later. She could survive with no source of income if she really wanted.

A snake of anger wiggled under my skin and wrapped around my heart. As if her life wasn't easy enough already. Not that I thought she would actually live solely off magic. All magic had a toll, from my understanding. I didn't know the exact effects—Alyra never bothered to share, even after my questioning—but I did know having an amplifier lessened the cost along with making magic stronger. What else would I be good for beyond making my sister better?

"Come on." Alyra tugged me into a small cafe tucked into the corner of the square, one of the few that didn't have a stall in front of it. Strange. How did she know about this place? Just blink, and you'd miss it.

"Magi Barakat!"

Alyra waved eagerly at someone inside. I stepped into the dark restaurant, the oil lamps sparse along the walls. A towering figure straightened from the back of the narrow space and slowly turned to face us.

She pulled me closer, his silhouette sharpening into a lean figure dominating the room. Oddly, he didn't wear Magi robes—I didn't think they were ever allowed to take those things off. He dressed in a sharp dark suit with a lilac cravat, the standard style for men these days. I tilted my chin to get a better look at him. Sharp planes cut his jawline and cheekbones in smooth, dark olive skin. He clenched his jaw before he managed a smile. My heart skipped a beat. Magi were *not* supposed to be that young. Or attractive.

"I thought I told you to call me Tarin while we are here, Miss Nilas."

"Right, Tarin, sorry." Alyra flushed red as she ducked her head, hands twisting in her skirt. I glanced at her with my brow pinched. Did she actually feel ashamed, or did she *like* him?

He sighed. "It's fine, Miss Nilas. Fortunately, this is a Magi establishment; they already know me here."

I tilted my head and looked around. Once in the Tower, I didn't think anyone left.

The shop was barely wider than an alley, single booths carved into the left side, a bar carved into the right, and just enough space for two people to pass each other in the middle. An older woman stood behind the bar, wiping a glass down with a rag, and a few people sat in front of her, but no one wore robes. With the low lighting and stretching shadows, it could easily fit into the seedier part of town. Though this place was certainly cleaner than the vomit and blood-covered floors in the taverns past Kaster Street.

"Who is this?" His eyes, dark and narrowed, peered down at me, and I stepped on the need to tuck myself behind my sister's skirts.

Alyra barely flicked her gaze my way. "This is my sister, Alessa. She's an amplifier."

I shot my sister a dirty look. Too enraptured by her mentor, she paid me no mind.

"Alessa," he repeated, and I wanted to melt in my boots. His eyes trailed slowly down my figure before they came back up to meet mine, and the corner of his mouth curved upwards. "Interesting."

"Nice to meet you..." I paused. If Alyra wasn't supposed to call him Magi here, was I?

"You may also call me Tarin. Apologies, Miss Nilas, I know I said we'd have lunch, but duty calls. It appears you're in good company, anyway. I'll find you later." He bowed his head towards me. "A pleasure, Alessa. I'm sure I'll see you again."

Hopefully. He slid past me, and his shoulder brushed mine. A brief whiff of frost hit me, and I swore he smirked. I watched him leave with curiosity. He was not what I pictured when Alyra said she came here with a Magi.

"What's his tendency?" I asked, turning back to Alyra. The scent wasn't familiar.

She looked at me with twisted lips for a moment before sliding into the booth he just abandoned. "He's a telepath."

My eyes flew wide. While Alyra's ether magic was amongst the rarest, telepathy was a type of psyche magic not often found.

What if he heard me hoping I'd see him again?

"He's the youngest Magi in over a century," Alyra continued, unconcerned by my swirling mind. "He's only twenty-five. Can you imagine making it from Novitiate to Apprentice to Magi in only seven years? Most can't even go from Novitiate to Apprentice in that amount of time, if they ever get there at all."

Her admiration glowed through her far-off stare. "Was he the one who chose you to accompany him on whatever business you're here for?" Not that I cared why they were here, as long as it didn't interfere with my rituals. The Magi had better things to concern themselves with.

"I'm not sure, actually." Alyra's face dropped into a frown, brightening only a moment later. "But he hasn't protested at all, so it doesn't matter."

The barkeep came up a moment later, and while Alyra ordered tea and a meat pie, I ordered ale and a stew. No more pies for me unless I knew for sure they used something like lard rather than butter.

"Why didn't you tell me we were meeting up with the Magi?" I finally asked her. I thanked the barkeep as she dropped off our drinks and took a long sip. Alyra barely touched her tea.

"I wasn't sure you'd agree," Alyra admitted after a moment. "I wanted you to see that part of my life."

"Really? Because it sounded like you wanted to push me into going there." It hadn't bothered me much at first; I had been too distracted by Tarin. But now that I had a moment to dwell, my irritation grew.

"No!" she immediately protested. "I did want to introduce the idea to him early, I'll admit. I didn't want you to decide you wanted to work at the Magi Tower and then have the Magi be against it."

My annoyance mounted, but I tamped it down. My sister didn't have an impure bone in her body. Even if she hadn't gone about it the right way, she meant well. "Just talk to me before you go spouting things off next time, yeah?"

Alyra nodded immediately and I sighed, turning my attention to the food as it came out, ash wafting towards me. Frowning, I lifted a spoonful. Rosemary. I could taste it, but the smell was gone. I ate slowly before I focused on my sister again. "Did you want to shop more?"

I needed to see Resheph at some point, and check in with Marek too. But I couldn't drag my sister along to see the former. If sweet, innocent Alyra crossed Kaster Street, she'd probably faint.

My sister nodded, and after dropping crowns on the table, we exited back into the brisk air. The sun arched overhead, combatting the sharp points of the wind that sought any bare skin. I tilted my face up as my sister conjured a large hat for herself. I rolled my eyes. Queens forbid she get any color from the sun.

"Did you want anything?" Alyra asked as we approached a stall with leather goods, holding up her crown purse.

"Are they conjured crowns?"

Alyra looked hurt. "That's illegal, Alessa."

I shrugged and pretended to look over the stall. While lovely, these goods were mostly decorative. Stylish belts, crown purses, delicate gloves. Things I wouldn't use even if leather didn't scratch my skin.

Alyra led the way inside. And while she haggled over a set of gloves, as if the cream kid gloves she wore weren't enough, I wandered the store, pausing when I spotted a familiar figure through the window nicking a crown purse. *He's going to kill me,* I thought gleefully.

"Marek!" I called as I stepped into the doorway. He froze, only half a foot away from the man he stole from. His eyes found mine, and I could sense him cursing me from across the square. Smiling, I leaned casually against the frame.

He straightened, plastering a beatific smile across his face as he strode towards me. With his neat dark suit, he blended in well with the nobility that surrounded us. Interesting. I didn't think he worked this market.

"Alessa," he nearly growled as he approached. "How good to see you." Marek grasped my hand and leaned in close as if to kiss my cheek. "What the queens are you doing here?"

"Just shopping with my sister," I told him amiably, nodding back into the shop.

My sister lit up when she saw him, gloves in her hand. "Marek!"

Her tone was too close to the one she had used with Magi Barakat. *Does she like any man that moves?* She barely knew him. I supposed Marek was attractive in a way. Tanned skin, pale blond hair, soft brown eyes. He wasn't tall, though, and he was more like a brother than anything else. An obnoxious, nosy, overprotective brother.

He plastered a charming smile across his face, but I didn't miss the tense set to his shoulders. "Alyra. It's been a while."

"Indeed it has." Her voice went slightly breathless as a deep bell rang across the city. And rang again. "Oh, I have to go. I didn't think it was so late." She turned to me. "I'm so sorry, Alessa, I thought we'd have more time. Are you going to be okay getting home?"

Nodding, I kept my face carefully blank. I had no plans on going home any time soon.

"See you for dinner then?"

I bit back a sigh and nodded. That would give me enough time to find Resheph at least, and hatch a plan for my first test.

A hint of a smile lifted her lips before she bowed her head towards Marek. "It was good seeing you, Marek. Hopefully I'll run into you again before I go back. Perhaps you should come over for dinner one evening." His eyes went wide before she added, "I'll see you later, Less," and walked out the door.

I cringed. I hated that nickname. Watching my sister cross the square, I asked Marek, "Are you actually heading to 'work?'"

He shot me a deprecating look, and I smirked before looping my arm through his. "Good. You can accompany me to Resheph's."

His mouth twisted. "I don't like them."

"You don't have to like them. You're not the one doing business with them."

"I don't understand why you need to see them so often," he continued, still looking like he sucked on a lemon. "Surely other people make...that stuff."

"Just say it, Marek. 'Menstrual cycle relief.'" That was the story I had spun after Marek caught me leaving Resheph's alley. I even made sure Resheph knew, in case Marek went snooping. He didn't need to know what I did in my time outside of work, what those bigger jobs truly funded. Having him believe I spent all of my money on special pain potions and sweets kept him out of danger.

His face twisted even further, and I patted him on the arm before changing the subject, filling the space with useless chatter until we reached Resheph's alley off the outskirts of Vant Market. Marek paused.

"I'll wait here. I don't need to hear any details." He dropped my arm.

I only nodded and stepped past him, winding my way through the crates and into the shadowy end of the alley. All the better he stayed out there, really. Too many questions for Resheph burned my mind.

A hooded figure stood behind the stall, their back turned, not another soul around. Now that I thought about it, I didn't think I had ever seen another customer near their stall.

They turned as I approached. "Back so soon?"

Glancing over my shoulder and ensuring Marek kept to his word, I muttered, "It's not working."

"You'll have to be more specific than that." They waved a golden hand, too smooth. Everything else about Resheph spoke of an aged person. Yet their hands were as smooth as mine.

I let out a huff. "Since the first ritual, nothing has lasted longer than a few weeks at most."

Different colored eyes flashed beneath the hood as they shifted forward. I looked between them—blue and vivid green—before dropping my gaze to their shadowed mouth.

"You mean when you killed a man."

I stiffened. *How do they...?* I tried to push aside the flood of memories, but they crowded my mind. *Blood spattered across the space. Screams in the air. Ripped power. Sharp cinnamon. Color draining from an already pale face. A limp wrist. Empty eyes.*

Those eyes.

A hazel so light they seemed gold. I shuddered. I'd never forget them.

Rituals required sacrifice. That had been my first success, the first time after I had found—okay, stolen—the grimoire. Except I hadn't done it right. Done the right way, the way I did now, the sacrifice came from more than one source: me and my subject. By ensuring I expended energy at the same time they did, through blood runes, we were left exhausted, but alive.

"That can't be why it worked so well." My voice almost came to a whine, pleading with them to reassure me.

"Can't it?" They cocked their head. "He gave his energy fully, and you fully gained his magic."

"Then why didn't it last?"

They shrugged. "Perhaps the magic was not compatible."

"There has to be another reason," I insisted.

Resheph considered me for a moment. "Perhaps the magic was the most compatible. Perhaps his magic was the strongest. Perhaps you had the best combination of ritual ingredients so far. Perhaps you need the larger sacrifice. There are many maybes. Which will you choose to believe?"

"If it's the magic..."

"The further magic has to work through something else, the more extended, or diluted, it becomes." Resheph nodded soundly, as if they just gave me all the answers.

"Do you remember what version of the potion I used that time?" No matter the 'maybe,' I wanted to be prepared.

Resheph hummed and turned from me, rummaging in the crates behind the stall. They plopped a rotund bottle with night-sky liquid on the counter a moment later. "This one." They paused, then held up a slender finger before digging through the crates again and pulling out a long, slender bottle filled with lurid green. "You might want to try this one, though."

I took it from them, considering. My first instinct was to ask what it did and what it contained, but Resheph always refused to answer questions properly. They gave what they thought I needed, and I had to trust. And I always did. Even when I first met them, Resheph seemed familiar, comforting.

Unfortunately, whatever they thought I needed was generally wrapped in riddles. "With or without a change in sacrifice? And how much of this should I even use?"

Resheph lifted a shoulder, and I caught the barest flash of teeth. Did they just smile? "You tell me. Best wishes, Talitha."

My neck twitched. It caught me off guard every time. The first time they called me that, I had insisted my name was Alessa. Resheph had said, *"Well, yes, for now,"* and still called me Talitha. The name brought echoes, too many voices calling that name—some with laughter, some with anger. All familiar yet not.

Shaking away the unwanted past, I tucked the potions into my bag and tossed a few crowns on the counter. Resheph insisted early on that they didn't take crowns and my payment would come through other means. The thought left me uneasy, though, so I left crowns every time. Surely Resheph's fee would at least be less because of it.

"That took a while," Marek commented as I exited the alleyway.

"Dealing with Resheph always does," I grumbled. Taking his arm once more, I led us back in the direction of Kaster Street. Marek's apartment sat a few blocks on the other side—close enough to be cheap without as much risk for crime. "Any chance I can store a few things with you while Alyra's home? She always asks too many questions."

"Why don't you just move in? Then you wouldn't have to deal with your parents either." Marek halted us in the middle of the market. People shoved past, jostling us with curses.

I pulled us next to a stall. "I can't afford to pay rent, Marek. Not right now."

"Where does all of your money go?" he muttered before throwing up his hands. "Fine. Leave stuff. But don't expect to be able to get it at all hours. I'm not giving you a key."

I smirked and patted his arm once more. "Since when have either of us needed a key?"

~

Why isn't it working?

The question echoed in my mind as I stalked my next target, the previous mark's magic a bare whisper of power in my veins. Trying to determine which piece of the puzzle mattered most, I had tried the original potion, but with an earth-tendency. I still didn't have my answer. Despite seeming stronger than many I encountered, the power only lingered a few days. Perhaps I needed a new ritual entirely. Perhaps the more I used it, the less effective it became.

He gave his energy fully, and you fully gained his magic.

Resheph's words chanted in my mind as I shifted around the corner. My mark ducked into a tavern. I let a few people pass before I stepped back onto the street. Not finding my mark past Kaster Street left my heart pounding and my head buzzing. I didn't know this area well enough if something went wrong. And while I had the route mapped in my mind between here and Marek's apartment, as well as to the closest no-questions-asked inn, anxiety crept up my spine and left it rigid. Hunting outside of my grounds left me feeling more like prey than predator.

I took a deep breath as I reached the tavern door and exhaled the tension. With the deep red wig and padded undergarments beneath a freshly conjured dress—*thank you, Alyra*—I was unrecognizable. And since I specifically requested something more plain than the gold-embroidered dress she initially gave me, no thief would cast a second glance my way.

"Gonna stand there all day, sweetheart, or are you actually going in?"

Squeaking out an apology, I yanked open the door and hurriedly ducked in, stepping to the side before scanning the area. My mark sat at a table with a few others, an ale mug clenched in his meaty fist.

His round face was already reddened, dark eyes squinting in the low light. He was wide and muscular enough that if I didn't know better, I would've thought his craft magic was blacksmithing. No, this man had a tailoring tendency, and used it to run a shop a few blocks away. Other than morph magic, craft was the only type I hadn't tried yet. And since morph was so rare—and difficult to discover—craft became the next mark before the festival started in a few days. I wanted to exhaust as many options as I could before I had the plethora of possibilities the Magi would provide.

I planned my path past him before I went to the bar and ordered my own mug of ale and bowl of whatever stew they had on. With a clack of crowns, I got my meal and carefully wound my way towards an empty table against the wall. I stumbled a bit as I passed the tailor and brushed against him as I passed, just enough to catch his eye.

I ducked my head. "I'm so sorry. Excuse me."

Hoping I was the picture of embarrassment, I scurried to my spot and sat down. I brought the mug to my lips and caught his stare before smiling and quickly tearing my gaze away. Perfect.

I ate my meal slowly, not wanting to cast suspicion by running into him twice in such a short amount of time. Twice could seem purposeful if I wasn't careful, and I didn't need anyone accusing me of being a thief tonight. This wasn't a tavern past Kaster Street—I couldn't get them to look away with a handful of crowns or the promise of some noble's jewels.

The tailor seemed wholly absorbed in conversation when I finally stood and skirted past him to go to the bar. I placed the empty stew bowl on the counter while the bartender narrowed his gaze at the still-full mug of ale. Shrugging, I placed another crown down and kept my back to the crowd while he poured a replacement I'd never drink. I needed a clear head tonight if I wanted the ritual to work.

With a deep breath, I turned. It was now or never.

Adding a bit of tilt to my walk and glazing my vision to the wall across the tavern, I stumbled through the crowd and promptly ran into the tailor. My ale flung across his back as I slapped into the floor with a groan. His chair scraped against the stone as his companions shouted in protest. He loomed over me as I glanced up, blinking blearily. My eyes flew wide with shock as I noted the wet patch on his sleeve. It likely covered his back, too.

"I'm so sorry!" I let my lip wobble, scrambling to my feet and stepping too close. I dabbed at his arm furiously with my sleeve. When I let myself look at him, his cheeks were tinged pink, and his friends' shouts had turned to smirks and appraising looks.

"It's all fine. Accidents happen." He patted my wrist awkwardly, like he considered removing it.

I only pressed harder and brought tears to my eyes. "No, no." I let out a little moan. "I'm so clumsy. I'm so sorry. Please, let me get you cleaned up. I'm staying not far from here." I pretended not to see the leer on the one friend's face or the way one of the others nudged him. "I'll even pay for a new shirt. Please, please."

I kept my eyes wide, hoping the kohl I brushed over my lashes helped my green eyes look enticing rather than strange. Unnerving. If this didn't work, I'd have to ambush him, and I had no interest in trying to haul this beast of a man anywhere.

He considered me for another moment, and my cheeks pinked as he swept his gaze down my padded form. My mouth spread in a demure smile as I stopped myself from clenching my jaw. Men preferred curves. He probably never would've looked my way if I looked like myself. Not that I particularly wanted his attention.

I lifted my chin, ridding myself of that unhelpful train of thought, and cocked my head. "What do you say?" A tear slipped down my cheek, adding to my desperation.

He took my hand gently from his arm and patted it. My breath hitched, expecting him to pull away and refuse.

"No need for a new shirt, my dear, but I will not say no to getting cleaned up."

I smiled broadly, the innocent drunken tourist out of her depth. "Oh, thank you. Please, this way. I'm Leesa."

"Vardin."

He took a moment to drain his own mug before letting me lead the way out, his hand still in mine. I wove through the press of tables, ignoring the stares, pausing when the door opened to let in the newest patrons.

My entire body stiffened. A familiar giggle broke through the buzz of the tavern as a semi-familiar towering figure stepped inside, a glimpse of skirts hidden behind him. *Shit.* I ducked my head. *What are they doing here?* Tarin's eyes skipped over us as he took in the tavern, and I quickly tugged my mark past them. While the Magi shouldn't recognize me, my sister *would*, especially since she was the one who created this dress.

In my haste, I bumped into Tarin. I pitched my voice high and stuttered an apology, Vardin echoing one much louder. But I caught the Magi's gaze, and I saw the slow blink. The press of lips. The tilt of his head. My heart pounded. *Telepath,* my mind reminded. He just needed a brief touch for surface-level thoughts. He knew exactly who I was.

I shoved through the door, expecting him to call after me. Yet when I glanced over my shoulder, he only dipped his chin in acknowledgment, his eyes dancing. My pulse skipped. Something within me protested at the idea of him assuming I was sleeping with another man, especially when he didn't seem to care. Maybe he did want the attention of my sister, who thankfully at the moment only had eyes for him. My stomach twisted. What else should I expect, though? Everyone wanted Alyra.

Mind swimming, I led the way to the inn in a daze, answering Vardin's questions automatically. We went in through the back, and wound our way up the stairs until we reached the room at the far corner. I apologized for the meager accommodations as I fished out the key and unlocked it.

"If you give me your shirt, I can clean it," I offered once inside, holding out my hand expectantly.

Vardin frowned for a minute before he shucked it and handed it over. I smiled, letting my eyes flick across his broad chest for a second. "Would you like some wine while you wait? It might take a moment."

He nodded and settled on the bed, his back to the basin that stood in the corner. Good. It would be easier to pretend like I was actually cleaning when he wasn't looking.

I quickly poured him a glass from my tainted bottle, making a show of taking off the seal and pouring myself one too before pretending to take a small sip. Small things to ease his trust. With the wine in one hand and his shirt in the other, I went over to the basin and tossed in the latter, grabbing the nearby ewer and letting the water splash loudly over the stain. *Drink*, I pleaded silently. It wouldn't take much to knock him out, but the more he drank, the faster it would go.

"What brings you to Latheria?"

I let out a giggle. "Is it that obvious?"

"You speak like a native," he admitted, and the bed creaked. "But no one here has red hair, and your dress is a different style."

"Oh." I took a moment to look down at myself in case he watched. "I didn't realize." The lie slipped out smoothly.

"It *was* a style here," Vardin reassured me. "But about a decade ago."

I released a sigh of disappointment. This was taking too long. "How do you know so much about fashion?"

"I'm a...tailor."

Was the pause purposeful because he wasn't sure how I'd react, or was the wine finally taking effect?

"I never would've guessed," I told him honestly. "No wonder you don't want a new shirt."

He was silent for a moment. "Right... I can just...make...another."

The wine. I pretended to rub at the stain for a moment, before a heavy thud made me pause. "Sir?"

I turned to find him collapsed on the floor. Good. Hauling him off the bed would've taken a lot of work. And made a lot of noise.

"Sir!" I exclaimed, rushing over to hastily check his pulse. Slow and steady, his breathing deep and slightly labored. His eyelids stayed fully shut even as I plucked his cheek. I lifted his arm and let it drop onto his chest. Nothing. Good. I'd have to work quickly. While I had added more tyfen petal to accommodate his build, half the wine was sloshed over the bed, so who knew how long it would be until he woke?

I fished my bag from beneath a loose floorboard and pulled out the necessities. The new potion from Resheph. Candles. An athame. A seraphinite tower crystal. A compass. And a silver goblet.

Checking the directions, I dragged the tailor until he laid at an eastern point. The grimoire was explicit in the ritual's need of cardinal points. Something about east to west being the natural transfer of energy. The crystal went in the middle, runes in the north and south.

I grabbed the athame and the tailor's hand, carefully cutting across his finger and leaving it a little jagged. It had to look like he caught it on something other than my knife. I squeezed below the cut, dripping crimson into the goblet. Lifting my skirts, I cut a line across my thigh. I needed to keep my hands uninjured, and a cut on my arm would raise too many questions if noticed. Blood slid into the goblet as I pushed it into a scar from a previous cut right below the current one. If anyone ever saw my thighs, they would likely question the crisscrossing scars, pale against my olive skin.

I swirled the cup, letting our bloods mix before uncorking the potion and pouring half of it in. Why waste it if only half would be enough? And if I needed more before the festival, I could always go to Resheph. Hopefully.

The blood tingled against my finger as I dipped it in and carefully drew a circle around the tailor, shoving him onto either side to finish it beneath him. I redipped my finger and painted curling runes at north and south, still comparing them to their images in the grimoire despite having drawn them so many times previously. One final rune in the center before I placed the crystal over it and took my seat across from the tailor.

Inhaling deeply, I recited the spell from memory. Once foreign and heavy on my tongue, the ancient words wove through the air almost lazily, pulling on the ether that ran through the world. The scent of leather blanketed the room, tendrils of bright yellow stretching from the tailor towards me. My body hummed as the magic reached me, sinking into my skin and racing through my veins. They gathered at my core and exploded. The world flashed yellow like being blinded by the sun.

I doubled over and panted, blinking until the yellow dissipated. Something was different this time. I closed my eyes and sought the answer. My bones ached. My eyelids fought to stay shut. My head pounded. All normal.

The magic coiled like a slumbering snake, waiting for me to reach in and use it. *That*, that was different. A frown twisting my lips, I gripped my skirts and prodded the magic. It stretched, winding through my veins, into my fingers, and into the skirt. Releasing it, it sank back and coiled again, waiting patiently.

I peeled open my eyes to find my skirts had shifted from deep blue to the same green as my eyes. I reached for the magic again, willing the skirts to cut in two and bind themselves back in separate swaths. Like I wielded a pair of scissors, the skirts split up the middle, and a pair of invisible hands hemmed the pieces into pants. The seam was a little jagged, but considering I had no sewing skills to start, I was still left impressed. This magic was *strong*. And with the way it retreated, waiting to be used, rather than constantly running through my veins, I had a feeling this would last far longer than the rest.

A genuine grin stretched my lips. Now to find a Magi that had magic I actually wanted.

～

A KNOCK RESOUNDED through my bedroom, and I glanced at the door over my shoulder. "Come in."

Alyra pressed inside before I even finished the words. She halted near the door with a scowl. "You're not even close to ready!"

"I know," I sighed. I waved a hand towards my wardrobe. "I don't know what to wear."

I thought I had the outfit picked out for the festival, but the blouse had gotten a stain I couldn't get out, and the skirt didn't match with anything else. Admittedly, I wasn't even sure I wanted to wear the skirt anymore. With the tailoring magic still lingering in my core, I could've created something, but my mind wasn't that creative, and Alyra would've asked too many questions if I suddenly had new clothes.

"You could've asked me to conjure something for you. You don't even have your hair done."

"I know, I know," I muttered. I hated asking her to use her magic, though. The thought of owing her something twisted my stomach into my throat.

Alyra scanned my wardrobe with a shake of her head. She looked resplendent in warm autumn hues, a rosy billowing shirt paired with a dusk-orange skirt embroidered with tiny red flowers. Her hair spilled in perfect curls down her back, a red ribbon pulling it from her face, which glowed with hints of golden paint along her cheekbones and eyelids. Whatever she came up with, I would only pale in comparison.

"Pants or a skirt?" she asked me after a moment.

"Pants like a skirt?" I suggested. I couldn't show her the dress I had changed without a thousand questions, so hopefully she understood. That simple shift had left me more mobile without the additional stares I got when wearing tight pants. Women wore pants in Enssa, but normally only if they worked certain jobs. Silly, really, since half of the statues I had ever seen of Aveis, Halia, and Caralin showed them in pants.

Alyra shrugged and reached out to grab my shoulder. The

tailoring magic recoiled from hers, my amplifying ability taking a moment longer for her to reach. She didn't seem to notice, though, her eyes shut as an outfit appeared at the base of the wardrobe and sweet honey filled the room. I gaped at the set, picking them up gingerly.

My sister had conjured a matching outfit of pure gold, the blouse silky smooth and form-fitting until my elbows, where the sleeves split and spilled down past my hands. The pants would look like a skirt from afar, yet were lighter than any skirt I had ever worn. A pea-green bustier came with it, embroidered with swirls of gold that tied the whole things together while managing to give my figure the illusion of curves.

"Now let's see if we can wrangle that hair." She *tsked* and grabbed barely used products from my vanity. I closed my eyes as she pulled my hair and prodded my skull with pins. Something tickled across my face. By the time I looked into the mirror, I didn't recognize the person staring back. My curls weren't a pile of frizz but oiled ringlets carefully pinned back with a few pieces loose around my cheeks. Our faces were done identically, the only difference the color of my eyes and the deep tan to my skin.

"Come on," Alyra said, grinning and grabbing my arm. "We have people waiting for us."

My brow pinched in confusion as she dragged me out of the room to find Tarin and Marek standing with their arms crossed near the front door. I blanched—this was not the plan.

Tarin was the dark to Marek's light. Tarin's hair swept in inky waves while Marek shone golden. I could finally tell Tarin's eyes were actually blue. Ink blue to his ink black hair. Marek wore colors appropriate for the festival—golds and reds and deep greens— whereas Tarin still wore a dark suit like before, only embellished with a little gold. The same shade I wore.

Maybe Alyra didn't like him. She matched Marek better than Tarin, and she could've conjured anything after seeing them.

Marek blinked like he didn't recognize me while Tarin gave a slow smile. When he met my gaze, I could've sworn he winked.

"Shall we go?" Alyra asked, seemingly oblivious. My sister started walking toward the men, but before she had the chance to approach one, I hastily linked arms with her and dragged her past them. I could deal with that mess later. I had a festival to enjoy and a mark to find.

We left the house and joined the crush of people headed toward the square as the sun dipped below the tops of the houses. Most people wore similar colors to Marek and Alyra, but some wore blue-grays and red-browns and a washed-gray color I assumed was supposed to be pink. Another thing gone from the rituals.

Unlike Tarin, at least some of the Magi wore their robes over their festival clothes, the deep black marking them against the rest. The trim of their robe declared their magic, and I wanted to do a slow turn to take in all of the possibilities. Some of them I had already taken—bright red for enhanced senses, chartreuse for plants, white for sunshine—but some were new. Maroon for bone manipulation, periwinkle for dreamreading, even the pale gray— pale pink, in actuality—of a human morph. The sheer possibilities...

The square had transformed. Orange and yellow streamers wove around the square, marking the boundaries of the main festivities. Red lanterns dotted the area, providing much needed light as the sun disappeared. A long table divided the space, overflowing with free food and drink, while merchants hawked their wares from their stalls, warning the crowd they would close at dark. Musicians sat tucked into a corner, their instruments a discordant hum in the air as they prepared.

"What do you want to do first?" I asked my sister. Eventually, I would need to lose her in the crowd, but I had time yet. I'd need to choose my mark first anyway.

Alyra looked at me expectantly, then turned and pointed to a stall near the entrance. An artist sat there painting a child's face. We did this every year, despite likely being the woman's oldest clients.

She started pulling me to stand in line while Marek said, "We'll get food and drink."

The woman greeted us warmly and made small talk as she painted each of our faces—pretty flowers for Alyra and winding vines for me. We found the men standing not far off, their arms laden with goodies. Marek passed out drinks while Tarin handed us small bags. The bags made it easy to walk around, digging out fried balls of spiced ground meat, crispy potatoes, and squares of gooey cheese. Either Tarin didn't believe in sweets, or he hadn't seen them. But that was fine. Most of those would have butter in them, and I didn't want the taste of ash in my mouth.

I took a cautious sip of the drink as we wandered the festival together and was pleasantly surprised to find simple, mulled apple cider, no hint of alcohol heating my throat. While Marek knew I didn't often drink, the festival was normally an exception.

Ignoring Alyra as she gushed over something in the closest stall, I scanned the crowd. The Magi seemed old compared to Tarin. The youngest might have been forty. Age didn't matter from a power perspective—if they made it to Magi, they had to have a certain level of power—but it would make seduction more difficult. They were more likely to be wary of a woman half their age. And if they weren't wary, well... I shuddered. That was a different issue.

"Are you well?"

I glanced up at Tarin, surprised to see concern etched into his sharp features. "Fine," I told him. "Just thought of something unpleasant."

Him, just take him. The thought seemed treacherous. I'd never second-guessed choosing a mark before, but something didn't feel right. Knowing him, finding him attractive—that should have made this easier. *And more dangerous.*

"You're not cold?"

"No." I shook my head, waiting a few steps off as Alyra bought her first trinket for the night. "Thank you for asking." I paused. "And thank you for not mentioning the other night to my sister."

Tarin's smile lit up wicked parts of my mind. Parts that never woke. Not even in other lives. Not with the village boy as Talitha. Or the artist as Giovanna. Or the bootlegger as Millie. Trysts had happened, I knew, but they were done for distraction—or many times in an attempt to make my younger sibling feel an ounce of what I suffered by taking something they coveted.

I blinked away the memories. That was *not* what I was trying to do this time.

"What other night?" Tarin asked.

"I see some friends. I'll see you later," Marek announced. He disappeared into the crowd, but not before I caught his wide eyes and reddened ears. I wasn't sure I wanted to know what he imagined had happened between us.

Alyra frowned when she noticed Marek left, but continued on to the next stall as the band finally struck up the first song.

"She'll be shopping for as long as they're open," I told Tarin as I tossed my trash into a waiting bin. My heart pounded in my ears as I built up the nerve to ask, "Would you like to dance?"

Dancing would probably present the most danger. With the constant touching, he'd have access to my thoughts, and more than just the passing, top-of-my-mind stuff.

"I believe you beat me to my question." He offered his arm, and I took it, marveling at the height difference. My nose was squarely at his sternum. This would be...interesting.

Alyra didn't even glance our way as he escorted me into the crowd gathering in front of the band. People already danced a lively jig, and the only warning Tarin gave was brief eye contact before he swept me into the same. Together, apart, together. Feet flying faster than I thought possible. Laughter splitting our faces in two. I couldn't even conjure a thought beyond the movement, desperate to keep up with his long legs. When the band finally came to a bright halt, our arms caught around each other, swinging to a stop. His chest heaved in time with mine. I pressed into him as a light scattering of applause started and the musicians picked up another tune.

"I can't believe you left me!"

Alyra's voice cut through just as he dipped his chin. Tarin's jaw clenched, and he straightened, dropping his arm from my waist. Her purchases were gone, likely locked within the chests the city provided, or even teleported home.

I bristled and folded my arms across my chest, trying to ignore the cold spot he left. "You were quite content shop—"

"I believe it was my fault," Tarin cut smoothly across. "The last was one of my favorites, and as you were occupied, I asked Alessa to dance."

As you were occupied echoed in my mind, and I stepped away from him. The words cut to my core. Of course I was just a distraction. How could anyone look at me when Alyra was around?

This wasn't anything new, so why did I blink away tears? "I'm going to find Marek," I muttered, tearing away before they could respond.

Every time. Every time I wanted something, Alyra swooped in and took it without a thought, unless it was simply handed to her first. My vision flooded pea-green, and I ducked into the shadows between the closest stalls.

Not this time. Tarin would be mine, one way or another, and so would his magic.

My sister danced with the biggest smile on her face, yet Tarin's demeanor had changed. His grin was tight, and despite the frequent catch and release of the dance, he kept my sister at arm's length. Who knew how long he'd be able to keep his distance, though. I was sure he'd succumb to my sister before long.

The song changed again to a dance that frequently changed partners, and I approached the closest man with my gaze flitting away as if I was nervous. He agreed without hesitation. I gave him a coy smile, and he took me to join the long line of women standing across from the men.

Glancing down the line, I did the math. Three partner changes and I would be with Tarin; two more after that to get back to him.

Good; that would give me multiple chances. With his telepathy, all I needed to do was concentrate.

My feet moved automatically—the dance was one done every festival, so I knew it well by now—and I focused on conjuring an image in my mind. A daydream.

The warm glow of the sun across rumpled sheets. Bare skin slick with sweat. Slow touches and gentle kisses. Roving tongues.

My cheeks flushed, and I stumbled. Tarin caught me around the waist and I latched back onto the daydream, letting it slam into his mind as his magic thrummed between us. He coughed, and his eyes latched onto mine. I smiled innocently, even as I let the images in my head shift from warm and romantic to heated and passionate. Tangled limbs, hair yanked back, breaths coming out in short puffs. This body had never experienced such intimacy, but my mind knew it well enough, conjuring semi-familiar sensations from my past lives.

His eyes trailed after me as I was swept away by the next partner, and the next, and when Tarin had me once more, his grip tightened and he practically dragged me out of the crowd into the nearest alley. Pressing me against the wall, his mouth hovered only inches from mine.

"What are you trying to do?"

I blinked, my eyes going wide. "What do you mean?"

"Don't play innocent with me." His knee pressed into my thigh, further trapping me. "I know your sister told you of my magic. What game are you playing?"

I cocked my head and gave him a demure smile. "Did you not like what you saw? Would you like something else? What about this?" A roaring fire and bare skin pressed together beneath fur rugs. "Or this?" Waves crashing over us as we knelt on wet sand, hands fisted in hair. "Or—"

Tarin's mouth crashed onto mine. There was nothing gentle in his touch as he dragged his nails down my waist and around to my thigh, hoisting my leg around him. His tongue pressed through my lips and captured mine. I could barely breathe, my mind going blank in the wake of reality.

He tugged on my bottom lip, and a moan escaped my lips. I tried to pull back, but there was nowhere to go. I pushed my hands into his chest, my breath uneven.

"Not here," I murmured, peering pointedly past his shoulder and back towards the festival. "We'll need to leave separately if we don't want to catch Alyra's suspicions."

"What does it matter?" He nuzzled into my neck, nipping my earlobe.

What does it matter? My mind echoed the words. Let Alyra wonder what she wanted. Let her be jealous that I succeeded in taking Tarin.

"Do you want her incessant questions?" I asked him.

He huffed, his breath warm against my skin. "No, but perhaps she would stop dogging after me."

"She won't let me hear the end of it," I told him. "Please."

He pulled back and considered me for a moment before nodding. I wanted to get lost in those eyes. "It won't be hard to say I have to leave for work purposes."

"Despite her being here to work with you?" I frowned. He inclined his head. "Very well, you can go first then. I always leave earlier than she does from these things anyway, so I'll just say I'm tired and going home."

"And when she doesn't find you at home?" He lifted a brow.

I tilted my head side to side, pretending to consider. "I'll tell her I went to Marek's instead because it's closer. Meet you here?"

He nodded his assent and I pushed to move past him. "What's between you two?"

"Why? Jealous?"

He shook his head. "I don't like making messes."

If he didn't like messes, he wouldn't be involved with me at all, but I wasn't about to argue that point. "We work together. He's like my older brother."

For a moment I thought he would tell me he didn't believe me, despite being able to sift through my mind if he so pleased. That hint of disbelief lingered when he finally grunted his acknowledgment and stepped back, sweeping his arm wide. "After you."

We returned to the party separately, and I smoothed out my hair and skirts as I walked. If Alyra noticed anything amiss, she didn't say, dragging me into the next dance. I begged off from the next one, going to the food table and dragging my hand along the edge as I considered. No pies were safe, and even the lavender decor was tainted with its ashen scent. I settled on an apple, not wanting to chance anything else, even as a blackberry pie called my name.

Tarin danced with my sister again, and I waited for the anger to flash through my veins. This time my heart stayed calm, my jealousy a tamed beast for now. It didn't matter if they danced for a few minutes—Tarin was mine.

He bent close to her ear at the end of the dance, and my sister's shoulders drooped. Good. It would be my turn soon enough. I faced the table once more, pretending not to notice the exchange while munching on the apple. Alyra came over in a huff, her arms folded across her chest. It wasn't often she didn't get what she wanted.

"What's wrong?" I asked her, my eyebrows pinched together.

"Mag—Tarin had to leave. He said on business, but he insisted I stay."

"What you're here for still isn't resolved?"

She shook her head. "No. You'd think it wouldn't be so hard to find someone stealing magi—" Alyra's hands flew to cover her mouth. "I shouldn't have said that."

My heart thundered in my chest as ice dropped into my stomach. I fought to control my face as I looked at my sister. "Who am I going to tell? Marek?" Alyra gave me a hard look. My hands flew in the air, nearly tossing the apple from my grip. "Come on, you know I wouldn't tell him. He probably wouldn't care about it even if I did. Someone's stealing magic? That's possible?"

"Apparently. No one's ever heard of such a thing, but there are reports in the city of people waking up unable to use their magic for days—even weeks."

"There's not something wrong with magic, right? It's not like we have a source—unlike the continent, or even Sitia—so maybe it's just...running out?" The words sounded lame, even to me, but my sister assumed I understood little about magic, and I needed to keep it that way.

"I don't even know if that's possible." Alarm flashed across her face. "I need to find Tarin."

I caught her arm as she turned. "He's likely long gone. Stay, enjoy the festival while you can." I swept an arm to the massive swarm of colors surrounding us. I paused, considering my friend in the distance. "Go dance with Marek," I suggested. I smirked. "Or...more than dance."

Alyra's eyes flew wide. "I thought you liked him."

Hadn't I just explained this to her? I snorted. "No. Go, enjoy yourself."

"But what about you?" she asked, even as her eyes sought out the tall blond lingering with a group of men off to the side of the musicians.

"I'm getting tired. You know me." I shrugged. In the past, I would go thieving while everyone was out of their homes. I guessed I was still thieving this year, just something far more valuable. "Go on."

I nudged her, and that was all she needed to cut a path like an arrow through the crowd towards Marek. Turning on my heel, I found Tarin in the alleyway and promptly grabbed his hand, dragging him away from the city square.

"Where are you taking me?"

"Somewhere we can be alone." I shot a smile over my shoulder, and he returned it, his long strides quickly catching him up to my side, where he let go of my hand. We were headed to Marek's, but I didn't think he'd appreciate that detail. Marek's apartment wasn't particularly far, and he typically stayed at the festival until the wee hours of the morning, so I should have plenty of time.

Once we wound our way to the third story of the apartment building, I knelt at the door at the end of the hall and pulled out a few pins from my hair, a chunk of curls tumbling down my spine.

"What are you doing?" Tarin's voice suddenly sounded hesitant.

"Forgot my keys." I shrugged. "When you do that as often as I have, you learn how handy hair pins can be."

My lips curved upwards as the tumbler clicked, and I turned the knob, shoving open the door. I pulled him into the dark before pressing a kiss to his cheek. "Give me just a minute."

I took a moment to light a few candles in the space before grabbing my bottle of wine and holding it out to him. "Drink?"

He shook his head and tugged me close, pressing his lips to mine. I forced my panic aside. Let myself linger in the kiss. Tarin pulled back and pressed his forehead to mine.

"Do you think I need a drink to want you?"

I bit my bottom lip, hating how close he hit to the truth. "It seems to help calm nerves."

He shook his head. "I'm not nervous. Maybe you need some?"

I shifted back, out of his grasp, and pretended to consider the bottle. If he wouldn't drink, I would need another plan. But if I thought at all about another option while touching him, he'd stop me. *Queens, I'm screwed.* I had once chance to get this right.

Placing the bottle on the nearest side table, I approached and pressed my body into his. I lost myself in languid touches and eager lips, letting him push me against the side table as he fumbled with my bustier.

Now or never. As soon as the thought crossed my mind, he paused and looked up, eyes widening as I gripped the neck of the wine bottle and hoisted it overhead. Tarin caught my wrist as he straightened.

"What do you think you're doing?"

"Sorry."

I kneed him in the groin and yanked my arm from his grasp. He doubled over as I swung the bottle down on his head. *Thunk.* He crumpled to the ground, and I looked at the bottle, surprised it was still intact. I let it drop to my side and turned to get my things from the other room. Who knew how much time I had?

His hand lashed out and grabbed my ankle before I could step, yanking me back. I crashed to the floor. His nails dug into my skin and I bared my teeth, scrambling to hands and knees before shoving my free leg back. Something cracked.

With my ankle free, I spun around. Tarin cradled his nose, scarlet dripping freely between his fingers. I fumbled for the bottle. His eyes met mine. He reached. I swung the bottle sideways and it collided with his temple.

Tarin dropped like a stone.

Some small part of the back of my mind panicked, but I was already rushing to my satchel and setting up the ritual. I used the blood from his nose to mix with mine, drawing the runes with haste. I would have his magic.

With everything in place, I spoke the words and let his magic sweep over me.

And my world exploded.

I stumbled out of Marek's apartment with my mind on fire.

Ugh, yes, take it.

Who the queens does she think she is?

I can't believe he just left her like that.

I wonder if we have food at home.

I'll just take that.

Queens forbid we do anything improper.

My mind spiraled with unfamiliar voices. It was all I could do to pack my bag and get out of there. I couldn't concentrate long enough to do anything with his body. Marek would find evidence of the ritual on his floor.

I couldn't care. My body threatened to eat itself alive.

My feet somehow found their way to my parents' house, and a

flurry of unsolicited thoughts later, I was in my bedroom. I tore at my hair. *Make it stop.*

Who does she think she is?

I don't know why we let her stay here.

Coming in at all hours of the night.

We should really make her get her own place.

Disturbing us constantly.

She has a job.

Why can't—

I just wish—

She be—

She was—

More like her sister.

"Make it stop!"

The scream tore from my throat as I collapsed onto the floor, tears streaming down my face.

"Get it out, get it out, get it out."

I clawed at my head, chunks of hair flying from my skull.

Alessa?

The word echoed aloud. I couldn't look at her as I sobbed. "This is all your fault."

What is going on? What happened to her face paint? What's my fault? Stop doing that. Stop!

She grabbed my wrists and I shook, rocking back and forth on the floor.

"Get it out. Now!"

Get what—what in the queens' names is she talking about? Is she injured? There's no—wait, there is blood. Oh queens, where is she hurt?

"Not. Hurt," I gritted out.

I'm going to die like this.

What does she mean— Wait. "You're the one stealing magic." I couldn't argue. I only sobbed harder. Alyra let me go and took a step back. "Where's Tarin? What did you do to him?"

I just shook my head. "Please...Alyra..."

"It's his magic." *How could she?* "Is he dead?" *He can't be dead. None of the others were dead. He's fine. He has to be—*

"I don't know," I told her. *My brain is melting.* "Please. Please."

Alyra looked at me, and the tumult of her thoughts shoved their way into my brain. She was at war with herself. What would win, her loyalty to her precious Magi, or her love for her sister?

I closed my eyes and wished for a quick, quiet death.

"How?"

My eyes flew wide. I pointed numbly to my bag where the grimoire lay hidden. There were other spells beyond the ritual within. Surely there was something for this.

I pressed my fingers to my temples and tried to destroy the foreign thoughts with my own, but they were loud and insistent and impossible to overcome.

"Which one did you use?" she demanded, and I pointed out the spell after a moment's hesitation.

Well, I can't use that, clearly it's temporary.

But if it's temporary, why not let her wait it out until it's gone?

No. Who knows how long that would take. She can't handle that. I need to find...That should work.

"I need you to stay still."

A whimper escaped my lips, but I managed to nod, my whole body shaking instead.

So much for still. Alyra's thoughts echoed my own.

My sister grabbed my hand and slashed across it with my athame. I hissed as she did her own. She slapped our palms together and held tight.

Words of power slipped over her tongue before lingering in the air and settling over us both. Lilac magic yanked from my veins and wove through the air as pale gray magic coiled out of Alyra. The powers wound around each other and shot into the other person. We flew apart, banging into opposite walls.

Alyra winced and held a hand to her head. I mimicked her, but my face split with wonder.

The voices were gone. My head was mercifully quiet. A dull ache pounded behind my ears, but that was all. I blew out a sigh of relief. Never did I think I would be grateful for not having magic.

I needed a cup of tea.

Bergamot abruptly wove through the air, and I scrambled back when I spotted a mug on the floor in front of me. *No.*

"What did you do?"

Alyra straightened slowly. "I traded magics," she said simply. As if anything about that was simple. Her whole face fell as she examined me. "Why?"

The disappointment in her voice made me want to hide. My shoulders shrank down, and I studied the mug of tea, unable to meet her gaze. I could lie, say it was just some conquest for power, but what was the point? And after the disaster she just saved me from, I owed her an explanation.

"You have everything." My sister opened her mouth to protest, and I held up a hand. "Please. Just. Give me a moment." I took a deep breath. "We used to be the same. But then you got magic. And I didn't. Our worlds changed. You became the star, the coveted child, and I became...nothing. Practically invisible. I only existed to make you even better. That's all you ever came to me for, anymore, my ability to amplify your magic. How was that fair?" I choked on my own words. "I just wanted my own magic. Maybe then I would've been seen."

Tears slipped down my cheeks and dropped to the floor. Who knew how long I would have Alyra's magic? And even with it, there would be no pride in my parents' eyes. Only horror. To them—to her —I was a monster.

Arms encircled me in a tight hug. I collapsed to my knees. She shouldn't have been hugging me. She should've wanted nothing to do with me.

"You are not a monster," Alyra whispered in my ear. I cried harder. "And I never meant to use you. I am sorry. I am sorry you feel this way, and I am sorry that's how I came across. I just wanted you to be my sister. I just wanted you to play with me like you used to— to do everything together, like we used to. I didn't realize..." She shook her head. "You don't need magic to be seen. I'll prove it."

Alyra pulled away and went over to the grimoire. My eyebrows pinched tight, tears still slipping unwillingly down my cheeks. "What are you doing?"

"There's a spell in here that gets rid of your magic entirely."

I had seen that one. I had even considered trying to incorporate it into the ritual, but I couldn't figure out a way to consume the magic the person would sacrifice. Plus, they had to strip the magic willingly, and once gone, they would never be able to touch magic again. They wouldn't see it, wouldn't smell it, wouldn't be affected by it. Both a curse and a protection.

It took me too long to realize what she was doing.

"No! Alyra, you don't—"

Too late. She had the grimoire in her lap and the words on her lips. Power pulsed through the space, and the borrowed magic twisted its way back out of her. Her hair went dull, her skin turned pallid, her body sagged. And the magic disappeared.

"There," she breathed.

I could only gape at her. She tilted her chin to look at me and planted a shaking arm on her hip.

"Am I any less without magic?"

I wanted to shout *yes*. Yes, she was less. Less shiny, less golden, less perfect. But was that magic, or just the effect of the spell?

I looked down at the bergamot tea. Stroked the pale gray magic coiled inside me, waiting to be commanded with the simplest thought. Then looked at my sister. My sister, who just sacrificed her own magic to prove a point. My sister, who knew I might have killed her mentor, yet still decided to help me.

I didn't deserve her. And I certainly didn't deserve her magic.

Moving over to the bed, I sank into the mattress beside her and took the grimoire into my lap. I stared down at the spell, perhaps the simplest one in the whole book. Years of planning, years of wanting, gone in a matter of seconds. Alyra wound her fingers through mine. I met her eyes, and she gave me a small smile.

Perhaps that was for the best.

I cleared my throat and recited the words. Alyra's magic shot out of me like a lightning bolt. With the last word, it snapped free, and I shuddered. Exhaustion riddled my bones, and I dropped my head onto my sister's shoulder. I waited for the regret, the anger. Nothing but tiredness hollowed my stomach.

Alyra squeezed my hand and bumped my shoulder. "We'll need to take care of Tarin."

Maybe she should've been born first, always cleaning up my messes. I straightened and nodded. Since Alyra rid herself of his magic, would he get it back—assuming he was still alive? Or would it be gone forever?

Why did I suddenly care when I had been so easily prepared to take his magic forever without a second thought?

"Um, Alessa?"

I turned fully to my sister. "What?"

"Your eyes."

"My—what?"

"Go look in the mirror."

Scowling and bemused, I wandered over to the mirror on my vanity. And did a double take. I leaned in close, disbelief dropping my jaw.

My eyes were no longer the pea green of envy, but the same warm blue as my sister's.

Bittersweet

Maddie Jensen

CHAPTER 3
BITTERSWEET
MADDIE JENSEN

I recognised the omens. Crows circling in the sky like vultures over a carcass. The stink of sulphur on a morning breeze. One desperate scream joined by another, an unholy choir of pain and suffering. The metallic tang of blood thick on my tongue.

Tonight, the skies were clear, the stars shimmering overhead without obstruction as my faded red 2002 Mitsubishi Magna passed a sign that heralded fifty kilometres until we were back in our hometown of Eris.

The warm summer air caressed my blonde hair, a cooling balm against my sweat-slick skin and the tank top that stuck unpleasantly to my back. I much preferred the icy cold of winter, curling up under a mound of blankets with a mug of hot chocolate in my hands.

"Seriously, are you and Conrad just never going to address it?" Dana asked from the passenger seat. Her head was tilted back, a mischievous smile across her lips as I chanced a look away from the road to observe my best friend.

"Address what?" I was momentarily drawn out of our conversation by my own thoughts of impending doom, before I groaned as I remembered the topic of discussion. "For fuck's sake."

"The sexual tension," Dana sang as she leaned forward to tap on the car's inbuilt stereo as the Bluetooth cut out again, a frequent occurrence in a car almost as old as we were.

"I thought we promised we weren't going to talk about Conrad on this trip," I complained, drumming my fingers on the steering wheel.

My heart raced, heat that had nothing to do with the summer sun flaring in my cheeks. Conrad was our other best friend, and someone that I'd admittedly had a crush on for years. He was gorgeous, with the most piercing blue eyes I'd ever seen. I had never let it go beyond friendship. Conrad and Dana were already as close to me as I'd ever let anyone get.

Across my many lives, the golden thread the Fates had woven me bled crimson. The lives I had taken, the battles I had fought. Battle and bloodshed were woven in the fabric of my identity. My future was a concoction of anger, hatred, and violence, a vile taste I'd become accustomed to. There had never been room for a blossoming romance, not since Dimitrios. Not since I had been Athene.

This is the gift you gave me, dearest Dad, I thought bitterly. The curse of ending lives and harming others, over and over again.

"Then why don't we talk about you?" Dana said, her tone dropping and losing its light teasing. "I worry about you, Minnie."

I scoffed. "What? Because I didn't go to some fancy college like you and Conrad? If this is about my job again, I like being a mechanic."

Dana and Conrad were from wealthy families, well-known in our small town. By contrast, I grew up in shabby second-hand clothing from the thrift shop, my school backpacks old and stained. I spent my childhood in the back of the beat-up Magna I now drove, constantly surrounded by the smell of stale McDonalds chips and damp towels.

I had been guiltily eager to leave my childhood house, the memory glowing with a bright spring afternoon and the sunflowers my mum had planted in the front garden. I still visited a couple of times a month, but I had always known that place was not my home.

Where was home? I didn't associate it with the one-bedroom apartment I rented either. Home was in a time long forgotten, a place that existed only in the dreams I'd started having in primary school. I could feel the splash of ocean salt across my skin as the waves crashed over the rocks, could hear the cries of the gulls overhead.

Once I realised who I was, what I was, loneliness crept in like a heavy shroud. I didn't belong anywhere, not when my purpose was to destroy.

"Not your job," Dana chided, kicking her feet up on the dash. "You just seem...I don't know. Distant."

Silence sank over us like a warm blanket, Dana's words pricking through my skin like my enemies' blades had in my past lives. No one had ever dug as deep as Dana. No one had wanted to.

Dana was the one person I wasn't distant around. With my best friend, I could forget the thick cloy of blood on my tongue. Dana took the hollow I'd carved inside myself and filled it with joy rather than the ancient rage that thrummed through me with every heartbeat.

"I'm not distant." The words were flat, my fingers tightening around the steering wheel. "We just spent a week together. I don't think you can get any less distant than that."

"It's like..." Dana dropped her legs, twisting in her seat to inspect me, pushing down her heart-shaped sunglasses. "You go someplace else. You have since we were kids. Like you daydream, but go all solemn and quiet."

"I don't know where you think I'm going." I shrugged, hoping it was nonchalant, a taste like sour lemon in my mouth at the lie.

"Okay then." Dana switched the song to something more upbeat, raising her arms above her head and waving them from side to side. I fought the smile that tugged at the corners of my lips. Dana's happiness was infectious, the grin on her face eventually echoed on my own as she shimmied in her seat like it was her own private disco.

I was usually more observant; many lives of being aware of my surroundings putting me on edge. Dana had filed those edges down into something softer. I was so caught up in the euphoria she exuded, the vanilla scent of her perfume, and the chirp of crickets, that I didn't see the car until it was too late.

The screech of tyres and the bright blue-tinged glare of oncoming headlights were the only warnings I had before the shiny Porsche hit the passenger side of the Magna.

I slammed my foot on the brakes as we spun out of control, whirling like a terrifying carnival ride. The car crunched over dirt and stones as we careened off the road, a sickening crunch making bile rise in my throat as we hit a tree. The front of the car folded in on itself. Smoke rose from the bonnet, and the windscreen shattered. I raised my hands to protect myself from the falling glass.

In a battle, one must stop to assess the damage done when wounded. This was a constant throughout my lives, though I had yet to see war in my current life. I reached up to touch my temple, my fingers coming away stained scarlet. The tree we'd hit obscured Dana from view, but I could hear her ragged breathing. Pushing aside the dull ache of a bruised rib, I kicked open the driver's side door and tumbled from the wreckage, breathing ragged with exertion.

Shouts from the road snagged my attention, the familiar scents of smoke and blood pushed from my mind as I shielded my eyes from the harsh street light to examine who'd hit us. Three guys, probably similar age to Dana and I. They stumbled about their Porsche to survey how bad a hit it was. At first I thought their staggering alluded to hurt limbs or broken bones, but my blood ran ice-cold as their slurred speech betrayed the truth.

They were drunk.

"Fucking great," one of them said, though the Porsche was in far better shape than my Magna. "Nice job, Jeremy."

"Whatever, man, you told me to drive," Jeremy retorted, raking his fingers through his hair. "Let's just get out of here."

"Wait!" I exclaimed, pulse hammering in my throat as I waved my hands to get their attention. The three stopped to stare at me, but their glazed expressions made me think they were looking right through me. "We took that crash worse than you. We need help."

The boy who had first spoken took a faltering step toward me, darkness and light clashing over his face as he stepped into the shadow, but Jeremy reached out and rested a hand on his shoulder. He shook his head fervently. "We need to go."

"Minnie!" The cry from the Magna, Dana's cry, made me spin around. She was the most important thing in this moment. I turned away from the idiots who'd hit us, curses surfacing and then dying on my lips. Even as I heard the Porsche doors slamming and the engine revving as the guys sped off into the night, I stumbled back to the car, yanking open Dana's door.

My anger toward the trio faded instantly, replaced by a cold horror that tasted like burnt sugar. Dana's body was broken, her torso blooming with so much red that it was like a disease, taking her over and swallowing her piece by piece. Her face was pale as bone, and alarm flared in her brown eyes when she saw my expression.

"It's bad, isn't it?" Her words were hoarse, and judging by her wince, it must have cost some effort to speak.

I had seen wounds like this in wars past. Practicality caressed me with cruel talons and told me there was no coming back from it. Desperation gripped me tighter though, the knowledge that I would do anything within my power to save Dana, even if I fought on the losing side of this battle.

I took my phone out of my pocket, swearing as I examined the cracked screen. Getting Dana's phone from her would only jostle her and cause more pain. My stomach twisted, tying itself into nauseous knots as the bleak truth stared me in the face. I could fight this, as I fought everything, but the result was inevitable.

My knees trembled and threatened to collapse from beneath me as I rushed to Dana's side, taking her hand in both of mine. She tilted her head back, managing a grim smile across blood-flecked lips. A warm smile, one that broke my heart, because that smile was for me. Even in these final moments, she wanted to comfort me.

"Please don't go," she whispered.

"I won't," I choked out.

It had been a while since I had delved into my power, something I kept from using to keep up the charade that I was normal. When I was younger, it wasn't as easy. I remembered sending schoolyard bullies screaming as I created the illusion of monsters from the books Conrad and I read in the library at recess. I could give someone the sweetest dream they'd ever had, or send a nightmare slithering into their subconscious like a vicious serpent.

Creating illusions had served no purpose, especially when I didn't need magic to create the biggest illusion of all: that I was simply Minnie Jameson.

Not Athene. Not Wrath.

As Dana's breath rattled through her lips like a bitter winter breeze against the window panes of my apartment, I created illusions of our happiest moments. The days we had spent by the creek, splashing through the water and shrieking when we almost stepped on an eel. Laughing out in the summer afternoon, Dana's home-brewed lemonade sticky on our lips.

I conjured a dream for her, ensuring her last moments were not spent in pain and fear, but being reminded of how much I loved her.

There was a sudden stillness to death, a final exhale before the life left a person and they were simply flesh, their soul departing to someplace better...or worse. Dana's head lolled to the side, her eyes glazing over, fixed on the stars that sparkled overhead. A sky she could no longer see. Her fingers, clamped around mine like a vise, went slack.

A scream ripped from my throat as all the rage I had suppressed, the fury and hatred I had accrued through centuries and lifetimes, erupted like lava from a volcano. I'd been told about the five stages of grief, but I'd always launched straight from denial to anger.

I had been stabbed. I had been shot. I had been injured in a myriad number of ways, but there was something about loss that tore me apart with more violence than any physical injury. Cuts either heal, or you die. Loss holds you somewhere between the two, a purgatory where you do not die, but sometimes you wish you had.

Tears streamed down my face, obscuring my vision and blurring the harsh lights of a car stopped at the side of the road. A man stumbled toward us, and he said something about calling an ambulance, but nothing mattered in that moment other than the fact Dana was gone. I howled when he tried to pull me away from my best friend, and he settled for taking his jacket off and gingerly putting it over my shoulders.

When the ambulance arrived, I was still holding Dana's hand, terrified to let go of the one person who had anchored me to reality, to a place and a time where I could be more than just a whirlwind of destruction.

Minnie Jameson died that night too. From the ashes of that crash, Athene rose with a hunger for vengeance and a thirst for violence.

No one said it, but there was a timeline for mourning. My work gave me two weeks off to grieve, and my parents brought over food to my apartment when Mum suspected that I wasn't eating properly. The only person that I actually wanted to see was Conrad, and he would show up every day at my apartment without fail, even if it was just to sit with me while I wrapped myself in a blanket burrito.

"They identified the guys who were in the other car."

It was the morning of Dana's funeral. My kitchen filled with the scent of cloves as Conrad went about making a tea, dashing in some milk that was on the brink of expiry. He raked his fingers through his shaggy black hair, his movements assured and precise.

"Who?"

"They were in the year above us at school, I think. Jeremy, Oliver, and Lionel."

I nodded slowly as though disinterested, but the cogs in my mind spun as I committed the names to memory, tossing them into the dark pit of revenge that I could never tell Conrad about. I vaguely recalled they were from wealthy families. Not one of them would see the inside of a jail cell.

Conrad took a mug in each hand, crossing over to the circular dining table and setting my tea down on a glass coaster. The mug was my favourite, little spanners and screwdrivers printed across it. Dana got it online for me two years ago. I traced my fingers over the chink at the top where I'd once knocked it off a bench.

Tears blurred my vision as I raised the mug to my lips with shaking fingers. So much of my current life was intertwined with Dana. The sweet happiness she had brought into my life threatened to be destroyed with her death. Conrad's silence as we drank our tea was peaceful, a mercy after the barrage of questions on how I was doing and how I was feeling from everyone else we knew.

The last time I had been to Eris's small graveyard had been for the funeral of my nan, some seven years prior. I climbed into the passenger seat of Conrad's Audi and stared at the familiar scenery that rushed past. The green haze of trees that lined the quiet suburban streets, the Tudor-style houses that I once dreamed I would have enough money to buy.

I could almost taste the chocolate chip mint ice-cream from Pendulum Parlour, one of our favourite haunts in town. The sharpness of the mint and the creaminess of the chocolate chips would always mix on my tongue, a flavour Dana had wrinkled her nose at in distaste. How could I ever return to the places that had become associated with her, with us?

Conrad pulled into the graveyard's parking lot. When he put the car in park, he reached across and touched my hand, a jolt of electricity flaring through me. My head snapped up and my eyes met his, and I was startled by the tears on his face. Conrad was always the level-headed one of us, but Dana's death wrenched the grief from us all.

"I know this won't be easy for you." His voice was soft, like a gentle caress. "I'm not going anywhere, Minnie. I'll be by your side the whole time."

I nodded, chewing at my lip and tasting the coconut and pear lip balm I'd applied before we left the house. I wasn't ready to say good-bye, wasn't ready to watch the light I'd found over my many lives be buried in the ground. Fates and furies damn us, for they must look on in cruel indifference to my plight.

I slipped out of the car and followed Conrad to the graveyard. I moved like a robot on autopilot, embracing my parents and Dana's parents and everyone else in the goddamn small town that I knew. Across the sea of grim faces, I saw one that I recognised, standing a respectable distance from those of us who had gathered to pay our final respects to Dana.

He was in his mid-thirties, tall with dark hair and eyes that possessed a mixture of solemness and compassion that I would recognise in anyone. In all my lives, he looked different, but I would recognise my dad anywhere. Not the Jamesons who had brought me into this life. The man who had given me my first life, and in doing so, damned me. His real name was Thanatos, though I couldn't have said what his name was now.

I nudged Conrad. "Who's the guy over there?"

Conrad's brow furrowed. "Not sure. I think it might be Tristan. He was Dana's therapist back when we were in high school."

Tristan. A name that truly reflected the man my dad was. He didn't approach me, nor did I expect him to. Dear Dad waited for me to acknowledge him on my terms. I respected him for it.

Dana's parents gave the eulogies, along with some other members of her family. They'd asked me if I wanted to say something, but words couldn't convey exactly how much Dana had meant to me. The scent of turning soil was rich with the roses and daffodils that everyone had brought with them. By the time they lowered

Dana's coffin into the ground and buried earth atop it, Tristan was gone.

That was my burden; people leaving me, some in more violent ways than others. The memory of Dana begging me to stay with her hit me with the force of a blunt axe, and I pressed a hand over my mouth to stifle a sob. Conrad's hand was a warm weight on my shoulder as he pulled me close, lips brushing the top of my head.

Family and friends moved forward to put their flowers atop the earth, but I didn't want to step any closer to that headstone. I didn't want to see the dates that reminded me Dana had been only twenty-two years old. I denied myself the finality of her passing, because there was something deep and dark within me, slumbering for a long time, that had finally awoken.

"I want them to pay." The words were hoarse, rasped from a throat thick with a lump I couldn't swallow.

Conrad drew back to look at me, those beautiful blue eyes bewildered. Then he pressed his lips into a firm line and nodded. "So do I."

"No." I wrenched away from him, frustrated by his inability to understand what I was even though I had never given him the opportunity to. "We both know they won't do jail time. I don't want them to get a slap on the wrist. They killed Dana. I want them to suffer."

It was the first time I had revealed a true indication of the rage that burned in me. I expected Conrad to look at me with shock or revulsion. Part of me wanted him to chastise me, so that I would feel guilt about the violence I craved. Instead he examined me the way he'd examined the Christmas lights on the main street every year— with wonder.

"Sometimes..." Conrad broke off, his voice trembling with barely concealed trepidation. "Sometimes the law isn't enough."

∾

I DREAMED OF A PAST LIFE, of a battlefield engulfed in smoke and littered with corpses. The copper taste of blood was thick on my tongue, its metallic scent flooding my nostrils. It was suffocating me, and yet as I nudged an armoured corpse aside with a careless boot, I could think of nothing but the victory I had achieved. Violence was glory, as my uncle had constantly assured me.

"You did well today, Athene."

My uncle had many names. The most common of which was War, a horseman of the apocalypse. To me, he was Tyr. No matter what life I had, I would always be Athene to him. His praise bolstered me, though I concealed it beneath a veneer of indifference.

None of my siblings had ever understood the fury within me. Even my father, a horseman himself, did not feel the call to it as I did. Tyr was the one who saw my potential, who did not look at my rage with concern or trepidation.

A crow cawed above us, and I shielded my eyes from the afternoon sun as it glinted off my sword, more caked crimson now than shining silver.

"I should hate this. I should look at our enemies and mourn them."

"Why?" Tyr arched an eyebrow, lips twisting into a cool smile. "We do not weep for fallen enemies. They are deserving of your righteous wrath."

Once, I had possessed morals. The thing was, over the centuries and the various lives, I'd crossed many boundaries. Each vow to myself I claimed I wouldn't break, each shred of morality I stubbornly clung to...they all faded away in the end. It had left me void of mercy, a weapon to be twisted into whatever shape Tyr saw fit.

I could not blame my uncle for what I was. I had always been a monster. Tyr had just helped me cast aside any guilt I may have felt for what I'd become, the terrible things I had done. The odour of rotting flesh mingled with the thick smoke, though it had long since stopped turning my stomach.

"Sometimes, I don't know why I do this." I took a ragged cloth from my belt and wiped the blood off my blade before it could dry. "War is your art, not mine."

"We both know why, dear niece." Tyr rested a hand on my shoulder, a light squeeze coaxing a grim smile to my lips. "You enjoy it. You cannot admit as much to the rest of your family, but you can to me."

Tyr had a way of making me feel special. His understanding of my nature, of my ruthlessness, meant I did not have to hide what I was. Yet with each new life, I strived to conceal that darkness, the anger and the violence that flooded my veins with each heartbeat.

There are few things more horrific than a monster who knows what they are and embraces their cruelty anyway.

As I woke up gasping, sweat-slick limbs tangled in my cotton sheets, I realised that though my joy with Dana's summer-sun warmth had been real, it had been snuffed out. Like an expelled candle on a starless night, only darkness was left.

COMMUNITY SERVICE. Two words that really meant "You're white and your parents are wealthy with connections, so of course you aren't going to be punished." I wondered, through a rage so great it made me shake and my stomach churn, what kind of fucking service these murderers could actually do for our community.

Everyone wanted me to move on. Conrad suggested therapy, which was almost laughable when I considered what I could even tell a therapist. I was almost certain I had PTSD from all the wars I'd participated in during my past lives, but how was a woman in her early twenties supposed to explain wartime PTSD when realistically she wouldn't have experienced it?

It would be like talking to my dad, who was a therapist himself. No thank you.

I didn't want to move on and put it all behind me. I wanted

something darker and more satisfying than closure. I wanted revenge.

I knew where that road led. Revenge was a road full of potholes and speed bumps, dangerous and unpredictable. There was no way back once I went down there, and it wasn't what Dana would have wanted for me. Unfortunately, the siren's song that was vengeance was a lure too strong to ignore—unless I uprooted the whole thing entirely.

My eldest sister, Mnemosyne, worked at the Great Library. She would be able to remove any memories of Dana, of the crash, of anything that threatened to lure me into the merciless killer I somehow always became. She could wash my hands clean before I had the chance to sully them further.

I took the train into the city. The idea of being behind the wheel of a car made bile rise in my throat. I sat by the window with a steaming paper takeaway cup of lukewarm coffee in my hand, distracted by the scenery that whirled past the window. The pine trees made me reminisce on a pine air freshener Dana had gotten for my car to help banish the stink of stale food.

Would Mnemosyne wipe away every trace of the people I loved? Or would I pass by a bakery and feel a tug of familiarity when I inhaled cinnamon scrolls, Conrad's favourite baked good? Could she really rip the memories out, root and stem, or would seedlings grow in their place?

It had been lifetimes since I visited the Great Library. I'd never had a reason to, preferring to distance myself from my siblings lest I bring violence into their lives. I didn't know if it appeared differently to everyone who visited, but I stepped inside to shelves of books stretching as far and high as the eye could see. It smelled of old paper and leather, reminding me of whenever I'd visited Conrad and Dana on campus.

A stunning woman in her thirties appeared at the front desk and offered me a kind smile that I didn't reciprocate. There was a prickling up my spine, like a zap of electricity, that coursed through my body whenever I was in close proximity to one of my siblings.

Mnemosyne and I shared a tendency to exude warmth. Hers was like rays of sunlight dappling through red and yellow leaves on an autumn morning. Mine was the molten fire in the blood that preceded impassioned acts of extreme violence. Gentleness versus brutality. We could not have been more different.

"Mnemosyne."

The patience in her smile prickled across my skin, a sour taste building beneath my tongue. "It's Naomi now."

Naomi—a name that tasted like rich mulled wine in the depths of winter.

I shrugged with practised nonchalance. "Well, I'm Minnie."

"I know why you're here." She led me into a sparsely furnished office, gesturing for me to sit in one of the leather seats on the closest side of the desk. "It's about your friend, isn't it?"

Had she been in contact with our father? Bitter tears welled in my eyes at the mention of Dana, at the piercing sting that her name elicited. This was why I needed the memories of her gone: because now the sweetness of our friendship would be forever tainted with the pain of losing her.

"My lives have always been short." My hands gripped the hem of my shirt, toying with the frayed edge. "I usually die violently, and that's just...it is how it is. But I'm so tired of losing the people I love. I didn't think it was going to be Dana this time."

"Who did you think it would be?" Naomi tilted her head to the side, eyes gleaming with curiosity.

It would be too easy to claim I didn't know the answer, but I had for years. Conrad. The man I loved without hope, pushing aside my feelings because I feared they would cost his life. Instead we had been drawn closer together by Dana's death, and the anger we shared for the privileged scum who had murdered her.

"A man this time." I fought against the lump forming in my throat. "His name is Conrad. He, Dana, and I were best friends."

"So your memories of Dana are tied into your experiences with Conrad." Naomi's words were soft and contemplative. Dread twisted my stomach into knots, and I inhaled sharply, the scent of freshly polished wood invading my nostrils.

If I lost Dana, I would lose Conrad. To forsake my memories of my best friend was to abandon the man I loved. I weighed the odds, trying to determine if it was still a sacrifice worth making.

"It hurts." My voice wavered with the weight of my grief, and I cursed myself. The last thing I wanted was to bare my weakness to my oldest sibling. "I just want the pain to go away."

Naomi reached across to rest a hand over mine, a hesitant brush of skin, as though she feared I would rip my hand away.

Tears blurred my vision, and as they spilled down my cheeks, I was thrown back into a hellscape of bright lights and screeching tyres. I would always have the peaceful memories of Dana, washing over me like a soothing trickle of water, but her violent demise would forever be my last memory of her. Did all the joy we'd shared outweigh the final few minutes of her agony, fear, and confusion?

I had never considered myself prone to tears. Tears were not weapons of my arsenal the way they were with others. But since Dana's death, I had cried more than in the rest of my current life.

I had come here with a single purpose in mind: erase the pain that Dana's death caused me. Now I realised that Dana was so woven into the fabric of who I was that I would be losing not only Conrad, but myself.

I couldn't let go of that. I couldn't let go of her, even if it meant succumbing to vengeance. I gripped Naomi's hand like it was an anchor, the only thing keeping me afloat in a storm that meant to drown me.

DEATH HAD a way of making the rodents crawl out of the woodwork, and that could not have been more true than in the case of Tyr.

Father and Naomi sensed loss, their compassion as much a thorn in my side as it was a comfort. My uncle sensed an opportunity. It was always when I was at my lowest that Tyr imposed his presence into my life, encouraging the violence I was so prone to.

Tyr stood outside the Great Library, and when the breeze rustled my blonde hair, the thick scent of sulphur and smoke carried on the wind. An indulgent smile crossed his handsome dark features, and he spread his arms wide.

"Dearest Athene."

I didn't embrace him. Instead I planted my hands in the pockets of my coat, the thick wool a warm comfort against my fingers. It was bitterly cold for a summer's day, but I attributed that to the unnatural chill I experienced in Tyr's presence. Some thought that War was all heat, but there was an iciness to it, a cool calculation.

"I go by Minnie now."

"Of course." Tyr's brow furrowed. "I was so sorry to hear about your friend. Such a devastating loss."

I clenched my jaw and tilted my chin back to stare up at him. He had almost a foot on me, but there was a power in Tyr's presence that went beyond height. There was an undercurrent of menace, like something could shatter like glass at any given moment, the threat of untold horrors behind his eyes.

"She was killed, wasn't she?" Tyr sighed and shook his head slowly, a mockery of the vexation he didn't feel. My stance remained rigid, shoulders tensed. "Those boys in the other car, they got off so lightly, considering what they did."

Once, when I was newer to the world and to Tyr's manipulation, I might not have seen what he was doing. The infuriating part was the dangerous temptation in what he offered, the sweetness of revenge.

"You want me to work for you again." I tilted my head to the side, the memories of World War II like bitter ashes in my mouth. I could never forget the devastation that Tyr had me wreak, pushing me toward violence and death, aiming me like a gun.

"So blunt." When Tyr smiled again, his eyes lit up with glee. "That was always what I liked about you. Straight to the point. You never did want to play games."

"But you did," I reminded him, unable to keep the accusation from my tone. "You claimed I was your favourite because it made me compliant."

"Or perhaps it was because you are the most like me."

"Don't." The word came out a snarl. The comparison would have once filled me with pride, but now it made my stomach twist.

"I could help you." Tyr stepped closer, expression earnest. "We could bring those boys to justice together."

"In exchange for me helping you."

A smirk twisted his lips. "Look at it as a compromise."

The thing about War was that everyone viewed it as battle. But it was more than that. It was the tension that rose up, a spark ready to ignite. I had learned over many lifetimes that the dangerous part of War was everything that led up to it. It was in those early stages, pushing pieces around a chessboard, that Tyr was the most deadly.

"I can deal with my business myself."

Tyr smiled fondly, reaching out with a finger to tilt my chin up.

"There's so much rage in you." He inhaled sharply, like he could breathe all that anger in. "You really are a delight, Athene."

I smacked his hand away from my face, which only caused his grin to widen.

"Once your business is done," he said, "I'll find you."

I couldn't decide if it was a promise or a threat, but the implications made a cold shiver race down my spine. Tyr kissed the top of my head and drew back, feral delight dancing in his dark eyes as he turned on his heel and sauntered down the street. I fumed at his attempt at paternal affection, something he had always employed to try and get me on side.

I had changed, become something different from the furious, naive girl that Tyr first recruited back when I was Athene. I was weary of being dragged into the battles of others when all I wanted was to fight my own.

Tyr was a problem for another time. As I walked back to the train station, my mind remained fixated on the task at hand. Since I had chosen to remember, chosen vengeance, I needed to decide what that meant.

Perhaps once, it would have meant a cruel and drawn-out punishment, but my heart was broken and my soul was heavy. I was not sadistic, and I did not take pleasure in torture. I was practical despite my rage.

Jeremy. Oliver. Lionel. I committed their names to memory.

They had taken my beating heart and ripped it from my chest while I had been forced to watch.

That made justice very, very simple.

They had killed Dana. So I would kill them.

ERIS WAS NOT RENOWNED for its nightlife, though there were several clubs along the main street that Conrad, Dana, and I frequented. I thought back fondly to our late teenage years, stumbling down that street with our arms linked, raucous laughter bellowing through the early hours of the morning as neon lights flashed overhead and music pulsed beneath our feet.

A mutual friend had posted on Facebook about an event occurring at Bad Apples, and when I saw the invite list and that the murderers were going to be attending, I pressed Going. I told Conrad that I wanted to start integrating back into society after Dana's death, my stomach squirming with guilt. It was a blatant lie, but how else was I meant to explain my plans to him? He would never understand what I was capable of.

I dressed to kill. Literally. I was typically fresh-faced, with Dana the make-up goddess working her magic every time we'd needed to dress up. I stared hard into my compact mirror as the taxi we'd caught jostled over another speed bump. I hadn't braved false eyelashes, but I'd managed a pretty decent smoky eye, complete with a light sheen of lip gloss.

Over the years, my preparation for battle had changed. In past lives, there had been ritual sacrifice, the smearing of animal blood across my cheeks. In this life, the make-up was my war paint, conveying a ferocity that my natural baby face wasn't capable of. Conrad reached across and squeezed my hand, and my heart did a somersault in my chest as a smile flew unbidden to my lips.

Would Conrad still show me such affection once he realised I intended to confront the murderers?

I stepped out of the taxi in white platform heels, craning my neck back and shielding my eyes from the flashing green image of an apple outside the club. I marched up to the door with purpose, Conrad and I showing the bouncer our IDs before we slipped back into what had once been a familiar atmosphere.

It reeked of an unholy combination of Lynx body spray, an overabundance of tequila, and a sickly-sweet watermelon mist that sprayed out every now and again, a fine smoke that added to the gritty atmosphere of the club. Neon lights flashed overhead, the electro beats that we'd once danced to making my head pound. I could already see my targets: they were piled into one of the booths across the far side of the club, laughing and taking selfies with no remorse for the life they had carelessly stolen.

"Minnie." Conrad caught my arm, and I spun to see dread in his blue eyes. How beautiful those eyes looked, flashing with the colours of the neon rainbow around us. "You really want to do this?"

Any response I had caught in my throat as I realised that Conrad perceived my intentions immediately. I hadn't given him enough credit. He had known me since we were kids, after all. A relieved laugh bubbled up in my mouth, but I swallowed it whole. I jerked my head in a sharp nod, expecting him to dissuade me, the voice of caution. Instead, his lips pressed into a thin line, and he returned the nod.

Understanding. And permission.

One of the boys stood by the bar, raising a bright green shot high before tilting his head back to knock it down. Jeremy. It was a blur trying to remember which of the boys was which from that fateful night, but I did recall that he was the driver. An icy cold seeped through my veins and I strode over to the bar, nudging my way to Jeremy's side.

When he noticed me, he lowered the shot glass, eyes flashing with panic. I offered him a saccharine sweet smile. He knew precisely who I was, and the fear in his expression made me all the more powerful.

"Why are you here?" he demanded.

"Small town, Jeremy." I hailed the waiter and ordered a vodka shot of my own. I savoured his trepidation more than the alcohol, the taste of it far sweeter on my tongue than the shot I poured into my mouth. Once I swallowed, I swiveled back to him, apparently frozen in place.

My power had always been strongest when I was angry, and I was fucking infuriated. How dare he stand there, laughing and drinking with his friends while Dana's corpse rotted beneath the earth? I pushed an illusion upon him, a savage vision of being buried alive. Jeremy pressed his hands to his temples and screamed, causing several people to jump and stare at him as if he'd grown a second hand.

My lips curved into a cruel smile. It was true that I did not enjoy torture, but there was no harm in a taste of pain.

I knew dozens of ways to commit murder. Tyr had taught me all of them. It would be easy to do it here and now, witnesses be damned. My uncle would certainly have approved of such a bold, violent course of action.

It was too crowded in Bad Apples to kill Jeremy. My time would come. In the meantime, I had pushed a sliver of terror beneath his veins. He gripped the counter, knuckles going white, and stared at me with a horror that made my power pulse beneath my skin, itching to be used once again.

"What the fuck are you?" The words were barely more than a whisper, but I heard them nonetheless.

Conrad appeared at my elbow, but I held up a hand, and he paused. I smirked at Jeremy, hoping that he felt at least a touch of the pain and confusion Dana had the night she died.

"Something you should fear."

Jeremy sneered, false bravado filling in the shadows that horror had previously touched. "You want someone to blame, right? For the way your friend died. I don't even remember her fucking name."

It was the wrong thing to say. My blood boiled with rage. How dare his worthless lips utter a word about Dana? He should have been on his knees begging for forgiveness, but sometimes my ability to conjure nightmares in the minds of others prompted indignation. Jeremy had almost a foot on me, but it was easy to grab him by the front of his shirt and swing him around, slamming my fist into his face.

Jeremy staggered, hands raised to his nose as though he couldn't believe I'd dare strike him. I braced for a fight, knowing that despite Jeremy's size, I had killed larger and more formidable men. My hands were drenched red in the blood of my enemies, and with the pulsing tempo of the music mixed with the strong taste of vodka on my tongue, I was more than ready to kill again.

Jeremy dove at me, but a quick sweep of my foot across his shins sent him to the ground. Cheers and shouts rang in my ears. I could barely hear them over the roar of the blood rushing through me. I planted a foot hard on Jeremy's chest to prevent him from getting back up.

"Minnie!" Conrad caught me by the waist, dragging me off Jeremy. If it had been anyone else, I would have thrashed and fought, but Conrad's presence always had a way of calming me. I stepped away from my enemy, Conrad's fingers linking with mine. The metallic scent of blood, of war, permeated my nostrils as Jeremy wiped it off his face.

Conrad marched me outside, even as the other patrons of the club began to whisper amongst themselves. The cool night air was bliss as it caressed my skin, its freshness a stark contrast to the stifling abundance of scents within the club.

"What was that all about?" Conrad demanded.

I wrenched my arm from his grasp and whirled to face him. "You know what it was about."

In that moment, the desperate urge to tell him the truth became a physical ache. How lonely it was, unable to share the secrets of my past with those in my current life. I had wanted to tell Dana, and now I would never get the chance. I had the opportunity with Conrad, and yet there was something holding me back. Fear that he would think I was crazy. No, there would come a moment, but it was not this moment.

"Is this what you think Dana would have wanted?" he asked, exasperation colouring his tone.

"I don't know what Dana would have wanted." A sob clawed its way up my throat. "Because she's dead, Conrad. She's dead, and it's their fault."

Sorrow and sympathy clashed in Conrad's beautiful blue eyes before he wrapped his arms around me and tugged me close. The scent of musk and leather washed over me as I buried my face in the soft fabric of his shirt. My hot tears dripped onto his chest as I tried to choke back my grief.

For so long, I had been searching for home. I had found it in my best friends. I might not have had Dana any longer, but I still had Conrad.

I walked a dangerous tightrope when it came to vengeance. Pushing too far would drive Conrad away, but fighting my instincts felt like an insult to Dana's memory. My actions at Bad Apples had left a bitter taste in my mouth, seeing the way the town denizens who I was familiar with looked at me: with fear and uncertainty in their eyes. My next move was one that Tyr would have been proud of, for it was far more calculated.

The heat of summer was beginning to disperse from the town, which was the cue for a beach party. Technically, we were too far inland to have a true beach, but there was a man-made inlet that was made up to seem like one. Everyone dressed for the occasion, rainbow towels and inflatable flamingos covering the white sand.

I hadn't told Conrad that I was going to the party. Guilt squirmed in my stomach about that, but I refused to be daunted. Conrad knew me too well, and he would be a distraction. Jeremy certainly gave me a wide berth, still nursing bruises from my attack in the club. His friends, Lionel and Oliver, were not so cautious.

It was Oliver whose attention I got first, mainly because of the little black bikini I wore that left little to the imagination. I had done my research: Oliver was renowned for his trysts with girls both in and out of town. It didn't take much to garner his interest, and I was confident enough in my appearance to know that I was pretty.

"Hi." I offered him a sugar-sweet smile. It didn't come naturally to me as it had to Dana, a notorious flirt who gained interest from guys with nonchalant ease. Every fibre of my being burned to slam a fist into Oliver's face, but I resisted it. Patience.

"I heard what you did to Jeremy." Oliver took a drag from his vape, blowing out smoke tinged with a strong artificial grape scent. "Going to hit me too, then?"

"No." I did my best to look demure, dipping my head to look down at my feet. "That wasn't...it wasn't my finest moment. I was just angry and upset, I had a few drinks. I knew Jeremy wouldn't talk to me, but I hoped you might."

"All right." Suspicion and curiosity mingled in Oliver's eyes, but he followed me as I walked away from the bonfire and laughter, forsaking the warmth of it for a familiar dark quiet. The noise faded into nothing, our feet crunching through the sand the only sound above the chirp of crickets. When Oliver was distracted by someone setting off a firework, I reached into his pocket and stole his phone.

I spun to face Oliver with vengeance beating in my heart, and I delved into the depths of my power. I conjured up a vision in his mind, a pontoon out in the inlet with fairy lights and beers and weed. Oliver blinked slowly, dazed, before he walked back toward the party, shuffling his feet like he was sleepwalking.

That was the important part: people seeing Oliver. If it was just him and I, alone in the dark, then suspicion would fall on me. I needed everyone to witness that this was supposedly Oliver's own doing. He staggered into the water, arms outstretched, his vape falling from his fingers onto the wet sand.

"Oliver?" Jeremy and Lionel appeared at the water's edge, watching as their friend paddled deeper. Oliver could swim, but the illusion I'd pushed upon him would take him far beneath the water's surface. As he plummeted under, someone screamed. I folded my arms and watched from the shadows, a cruel smile crossing my lips.

The average person could hold their breath for around two minutes, but the average person wasn't underwater thinking they're breathing in air, their lungs filling with liquid without any inclination to stop. By the time a few of the group had pulled Oliver from the water, the music was off, one of the flamingos had deflated, and Oliver was dead.

People sobbed as one of the girls attempted CPR, but I had done my job too well. I should have felt remorse, but there was an emptiness yawning open inside of me, and it only had room for savage victory.

Conrad was uneasy after Oliver's death. Once he found out that I had been at the beach party, that Oliver and I had walked off alone for a few minutes, he wanted answers. I said I would give them to him, luring him over to my apartment with the promise of pizza. Unfortunately, even the rich tastes of chorizo and smoky barbecue sauce were like ashes on my tongue as my mind whirred with what I was going to say.

Conrad and Dana had both known me for years. I had the impression my behaviour lately was alarming to Conrad, but what would he do if I told him the whole truth? There was only one way to find out, and despite my more guarded instincts pushing me to hold my silence, the fact that I loved Conrad made it so much more easy for honesty to glide off my tongue.

He was my best friend. I loved him. He was suspicious of me, and it was when I realised that I no longer made sense to him that I knew it was time to crack open the vault of secrets I had guarded for so long.

At first, my intention was to filter through the truth, one revelation at a time. But finally divulging all of myself to someone was too much, and everything flooded out of me like water from a broken dam. I told him about my original family, my role as Wrath, the lives that I had lived, my abilities. Conrad munched on his supreme pizza in silence, blue eyes glazed over like he was processing everything.

"So you're Wrath." It was hard to place the emotion in Conrad's level, thoughtful tone. "You can create illusions, and your family... your real family, they're all the rest of the Sins as well. And your father is a Horseman of the Apocalypse."

"Death," I provided helpfully, raking a hand through my blonde hair. My pizza lay in its box, hardly touched. I barely had an appetite for it, more focused on just how much I was trusting Conrad. "I know it's a lot to take in."

"Minnie..." Conrad licked his lips, and there was something pained and concerned in his blue eyes when he finally looked at me. "I know that Dana's death hasn't been easy. You should really see someone."

Fury flashed through me, as well as hurt. "I'm not crazy, Conrad."

"None of this explains what happened at the beach party."

"I killed him." I pushed myself to my feet, my knee bumping against the coffee table and jostling my can of Coke. "Oliver. I put an illusion in his head. It was like...putting a lighthouse out at sea and watching a drowning man swim toward it."

Conrad's eyes widened, the pizza slipping out from his fingers. He was searching my face for any sign of madness or lies, and his lips parted as he found none. Tears blurred my vision, my shoulders shaking with sobs. Not for Oliver, but at the fear that my honesty might cost me the person I held dear. I had already lost Dana. I didn't know what I would do if I lost Conrad, too.

"Why?" The single syllable was a broken word, cracking with despair. Conrad got up as well, catching me by the shoulders. The scent of his cologne washed over me like a caress. So close to him, I could see how thick and dark his eyelashes were. I could feel his breath, warm against my cheek.

"We said the law wasn't enough." My voice was soft, barely above a whisper. "I meant it, Conrad. I wanted them to suffer. You just seemed to think my words were worth nothing."

"Of course I don't." Conrad inspected me, reaching out to tuck a strand of hair behind my ear. "It's just...this is a lot, Minnie. Whatever you are, whatever you've done, this isn't what Dana would want for you. I want revenge, too. But sometimes, you need to choose to be the bigger person."

"Be the bigger person?" I wrenched away from him, anger coursing through me with its familiar searing heat. "That works when you're talking about someone calling you names on Facebook. They committed murder, whether the law wants to recognise that or not. I'm simply returning the favour."

"I don't care about them!" Conrad snapped, the same fury that burned within me rising up in him. "I care about you!"

His passion stunned me into silence, and I stared up at him, wondering if I was reading too much into things. Conrad stepped back, raking his hands through his hair, frustration in every rigid line of his shoulders. The quiet between us stretched on a few more moments as his eyes fluttered closed and he took a deep breath, composing himself.

"I'm in love with you, Minnie. I have been for...I don't know, a few years now. I didn't want to jeopardise our friendship, but fuck it. You told me everything, so you deserve to know how I feel. I'm not scared of you. I'm scared for you."

Conrad was in love with me. Conrad believed me, as insane as my claim to be a reborn Sin was. Relief crashed down over me like a tidal wave, new tears filling my eyes as a weak smile tweaked at the corners of my lips. Conrad didn't fear my darkness, like everyone else seemed to. He worried what being consumed by it would mean for me.

"I love you, too." I reached forward, taking his hands in mine, linking our fingers. "I can do better than just telling you what I am. I can show you."

Conrad took a shaky breath. "Okay."

I gave his hands a light squeeze, and the illusion this time was something soft and beautiful. The last good illusion I brought forth was for Dana in her final moments, so my entire body trembled as I closed my eyes and gave Conrad peace. Dana on a swing in the summer sun, flowers threaded clumsily through her hair, her laughter like the sharp peal of a bell. I gave him the illusion that there was something for Dana after death, something gentle.

Conrad jerked away from me with a hoarse gasp, tearing his fingers from mine. Tears streamed down his cheeks as he stared at me with a terrible understanding. He might have believed me before, but he didn't realise what being Wrath meant. Now that I had shown him what I could do, the full magnitude of it weighed down on his tense shoulders.

"This is..." Conrad shook his head vigorously, as if trying to rid himself of what I had put in his head. "I have to go, Minnie. I can't do this right now."

He scooped up his box of pizza, his unopened can of Fanta, and swept from my apartment without a backward glance. I watched the person I loved most walk out, and sudden terror struck me. Maybe he wasn't coming back. As I had lost Dana, perhaps I was losing Conrad too.

I pressed my face into my hands and cried, raw sobs that grated against my throat and burned at my eyes. Perhaps, in the wake of my violence, I was always destined to be alone, forsaken for what I had done and what I planned to do next.

I TEXTED Jeremy and Lionel from Oliver's phone.

Meet me where she died.

Perhaps a bit dramatic, but it punched home the message. They knew who it was texting them from their dead friend's phone. Maybe they would take this to the police, but since the police had been the ones who had given them a slap on the wrist for their behaviour, they probably realised just how seriously the law took such matters.

I hadn't driven since the car accident, so I took an Uber out to the crash site. If the driver had questions about why he was dropping me off in the middle of nowhere, he had the good sense not to ask them. I shrugged my jacket more tightly around me, my boots crunching through gravel and dry leaves as I headed down to the place where Dana had died.

Torchlight in the black oblivion told me I was not alone, and I shielded my eyes from its harshness as they adjusted to the sudden light. I inhaled the smell of petrol and freshly turned soil as I made my way down to Lionel and Jeremy, their expressions caught in a mix of trepidation and contempt. A quick scan of the pair and I could see that Jeremy had a gun tucked into his belt, poorly disguised by his jacket.

"What is this about, Minnie?" Lionel sounded resigned, mouth pulled into a grim line.

"Closure." I stuffed my hands in my pockets. Reading their body language, Lionel just wanted to get this over and done with, while Jeremy seemed ready for another fight. I was far more relaxed, used to tense confrontations with the promise of becoming violent. "I want an apology for Dana's death."

"Are you serious?" Jeremy's eyebrows flew upwards, his lip curling in a sneer. "All of this is still about your friend?"

"Jeremy, leave it," Lionel muttered, resting a hand on his friend's shoulder that Jeremy promptly shoved off. He marched over to me. I didn't move an inch, unfazed by his determination to prove he was in charge in this situation.

"I was the driver that night." Jeremy folded his arms over his chest, glaring down at me as the wind whispered through the trees around us. There was no guilt in Jeremy's words, no regret at what had happened, just petulant indignance. "What happened was an accident. Okay? It's done. You need to move on. It was as much your fault as it was ours, so..."

"What did you just say?" My words, cold and filled with every part of the icy rage that has settled over me like winter's chill, cut out whatever Jeremy was going to say next.

"Dude." Panic flared in Lionel's eyes. Maybe he didn't quite know why I terrified him, but it was clear that I did. A wise response.

Jeremy was less wise. "I said it was your fault, too."

My savage backhand knocked him off his feet. Adrenaline coursed through my veins, giving me a frightening strength that someone of my build shouldn't possess. Jeremy sputtered amongst the dry leaves, spitting out dirt. That was where he belonged: on the ground amongst the insects and the mud. I tilted my head to the side and pushed every nightmare, every creature that children are told to fear in the dark, into his mind. I wanted him more than just afraid. I wanted him scared shitless.

Jeremy screamed, clutching at his head and writhing around in the dirt, haunted by monsters only he could see. My lips curved into a cruel smile, the cries that would curdle the blood of mere mortals like a melody to my ears. I was used to the sounds of death, the sounds of pain. Lionel's breath came in ragged pants as he took a few steps back, staring between Jeremy and I with growing apprehension.

"What are you?" Jeremy demanded on a hoarse breath, a question still unanswered from my initial attack in Bad Apples.

Did I enjoy causing torment? Or was it only in seeing those who deserved punishment but had evaded it that I found exhilaration? I had wanted to put the path of war and violence behind me, and yet here I was, a monster in the woods.

"You can call me Justice."

Jeremy rolled over, reaching into his jacket. I sighed heavily at his tendency to resort to utter stupidity instead of sense. When Jeremy pulled the gun on me, I kicked it out of his hand, pressing my boot down on his fingers and pinning them to the ground. A sharp twist of my heel resulted in a crack that made Jeremy scream again. Keeping my foot firmly on his broken fingers, I reached down and picked up the gun.

Weapons had evolved over the years, but I always learned to use them. I was the true weapon, and I would make sure Jeremy knew it.

"One last chance." I removed my foot, eliciting a whimper from Jeremy, and took a step back. I clicked the safety off the gun, and glanced at Lionel to see tears streaming down his cheeks in the pale moonlight, his whole body trembling. I turned my gaze back to Jeremy, lips twisting in scorn. "Get down on your knees and beg me for mercy."

Was there truly mercy to be found? The concept was still foreign to me. I was not a woman who backed down, and I did not spare a life when I had already made the decision to take it.

"Fuck you, bitch," Jeremy snarled the words with pure loathing, lunging at me with his hand curled into a fist.

The sound of a gunshot ripped through the quiet as I pulled the trigger. Whatever can be said of killing, this much I knew: I made it quick. I did not aim to delay the inevitable. The bullet went clean through Jeremy's head, killing him instantly. His corpse hit the ground with a dull thud, and I swallowed the lump in my throat.

I did not regret killing Jeremy. I hardly even felt it. I remembered Conrad's words, his concern about what I would become if I went too far.

My eyes flicked to Lionel, who was openly sobbing, clutching his jacket tightly around him as he shrank away from me. Tears and begging had not moved me in the past, especially when it came from a witness to my crimes. Covering up what I had done was imperative, and I had silenced any voices that might speak up against me.

If I didn't kill Lionel, he could tell everyone what I had done. I could go to prison for shooting Jeremy. If I did kill Lionel, the blood that stained my hands would never be washed away, and I would be constantly repeating the sins of my past.

I thought of Dana, of what she might say in that moment. It was the thought of her hurt, not Lionel's tears, that gave me pause.

Dread coursed through me with the piercing sharpness of a knife. Was this what I wanted? To be the woman who could only be feared? No; I had possessed Dana's love, and I also had Conrad's. There was something more for me now, something other than violence and murder.

"You...you aren't even human." The words came out choked as Lionel collapsed to his knees, staring up at me with blatant panic. "You just killed him in cold blood."

Somewhere there was a line, even for a creature like me. Had I crossed it? I wasn't certain, but there was a chilling knowledge that if I shot Lionel too, I would have. There could be no chance for redemption, no chance for forgiveness. Lionel was not fighting me. He was crying in fear for his life.

Athene would have killed Lionel without hesitation, but I was not Athene anymore. I was Minnie, a woman who forged her own destiny.

This time, the scream that pierced the midnight air was mine. Frustration and desperation consumed me, and I hurled the gun to the ground. I joined Lionel in tears, mine born of sorrow and confusion. If I wasn't a killer, if I didn't succumb to vengeance, then what was I? The idea of becoming something new was terrifying, and yet I kept picturing Dana's soft smile, Conrad's beautiful blue eyes.

"I finally had everything I could have wanted." I didn't know if Lionel was listening, but I had to make him understand. "People who loved me. You three ripped it all away from me, and I don't know what to do with the empty space you've left me with."

I closed my eyes and inhaled the scent of pine, running my fingers through the dirt. If Lionel picked up the gun and shot me, I wouldn't blame him, but some part of me knew he wouldn't. When I opened my eyes, Lionel's fear had morphed into what I had wanted all along: guilt and regret.

"I know you won't believe me, but I've lived many lifetimes." I picked up the gun, putting it in my pocket. "In every one of them, someone I love has died violently. I have died violently. That and bloodshed are all I have ever known, and I'm tired. I'm so tired."

John, beheaded during Henry VIII's reign. Alice, executed during the Salem witch trials. Claire, killed during the bombing of Pearl Harbour. Just some of the awful deaths of people I had loved over the ages, deaths etched deep beneath my skin.

"I'm sorry." What surprised me the most is that the words were so genuine. "Minnie, I'm so sorry. Dana deserved better. What happened was...we did something terrible. It was wrong. I will spend the rest of my life regretting it."

I could have killed him, used his words as his final confession. Yet I wanted to be someone better. For Dana, for Conrad, for me. After so many lives being consumed by anger and hatred, it was time to move on. It was time for me to forsake Athene and simply be Minnie. Dana had deserved better, and maybe despite my innumerable sins, I did too.

I had no reason to believe that Lionel wouldn't report me to the police the first chance he got. I had no idea what he was going to say when Jeremy's body was found in the woods, a gunshot wound carving a hole open in his head. Yet despite so many unknown variables, I chose to walk away, and this time I didn't look back.

~

CONRAD MET me at the library at dawn, pale blue and pink hues cast across the cloudless sky as he slid me a chai latte. The scent of cloves and cardamom soothed me as I drummed my fingers against the recyclable paper cup. The silence between us was peaceful, and I realised just how much I had yearned for this: moments of quiet.

"I asked Jeremy and Lionel to meet me out where Dana died." The words were soft so as to not disrupt the others, the handful of early morning risers who sought out books as solace. We sat down on a pair of plastic chairs in the reading area.

"What happened?" Conrad leaned forward in his chair, curiosity and anticipation battling in his eyes.

"Jeremy tried to attack me, twice. He was armed." I took a deep breath, knowing I stood on the precipice, ready to jump over the edge. "I took his gun from him, and I shot him in the head."

Conrad raked his hands through his hair, a whirlwind of emotions dancing across his face before he settled on uneasy acceptance. He nodded slowly, and reached out to take one of my hands in his. The gesture of support warmed me even more than my chai latte, but I couldn't bring myself to smile.

"Lionel...he apologised. It was sincere. I left him out there. I don't know if he came back or not."

Conrad's brow furrowed. "You aren't worried that he's going to report you for Jeremy's murder?"

I chewed at my lip. "No. But I wasn't...I couldn't kill him too. He didn't deserve it. Not like the others did. Whatever he does now, it's up to him, and I'll accept that."

"Minnie." The way Conrad said my name tasted like sweet candy. "Are you...are you okay?"

It was far past time I stopped lying about what I felt. I bit down on my trembling bottom lip and shook my head.

"No. But I will be."

Time did not heal all wounds, not completely. Sometimes they reopened to bleed all over again. Healing was a slow process, filled with as much regression as progress. Dana was a fresh wound, something that stung when salt was poured into it. The older wounds... some of them were scars now. I would never forget they existed, but they had stopped hurting.

Conrad took my face in his hands, his fingers gentle against my skin. He leaned forward to rest his forehead against mine, and I closed my eyes and wished I could stay in the moment forever. Maybe he didn't forgive me for what I had done, but there was no blame, no accusation. He understood.

When Conrad pressed his lips to mine, I could taste cinnamon and sugar. My hands moved to grip onto his shoulders, as if he and this precious moment could be ripped from me in a moment. If I had been the ship roiling in a turbulent ocean, Dana had been the anchor keeping me safe and secure. Conrad was the lighthouse guiding me home.

In my past lives, these moments had always led to destruction and sorrow. This time, I had chosen peace. This time, things would be different, because I was forsaking what I was to become who I wanted to be. I had ripped away all that I was, my past selves dead and buried, to be the woman I was now.

"I love you." The words came out choked as I drew back, Conrad's breath warm against my face as hot tears spilled down my cheeks. "Wherever I go and whatever I do, I want to do it with you."

Conrad gripped my hands in his, pressing a kiss to the back of them. "I'm not leaving you, Minnie."

I laughed. Had I laughed since Dana had died? Had I even really smiled? Conrad had a habit of drawing out the best in me, just like Dana had done. The laughter bubbled out of me like water from a fountain, because I was free. Of my vengeance, of the call to violence, of everything that had shackled me to being Athene, the young warrior who had died with five arrows in her chest.

There was beauty in my love for Conrad, finally something other than the ugliness of death and destruction. We exchanged a few more kisses, soft as a feather's caress, before one of the other library dwellers told us to get a room. I stumbled out of the library with Conrad's fingers firmly twined through mine, feeling more alive than ever. The morning air was a rush of citrus against my skin, and I tilted my face up to the sun and let it warm my skin.

"Minnie." A familiar voice, and an unwelcome one in my home town. I staggered to a halt as Tyr approached me with his hands in his pockets and a wry smile across his lips. Conrad gently squeezed my hand in reassurance, and I glanced at him.

"I'll meet you at the bakery."

Conrad's eyes darted between us before he pressed a kiss to my cheek. No argument, no questions, just an understanding that this was something I must do myself. The tension that had fled from my body returned, creeping into my shoulders as my hands balled into fists. I inspected my uncle with apprehension.

"What are you doing here, Tyr?"

"You know exactly what." Tyr arched an eyebrow. "Your business is done here. It's time to embrace what you are and return to my side."

This time, the laugh that left my lips was mocking and mirthless, and Tyr's smugness faded as if wiped away with a cloth.

"This is what I am, Tyr. I am not Athene. She died centuries ago. I have been changing ever since, but you've been too blind to see anything but my role in your ambitions."

A dark shadow crossed over Tyr's face, and I recognised the threat of what he was capable of, the havoc he might choose to wreak upon my life. Once it would have bowed me like the branches of a tree in a harsh storm. This time, I held my head high.

"So that's a no, then?" The words were light, but I could see the anger simmering in Tyr's dark eyes.

"I've had enough." It was a relief to say it, to turn my back upon a life I no longer wanted. "I'm done with war and fury. I'm done with retribution. I want peace, Tyr, and I feel I've more than earned that right."

I anticipated a strong response, for my uncle to convince me that I would serve his aims no matter what I wanted, to wheedle his way into gaining my approval. Instead, a slow smile spread across his lips and he folded his arms over his chest, appraising me with a curious look.

"You really have changed. Very well, niece. I will leave you to this mortal life. But remember this: once you tire of the boy, your family are the ones who will be there for you."

"I have a new family now." Although I found it disconcerting how easily he surrendered, I wondered if perhaps I was not the only one who had changed over so many lives. There was no doubt in my mind that this time, things were different. Tyr could no longer convince me or manipulate me. I had well and truly broken those shackles.

Tyr stepped forward and I tensed, prepared for an attack. Instead he pressed a kiss to the top of my head, drawing back to examine me with a rare fondness.

"Then I give you your freedom."

"No." I shook my head fervently, swelling with an emotion I hardly recognised: hope. "My freedom is not something you can give. It's something I've fought for with every breath, and something I've chosen myself."

I spun on my heel and walked away from him for the last time. Instead of dread, elation coursed through my veins like lightning.

I would go to the bakery with Conrad and have cinnamon scrolls as sweet as his kiss. We would visit Dana's grave to pay our respects. It was time to move through this world with love in my heart instead of hate. Conrad had shown me that I had a purpose beyond anger, beyond violence.

I breathed in the crisp air, a slight chill to it that burned its way through my lungs. There wasn't a single cloud in the forget-me-not blue sky, and the sun caressed everything it touched with gentle warmth.

It was a beautiful morning.

Dana would have loved it.

Lovesick

Kayla Whittle

CHAPTER 4

LOVESICK

KAYLA WHITTLE

I breathed in the scent of brewing coffee and wilted passion. Exhaled, pushing out the threads of my power into the cup held between my hands.

It was the morning rush at Bean Me Up and so many of my customers were desperate. Shadows lingered beneath their eyes; their fingers twitched as they held up their phones to pay for their morning coffee. The shop was chaos, customers shuffling into line while others loitered waiting for their drinks to be made. Through it all, the tired scent of their aspirations lingered like spoiled meat. Breathing too deep made my stomach roil.

With my centuries of experience, I could slowly sort through the mess of passions writhing around me. There was the regular in the corner who smelled like old books and wanted to write a bestseller. The tourist stinking of motor oil with a fondness for fast cars and beautiful women. The coworker on the other end of the counter exuding coffee and the rot of expired pastries.

Then there was my latest customer, Tom, whose emotions smelled like withering rose petals and tasted like old wine. Looking at him, feeling the heavy flavor on my tongue, I knew he struggled over the decision to propose to his boyfriend.

My hands flexed around his drink. It only took a little push, a little intention, to pour some of my power into his coffee. Enough that when he drank, Tom's passions would be heightened, bringing some clarity for him. Either he'd see that what he wanted most was right before him, or realize that wasn't what he wanted from life after all. My fingers warmed and the coffeeshop seemed too loud, too much, until the transfer was finished and his drink was complete.

I popped the lid onto his coffee, sliding it over to the pick-up window.

"For Tom?" I called, sparing a moment to watch the short, hunched man snap up his order. No *thank you*, no regard for the young mother he nearly slammed into on his way out the door.

I hoped his passion would carry him well. Hoped, but there was nothing I could do to control the future, the consequences—and hard as I worked, my success rate sat somewhere around fifty percent. Half the customers who drank my passion-infused beverages were inspired, elated. They asked out the right person, aced the exam, painted a masterpiece.

The other half allowed their passions to consume and ultimately destroy their lives.

Lust was unpredictable that way.

THE NUMBER of customers dwindled when the end of my shift neared. Bean Me Up, the coffee shop I'd worked at for the past few months, was small but well-established. The shop's reputation was good enough to keep regulars and attract tourists. The front room was spacious for a spot in the city, filled with café tables and lounge chairs. By the back wall sat a miniature stage coated in silver. Overhead, a cutout of a spaceship hovered, directly over the performer's area. Typically, Bean Me Up closed by early afternoon, but a few nights a month the shop was open late with local musicians or comedians drawing in a crowd. The space usually reeked of aspirations toward fame—unwashed skin and hair dye—after those events.

Situated in south Philadelphia, the location was close enough to the convention center to draw in traffic from their visitors. It offered the perfect chance to connect with customers from around the world.

That was exactly what I looked for: places where large amounts of people connected. In the past, I'd worked in taverns and roadside inns, the kinds of places that attracted weary travelers. I could deliver tastes of my power to those who would drink deep, passions rising, and then take those enhanced emotions onward. I'd served bards who ended up traveling the globe, and others who'd become so fixated on finding the correct words for their next piece they'd ended up locked inside their own heads. I'd prodded artists toward muses, and locked others onto ideas that would never be worth a penny. There was absolutely nothing I could do to control the outcome; my power demanded to be used, and I tried to use my best judgement on who I served.

Half the time, the lust I gave my customers was used wisely. For art, for life, for hope. The other half—

I was lucky some of my family continued to keep in touch with me. My brother, Joseph, remained willing to maim any customers trying to harm me. Like that man several decades back, one I'd served at a bar called Beer We Go. He'd left for the night, emotions swirling with sweetened determination to find love. Only to return the next afternoon, looking for me. Sometimes, lust latched onto something—someone—unintended, and sometimes, the customers wouldn't accept *no* as an answer. The man had figured out my name, my schedule, and where I'd lived. His smile had been more like a smirk, tinged with the kind of lust my power had enhanced, taking something evil within the man and making it worse. I'd rang Joseph on the old phone at the back of the bar and he'd come to take care of him, few questions asked.

I did not want to ever experience something like that again.

Scrubbing at a stubborn stain on the counter, I mentally tallied up my day. Most customers had been served boring, run-of-the-mill menu items; I'd gifted five with something extra, including Tom. A little dose of power, a gift, or a curse; I might never be certain of the individual outcomes.

Even then I felt it, the pull of passion around me. Erik, my manager, lusted after the woman living in the apartment below him. The woman in the corner wanted a promotion more than anything; the person beside her wished they could break free of their writer's block. Their passions ebbed and flowed, caught up in their heart-beats, the pulse in their veins. I couldn't quite see it, not physically, but I could feel it all there, the emotion so strong it made my ears ring and stomach turn. I could taste it all; when my lips parted, their passions sat heavy on my tongue. Rich and bitter, though I chased after the ones that could be sweetened.

My successes. The fifty percent who thrived. The ones who found real love, real contentment, real success. The humans who sank into the embrace of their passions without letting it consume them. There was no option for me not to use my power; the best I could do was direct it toward the people I thought would grow brighter, stronger, with a little help from me. I'd never stop trying to get my customers their chance at happiness.

I'd never use my ability when there was a chance that lust could turn toward me, never again.

My failures could be cataclysmic.

I scrubbed harder at the stain, fingers stinging.

There were writers I'd worked on who'd forgotten to eat, to sleep, too enamored with their projects. People fighting for the wrong part-ners, clinging to those who weren't good for them, relationships ending in fire and blood. It was difficult to track my magic after the customers left. I had little control over where their passions took them or which of their wants my power enhanced.

That man at Beer We Go hadn't been my only mistake. There'd been customers who decided to take out their competition, who turned toward violence and rage. My power amplified the emotion already within them, writhing beneath the surface; I drew out the best and worst in humanity.

I tried my best to make things good. I tried to provide humanity with the push they needed to be the best versions of themselves. In those moments when it all fell apart, I asked for help. Joseph, consuming and tearing through those who'd become dangerous. My father, helping to numb the emotions my power had heightened. It often felt like my family was around only to look after my mistakes. They always knew how to find me, though I typically switched between businesses every few years. Easier to reach more humans that way.

Every time lust went awry, I told myself it would never happen again. That humanity would behave better, that I would choose better. That I would *be* better.

My fingers twitched and I laid my cloth down on the counter. The stain remained.

I felt terribly alone.

Folding my hands on the counter, I rested my head on them with a thunk—and lifted my head again, eyes wild, when the shop door opened with a jangle.

It was *her*. I knew her from the taste. Her passions were sweet like breaking open a ripe apple. They smelled fresh, like pine and the few minutes after a rain shower, like hope.

Oh, *no*.

I swiped my hands over my hair to try to pat down any flyaways, already knowing it was a lost cause. My apron was splattered with one of our syrups, and my collar itched like some had splattered there and dried on my skin.

"Hi!" I started—no, that was too enthusiastic. I cleared my

throat. "Hello. Welcome back to Bean Me Up. I mean, I saw—I've seen you—well—"

"You recognize me?" The customer smiled. I wanted to melt into it like a cat in a pool of sunshine.

"Lex," I blurted, like I was being quizzed and had miraculously remembered the correct answer. "You, well. You've been in."

"A few times." Lex smiled, leaning forward. Her hair was short, curling around her ears, deep brown like the earth after a storm. She nearly always wore a denim jacket—dark, heavy, and covered in patches from bands I didn't recognize. Her shoes were always worn, smile always sharp, and she was one of the loveliest humans I had ever met.

I could not afford to ever want more than this, a few minutes of conversation spent with the dirty counter sitting between us.

"Whitney?" Lex asked, raising an eyebrow.

I slapped a hand over my nametag—having, as usual, forgotten it was there until someone decided to call me by name.

"Wit, actually. It's Wit. You could—could call me that, if you want," I offered, hesitating a moment longer before hurrying off to start her drink. Only to belatedly hate myself, again, because I'd forgotten to confirm Lex's usual order.

I really needed to get my nametag fixed. A simple *Whitney* shouldn't leave me so flustered, but it was the only explanation for why my heart was beating so fast.

Every lifetime, I had no control over what humanity named me. I was busy being borne into existence, then remembering my purpose. Or burden, or power, whatever it should have been called. This ability of mine had been forced upon me, over and over. There was strength in it, but also immense isolation. There was little I could do to control the fate I'd been dealt. But I could control a name. No matter when or where in the world I dwelled, I took the name I'd been given and made it my own. Whitney became Wit. Last century in England, Lorraine became Lori. In the beginning, before it all went wrong and my lives became entangled with lust, I'd been known as Edana. Eddie, to my family.

It would have been nice if some of them stopped in more often.

I pumped syrup and poured coffee and decidedly did nothing more or less than that. Lex would never drink anything enhanced. She would never taste my power. Ever. I couldn't risk it. There'd been people who'd captured my interest over the years, around the world. I felt attraction in the very heart of me, in my soul, not so much with my body. It had taken me long, long lifetimes to find the right words for how I felt—biromantic and asexual. I liked those terms, even if I knew I was too dangerous for any human.

Even if she was nice, and kind, and smelled like my favorite kind of weather.

"Same price as usual?" Lex asked when I set down her drink. I shook my head, and her eyebrow went upward again.

"If we had loyalty cards, I think you would have already earned a free drink," I said, nudging her coffee forward. "Don't—don't worry about it."

"Really?" Lex asked, lips pulling wide. "Thanks, Wit. I'll see you again soon."

She stuffed a few dollars into the tip jar and left, taking all the air in the room with her. I slumped against the register.

"You know you'll need to take care of that," the current manager, Erik, called from the other end of the counter.

Grumbling, wondering if I should risk giving him a taste of his greatest passions, I dug out my wallet.

It'd been worth it, to see Lex smile.

"No, Joseph," I whispered into my phone. Technically I was on break, and *technically* my coworkers weren't supposed to eavesdrop, but that'd never stopped them before. "I've dealt with worse than Erik.

You know you're always welcome to visit, but please, you can't consume my manager."

Even Joseph's grumble sounded irritated, but I was just relieved to hear from him. Something had been off with him lately—though things were never simple, not in my family.

"Say the word, Wit, and I'll have it handled," Joseph said, voice crackling through the distant connection. "I've taken care of worse."

"So have I," I reminded him. Sometimes it felt like my siblings, my father, only ever saw the desperation that leaked so freely from me. Beneath that, hidden by the loneliness, were my sharper edges. Modernity had softened them, made it so I was more likely to ask others to help with my problems, but that didn't mean I'd forgotten my dark ages.

Fueling enthusiasm for revolutions against tyrannical governments. Choosing my customers carefully, selecting those who most deserved to have their lust tear them apart. I'd reveled in it. I'd wanted, for once, wanted so much that it only took selecting a few wrong clients to nearly destroy me. If Joseph hadn't been able to arrive so quickly, if we hadn't been able to stop the man who'd followed me back to Beer We Go, I knew I wouldn't have been the same. I knew my version of lust would have begun to look more like wrath.

Athene—Minnie, now—probably wouldn't have liked that.

"Keep me updated," Joseph demanded, and the line went silent.

"I love you, too," I sighed.

"Wit, finally," Erik said when I made my way over to the counter —as if I hadn't been in full view the entire time I'd attempted to take my break. He shoved some papers into my hands.

"Put these up, will you? We'll need you to think of other ways to market the thing, too. Maybe you could spend your next break brainstorming for us," Erik said, with that cold little smile that meant his suggestion was really a demand.

I hated the collective 'us' and 'we' Erik tended to use when referring to his team. *We're all family here. We all need to pitch in.* Such a grammatical scam. Maybe Joseph had a point. I'd already suffered enough, hadn't I?

By the time Erik walked away, I'd mostly convinced myself not to call Joseph back. My attention turned to the flyers shoved into my hands.

OPEN MIC! FRIDAY NIGHT!
CASH PRIZES FOR BEST ACTS
MUSIC, COMEDY, AND MORE

The largest text in bold mentioned how the most popular act would get a steady gig at Bean Me Up. Fridays for the rest of the year —something I had to look forward to, then. I'd probably need to work late. I'd probably be expected to somehow ensure a good crowd was there, too. Even in my tavern years at Do Ye Want a Piece of Mead I'd never been expected to double as an event planner. A good bard would wander in, get themselves set up on their own.

I missed the days when marketing wasn't a concept because most humans died before they traveled farther than they could throw a stone.

It was a task that got me away from the register, at least. I plastered signs around the shop, on the windows in front, at the tables struggling artists preferred to grab. When I rummaged around for a few thumbtacks for the back wall bulletin board, I inhaled deeply. Above the scent of coffee and the recently single girl sitting in the corner, I smelled rainwater. The thick, rich taste of chocolate coated my tongue.

"What's that?"

Lex's voice, so low and close to my ear, startled me. My hands rattled and flyers slipped free, raining from my hands in a flurry of ugly neon yellow.

"I'm sorry," I said immediately, dropping to the floor to clean up my mess. But Lex knelt as well, to help, and my embarrassment ratcheted higher when I realized how close that brought her face to mine.

"Why are you apologizing?" Lex asked, scooping fallen flyers into a lumpy pile. "I'm the one who startled you."

"I shouldn't—should have—you know," I winced, taking the papers from her and lurching to my feet. I'd spent countless years traveling the globe, learning new languages, lingo, slang—and still, a look from Lex knocked the words from my lips. I needed to pull myself together, but surely it would be fine, as long as I kept her at arm's length.

"I'm not sure I do," Lex said, but she smiled, and it didn't seem like she was laughing at me. She nodded to a flyer still clutched in her hand. "Is this something anyone can come to?"

"Yes," I said before I could worry about sounding too eager. "I mean, yes. You could sign up. You should. If you do that. Things like that."

How could I explain to her that I already had the taste of her music on my tongue? I could feel the weight of her passion threading through the air as she leaned closer to me, reading Erik's shitty flyer. Her talent was wild, unclaimed, sitting there waiting for me to grab it in both hands and wrangle it into something *more*. For better, or worse.

I couldn't. I wouldn't. With my luck, lust would ruin her.

"I do," Lex said. That smile was still there, smudging her lips. "I do things like that. Never professionally, but that's the dream, isn't it? A regular gig here could make a huge difference."

"You should come," I said before I could stop myself. She would never taste my power, but I couldn't stand between her and opportunity.

"You think so?" Lex lit up. "Will you be there?"

"Yes," I answered; I didn't need to check the schedule or check in with Erik. Of course he would leave me with responsibility for an event he'd created.

"Good." Lex folded up the flyer, putting in her pocket. "I want to hear what you think after I play."

One of my coworkers called Lex's name, Lex went to get her drink, and I was left with the weight of her dreams hanging around my shoulders.

SLEEP EVADED me as my work hours grew longer and the open mic neared, with the promise of an extended visit from Lex. She'd never lingered in Bean Me Up longer than a few minutes after picking up her coffee. Good for me, because it made it less likely I'd say something I wouldn't be able to fix. Bad for me, because it kept me up late wondering what would truly happen if I set Lex's passions free. She could climb to great heights. She could crash and burn. It was vain, probably, to think that any of those wants could be twisted toward me. Selfish, not to use my power.

Her music could take off. First a gig at Bean Me Up, then a chance at bigger venues. A real career, dreams coming true.

Or, the music could consume her. The notes would emerge wrong, discordant, her focus wrapped so tightly around the songs that every other piece of her life would be neglected. Sometimes greatness required a sacrifice. Marriages had dissolved because my musicians were never at home, constantly working on their music. Distraction led to danger, and my customers might become so fixated on their notes they lost the road and crashed their car, or slipped and fell from above.

There was no guarantee music was what she would become most passionate about. I could taste the truth of it each day I saw her, the sweetness that'd invaded her wants. The possibility. The potential.

I could never involve myself with a human I'd used my power on. It'd be impossible to say which emotions were genuine, and which had come from my meddling.

So, even though I knew I would never act on it, never be bold enough to do more than mumble and drop things whenever Lex arrived, I couldn't lose that possibility of *more*. Not for myself.

He arrived the next morning.

It was a regular enough occurrence that I didn't do the double-take I might have if it'd been one of my siblings. Most of them, I would be lucky to get an annual visit. Maybe more, if they happened to be in the area and I managed to guilt them into coming. It was so lonely when my family was so far. Humans were too malleable, untrustworthy when the way I dabbled in their emotions could falsify any friendships I formed with them.

Family was forever, and for mine that was a truer statement than for most.

"Black coffee," I offered, sliding the cup onto the table while my father, Thanatos—Tristan, in this lifetime—looked me over. When he was sitting, the differences in our heights weren't so prominent. It was easier for me to look him in the eye, and angle myself so fucking *Erik* wouldn't be able to see me chatting to a regular outside of my overbooked breaktime.

"Wit," he said, and that was all for a moment—as if that would be enough.

To be fair, in the past, that might have been enough. The validation of my chosen nickname combined with the weight of seeing someone who truly understood me, my past, and my power. I plastered on a smile, knowing my father would be able to see through the cracks. After all, he seemed drawn toward suffering.

Bean Me Up sometimes felt like another version of hell, but Father and I both knew there was much worse out there. Worse times, worse realities. I couldn't complain.

I *could*, but wanted to handle it on my own, for once. Maybe. Like old times, but with less inclination toward destruction and physical violence.

"How have you been?" I asked, ignoring the way his eyebrows drew downward. I'd never become skilled at steering the conversation away from myself.

"What's wrong?" Father asked, which was another way of saying to cut the bullshit, that he could see right through me and maybe neither of us liked what was lurking underneath.

I was a mess of loneliness with a crush on a minorly passionate musician. Part of me suspected the man I'd helped the previous week, working on a book of poetry, was currently stalking his ex-girlfriend. Part of me *knew* a teenager I'd served a month ago had turned his intelligence toward cybercrime instead of his college courses.

But I was fine. It was fine. Passion went awry, somehow, for some people. That was the balance. The risk I was forced to take.

"I'm thinking of moving on already," I confessed, surprising myself when the words poured free. To keep to my self-assigned pattern, I'd typically stay in this spot a few years longer before scoping out another area crowded with those needing a boost. Places that attracted too many customers, a lot of tourism.

"Is that such a bad thing?" Father asked. He could probably feel the tangle of emotion inside me, that it was more than an urge to move onward, or the thought that I needed to get away from a bad boss. But he was too polite to say anything about it aloud.

"No," I answered immediately—then, less certainly, "I don't know."

The bell by the door jangled, and I felt his eyes on me as I glanced over to see who'd walked in.

Lex. Of course. It was around that time of day, not that I'd begun anticipating her regular arrival. By the time my attention slid back toward my father, his expression had settled into something more knowing, involving both eyebrows this time.

Even after all the centuries, I knew it would be incredibly embarrassing to tell my own father that part of my conflict over staying revolved around a woman. I kept my love life away from my family, only in part because there wasn't much to speak of. Some people left after they realized I'd never want a physical relationship; some I shoved away, thinking I shouldn't be selfish, thinking I shouldn't hold someone back from their passions simply because sometimes I *wanted*, too. Afraid of what would happen if I did give them a taste of my power.

Then there was Lex. Denim jacket and dirty shoes, a current of honeyed interest trailing from where she stood at the counter toward where I loitered by my father's table.

"I'll let you get back to work," my father said. I refused to pick apart any amusement that might have lingered in his tone.

I was a professional.

"Wit," Thanatos said before I could leave. "Remember to consider your options. If you wish to change locations, I will see what I can do to help you get resettled. If you wish to stay, you won't be alone in that, either."

I hated that he could see how acutely my loneliness had cut into me. How hard it was to function sometimes, when I woke each morning century after century doubting whether most of the people around could feel any genuine emotion when it came to me. Fearing the worst, knowing what happened when things went sour.

Knowing that even if the worst happened, there were still those I could call, who would be there to help me fix everything. Who would keep me safe.

I left my father at the table, unable to say what I wanted next.

"Wit," Lex greeted me. My coworker had already taken her order and I didn't know whether I should have been embarrassed to see no one else had memorized it the way I had. "I was hoping you'd be working today."

"Oh! Oh, you were?" I asked, propping myself against the counter, trying for casual and looking more like I was white knuckling the wood. "Uh, why?"

"You're the expert, here," Lex said. "I wanted to know what kind of music you like."

"Oh." If I said *oh* to her one more time, I was going to lock myself in the backroom until Erik finally fired me. "I mean, I'm not going to be the one judging the open mic. The crowd will. It doesn't matter what I like."

"Yes, it does," Lex said. "You'll be here all night listening to sad poetry and bad comedy and the least I could do is make sure I'll pick a song to play that you'll enjoy."

"Are you going to play an original?" I asked, knowing she had the talent for that. I could feel it, seeping from her skin. Would it bubble over into an album, a record deal, if I took her coffee from my coworker and added a little passion?

"Sure," Lex agreed, as if I'd given her an answer.

Maybe her talent would fizzle out and die, stressed and over-worked, underachieving and arbitrary, if I interfered. Maybe she'd reach the point where I'd need to call Thanatos or Joseph, to fix things, to fix *her*.

"That's—that's great. I mean, I'm sure it'll be wonderful. Music you write, it's—it really encompasses everything about you, you know? I think you can feel the difference when the artist believes in the words they're singing," I said, because I truly *could* feel that difference. It would lay along the lines of my bones, steady as the weight of Lex's gaze. "Songs like that tell a story."

"I'll be looking for you on Friday, then," Lex said. I realized at some point she'd received her drink, and that she was already turning to go.

I didn't want to stop her, didn't want to enhance her passion, didn't want to interfere.

Lex passed Thanatos on her way out, and as she left, it looked like he was subtly giving me a thumbs-up. I only minorly wished for an elusive afterlife. My father had a point; I had options, a choice. Leaving might keep me away from Lex, but it wouldn't fix the worry that burrowed deep within me now whenever I used my power or a customer smiled at me a moment too long.

This was different. Lex was different. I would stay, at least for now.

It didn't mean anything that for the next few days, I avoided enhancing the drinks of anyone with threads of music in their passions.

As EXPECTED, Erik scheduled me to work the open mic, a much later shift than my usual morning rush to afternoon slowdown. I didn't mind; he kept himself busy with the friends he'd invited, leaving me to work the machines. And the register. And oversee the sign-up sheet. Surprisingly, our half-hearted advertising had managed to pull in a few comedians, a poet, an essayist, and a handful of musicians.

The stench of their passions was overwhelming. Rotting sheet music mixed with old sea air, the perfume of a fresh bloom mixed with trash rotting by a roadside. Riddled with nerves and excitement, or the calm sort of confidence usually covering a lack of natural talent, customers swarmed the sign-up sheet. Thick, vibrant notes of music tangled with the sharp sting of punch lines, swirling into a mix that had me suppressing a gag. Instead, I forced a smile, using my best customer service voice to wrangle them into order. It worked well enough; I'd hidden worse than my annoyance behind a bright smile. I'd once had to fend off a near-feral pack of guards fighting over a loaned lute.

The poet ordered an espresso. One of the musicians leaned way too far over the counter as he ordered a coffee—black, like that would impress me, like that order wouldn't just remind me of my father—and the overwhelming blanket of his music and lyrics and lust wrapped together in such a way that I didn't realize Lex was there until she was directly in front of me.

"Hi, Wit."

"Hi, Lex. Hello."

Looking at her made me feel silly, light and young in a way I hadn't in centuries. Her hair was like the night and eyes like the stars; I was the moon, drawn inexorably into her depths.

I coughed, then sniffed, trying to shake the lingering threads of passion stretching toward me. Overwhelmed, I felt a little like I imagined humans did with their seasonal allergies.

I needed to pull myself together. The night wasn't about me.

"There's a spot left for you, here," I said, pointing toward the bottom of the sign-up sheet. Not the very end; one of the musicians and a comedian had secured the very last acts. I tried not to focus on Lex's expression as I handed her a pen.

"I hope you won't be too busy to enjoy the show," Lex said after she'd signed her name along one of the lines.

"Even if there's a line, I'll listen to you," I said. "I mean—well— not that I'm biased. But I'm looking forward to hearing you. Your song. Your music."

"Thanks, Wit," Lex said, bending down to pick up the guitar case I hadn't noticed she'd settled at her feet. "I'm looking forward to you listening."

I lost sight of her in the crowd. Lost sense of her, too, because Lex's rainwater and pine passion blended so well in a group like this. It was hard to pick out a single stream of interest. Even so, there was a weighty familiarity to some of the passions stirring in the shop. Customers who'd visited me before. Faces were forgettable, but with enough concentration I could recognize even the most stubborn, hidden wants. I knew one of the comedians had been in the shop a month previously, stopping by before she'd started work on a new routine. I knew one of the musicians, too, but I could taste the way their interest had soured, that their attention had turned away from their music and toward their partner. Their love didn't feel like a bad fit, but that consuming passion could be a distraction.

Erik situated himself behind the microphone.

"Welcome to Bean Me Up's first open mic night," he said, speaking a little too loudly for the volume to be comfortable. "Hopefully, the first of many. Our most popular act tonight will win a regular appearance in the shop, so be sure to stick around and support your favorites. Visit Whitney at the counter and grab a drink. Treat yourself."

He grinned, but Erik's stare was hard as he gestured over toward me. I'd stopped reminding him to call me Wit. I'd also stopped caring about how he expected me to spend the night upselling all the pastries and specialty drinks we'd created for the event.

We. There I went, using Erik's old trick of referring to the shop as a collective, when I really meant myself and the two coworkers I'd spent the afternoon prepping with.

Something in his words must have done the trick, though, because a short line formed as the essayist was stepping up to start off the night.

Everyone liked a delicious gimmick; the overly sugared specialty drinks menu unfortunately became popular, which meant spending a lot of time on each order, which meant the acts passed in my periphery without much notice on my part. I served too many drinks named *Mic Drop* and *Punchline* and *Earworm*.

Whenever a new act took the stage, I tried to hide the way I needed to clear my throat or rub at my eyes. The overpowering hope and talent and cries for *more* clogged my mind whenever the artist's passions peaked and consumed their thoughts.

I was busy plating one of our *Note-able* pastries, coated in iced music notes, when I felt her. The strings of her interest were calm, tentative—polite, almost, when they reached for me. Soft, like flower petals. It felt like they nudged against the back of my mind, urging me to turn around.

"Five minutes," I said to the next customer in line, feigning an apologetic smile. "Need to take a quick break, sorry."

Thankfully, like most reasonable twenty-somethings who'd also survived working through the service industry, the customer seemed to understand.

I slipped out from behind the counter, tucking myself into a corner closer to the stage where I could see and, more importantly, where the line I'd left wouldn't be able to see me.

Inhaling, I felt the first notes of Lex's music before she even started to play. Exhaling, I realized with a shudder that there was an undercurrent to that passion. Another layer, nearly hidden, intertwined with her song and simultaneously meant only for me.

It had been a long time since I'd allowed myself to feel the smooth slide of another's interest and hadn't tried to turn that passion away from me. I didn't know what to do with that honey-coated sweetness, didn't know what to do with myself.

My hands, my heart, unsteadied. Lex was all slow, sticky confidence as she picked out the first notes on her guitar.

The heart of Lex's music slipped through the crowd, passion curling around my wrists, trailing up the backs of my arms. It thickened, seeping into me, nearly overpowering her voice as she began to sing. Technically, lyrically, I'd heard better. I'd felt more talent pooling in the air, allowed stronger wants to slip out of my shop. But Lex was best because her music was her own. I could hear the reverence in her tone, the twist of each syllable, the sharp tang of consonants ringing with belief. She knew what she wanted to say, what she wanted her audience to hear.

She sang of love and loss and loneliness. She sang of love found again, that promise of hope that needed to be held gently. My fingers tingled and heartbeat rose, mingling with the fresh spice of her passion somewhere over the gathered audience.

I thought Lex's eyes found mine in the shadowed café, but that could have been a trick of Erik's self-assembled stage lights.

As if a thought could summon him, a firm grip tugged on my arm, pulling me backward as the last notes of Lex's song faded. The sweetened lines of her passion wound back toward her, disappearing within the crowd.

"What are you doing away from the counter?" Erik demanded. It was creepy, the way he could snap at me while his face remained fixed in a smile in case anyone happened to see us talking. "I gave you these extra hours to work, Whitney. You need to serve our customers. Their needs come before yours."

As if he was doing me a favor, assigning me an extra shift I hadn't asked for. As if I didn't know how to do my job, and do it well, after literal centuries of practice.

I loved customer service. I liked dealing with unruly customers or setting my siblings upon them. I liked making peoples' days easier or brighter, getting them what they needed and sending them onward to where they needed to go. Even when I didn't meddle with their passions, there was something so satisfying in handing a human their order and seeing the way a few quick words could make them smile. There were probably other, easier ways I could exercise my power, but I liked being a hostess or barista, waitress or serving wench, and saw no reason to change that simply because of bad management.

My hands tightened by my sides. The concentrated passions inside Bean Me Up were beginning to give me a headache. Maybe some of the strain showed in my expression, or the way I felt my jaw twitching, because Erik's false smile thinned.

"Why don't you go in the back and start getting everything ready to clean?" Erik asked. "You're closing alone tonight, though."

That twitching muscle became more persistent. I swept into the backroom before I could lose my temper, and before I realized that meant I would miss the end of the open mic. With the door closed, the noise dulled, and the trailing bits of lust went off-kilter, too. I wouldn't be able to keep track of the last few entrants. More importantly, I wouldn't be able to see the outcome.

I wanted to find everyone Erik hated and give them a taste of my power so at least half would have the chance to realize their dreams. So that he'd watch them succeed where he couldn't.

All because I'd stolen a few moments for myself, time I'd

deserved. Time I refused to regret, not when it meant I'd had Lex for a moment. I could still feel the way her music had wrapped tight around me. For a moment, nothing had felt quite so impossible.

She'd seen me, I knew she had. It shouldn't have burned so badly to no longer be out there, seeing *her*. Had she looked for me again, after the song had finished?

It didn't matter. I couldn't want her.

I slammed my way through our ovens, ripped through plastic bags and nearly overturned trays of silverware in my rush to pull them into our sinks. I knew the least I deserved was some stress for all I'd done in the world, *to* the world, but could I not have one night? One moment, one song, which I could pretend had been sung just for me. For that minute or two, it hadn't mattered that Lex was human, fragile.

My fingers itched for my phone, to call Joseph or my father, knowing a few well-placed complaints would rain hell onto Erik's life. The downfall of one coffeeshop manager was child's play compared to my family's past works. I'd once asked Thanatos to interfere when a contingent of unruly outsiders had tried to overstay their welcome in an inn I'd been running. Sleep You Real Soon had easily kicked out the numb, shivering group when my father had finished with them.

It wouldn't be as satisfying anymore, handing off the hard part to someone else.

Stacking clean plates for the day shift, I moved too quickly, cracking one against the countertop. I stared at the large, sharp shards, broken irreparably, like half the lives I left in my wake.

Someone knocked on the door to the backroom.

My annoyance grew into a large, ugly thing, seething within me. I was allowed to have my passions, too. I didn't physically lust after anyone, but I could still *want* in so many other ways. I was tired of pretending I needed nothing and no one besides my family. In that moment, I wanted Erik to feel what he'd made *me* feel, and then some. To take his worst passions and elevate them until his lust tore him to shreds. I knew I was spiraling and didn't care.

"Why don't you—" I threw open the door, only to find myself face-to-face with Lex.

I should have known; Erik never would have knocked.

"Are you all right?" Lex asked, brow furrowed. "Your manager said he was heading home for the night, and I told him I'd let you know. I hope that's okay."

It wasn't okay, but that wasn't Lex's fault. Peering past her, I realized the shop had dimmed and emptied. The cloying swirl of passions lingered, leaving an aftertaste of sharp victory and pungent defeat. A few notes still dangled in the air, heavy with talent and care.

I shouldn't have listened to Erik. I should have left the backroom. I'd missed the end of the open mic, and Erik hadn't even bothered to tell me who'd won.

"I'm—I'm fine," I said, ignoring how Lex frowned at my lie. "Are you—did you—how did it go?"

Her lips parted, but before she could speak, I held out a hand—either to stop her, or to steady myself, or both.

"I mean, I heard you. Your song. Your music is beautiful," I told her. It was beautiful as the look in her eyes when she'd heard about the open mic, the smile she gave me every time she picked up her drink, the laugh caught in her throat when I stumbled over my words.

"I'm glad you liked it," Lex said. "It was for you."

I'd served countless cups filled with power, watched from afar as artists and lovers did what they could with their something *more*, but never had any of them directed that passion toward me, not in any way I'd liked. I could feel it, the pinprick of Lex's interest circling me, settling around my shoulders. Warm, and sweet, and familiar.

"I mean, I didn't win," Lex said. Her expression softened, fading to something sadder. "I lost pretty spectacularly, actually."

Maybe I should have rigged it. Maybe I should have ensured

none of the contestants had ever been touched by my power. Maybe it had been selfish, not giving Lex a better chance at succeeding. Maybe, maybe, maybe.

"I'm sorry," I told her. "Your work deserves better."

"It's all right," Lex said. "I didn't expect to win, really. It would have been nice, but—but really, I wanted the gig so I'd have an excuse to see you every Friday night."

"Me?" I should have tasted it within the strands of her music. Picked through her interests, digging down to the heart of her passion. I didn't want to pry, not with Lex, but I couldn't argue against the want sitting snug around my shoulders.

"If you'd want to, we could—I mean, I was thinking—me and you, sometime—" Lex picked at the ragged edge of her jacket, gaze sliding away from mine.

It was refreshing and wrong, to have Lex be the one stumbling over her words. Something lit within me, burning and bright with something dangerously close to hope.

She liked me. Lex had a song for me, and she liked me, and I liked her. My power had never come close to touching her, to manipulating her emotion.

I thought of my father, reminding me of my options. Eternity was a very long time to spend alone. Breathing deep, I sank into the cool, lively scent of Lex's wants, letting it steady me.

"I'd like to take you out some time," I said. "I don't think I'll be working here much longer, but I want to keep seeing you."

Lex's chin lifted, lips spreading with that smile that felt like sunshine.

"Yes," she answered, so quickly I could only believe her sincerity. "Maybe grab a drink? Something other than coffee. I don't drink it much, really."

Holding the door open for her as we left the backroom, I eyed Lex as she shrugged.

"I needed an excuse to keep coming back," Lex said. She fidgeted with her jacket again, before joining me in my surprised laugh.

I felt light, optimistic, the way I thought most humans might feel after drinking something I'd handed to them. Although I'd already lived through countless centuries, with who-knew-how-many years to come, here was a chance for happiness. To push back the loneliness. To allow *myself* to want, for however long this might last.

Perhaps the next shop I'd choose to work in would be a different venue, one more suited to music.

"Come with me," I said to Lex as we left Bean Me Up. I locked the door behind us, knowing I'd only return once more: to quit, and to serve Erik a cup of coffee. Perhaps a few enhanced passions would improve his life—or perhaps they'd overwhelm it, dragging him down.

I had no control over it, and for the moment, that was fine. I had Lex. I had more hope than I'd held in a century. Her shoulder pushed against mine as we walked down the street together, and her smile was brighter than the streetlamps lighting up around us.

CHAPTER 5

A MILLION DREAMS

CASSIDY CLARKE

The hush before the musicians took the stage was always the worst.

Something about that silence, edged with anticipation reminiscent of a dog drooling over a steak held aloft over its head, always sharpened the pain in my stomach. A self-wielding knife that stabbed with no thought of mercy, demanding a sacrifice that amounted to more than my own curses, something more than the pressure of a pillow jammed against my gut to muffle its eternal screams.

Not growls. Not groans. *Screams.*

The first absentminded tease of bow against string sent a flash of timid blue through my mind. Only a tattered scrap of a note, but enough to turn the hunger *rabid.*

"Seph." A long-fingered, golden-brown hand settled on my shoulder, its squeeze a silent command. "You're wearing a witch's eyes."

I couldn't help grimacing at Ben's crude attempt at humor. He always said I looked like I was being burned at the stake on my bad days.

"I'm fine," I muttered, prying his fingers free from my hollow-boned shoulder. I'd gone too long between meals; not by my choosing, but everything worthy of dreams had been closed down for the past week with the storms blowing in off the sea.

Thysia was not all that different from other places I'd lived; a beautiful city of stone that dwelled serenely on the coast of an ocean named *Antica*. I hadn't lived near water in lifetimes, but I'd discovered in my years here that there was something without compare about dreams accompanied by the melody of crashing waves. People slept deeper here, dreamed brighter, hoped harder. Something about the shore made for happier people.

Unfortunately, it also made for a hungrier curse. Spoiled now, constantly teased by the flavor of salt, it salivated for something better than simple imaginations. No, now it longed for something with substance. But beggars couldn't be choosers, and I was damned near desperate enough to get on my knees and *beg* Ben to read some of his horrendous poetry. "How long until the performance starts?"

"They're getting into place. Take a breath, all right? You need me to daydream a bit for you?"

"Ha. I'm not making that mistake again." Ben's daydreams tended to dip into lurid shades of red that I didn't particularly care for. Still, a spike of raging need drove upward from my stomach to my chest, a hunger cramp that nearly took my breath away. I bent against it, picking at the lace of my boot to disguise my agony. "Get the griffonia out of my bag."

Ben's hand shifted from my shoulder to my back, bracing me. "I thought you said it doesn't help when—"

"I know what I said, just *give it to me*." Something was always better than nothing, whether it worked or not.

Ben wrinkled his nose, but he dug his hand into my pack before offering me a small bag of green seeds, his mouth twisted in a knot that was holding back his judgment.

I couldn't blame him. Humans were inclined to scorn sin where they found it—to scorn it or salivate over it. Rarely was there a middle ground.

"You'd act the same if your insides were trying to eat themselves alive," I mumbled to him before shoving a handful of the seeds into my mouth. Their taste stirred pops of verdant light behind my eyelids, bitter juice and fibrous texture curling my tongue even as relief sanded down the edges of the knife stabbing my stomach.

"No, I know," said Ben, running an absentminded hand through his dark curls. "You can snap all you like, I don't care. I just don't get how you can stomach those things."

"I can stomach just about anything."

He offered me his program. "In that case, care to dispose of this for me?"

The seeds actually dulled the pain enough for me to laugh, driving my elbow into his ribs and snatching the program away. "Maybe I will, you ass."

Ridiculous though he might have been, I could never find it in me to be ungrateful for Ben's presence. I'd lived so many lifetimes— some in the past with horse-drawn carriages and worldwide wars, some in the future with television and the unmatchable wonder of ice cream, and some...some in different worlds entirely, like Thysia. Worlds that belonged in the storybooks I'd read in my other lives. But in none of those worlds had I ever had a friend.

We met on a hot, humid night, the evening sky tinted green with a coming storm, the crown of his head dancing with scarlet and rose dreams that tasted like floral liquor as he stumbled through his door, and I...well. I was rifling through his pantry for the third time that week. The fool never remembered to lock his door.

But rather than calling for the townsguard, he'd put on a pot of coffee, welcomed me to whatever I wanted, and made me sit with him. "If you're that desperate for a bite, I want you to at least enjoy it," he'd drawled, urging me to take more when I dithered and stammered. I'd lived in his spare room ever since.

Ben was the one person in centuries who knew my story, my *true* story—or at least most of it. The closest thing to a sibling I'd had in... too long. Long enough that I couldn't bring to mind exactly who I'd been the last time I'd seen most of them.

Father, though...Father I still visited. Each and every life, somehow I managed that.

Not often. Not enough. Only two days out of the year.

Mother's birthday. And Mother's deathday.

Two days neither of us could pass without remembering. Without wishing we could forget.

The symphony slipped into its usual rise and fall, the pitch of flute and trumpet melding with the syrupy melody of violin and cello, and I closed my eyes, letting the music wash over me. Letting the sparks of color bursting in firework flares within the musicians' minds wash over my consciousness.

Imagination was not picky about where it found its muse. And in this music, in the pitch and hum and song, it found the color it was constantly craving.

Dull, maybe, and edging toward unsatisfactory, but it did the job. Whether this was the same aria they'd performed the week before the storm didn't matter. What mattered was the commitment of the artists to their craft; what mattered was their passion, their love, their hunger for the notes their instruments birthed into the world.

Passion, craving, even the stage nerves. All of it strengthened the power of the creativity, the *imagination,* that dulled the edge of my fang-toothed hunger.

So was my calling. So was my curse.

Selfish boy.

The hiss of my mother's dull, hopeless voice slithered between the periwinkle warble of a flute and the satin-like whorl of burgundy that always trailed behind a cello's mournful groan, turning the pit of my stomach sour.

Selfish—but she was the one who left.

I gave my head a vigorous shake, burying memory beneath melody until only music remained.

Not tonight. I was too far gone to let the memory of her drawn, furious face—and the memory of her blue-veined hands snatching a half-molded loaf of bread out of my trembling grip—distract me from sating my current needs. These musicians might feel a bit discouraged tomorrow, a bit disillusioned with their craft after my consumption of their dreams, but it wouldn't last long. It never did.

I was not selfish. I survived.

I forced my gaze forward, doing my best to ignore the burning of Ben's eyes against my temple, and let the hurricane of artistry drown out the keening of my own cravings.

It was getting worse.

I didn't say as much to Ben, who was chattering on and on about the poetry reading he was planning on dragging me to later in the week. For a mortal man, he seemed to possess a truly eternal well of patience for my...*ailment,* but if I couldn't even last the walk back to our flat...

Swallowing the hollow sensation climbing the column of my throat, I opened my mouth to tell Ben I'd catch up to him after I tracked down a more tangible meal...when a glimmer of carnation pink danced in the corner of my eye.

The cobblestones jammed into the toes of my boots as I skidded to a stop, twisting to peer over my shoulder—but the color had flickered out just as suddenly as it had appeared.

Odd. Hallucinations probably weren't a good—

There. Again, a flicker that came and went in the span of a blink, this one a pastel yellow that winked at me like sunlight peeking over the frothing edge of a cloud.

This time, it came accompanied by the sweetest croon of violin I'd ever heard.

The note coated my tongue in bursts of cherry-red sweetness, a taste so familiar I rammed to an absolute halt.

Color swirled, sang—settled. Hardened into memory.

"One each," my mother told us, working down her line of children with a practiced efficiency that only a mother of seven could wield so easily. She placed a ruby-red round of sugar in each of our outstretched palms, and it might as well have been one of those obscenely valuable stones for how much it mattered to me.

We barely had enough to scrape together a meal these days. To be handed something as rare as candy...

My mother's thin, blue-veined hand closed around mine, folding my fingers over my candy. She leaned down until I was forced to look at her instead of the sugar in my hand. "One, Eris," she repeated, gaze sharp as the bones straining against her skin. "Once it's gone, it's gone."

I was walking before the memory had even handed control of my senses back to me, blindly chasing that trail of sunshine sweetness.

The dancing lights of a dreaming mind called me from street to street of brick dwellings and pastel-painted shops, and the louder the music sang, the quieter the constant roaring in my stomach became.

I'd never seen dreams like these—all familiar colors, all red and blue and yellow and purple, but their shades were just vibrant enough to defy naming, just otherworldly enough to escape the shackles of familiarity. Even if an artist spent decades putting brush to palette, I somehow doubted they could find the proper mixture to match these...these...

They were more than dreams. They were *hopes*.

Just as the name for what lured me through the twilight streets burst to life in my mind, I crashed through an alley into the next street over, ignoring the curses as I collided with a knot of taverngoers, and—

And all at once, for the first time in so many lifetimes I couldn't count them all...my slavering, starving curse went utterly silent.

Like it, too, wanted to stop and listen.

Despite the silvering of the moon blanching everything it touched, despite the only other light coming from flickering lamps mounted outside what few businesses were still open...I still saw her in perfect color. A creature of riotous joy danced barefoot across the cobblestones of the town square, her chestnut hair tied up with a yellow ribbon, each shivering curl bouncing in tandem with her flying feet. On her shoulder she braced a violin so fine that any one of the symphony players would have salivated to see it, a masterpiece of lacquered rosewood and shimmering strings that fit against her chin like it had been carved for that exact perch. Her face was dotted with droplets of white and yellow cosmetics meant to mimic freckles of sunlight, her eyelids were glazed with something gold, and her lips...

Her lips, spread wide in a grin of sheer delight, were the same shade as cherry candy being placed in a hungry child's hand.

I only realized my jaw was hanging open when some night-dwelling bug flew straight into it.

I might have been hungry enough to nearly devour a paper pamphlet or raw seeds, but I'd have to be worse than dead before I fell far enough to eat an insect. I gagged, twisting around to scrape the intruder off my tongue, coughing so hard that I didn't even hear the music stop until—

"Are you all right, sir?" chirped a voice like a songbird, amuse-ment dancing a jig over every prettily-pitched word. A fist jammed into the small of my back, adding a bit of *oomph* to my grinding coughs.

Fates, she even *sounded* happy. Like a song given form.

I turned quickly, finally dragging in a deep breath as I laid eyes on her. She stood before me with a carefree grin, her violin propped up on her shoulder, her other fist curled around her bow. The tattered edges of her daffodil-yellow skirt fluttered around her ankles like it hadn't realized she was no longer dancing, and sweat glimmered in the hollows of her clavicles.

Moon and sun, stars and glitter.

"Sir?" she prompted once more, and I tugged myself to with a silent curse.

"I'm all right," I croaked. "One of those damned mosquitos..."

"Ugh, they're a menace, aren't they?" Her long, hooked nose wrinkled. "I've got more bites than freckles, I do. The price you pay for outlasting the sun, it seems."

"Indeed," was all I managed, and that only barely. The flickers of constant color flitting around her head like a halo kept pulling my eyes upward, their light washing over my senses in waves of cherry red and lemon yellow and berry blue—even morsels of herbal green here and there, a green spicier and far more pleasant than the bitter seed fibers still caught in my teeth.

"I'm Jemma, by the way." She stuck out a sun-kissed hand, the tiny false jewels on her lacquered nails twinkling like pigmented stars. "Jemma la Rue."

"Joseph." I took her hand, silently marveling at the harsh span of her palm—she had cal-louses to match any warrior or worker. "Joseph Erisichthon."

Wrinkles traced themselves over the bridge of Jemma's nose as she grinned once more, her blue eyes reflecting the silver of the moon. "That's a mouthful."

"I've been told." I didn't bother to tell her it was my mother who'd chosen it, or that I'd done my best to leave it behind for the first handful of my lifetimes. I'd only taken it back on so my family could track me down when need be. It was harder when we ignored our first names.

Caedmon, at least, had come up with something close. It made it easier for *me* to find *him*, every other lifetime or so, just to make sure he hadn't sunk between his chaise cushions like a stray coin, never to be found again.

It was the one favor I did for my father. Caedmon might want nothing to do with me anymore, with *us*, but he was my brother, whether he liked it or not. The baby of the bunch.

The rest...the rest I generally left to their own devices. Particu-larly my older siblings. Particularly the oldest. We had...conflicting needs.

It was only when Jemma tapped me—tapped me on the *nose*—
that I startled out of my reverie. She quirked an eyebrow, pink lips
thinning against a laugh. "Just coming from the tavern, are you?"

"Ah—no." Alcohol only sharpened the cravings, never dulled
them. I hadn't touched the stuff this entire lifetime. I rubbed the tip
of my nose, a hurried dash of knuckle against skin. Her touch made
my skin buzz. "Sorry. Lost in thought. Your music is…"

That smile twisted into something expectant, disappointed. She
crossed her arms over her chest, chin raised in challenge, a girl ready
for a fight if I ever saw one. And with four sisters, Fates knew I'd seen
far more than one. Especially growing up with Athene, who'd once
grabbed hold of my hair and refused to stop pulling until I apologized for *accidentally* stepping on one of her toys. "Loud? Disruptive?
An insult to the muses who blessed us with the gift of song?"

I frowned. "It's beautiful. Without compare, actually."

Jemma blinked, surprise dropping her jaw, and for the first time,
the sass in her demeanor stuttered. "Oh. I—well! Thank you, Mr. Eris
—Erisich—"

"Joseph's fine."

She blew out a breath of relief, settling a hand over her chest.
"Oh, bless you."

"Do people really tell you off for your playing?" Impossible. It
had to be a joke.

Now her lips bent into a wretched shape, golden joy diving into
vivid blue gloom, and she shrugged the shoulder that bore her violin.
Behind her, the fountain in the center of the square suddenly ceased
to bubble, as if it had only just realized that night had fallen. "It's not
about the playing, really. People don't like to see penniless people
with things of luxury. Makes them feel like they have one less thing
to lord over us."

I knew that feeling. "It is a handsome instrument."

She fondly stroked a gemstone fingernail down the violin's neck.
"My mother's. She passed when I was little."

"I…" I tried to read the emotion in her eyes. Was she grieving?

Angry? Was it simple sadness that lined those blue-sky eyes in threads of silver? "I'm very sorry. That's a hard loss to take."

"You know it?"

My mouth dried out. "I do."

That bow tapped lightly against her hip. "You miss her?"

The girl might as well have slapped me across the mouth.

I'd told the lie so many times that it should have been easy. It should have been out of my mouth the second she finished the question.

But looking into her inquisitive eyes, ready and eager for any answer I might give...

"No," I admitted. "I wish I did, but...no."

The memory of my mother was soaked in a shame that I never quite managed to shake. A rage that never dulled. There was no real way to *miss* that. Everyone else, yes, but...

She'd abandoned us.

Selfish boy.

Selfish. But *I* was the one who stayed.

Her chestnut ponytail bounced as she smacked the heel of her hand to her forehead, cursing softly. "I'm sorry, I'm such an arse. My father used to say I had a knack for asking awful questions."

To my surprise, I found myself...smiling. "I find it refreshing."

"Then I really don't believe you haven't been frequenting the taverns." Jemma stepped back and bobbed up and down—a curtsy so quick I nearly didn't realize what it was. "I'll bid you goodnight, Joseph. Get home safely."

"You as well, Jemma."

A gentleman would've offered to walk her home, but that didn't occur to me until I was already halfway back to my own flat, the memory of her dancing feet and blinding grin twirling through my mind in spinning circles that might as well have been whiskey-induced—another taste my father and I shared, a vice we both did our best to avoid.

If there was one thing I cursed the Fates for, it was the fact that I bore both of my parents within me—too much of my mother in my looks to forget her face, and enough of my father's heart that it hurt to look in a mirror. That never changed, either; my appearance shifted somewhat from lifetime to lifetime, but never enough to shake them both.

I had her eyes, my father said sometimes on the rare occasions he *did* have a bit too much drink—not quite the same, with flecks of darkness that belonged to him and his, but close enough that he couldn't quite look me in the eye.

I'd started wearing painted glass lenses in my eyes after that, dulling them from sea green to something closer to hazel. It made our visits easier.

If he noticed the change, he never said.

Those thoughts distracted me so thoroughly that it wasn't until I was huddled in bed back at my flat, thick knit quilt tugged over me and a pillow pressed to my gut to muffle the inevitable growls, that I realized why I'd been able to lose myself to memory like that:

I wasn't hungry.

Sitting up, pulse racing, I put one hand over my ever-hollow stomach, waiting with bated breath—waiting for the dream to end, for the pain to begin, for the cramps to seize me in iron claws until I was forced to take to the streets once again to hunt down wisps of sleeping dreams.

Nothing. I wasn't full, not by any means, but...I wasn't craving.

Wonder tightened my throat as tears budded on my lower lashes, a choked laugh squeezing between my ribs.

I *wasn't hungry*.

And that could only mean one thing:

I had to taste Jemma la Rue's dreams again.

Erisichthon!"

Mama's voice preceded thin arms grabbing me around my ribs, tugging me out of the hiding place I'd fashioned out of broken crates and a moth-eaten blanket, its floor nothing but lifeless dust; the dirt hadn't given us anything useful in too long, and food was running low.

We weren't starving, not yet; but everything was carefully rationed out, equal portions to seven hungry children.

What filled some of their bellies, though, did nothing for me. Little Caedmon, perhaps, and the others smaller than me, but I was balancing on the precarious edge between child and man, growing inches in mere weeks. The portion given to me didn't even take the edge off the awful cramps in my belly, the pains that drove me to tears at night, pain that drove me to my parents' bedside in hysterics, believing wholeheartedly that I was dying. Only my mother's soft lullabies—and my father's reassurances that Death knew better than to prey on his children—were able to soothe me to sleep.

But the pain never stopped. Which found me here: huddled in a pile of rubbish, hunched over my own pile of secrets, dragged out by my mother's tight grip on my arm.

"Wait—" I pleaded, but in my flailing resistance, I accidentally knocked my refuge over...revealing the treasures hidden inside.

My mother froze in her tracks.

"What is this."

Fear...embarrassment...shame turned my hollow cheeks red. "Nothing."

"Nothing?" Brittle shock broke into blazing fury, and she kicked the rest of the rubble aside, revealing the source of her anger: a pile of scraps that was hardly good enough for a dog's dinner. Loaves of bread that were well past stale, nearing the point of molding; pieces of dried meat, tough enough to patch up a wall if need be; and nestled in the center, two pieces of cherry candy, glistening red orbs that had gone missing from Mnemosyne and Caedmon's possession in the dark of one desperate night. "Nothing? Erisichthon, this—this is meant to feed all of us, do you understand that? This is all we have—"

"Mama, please, I was just—"

"I can't believe this." She choked on a sob, her accusation thinning to

something awful, something hateful: "You selfish boy. Did you even think of what this would do to the rest of us? To your brothers and sisters? When they starve to death, whose fault do you think that will be?"

Shame, hot and horrid and tasting of tears, slid down the column of my throat, festering deep in my belly. Any hunger pangs dulled to nausea in its presence. "I'm sorry. M-Mama, I'm sorry—"

"Sorry won't feed your siblings!"

"Chara, enough," chided my father, who'd approached without either of us noticing. His hands slid over her shoulders as he took in the scene: me on my knees, tears streaming down my dirt-streaked cheeks; her trembling with rage, crying harsher tears than mine; the pitiful pile of food in the center of it all, barely enough to feed one of us to satisfaction. His eyes were always dark, but taking in the scene, they almost seemed to blacken entirely—no anger, only pain. "Eris, what happened here?"

"I was just..." My voice caught on a sob. "I'm so hungry, Papa."

My mother's anger guttered—softened—broke. "I...Eris—"

I didn't wait for the next accusation, the next glare, the next broken-hearted sob. I rocked to my feet and ran all the way back to the house, ignoring their cries for me to come back.

"You're starting your day late," Ben commented, his words garbled by the spoon in his mouth. He sat at our table with his ankles propped up on the edge, his bowl of oatmeal balanced precariously on his lap as he watched me drag myself down the steps. He was already dressed, his dark curls smoothed back with pomade, navy blue waistcoat done up perfectly, silver pocketwatch dangling from its chain.

"You're starting it early," I grumbled, shuffling to the stove. I grabbed the pot of oatmeal, not bothering with a bowl, and fell into the seat across from him. No use pretending I wasn't going to eat whatever was left; Ben knew to take what he wanted before I came down. I filled the serving spoon, warm steam wafting the smell of cinnamon and oats over my senses.

Not selfish; just surviving.

"Are you going to see that girl again?"

I paused with the serving spoon poised over my mouth, ready to dump a hearty bite down my throat. "Hm?"

"The girl. The hyper little thing with the violin." At my blank stare, Ben sighed, dropping his feet to the floor with a sharp *thump* and setting his bowl on the table. "Seph, I got home and turned around to see that you'd vanished into thin air. Did you think I'd just tuck myself in without tracking you down?"

Heat flushed across my cheekbones. "I didn't mean to worry you."

"And yet, worry I did."

"So you saw...?"

"Did I nearly see you choke to death on a bug in front of a pretty girl? Yes, and thank you for that, that'll bring me joy for a good while yet."

Pretty. The word seemed so frivolous compared to the reality of the dreams she carried around with her. "I plan to see her perform again, yes."

"So soon?"

I let the serving spoon fall back into the pot. It plunged in with a sad *squelch.* "Is that a problem?"

Ben shrugged, but in spite of his blasé look, there was a tension in his shoulders that belied deeper thoughts. "No. I'm just making conversation, Seph. Relax."

It wasn't just that; Ben wasn't any good at hiding his feelings, and there was something in his voice I didn't care for. But if he didn't want to share, there would be no dragging it out of him. He was stubborn like that; stubborn and proud. It reminded me of Balshasar a bit. Maybe that was part of why I enjoyed his company.

Though Edana and I had always been closest, and Caedmon had always felt like my responsibility...my older brother was the one who used to make me laugh. Who would pluck "lucky" coins from behind my ears and make them vanish again with a wink and a nonsensical *magic word*.

A silent, serrated pain—not a hunger pang—drove itself to the hilt in my heart.

I tried not to, but I couldn't help it—I missed the days when I sat in the middle of the table instead of at its head. When there were nine chairs instead of two. When there was endless chatter, giggles, and mooning looks between my parents instead of this...quiet.

Even with Ben's gossip, everything seemed quiet compared to a table filled with family.

I shoved up from the table abruptly, cutting off whatever story Ben had launched into while I was lost in thought, tossing the pot and still-full serving spoon down in front of him. "I'll bring dinner home. Least I can do for worrying you."

"Certainly is," Ben agreed wryly, but his grip was warm when he caught my arm and gave it a friendly squeeze. "Be safe out there."

"Always am." I squeezed his arm back, giving him a quick kiss on the head—he yelped in protest, waving me off with curses and complaints about how I'd surely ruined his hair. I chuckled quietly, snatching up my coat and throwing it over my shoulders as I made my way out into the city—and ducking to avoid the spoon he tossed at my head.

It wasn't long before color caught my attention: flickers of pastels this time, gleams of periwinkle and eggshell and rose and sage tumbling through the chilly autumn breeze like wrestling kittens. I'd never seen dreams with such life infused in them; excitement tickled at my heels, pushing me into a faster gait, my neck craning above the bustling crowd of morning shoppers to catch a glimpse of—

There.

Today she was dressed head to toe in brilliant turquoise, ribbons tied to her waist that fluttered and danced to their own rhythm as she twirled through the square, her bow flying at a speed that rivaled her feet. As I watched, she leapt up onto the fountain—the center of which boasted a sculpture of white marble carved in the shape of a masculine figure, his form lithe and sharp, a scythe in one hand and a dove in the other. The form of Death in this city's mythology... the irony of which certainly didn't escape me.

Jemma spun absolutely precarious circles around the fountain's perimeter, every step a dare to the scythe held up in warning by this world's imitation of my father. At the base of the fountain sat an open violin case; within, a meager handful of coins glimmered in the thin autumn sun. Hardly what she deserved for such a performance.

My anger had just begun to well on her behalf when she caught my eyes—and her entire face lit up.

When was the last time someone had looked so happy to see me?

"Joseph!" She hopped down from the fountain with perfect grace, landing on her tiptoes and spinning over to me, drawing one final, lingering note out of her violin before letting her hands fall limply at her hips. She was gasping for breath, dripping sweat, and smiling from ear to ear. She wiped her forehead with her wrist, blowing out a wheezing breath. "Miss me already?"

"I'm afraid that after hearing your music, the symphony hall doesn't quite compare."

She scoffed—a sensible reaction, to be sure, but she had no idea how true it was. "I'd love to say that flattery will get you nowhere, but alas, I'm a vain creature. Thank you for the compliment. Where are you off to?"

I blinked. "Um."

To see you seemed a bit too forward. *To feed on the magic you create with your dreams* seemed marginally worse. I settled on, "Lunch."

"Well, take that home and name it serendipity. I was just about to take a break myself. Let's see, what can I afford with..." She muttered to herself as she turned away from me, scooping up her case and counting it, that smile slowly folding into a scowl. "Huh. Well, I could get some water with ice, maybe."

Even the sour taste of her frustration couldn't stop the smirk on my face. "I know a place where you could get a bit more than that."

One of her brows—painted in a graduation of shades of blue that went from navy to ice—arched in a truly impressive look of skepticism. "Is this some roundabout way of offering to take me to lunch?"

Panic seized every part of me that wasn't already in the relentless grip of hunger. "I—oh, ah, I didn't mean to imply—ah—no. Just a suggestion, and you needn't feel obligated to follow it—"

"A shame. It would've almost certainly worked." There it was again, that grin that lit the whole world up in gold.

I blinked. Frowned. Was she serious? "You've only just met me. I could be dangerous."

"Hmm." She nodded thoughtfully, giving me a long once-over, circling me like a farmer assessing a new piece of equipment. "You make a good point, of course. I'm not in the habit of keeping the company of total strangers, pretty eyes or not, but here's the thing— if you wanted to harm me, last night would have been a *far* better time to try it. So if you let me be last night, I can only assume you'll the same in broad daylight. Go on then, handsome. Lead the way to this magical little establishment."

Handsome. My cheeks burned. "Magical is...certainly the word."

"What was that?"

"Nothing. Follow me."

THE FIRST THING I saw when I walked into the tavern—the swinging wooden sign above the door reading *Brew the Day*—was a leering man shouting in my sister's face.

Edana's tavern was a pretty little place—the first she owned herself rather than serving as an employee. The smell of cedar and coffee and bacon grease sang in sunlight shades through the air, the leftover flavors of morning lingering well into the afternoon. Every lacquered, handcrafted table boasted bouquets of wildflowers in vases or baskets in its center, and each was surrounded by mismatched chairs, all upholstered in different fabrics or framed in woods of different stains. Unique, joyful, and utterly welcoming— much like my sister herself.

Edana stood at the bar on the far side of the tavern. Her hair was up in a twisted knot, nothing fancy, but the lavender and white shards of her daydreams still crowned her like a queen. She leaned on the floral-painted bar counter with her sleeves rolled up to her elbows, regarding the man before her with a pasted-on smile, her eyes deader than the plants Ben kept trying to revive in the window of our flat. Even with that practiced mask of composure, though, her hands rattled a bit against the counter.

I had more of my father in me than anything else. But sometimes...sometimes my blood remembered it had something in common with War, as well.

My sister's eyes slid past him and landed on me. Widened in surprise, then narrowed in warning.

Too late for that. By the time Jemma sat down at one of the tables, I was already halfway to the bar.

"Sir," Edana—Eddie, if I wanted to needle her—was saying as I walked up, "again, I'm very sorry you had an unpleasant—"

"Unpleasant doesn't cover it!" snapped the man. *His* dreams were all cast in gritty, storm-like colors—not one of them worth a taste. "If you don't give me my coin back, bitch—"

The empty glass by Eddie's elbow rattled as I dropped myself into the barstool closest to the man, giving him my biggest, broadest, most unsettling smile—the one Ben complained made me look like a cat who'd managed to catch the biggest rat in the room.

"If you call this kind young lady a name even once more," I informed him pleasantly, "I will eat each of your disgusting fingers knuckle by knuckle until you cry for your mother."

Mauve-tinted fury instantly paled to the special shade of chartreuse that only came with true terror, and the man stumbled back from the bar counter before turning tail and fleeing the tavern.

"Have a nice day!" I called after him in my best imitation of Eddie's placating voice.

When I turned back around, Eddie was glaring at me. "I was handling it."

"That's a funny way to say *thank you*."

She merely rolled her eyes, crossing her arms over her chest—but she did smile a bit, which was enough to convince me I wasn't *entirely* unwelcome. "What are you doing here, Joseph?"

"Just came for lunch, ah..." I paused. "Remind me, again—is it Abigail here?"

Eddie sighed. "Abbi."

"Abbi." Too many Fates-damned names, too many Fury-cursed lifetimes. "I'm here with a friend, actually."

That caught her attention—her brows shot up, and she immediately craned her neck around me to peer around the bustling tavern. "Ben's willing to be seen in public with you again?"

I scowled. "It's not Ben."

Those eyebrows were nearing her hairline now. "You have *two* friends?"

"Keep being a smartass, and I'm going to tell Father it was you who used to put salt in his tea to see if he would still drink it."

She blushed, scooping up her cleaning rag and throwing it at my face. "You *swore* you'd never tell!"

I caught it, grimacing at the stickiness, and tossed it back at her. "Look, can we just get two mugs of coffee and whatever you have in the kitchen today?"

"Two coffees and food for afriend, coming up." She caught the towel and slung it over her shoulder, walking back toward the swinging door that led to the kitchen. She twisted on heel briefly, stabbing a warning finger at me. "Remember, you're only allowed to eat *food* here."

"Yes, ma'am." No consuming the dreams of Eddie's customers—not unless she asked, anyway. Sometimes her magic got a bit out of hand, and my gifts could take the edge off for those customers who got too lost in their passions.

By the time I got back to Jemma, she'd made herself at home at the table nearest to the window, staring pensively at something beyond the glass.

"The magic is on its way," I told her, dropping into the chair across from her.

"Hmm."

Only the promise I made to my sister kept me from siphoning off some of those dreams drifting in calm twirls of blue around her head. "What are you thinking?"

"Do you think birds have feelings?"

I choked. "Excuse me?"

"Well, you know—look." She patted at my cheek, pushing me until I was looking out the window. A few birds were indeed pecking about the street, and a gaggle of children had positioned themselves nearby, throwing pebbles and cackling when the birds squawked and flapped around, breaking formation only to form it again moments later. "They'd never do that to a dog, right? Because it would be sad. Why do we respect the dog's feelings, and not birds?"

I couldn't help it—I laughed, watching as the avenues of her imagination formed a halo around her head, solidifying her path of thought. "You have...a truly unique imagination, Miss la Rue."

"My father used to say so, too." The path of her imagination broke down in the center—a shivering black fissure cutting through the color for a moment before it mended itself.

Gently, I asked, "Did he pass as well?"

Her blue eyes clouded with pain. "Just a couple weeks back. He was...it was sudden."

"I'm very sorry to hear that."

"I've been living off what he left behind, but it wasn't much—we hardly expected anything to happen. And people aren't being too generous lately with my playing, either." Her fingers tapped idly against her violin case. "I'm afraid I may have to start selling things off soon."

The way her knuckles whitened as she tightened her grip on the case made no secret of which item would bring her the most money.

Panic bolted straight into my heart. "You can't give up playing. You're entirely too talented."

A sad smirk. "You're kind to say so, Joseph. But talent won't keep me fed."

Mind racing, stomach churning, mouth drying out, I turned away to search for Eddie. She had yet to come out of the kitchen.

I couldn't lose the one *sliver* of relief I'd stumbled across in all these eons of living.

"Let me hire you," I blurted, twisting back to face Jemma.

She blinked at me, surprise shattering her half-drifting imaginings into pieces. "Pardon?"

"Let me hire you."

"For *what?*"

I hadn't thought that far forward.

"To teach me to play." Yes, that sounded almost like a reasonable idea. "I've been thinking about picking it up anyhow, and my friend Benjamin is always needling me to get a hobby."

For the first time, I saw her friendly demeanor dip into something stiff; something angry. "I appreciate the offer, but I didn't tell you that to earn your pity."

I cursed my own clumsy tongue. "It's not pity. Truthfully, *you'd* be doing *me* a favor." That, at least, was completely and utterly honest. "I could use a...distraction. Something to do besides languishing in my flat. I'm afraid I'm wasting away in there."

"I see." But she didn't seem quite convinced.

Before I could push further, Eddie came back out from the kitchen, now crowned in flyaway hairs rather than daydreams, her cheeks flushed and her hand bearing a tray. She beelined to our table and set our plates down, quickly followed by steaming cups of coffee. "Apologies. It takes a bit to brew fresh. Any milk, sugar...?"

"Both," I supplied, but Eddie held up her hand.

"I know how you like it. I was asking your *friend*." She smiled adorably at Jemma. "I'm Abbi."

"Jemma. And sugar would be lovely, but I should tell you, I can't—"

"I'm good for it, Abbi," I said quickly. "Get her whatever she likes."

"You don't have to do that," Jemma protested, but Eddie just shook her head.

"Don't think he's being gallant, Jemma. He eats here for free. As do his friends." She flashed me a smile that held a silent *we will be having words later* behind it before bustling off to fetch sugar.

Jemma raised an eyebrow at me. "Free, hm?"

"She's family," I mumbled. "Like a sister."

"Ah."

"So," I prompted, "lessons?"

She thought for long enough that I was forced to bury the nervous quiver of my lips against the rim of my coffee mug, which had indeed already been mixed to my tastes. But finally, *finally*: "I don't see the harm. When would you like to start?"

Relief threatened to consume what remained of my strength. "Tomorrow?"

There it was, that Midas-touched smile. "Tomorrow."

"Who are you?"

I looked up from my bowl of eggs to see Ben staring blearily at me from across the table, his hair a mussed-up jumble. He was out late last night, and it wasn't hard to guess where—the warm-toned colors of his lingering dreams rendered our entire flat in a rosy hue. "Fates, Ben, how much did you drink last night?"

"Not relevant. You—" he jabbed a finger at me and scowled, "—cannot possibly be *my* Joseph. You see, my Joseph doesn't use bowls, he doesn't restrict himself to what most would consider reasonable portions, he doesn't wear *colors*, and most telling of all, he doesn't *smile* before the sun's hit its peak."

I swallowed a mouthful of eggs, wiping the aforementioned smile off my face. "I'm not allowed to smile?"

"It's that girl, isn't it?"

That girl in question was Jemma, and as much as I didn't care for the winking that accompanied his accusation, I couldn't argue. The past month had been...without compare. And with the thousands—millions—of months I'd lived, that was truly saying something.

I was well-rested. I was eating meals at ordinary intervals. I was staying in at night instead of wandering the streets for errant dreams, I was sitting and laughing with Ben, I was visiting Eddie more often, I was...

I was...

Happy.

I shrugged. "She's good company."

"*I'm* good company, and things were never like this before. No, she's done something to you. Dare I say—?"

"No, you don't."

Ben pouted. "You don't even know what I was going to say."

"I don't need to. I—"

A three-beat knock on the door interrupted me, followed quickly by a singsong voice: "Chaos has come again!"

"And long may she reign!" Ben called, winking at me once again as I stood up to let Jemma in.

I decided to ignore that. I hurried over, flung the door open, and...

"What's wrong?" The words dove off my tongue before I could think better of them.

Jemma laughed, her brow furrowing as she came inside, shrugging off her wool shawl and hanging it on one of the wrought iron hooks mounted to the wall. Beneath it, she wore a blush-pink day dress that only showed a bit of wear and tear at its hem, and muddy boots that appeared a couple sizes too large. "What do you mean? Are the boots really that bad?"

It wasn't that—on the outside, she looked every inch the Jemma I saw every couple days for violin lessons, the same vibrant, excitable creature who danced through the streets and pondered aloud about the emotional well-being of birds. But where her presence normally came with a perfect storm of imagination and hope and unadulterated joy...

Today, her dreams hung in tatters around her head. Present still, and strong, but...paler than I was used to. Almost wan and sickly, if dreams could be so.

They weren't gone. They just seemed...tired. Something was missing.

But I couldn't very well say that to her, and on the outside, she looked...fine.

"No, they're...sorry. Come in." I moved aside, and she twirled in with all her usual flair, immediately engaging Ben in some charming tale involving a stray cat and its friendship with one of the horses kept in the stables down the street.

I trailed after her cautiously, breath held, waiting for her dreams to perk up, for any sign of the vivid colors I'd grown used to. But though there was an occasional flicker of something brighter...they never lit up, never spun, never danced.

Maybe it was just an off day. Humans had hard days all the time —Fates knew I did. Everything was fine; she looked fine. Better than fine.

Beautiful.

"Joseph? Do I have something in my hair or what?"

She was fine. And I was staring.

"No," I said quickly. *Pull it together.* "I'm sorry, I didn't get much sleep last night."

A frown turned down her lips—not painted today, which wasn't a common sight—and she put her hands on her hips. "I can come back tomorrow instead, if—"

"No, no, it's fine. I'm fine. Please don't go." Could I sound anymore pathetic? "Ahem. I mean, just—"

"Please don't go," Ben agreed, sliding behind her and shaking her shoulders playfully—all while shooting me a look over her head, mouthing *what's the matter with you*? before continuing, "He's been practicing night and day since you were here last, and I'm afraid he's not much improved. I'd be forever grateful if you'd fix it."

"Well, how can I say no to that?" she laughed, and just like that, the lesson began.

After a month of back-to-back classes—and what Jemma generously referred to as my *natural talent*—these lessons had quickly climbed from basics to more complicated melodies, and today... today, my first duet.

My siblings would howl their heads off if they saw me like this: their standoffish, anxious brother wearing a white shirt with a vest the same shade as a summer sky, a musical instrument propped on my shoulder, standing awkwardly in our tiny living area as a woman half my height adjusted my posture, my wrist positioning, even my lower stance. My face flushed hot as her hands settled on my hips briefly, twisting me into a different position.

Hopefully she wasn't saying anything important, because I couldn't hear a Fates-cursed thing past the pounding pulse in my ears. *What is wrong with you, Eris?*

"Okay, Green Eyes, assume the position."

Mentally shaking off the buzzing in my head, I raised the bow to my violin. Jemma spun to stand across from me, her own body slipping into the proper stance with an ease that suggested it was her most natural state; she always seemed most relaxed when poised for performance. Her chestnut curls were bound tightly to the back of her head in a single braid, and as her bow kissed the strings of her instrument, her blue eyes glazed with the look of a dreamer.

Had she always worn such dark shadows beneath those eyes?

"One, two, three, now," she instructed before I could ask again if she was all right, and then there wasn't time for asking *anything*—there was only the flying of our bows and the timing of the music and her voice coaching me through the steps my feet were supposed to take, a jumble of rhythm and music and giddy terror that left me breathless in seconds.

Somewhere beyond the bounds of our song, I could hear Ben laughing his ass off. And dimly, I was aware of how ridiculous I must look—spinning and stomping around the space that served as our foyer, nearly stubbing my toe on our single ragged chaise, bending my body at odd angles to try and frame myself around Jemma, who was *leagues* more graceful than I could ever dream of being. More than that, she wore such a thick cloak of confidence that even if she *did* look silly, you couldn't help but love it—couldn't help but itch to dance along.

So ridiculous or not, embarrassing or not, I danced. And I laughed. And as we twirled around each other, swapping lead on the melody and passing grins between each other like secret notes, her dreams finally began to perk up, fluttering like maypole streamers from the crown of her head.

My greedy curse did not wait for permission—it lashed out toward their pastel swirls with a snarl that briefly drowned out the music in my head.

Still, Jemma's stride didn't hitch, nor did her laughter. And for my part, well...I hadn't laughed myself hoarse like that since childhood, since well before my memories of my past lives drifted back into my mind.

And all at once, it was over. We both collapsed on the gray velvet chaise, soaked in sweat and dragging in breaths that sounded a bit like braying donkeys. The sunlight that filtered through the window tinged bloody; was it sundown already?

"You sound awful," I wheezed, nudging her in the ribs with my elbow.

"You sound worse," she laughed, shoving my hand back. "When was the last time you got any exercise?"

I pretended to ponder. "Mm...sometime in the past century, I'm sure."

"Ha." She flipped over to lean on her side, drawing her knees up onto the chaise as she scanned the foyer. "When did Ben leave?"

"About an hour ago. He keeps a strict schedule."

Jemma frowned. "Sleep schedule?"

I snorted. "I wish. No, he goes out most nights. He doesn't do well if he doesn't keep busy."

"Hmm. We have that in common." She smiled, and by all rights, it shouldn't have been any different than her other smiles—it bent into her dimples the same way, creased her eyes, wrinkled her nose. But it was the look in her eyes that did it—a strange, unfamiliar softening when she met mine, a tenderness that arrested my heart mid-beat.

There it was again, that curious heat that only seemed to make an appearance when she was around. I cleared my throat, twisting to face her. "I can walk you home."

"If you don't mind, that would be wonderful. I have more questions I prepared for tonight."

That, too, had become a ritual of ours—her coming up with utterly mad questions for us to debate on the walk back to her place. "Oh, I look forward to that. Is it about birds again?"

"Of course not. I have to keep you on your toes, you know. No, tonight I want to know if you think plants can feel pain. You see, my theory is..."

As we pondered that out loud, I helped her to her feet—helped her pack—helped her fasten her cloak. But even when we crossed into the autumn air, the chill skittering across my skin and raising goosebumps in its wake...even then, that heat didn't fade.

That was going to be a problem.

THE GARDEN WAS EERILY QUIET.

That was what stuck with me, after, whenever memory dragged me back to that unwanted place...how thick the silence was, nearly tangible, a wall trying to keep me from the horrid sight that waited inside. But I hadn't heeded its warning, had misread silence as safety, and now I was on the hunt.

It was worse now, all of it—the hunger, the illness, the tension building between all of us. My parents didn't smile anymore. Some of us were ill. Some of us were starving. All of us were terrified. And I could only believe so many empty promises from my father...could only ignore so many agonized looks from my mother.

And if I didn't eat something right now, *I was going to be the first of us to die.*

Selfish boy.

Not selfish. Surviving. It was just surviving.

It wasn't stealing this time; it wasn't hoarding what was meant for the family if I could find some scrap of sustenance buried in this dead span of earth that had once been filled to the brim with green and growing things. Everyone else had already given up on it.

I wandered the rows, dragging my weak fingers across the thick walls of crackling brown stems, wrinkling my nose as the stench of diseased crops shoved itself into my nostrils, a powdery kind of rot that smelled of festering damp.

Nothing. No clean fruit, no fresh vegetables, not even a stray dandelion. I only knew those were edible because of the time my mother had told us to rub them on our chins; if our chins turned yellow, it meant we liked butter. Talitha had misunderstood, thinking Mama had said they would taste like butter, *and had devoured the yellow bloom in one bite.*

I'd thought for certain that she was poisoned. Mama and Papa had assured me otherwise.

What I wouldn't give for a butter-flavored flower right about now.

I was just about to give up and go back to the house when a tiny noise drove the slightest crack through the silence—a hushed, wet cough.

"Hello?" I called, then immediately regretted—what if it was my

mother, and she got angry with me again? What if it was one of my siblings who would take a portion anything I found?

Nothing answered me but another muffled cough.

Fear was quickly replaced by worry—what if one of my sick sisters had come out here looking for me? Mama kept saying they needed to rest.

I went in the direction the cough had come from, rounding row after row until I finally broke out of the dead crops and into the section of garden my mother used to be most proud of—a hedged-off area filled with flower gardens, an explosion of brilliant color that didn't match the rest of this withered place.

Anything inedible, ironically, had thrived through this past year.

And that was where I found her.

"Mama?"

I didn't understand the sight in front of me—didn't understand why my mother was lying on her back on the dry earth just past the border of the still-living flowers, a vial clasped loosely in her trembling hand. Didn't understand why she didn't turn to look at me when I called for her. Didn't understand why her dress, her chin, her lips were stained in red.

There it was again, that cough. But this time, I saw it happen—saw her whole body jerk with the force of that clotted sound, a fresh gout of blood gushing from her mouth.

"Mama!" Hunger forgotten, guilt forgotten, everything else forgotten, I ran to her, already sobbing by the time I reached her side. Terror tied my insides in knots as I dropped down beside her. "Mama, Mama, what happened?"

At first, when she looked at me, nothing changed—her eyes were dim, lifeless in spite of the breath in her chest. But at my next desperate sob, my next plea of Mama, those eyes lit with recognition—with pain.

"Eris. Go...go back inside. It's all right."

It wasn't. Nothing was. Nothing ever would be again.

"Papa!" I screamed, twisting back toward the house, my entire body dissolving into bone-rattling shakes. "Papa, help!"

My father was not a man who rushed. He was the sort of father to calmly saunter into a situation, eyebrows raised and hands on his hips, ready with an even tone and a gleam of good humor in his eye to help settle whatever had gone wrong.

But parents knew—there were different ways their child screamed for them, and they knew which one meant something terrible had happened. When I shouted that day, my father came running.

"Chara! No, no, oh no—" His voice shattered as he dropped to his knees on her other side, gathering her into his arms, wiping at the blood that just kept coming and coming and coming. "Eris, go inside."

"But—"

"Go inside now, Erisichthon!" Wild, broken—nothing like my father normally sounded.

I knew then that my mother was going to die.

Still sobbing, still shaking, I got up and ran—ran straight inside, straight into Balshasar and Mnemosyne's arms and their panic and their demanding, horrified questions. But not before I heard one last wheezing whisper from my mother's mouth, words that barely made it to my ears: "... Can't watch my children suffer..."

Nausea twined hands with the terror in my stomach, the grief, and the feeling quietly named itself blame.

JEMMA DIDN'T ARRIVE for my next lesson.

Or the next.

Or the next.

After a week of missed appointments, a week of pacing the foyer while Ben came up with increasingly absurd reasons for her to miss our lessons, a week of my hunger pangs whetting themselves on the grinding stone of withdrawal...finally, I couldn't take it anymore. I had to make sure she was all right.

And if for any reason she wanted nothing more to do with me, if I'd offended her or stretched her patience or she'd simply tired of my company...I would find a way to be all right with that.

And I would try very hard to pretend that the ache in my chest was merely a misplaced hunger pang.

Even with that determination, I dithered in the doorway until Ben finally told me to stop being a coward and kicked me soundly in the arse, closing the door behind me before I could turn and wrestle him back. Huffing, I tugged my coat more tightly around me before making my way toward Jemma's.

Her home wasn't far from mine and Ben's flat, but that only meant I didn't have nearly enough time to practice what I was going to say before I arrived. Though the sun was only just starting to dip toward the horizon, the frosted glass windows were dim, and there was no sound coming from within.

I'd come here once or twice before for my lessons when Ben needed a break from all the noise, and I'd always been greeted with lit-up windows and singing, humming, or music. But tonight, all was silent.

Foreboding crept into my fingers, chilling them. I tugged my sleeves up to cover them before knocking on the door.

I waited one minute. Two. Five. No answer.

Another knock. Still nothing.

Worry nibbled at my stomach, but I tried to tell myself it was nothing—tried to make myself turn around and go home.

But what if she needed help?

Finally, cursing myself and the Fates and every step that had led me here, I turned around and tried the knob.

It twisted without resistance.

Something was definitely not right.

"Jemma?" I eased inside, closing the door behind me, shivering—the chill was somehow even worse in here. There were only four rooms in her home—the kitchen, her bedroom, the bathing room, and the living area—and there was no sign of her in the kitchen or the living area. The fireplace against the far wall was dark as night, not even an ember to be seen despite the cold, and when I peered deeper into the kitchen, the oven appeared to be the same.

"Jemma!" I called again, sharper, louder. Had she left? Had someone hurt her? If she wasn't here—

"In here," called a voice from the bedroom—I only recognized it as hers because I'd grown so used to its pitch. It was so weak, so tired...

"Eris. Go...go back inside. It's all right."

I hurried down the short hallway, knocking lightly on the door before easing it open. And what I saw...

Her eyes were dim, lifeless in spite of the breath in her chest...

Jemma was curled up in her bed, covered up to her waist in a floral quilt. The floor was littered with cast-aside clothes and dishes that still held barely-touched meals. Her hair was loose around her shoulders, dirty and tangled and lacking its ordinary shine, and her dreams...

My heart stopped.

There were no dreams there to see.

Nothing—no color, no light, no joy. Not even the tatters remained now.

Never, not even once, had I come across a human with *nothing*. No hopes, no dreams, no imagination.

She merely blinked at me while I stared in horror, not a hint of emotion on her face.

"Why are you here?" Even her voice sounded wrong, distant and dreary, like she was half asleep...or something worse.

"I was worried. You disappeared for a week." I barely even heard myself—all I could see were her dead eyes, her pale face, the colorless void where brilliant and beautiful dreams used to dance.

She blinked again—slow, languid. "That long?"

The genuine confusion in her voice only stoked the fear in my stomach, and I hurried to her bedside, dropping to one knee and reaching out to feel her forehead.

No fever...if anything, she was a bit too cold. "Jemma, talk to me. What's the matter?"

"Nothing. I'm all right, I just...I'm tired. I'm always so tired, I just…" A forced smile. "I'm sorry I worried you. I'm all right. I think I just need some rest."

She was the furthest thing from *all right*. I knew the look she wore in her dull eyes. I knew it, and I hated it, and worst of all…I thought I might have done it to her.

Because in that void where her dreams should have been…

Scars.

I could see them now that I was closer—shadowy wounds that resembled claw marks traced down her temples, phantom damage that carried a familiar taste with it.

Nausea painted the sides of my hollow stomach, and I covered my mouth with my hand.

I did this to her.

"I'll be back." Scrambling back from her, my hand still clamped over my mouth, I struggled to my feet. "Just—just rest. I'll be back."

She didn't answer—only looked away, her stare drifting back to the wall and staying there.

I didn't waste any time. The moment I reached the front door, I broke into a run.

"Give me a drink."

Eddie's only response to my demand—which directly followed my shoving one of her other customers out of my way to reach the counter—was a raised eyebrow. She got that from our father, that look of silent judgment. I didn't have time for it now. "How 'bout we try a *please?*"

"Edana, I don't have time for this!" Fates, I must've looked a frenzied mess—I could hear the shake in my own voice clear as day. But it didn't matter. "I need a drink. One of *yours.*"

Now her expression exchanged patience for pity. "Eris," she said gently, "you know it won't help you—"

"It's not for me. It's for Jemma. Please, I—" My voice cracked in half. "I think I hurt her."

"Hurt her? How?"

"She's—I don't know. This has never happened before, I don't —" A grinding sob tried to rise in my throat, but I swallowed it down, flexing my finger against the bar to ground myself. I couldn't fall apart here. "She's...drained. Not herself. She'll barely speak, she's got this *look* in her eyes like..."

There was a certain bond that formed between siblings who filled in the middle of the family, and I'd never been more grateful for it, because it meant Eddie understood without me having to say it. Her chocolate-brown gaze flashed with her own pain, her own grief. "I don't know if it will help. It could go poorly—"

"Misplaced passion is better than nothing. She has *nothing,* Ed. No dreams, no fantasies...nothing. And it's my fault. It's..."

Selfish boy.

Can't see my children suffer...

"It's my fault." A ragged whisper. "All of it. Please help me fix it."

Eddie's lips pinched in uncertainty, her fingers fussing absently with her apron. But just when I was about to grovel, to truly get on my knees and beg, she finally said, "I'll see what I can do. Wait here."

Relief threatened to drop me to my knees anyway, and I stretched over the counter to kiss her on both cheeks. "Thank you."

"Don't thank me yet." And with a quick pat on my hand, she hurried off to the kitchen.

The second she disappeared, a new voice spoke from behind me, rasping and dry as a dust storm: "It won't work, you know."

Tension banded my shoulders. I eased myself into one of the barstools, keeping my eyes forward as a familiar smell clotted my nose...diseased crops, festering damp. My mother's final breaths coated in nightshade.

"Erra." Careful. Quiet. Despite my distaste, my *rage,* I'd learned something from my father's failures: never disrespect a Fury. Even the gentler ones wouldn't stand for it. "I don't suppose you're just here for a drink."

"Erisichthon." The movement of bright ginger hair and golden-brown skin in my periphery told me my worst fears had been realized—she'd taken the seat beside me. "It's been a couple centuries. How are you faring here, nephew?"

I glanced at Erra out of the corner of my eye. She was perched on the stool with all the grace in the world, her delicate hands clasped on the bar counter. Her pale brown dress hung off her form like a wilting plant, like the limb of a dying tree, and her eyes...

Her eyes, the shade of black mold and nightshade berries and the despair that led to humans summoning my father of their own accord, were fixed on me.

"I'm afraid I don't have time to chat," I muttered, craning my neck around her to search for Eddie's return. "I have a friend waiting on me."

"Yes, the poor girl you drank dry." Tsking, Erra turned to face me fully, her thin lips pressing even thinner in disapproval. "I thought you'd learned better by now."

My hands clenched into fists. "What do you want?"

"I'm telling you, this plan of yours? It won't work. Even your sister's magic can't replenish what you took."

Fear tried to tighten its grip on my throat. I swallowed past it. "You're wrong."

"I'm never wrong." Not bragging—that was better left to Tyr. She was simply stating the truth. "Your sister's curse *increases* what passion is already there, Erisichthon—it can't create something from nothing."

"Then what do you suggest?"

"You know I can't help you, nephew. You'll have to solve this on your own."

I hated that answer—worse, I hated that her assessment made sense. But I had to try something. I shoved myself up from the bar as

Eddie came back out with a mug of coffee, her eyes drifting warily to Erra, who merely smiled and waved.

"Erra," Eddie greeted her softly.

"Edana. Don't look so worried, girl. I'm moving on soon. I just stopped in to visit Erisichthon for a moment."

"A pleasure as always, Erra," I muttered, grabbing the coffee and turning away. "Thanks, Ed."

"Erisichthon," called Erra, and I stopped just shy of the door. "I always liked Chara, you know. A pity what had to be done."

My stomach turned, and I twisted to face her, a snarl creeping up my face. "You don't get to speak my mother's name."

Erra met my gaze evenly, her brittle nails tapping out a rhythm on the bar counter. "A pity," she said again, "what *we* had to do. But I don't recall *you* taking part in it."

Now my stomach truly churned. "What are you saying?"

"I can't help you," Erra repeated with a shrug. "I don't envy you, though. It's difficult, learning to forgive yourself for what you *didn't* do so you can move on...so you can take responsibility for what you *did* do. I imagine her ailment will mirror yours...imagine what it would take to fix that."

I tightened my hold on the coffee mug, but I couldn't move—couldn't tear myself away from her probing gaze. "You can't help me."

"Not even a hint." She sipped at the coffee Eddie silently passed her, my sister's nervous eyes darting between us.

"Then why...?"

"Thanatos was always my favorite sibling, you know," she interrupted me. As if it was an answer. And maybe...maybe it was. "You should hurry. You don't have time to chat, remember?"

She hadn't helped me, so when I left, I did not thank her.

But by the time I got back to Jemma's, I had a plan.

~

My hands still smelled like grave dirt.

Days after my mother had been buried, days after we'd gathered around our father and wept our way through what semblance of a funeral he managed to perform, after we'd silently trailed back into the house and started trying to learn what life was without her...and I still smelled like the garden. Her deathbed turned gravesite.

"Eris." My father's quiet prompting barely reached me across the table. "You need to eat."

I looked down at my untouched plate, my unused utensils gripped loosely in my hands...my hands, the creases still stained dark from throwing mud atop my mother's wrapped body. I'd washed them so many times I'd lost count. Nothing worked. Nothing helped.

"I'm not hungry."

～

THE FIRST DAY, nothing changed. Jemma didn't feel up to standing, let alone teaching, but when I asked if I could practice so Ben could get a break from my company, she also didn't seem up to telling me no. She simply shrugged before turning her back to me, and I got to work.

I played the first song she taught me, a simple melody that she could perform in her sleep. I even missed some notes, half hoping she would come out to laugh me out of her house, but the bedroom door stayed closed.

The second day, I played something a bit faster, a bit happier, something reminiscent of what she'd played the first day I saw her in that square: a creature of unnamable colors and untamable joy shaking me awake from a dream of my own, a nightmare filled with pain and desperation with no hope of escape. Still the door remained closed.

The third day, I tried something new.

She had given me the gift of a few happy weeks. I would not stop until I returned the favor.

"What are you doing?" Jemma asked as I came into her room and coaxed her out of her bed, stuffing down the swell of panic that rose as I took in her own wasting form. She was beginning to look like I used to before finding her, all sharp joints and harsh angles and hollow, hunting gaze.

"I want to show you something," was all I said, praying the vague answer would be enough to entice her to follow. And follow she did, though slowly, and I didn't like the look in her eyes—a look like she was merely sleepwalking, and I was nothing but her spectral guide.

When we reached the living room, I gestured for her to sit on the chaise while I went to dig my violin out from its case. When I turned around, I found her watching me, her brow creased—the most emotion I'd seen from her in days. "You don't look well."

"I'm just fine." I wasn't. Each day saw me waking up weaker, spiraling back into old ways of coping to dull the pain. I had to carry griffonia around again. I wasn't sleeping. Everything—walking, talking, breathing—*everything* hurt.

I wasn't fine. But I would be—when she was well again, when I saw her *smile* again, all this would be worth it.

I propped my violin on my shoulder, breathing in—breathing out. Breathing through the ravaging hunger pang that tried to drag me to my knees.

I would not be selfish. Not with her.

"I call this *Joy*," I told her.

And I began to play.

Not a song we'd played before. This was something else—a collision of notes I'd put together myself, scribbling them down with ink-stained fingers while bearing down on every pain that wrung my insides with clawed hands, practicing them well into the night to stave off nightmares of my mother sobbing *whose fault do you think that will be* as she coughed up blood and poison.

Instead of nightmares, I leaned a different way—I lost myself in memories of Jemma's jubilant laughter, her sassy glares, her fierce and limitless love of her music. The way she'd gazed at me in the foyer after our first duet. The little curl of gold that always stuck out against her mop of chestnut, gleaming like a ray of sun through silk curtains.

I remembered Mnemosyne's proud smile when I first learned to read aloud, following in her shadow for hours at a time. Balshasar's lucky coins and indulgent praise over the scrawling doodles I created with a discarded bit of charcoal. Edana's very first attempt at brewing coffee for our father that nearly set the kitchen ablaze, ending in the hysterical laughter that only came after surviving something terrifying. Athene throwing a well-aimed rock directly into the eye of a boy who'd tried to pick a fight with me. Talitha climbing on my shoulders and demanding my wholehearted attention. Caedmon falling asleep in my arms, my awkward bouncing soothing his newborn wails.

My mother's warm lips on my forehead. *My little helper.*

My father's grinning face. *That means you have a good heart, you know. Babies can sense that kind of thing.*

A medley of memories that swirled, spun, took flight...became something better. Lighter. Untainted by sadness or guilt or blame.

I dreamed. I dreamed this melody, and now I gave it all to her.

I didn't know if it sounded pretty. I didn't know if it was even *passable,* but that was all right. If I looked ridiculous swaying along with it, all the better. I was willing to play a fool for her, if it brought her even a smidge of joy. If it made her smile.

And whatever state it left me in...that was all right, too.

A flicker of color caught my eye, hope blazing through me so fiercely that I missed my next note. I looked up to see where it was, but though Jemma was watching me with eyes brighter than they'd been in days...the color wasn't coming from her.

I slowly raised my eyes up to find a ribbon of gold dancing gently around my head.

A quiet laugh jammed in the back of my throat. Tears pricked at my eyes.

I'd never seen dreams of my own before.

But even those belonged to her. To make up for what I'd taken.

Because I was not selfish. I survived—I survived, and so had my siblings, and though we all carried the weight of what we'd done to ensure it...maybe there was redemption there for us yet.

All of us. Even me.

All of it, all of it. Who I was praying to, I had no idea. *Take it all. Give it all to her.*

I played until my fingers bled. Until my head pounded with fatigue. Until the room began to resemble a vignette, blackening at the edges, narrowing with every note I coaxed from those stubborn strings until—

There.

Yellow—a shy, barely-blooming bud of light coming to life over Jemma, who blinked as though she'd just come out of a very long dream. She rubbed her eyes with the heels of her hands, frowning as she looked up at me. "Did you write that?"

"I did." I lowered the bow, staring at her with bated breath. "How do you feel?"

A grin broke across her face—Midas-touched. Gilded in joy. The first stirrings of a reawakened spirit. "It was beautiful. Can you teach it to me?"

I laughed—a cracked, shaky thing that sounded like a violin string snapping. "Of course."

Then I was falling.

"WHAT HAPPENED?"

Ben—that was Ben. Even past the roaring agony, I knew that.

"I don't know!" Jemma. Hysteria lit the back of my eyes with blinding fuchsia light, a hundred worst-case scenarios twirling in her imagination. "He came to my place—I was sick, or something, I don't know—and he played something, and then he just fell over!"

"You carried him here?"

A pause. "It might have been a bit less graceful than—look, just help him!"

"Seph." A hand patted my cheek, and I grimaced, just managing to wrench my eyes open. Whatever Ben saw there, he cursed about it —a vile, creative curse I would've laughed at had I not been in blinding pain. "You idiot, what did you do? Your eyes are black as pitch!"

"What does he need?" Jemma leaned over to join him, and I could have crowed in relief at the look on her face—tear-filled eyes, pink cheeks, emotion sketched in every crease.

She was all right. She'd be all right.

Ben launched into a very abbreviated—and somewhat incorrect —explanation of my curse; he didn't know every detail of my origins, but I'd had to offer some explanation for why I ate so much more than my fair share of food. Why I often wandered the sleeping streets. Why it still wasn't enough to keep me out of pain. And when he was done, Jemma's hand—warm again, thankfully—settled on my cheek.

"Do I have what you need to fix this?" she asked shakily. "My dreams?"

I didn't want to lie to her. "Yes."

"Then take them!"

"Not from you." Fervor pushed past pain, and I reached up to cover her hand with mine. "Never again."

She might have said more. Might have asked why, might have begged me to open my eyes, might have said my name in the way only she ever had.

But I heard none of it. I was already drifting.

I was already dreaming.

"Erisichthon."

I opened my eyes to books.

Thousands. Millions. Everywhere I looked, books made up the fabric of the world, spines gleaming with finely embroidered titles I couldn't read from this far away.

This...was not my flat.

A throat clearing brought my eyes back down to the woman in front of me. She resembled a hawk, I thought—all sharp, pointed features and eyes that looked bored enough that she might just put an end to me if it would offer her a pinch of entertainment.

Eyes with no pupil, no iris. Just pure, empty white.

"Who are you?"

"You can call me Pennella." Her eyes never left me as she reached for something to her left—a teapot, I realized after a moment. A teapot as blank as her eyes. "Welcome to the Library of Souls."

The blood drained from my face. "I've been here before."

She watched me steadily. "Yes."

My gaze dropped back to that pot. "Is it...did I already...?"

Did I already die?

"Not yet." Pennella reached beneath the desk, her hand emerging with a teacup held between her thumb and forefinger. She set it down, lifting the pot and starting to pour. "But it seems you've earned an early release."

Earned, as if death was a gift.

Up until now, most lifetimes, it had been.

"How?"

She looked up at me, expression never wavering. "How do you feel? Hungry?"

I opened my mouth immediately, the quick retort of *always* perched on the edge of my tongue, ready to dive. But when I took a breath in...

It didn't hurt.

Nothing hurt.

There was no growling, no groaning. No desperate cravings, no agony twisting my stomach in fraying knots.

"Why?" Barely a breath.

"You gave everything up for that girl...offered everything up to save her, leaving nothing for yourself." Was it my imagination, or was that *nearly* a smile forming on her face? "Something you've never managed in any of your previous lives. All curses can be broken, you know...even yours. If you like, Erisichthon...you can be free."

She slid the tea across the desk.

Free. I knew what that meant—forgetting. Permanently this time. No traces of memory left to bring me back to my first life. Nothing to weigh me down.

Forgetting Ben. Forgetting Edana and Mnemosyne and Balshasar and...everyone. Forgetting the pain and the shame and the terror of the torturous ending to my childhood.

Forgetting Jemma.

I swallowed, my mouth suddenly dry as I reached out to fiddle with the teacup.

Freedom. I could live a new life, with a new name...finally be set free from this legacy that never should have been.

No more agony. No more nightmares.

No more rescuing Edana from shouting customers. No more chats with my father over glasses of whiskey. No more breakfasts with Ben. No more music with Jemma.

There were so many sins I had yet to repent for. Sisters I needed to visit. An older brother to track down and talk to, even if I feared he would turn me away for whatever part I'd played in my mother's despair. A younger brother who still needed me, who still needed *us*, whether he thought so or not.

I lifted the teacup, studying it for a long, long moment...

Then set it back down. Pushed it toward her.

"Not yet," I said quietly. "I'm not ready yet."

If those milky eyes could have shown surprise, I imagine they would have. "You'll keep reincarnating, Joseph. You'll keep remembering what happened to you. The hunger may or may not leave you, but the memories never will."

"I know." I took a deep breath. "But my family still needs me, I think. It would be...selfish...to move on now. And I...I'd like to finish this life out, anyway. I want to see where it takes me."

Not surviving. Not anymore. I wanted to *live*.

"Hmm." This time, there was a definite smile. "All right, then, Erisichthon. If that's what you choose."

"I do." I had never been more sure of any choice.

Before I could say anything else, Penella raised a hand and snapped, sending me plummeting back toward life.

Back to memories of love and dreams of redemption, gleaming in shades of ichorous gold.

CHAPTER 6

REFUSE THY NAME

LINA C. AMAREGO

MARCELLO | *TUSCANY, PRESENT DAY* | OIL ON CANVAS.

Art was meant to be witnessed.

Eyes–dozens of them–tracked my every move with predatory focus. The well-tailored black suit emphasized the warm olive of my skin, the crowd drinking me in like a top-shelf antique. My mother always said my good looks and magnetic personality drew people to me like moths to a flame; but that was a partial truth.

Our family name synonymous with respect and awe, every Corrente demanded attention.

I *savored* it.

The power was a high, euphoric and frenzied. Should I desire it, I could change every life in the room. I could triple the value of Mr. Arden's modest coffee shop just by walking through his front door— or ruin his reputation with one Yelp review. I could singlehandedly incite a reporter's promotion by deciding who received my exclusive interview–or sink the entire paper with the mere insinuation of my displeasure. While both thrilled a dark part of me, neither truly scratched the itch deep within my gut.

No, the potent, ancient *thing* thrumming through my veins—that was the real power. One touch of a finger, and I could change fate.

As always, luck was on my side tonight. I tucked myself into a corner of the gilded space. Always at a distance. Always unattainable. Men and women stared across the ballroom, their whispers snaking through the room in time with the orchestra's poorly arranged music.

Marcello Corrente in the flesh...He's Lorenzo's son, right?...Do you think he'll notice us?...Rumor has it he has the best eye in the family.... Should I buy him a drink?...He's stunning, but you never want to be on a Corrente's bad side...

After so many years—lifetimes, really—the lack of originality scraped beneath my skin. They saw what they wanted to see—a pretty ornament, the crown jewel of my father's gallery. A simple young man in an expensive Armani suit, a decoration to be ogled and auctioned.

They couldn't see the true gift humming in my center, a power that had decided wars and leveled cities.

I fought the eyeroll that ached to distort my face, but I couldn't risk such a dismissive expression with everyone watching.

And they were *always* watching, even if they couldn't *see*.

With a bit of luck, I could slip out before long. The gala was a disaster— an uninspired 'masquerade' theme run by some 'up-and-coming' gallery that'd petitioned for my father's patronage. They lacked the class and organization to run things right—their doors would be closed before the end of the month, if I had to bet. But disasters made for good entertainment.

If my father were here, he'd have walked out already, dooming the small gallery to utter devastation.

In the fine art world, my father's opinion was law.

But I lingered. With luck always on my side, it was occasionally a release to see misfortune play out so spectacularly.

A small part of me—a hidden, dangerous part I kept under lock and key—considered the thrill of failure. How glorious it would be to unravel and unwind.

But not tonight.

I adjusted the gold mask resting across the bridge of my nose, though it did little to hide my identity. My true facade was not a strip of silken fabric, but the smiles and lies I hid behind, the frame of Corrente certainty that gilded every decision I made.

Crops are dying, Balshasar.

I shook off the memory barging into my head. No, I wasn't the same pathetic whelp I'd been long ago. Those failures held no power over me now, and I needed no reminder.

My mother's seaside stare, lifeless. My father's broken screams, echoing from the garden.

I was a Corrente. I did not bow to ancient gods or meddling Furies. I did not mourn dead mothers.

I shuddered, the chill still clinging to my spine, focusing instead on the unraveling revelry around me. At least the food was edible. I snatched a small olive and mozzarella skewer from a passing tray and popped it in my mouth, savoring the sweet-and-briny contrast as it coated my tongue. This was not a Corrente affair, so I didn't have to entertain. I merely had to attend, a lovely wallflower to help brighten the space.

"Excuse me, sir."

I jumped at the sound of the unfamiliar voice. A bold move, to speak to a Corrente without invitation. I spun to face him.

My breath caught in my chest. Like everyone in attendance, a mask covered half of his face. But my gaze roved over his every inch, from the shiny polish of his black shoes to the cropped brown curls that twirled away from his face. Though the unadorned black fabric of his suit rang of cheapness, *he* still sparkled, his presence more commanding than some of the most prized art hanging in my father's gallery. In his hand, a silver tray balanced a singular crystal flute of champagne.

I blinked. A *waiter.*

"Champagne?" he purred, the sound rolling over me in waves.

"No thank you." My tongue knotted itself. I'd mistaken friendliness for flirtation before, but the heat burning in his dark eyes sang a language that spoke to my basest parts.

"It's a gift from a gentleman currying your favor," the waiter elaborated, velvet voice dipping low.

My chest deflated. This was all unoriginal too–wealthy businessmen looking to secure their investments by winning my favor first. All to get to my father. To use my coattails as a comfortable ride to the top.

Never personal. Never about me.

Just business.

I straightened out my diamond cufflinks, remembering who I was. "Did he give you his name?"

The waiter shrugged, endless eyes staring through my mask like he could see beneath. "He asked to remain anonymous."

"Hm." Surprise lifted my brows. Anonymous patrons were few and far between. Most in the city only wanted recognition.

Or revenge.

Correntes demanded attention. But we also garnered plenty of envy and contempt.

My eyes narrowed at the thin flute as I slipped on a different mask.

"Is the champagne the only gift, or do you come with the package?" I asked, a smile of my own stretching. I'd played this part my whole life–and in my lifetimes before–the confident, carefree prince dazzled by a pauper with a pretty face. "How kind of them to choose such a good-looking messenger."

Normally, my flirtations were met with stammered words or flushed cheeks. Or worse—scrunched noses and disgusted frowns. But the waiter didn't miss a beat, his dazzling white teeth glinting. "They couldn't have someone drab deliver it, or they'd faint in the presence of someone that looked like you, *sir.*"

The way he emphasized the word made my abdomen clench.

"Might liven up the party," I smirked. I rarely encountered dance partners that matched my pace. I was a Corrente–bred and trained for moments like this my whole life. The subtle espionage of flirtation, the intimate violence of a brokered deal. But this waiter didn't just watch me–no, those eyes saw. They knew.

And it wasn't hard to look at him in return. His mask graced the edges of his high cheekbones, regal despite his stature. Even beneath the drab attire, his lean form had an elegance to it I'd seen only in Bernini sculptures, the marble somehow hard and graceful at the same time.

He'd make an excellent exhibit for my gallery, if I allowed myself the pleasure.

If I was caught leaving with him, it'd spell disaster. I could see the headline now– *Tuscany's most eligible bachelor risks family name and legacy for sordid affair with the glorified pool boy.* My father would strike my name from the family tree for less.

Good thing luck was always on my side...if I was careful, no one would know.

Hundreds of lifetimes, and I'd had plenty of wonderful lovers in secret. Bernini himself spent a whole summer tangled in the back of his workroom with me, much to his wife's dismay.

But this man in front of me–without even a touch–I knew he'd be the star piece. More precious than any DiVinci or Rembrant I'd purchased and displayed.

I reached for the champagne, the gold satin of my gloves matching the fizzy liquid. "Care to join me for the next round?"

A smile crawled across his face. Gently, he nudged my hand with a single knuckle, tipping my glass towards my lips. Nectar-sweet liquid met my tongue, and his eyes studied the movement. A shiver ran down my spine as our fingers grazed. Even without direct contact, static electricity pulsed between us, more potent than a lightning strike straight to the heart. The hair on my body stood straight as the wave of sharp pleasure crashed over me. My breath caught in my throat as he withdrew with a smirk. "Maybe next time."

And then he did the unthinkable. The man turned his back to me, a *Corrente*, and walked away, off to entertain another guest.

I blinked, trying to stop my head from spinning. But my heart still thundered in my chest, a furious beat from the organ I thought long dead.

What in the twelve universes was that? No one had ever evoked such a reaction from me, my tongue tied, my brain clouded with desire. *No one.* Through the years, even with my siblings' influences– Edana's elixirs and Talitha's amplification–I'd never felt that powerful before. That *strong.* Was it his level of ambition? My gift often responded to the ladder-climbers, people whose boldness led their every choice. Though he hadn't seemed like the type of person who wanted to get ahead. In fact, he had appeared perfectly content with his station, an anonymous waiter living behind a mask.

Another poisonous memory surfaced to offer its own explanation. '...*Your heart has no place in this world, Balshasar.*'

My shoulders tensed, the name rattling around in my chest like a warning bell.

No one had ever riled me like this.

No one since him.

No, I was not Balshasar anymore. Not some starving, filthy little child fighting for his life in a shattered family. Not some unlucky, love-struck fool playing pretend in a house of cards.

Now I was Marcello Corrente. I had power in name and merit.

You can forget, but it does not change what you've done, child.

The edge of the glass was to my lips before I could think. I remembered. I remembered everything.

Every life, every cycle. I remembered what it felt like to be born and what it felt like to die; the disorienting newness, the empty nothingness. Every name I'd ever taken; Willian and Marius and Hector and Achilles, every face I wore still simmering in my mind's eye, even as the reflection changed. I remembered every family. Every brother and sister. Every parent. Their faces haunted my dreams, ghosts that lingered long after they passed, the uncomfortable burn of nostalgia stinging tears to my eyes.

None could ever erase the shameful stain of the first. No, I could not forget about them—about that...*failure*. About the things I couldn't do, the names I couldn't save.

Breathe, Marcello.

Right. It was different now. It had been different for a few centuries. Especially in this life —modern Italy was the pinnacle of luxury and culture. Art, both modern and classical, etched into the stucco face of every building, painted on the frescoed ceilings. Fashion teeming from every boutique, the stone-laid streets an endless runway. Food, fresh and decadent and indulgent. Culture, warm and friendly and festive. The rampant violence within the ring of powerful families was a risk I tried not to end up on the wrong side of, but it was a small con. A commoner might be surprised how much blood had been caked beneath the paint of the art world. Among the elite, espionage and underhanded deals were all a part of the job.

But my luck gave me an advantage.

That, and the fact I conveniently had been there when many of the pieces were created. Though my brother Cardan despised me for it, those who used him as the living muse loved me—and my money.

I was made for this world. And I would not be startled by a mere waiter with a nice face and a charming smile.

With a deep breath in, I drained my champagne and searched for the man. All eyes in the room on me, I would remind him exactly who he was dealing with.

I FINALLY FOUND him sitting behind one of the long buffet tables, puffing a cigarette with two of the other waiters. It had taken me nearly a half an hour of dodging other partygoers and asking the waitstaff if they'd seen him, which was way more effort than I preferred to put forth.

Correntes did not scurry after commoners. People came to *us*.

And yet, I stood before him, a slight sheen of sweat tickling the back of my neck, my arms crossed.

"You." I pointed at his chest, my voice an impassive calm edged with displeasure. It was the most emotion I'd ever show—Correntes did not let their feelings get the better of them. The other two waiters jumped to attention. "You have an awful lot of nerve."

His mouth curled into a smirk. He made no move to stand, lounging further across the marble floor, the cigarette dangling between his fingers. "Did I do something inappropriate, *sir?*"

This time, a different heat flared through me, my anger hot as the embers lazily flicked to the ground, but I stamped it down. He hadn't done anything wrong, not really. He'd done his job—offered me a drink and smile, as any well-trained caterer should. I was the one making a big deal about this. Still, I cleared my throat and rolled back my shoulders. People were watching. They were *always* watching. And a Corrente never backed down.

"What do you think?" The other waiters took their cue, scrambling away before they could get caught in the crossfire. With a heavy sigh, he stood, stomping out his cigarette against the stone, smearing ash against the white, and I stiffened.

I'd fought in wars through the centuries, and learned to hold my own with a blade. The body I occupied now was lean, used to exercise, but the waiter was larger than me, a fact emphasized as he rose to his full height.

He trained the full intensity of his gaze on me, burning holes into my flesh. He leaned in so close his stubbled cheek scratched against mine, the scent of smoke and something honey-sweet clinging to him.

"I think that you are bored." His breath tickled the sensitive shell of my ear. "I think that you've been bored for a long time. And you're tired of pretending."

My body stilled, heartbeat hammering against my chest as another wave of electricity rolled over me. My toes curled in my Oxfords. If I so much as blinked, I would explode. Every little truth I swallowed, every part of me I hid—they'd all burst free like fireworks, lit by the careless flame of a discarded cigarette.

I didn't know this man, yet he knew me. Like a piece hanging in a gallery that he'd studied intimately.

The thrill quickened my pulse. *Bored.*

I was—so terribly tired of playing the bystander. Tired of staying on my perfect pedestal, waiting for patrons to come and get a glimpse of *the* Marcello Corrente. So bored of being the perfect son, of being watched and assessed and invisible all at the same time.

But a Corrente did not answer to presumptuous pricks. Even if they were right.

I scoffed, shifting closer, my gloved hand pressing to his chest. If anyone saw me fraternizing with a waiter, my name would be trending on socials within the hour, but I didn't care. Rumor mills kept the world turning. "Who do you think you are, to tell me what *I* feel?"

A deep chuckle rumbled against my fingertips. Dark eyes simmered behind his mask. "Do you want to have a bit of fun?"

That word snagged on something jagged in my heart.

Fun.

When was the last time I'd had fun?

Fun didn't have a role in Marcello Corrente's world. I grew up in the quiet alcoves of galleries, staring off into paintings I wished I could escape into, silently entertaining myself as my father made deals and my mother garnered friends. As cameras captured my picture and spattered it across papers and the internet, the still images of a little boy sculpted to fit exactly in the frame I'd been given.

I loved parts of it. The attention, the praise. The appreciation for art and culture that most kids my age could never comprehend. The easy excuse for my 'old soul' tendencies.

But fun?

No, I hadn't had any of that in centuries. Lifetimes.

Not since the beginning. Since getting lost in the tall reeds that walled our mother's garden, chasing after Talitha and Athene. Since staying up far past our bedtime to listen to Mnemosyne's stories, munching on whatever sweets Eris snagged, whispering so Mama wouldn't catch us.

Not since it all crumbled around me. Not since I'd *failed*.

I'd always been a tool, a means to my family's ends. Whether it was art or business, a sewing shop or the aristocracy, every family I'd ever been born into needed me. Needed my gift. It didn't matter what I wanted, what I enjoyed.

I wouldn't fail again.

But the man in front of me...

The promise of fun and danger was written across his every inch, the signature of whatever surrealist artist created him.

I let one word slip; one I'd live to regret. "Yes."

He did not wait any longer, his fingers clasping around my wrist as that dazzling smile pulled across his face. "Follow me."

And I did.

My pulse thudded wildly in my veins as we rounded a corner, into a narrow hall lined with old stone. A servant's pass, back from when Tuscany was a city-state ruled by powerful families. I'd been Giovanni then, the son of a powerful banker with a touch of luck and a fondness for art. My descendants might have owned this building, the de Medici name reaching far and wide for centuries after I left them.

I never stayed long, a symptom of my curse. But I always left a legacy to be proud of.

Just as I would with the Corrente name.

As we walked, the tension knotting my shoulders dissolved...we wouldn't be seen here, these hidden corridors perfect for masked waiters and sneaky patrons to slink around through. But a different pressure built, my excitement brimming as he pulled me forward, down the hall and to the left, into an open room.

My breath stole from my chest.

Classical arches lined the space as floor-to-ceiling windows carried in the night breeze, rosemary and sage scenting the air from nearby planters. Moonbeams mixed with candle-glow in pools of light that warmed the stone floor. There was a worn-down aura to the room, cracks in the stucco and stone littering the space. But on the far wall, a mural captured in vibrant hues decorated the stone. A man—painted with an expert balance of light and shadow—danced around a tree, limbs twisted at odd, exaggerated angles as his pretty face smiled peacefully. Dangling on one of the branches, an angel rested, his harsh muscles a counterpoint to the perfectly soft ringlets painted in bright copper tones.

The style was unmistakable. Ireplicable.

"This is beautiful," I huffed out before I could stop myself, my chest seizing at the sight. The Mannerist styling, the expert, illusionary foreshortening... "The fresco is a—"

"It's a Caravaggio," the man spoke, stealing the words right out of my mouth. My head swiveled to him. His full lips parted in appropriate reverence as he stared at the art. At the *masterpiece* hidden in the backroom of a no-name gallery. "If only the idiots downstairs knew what they were sitting on, they'd be making a fortune."

It took considerable effort to scrape my jaw from the floor. "It's hard to spot the real from a replica. You need a good eye."

"I know how to spot quality." The man simply shrugged, dark eyes focused on me. He reached into his jacket pocket, pulling out another cigarette, fitting it between his lips.

I snatched it straight from his mouth before I could remind myself of my manners. "Don't you dare, you'll ruin the paint."

His brows lifted in surprise, a soft laugh escaping his still-parted lips. "You're not like the rest of them downstairs, are you?"

He took a step closer, his broad chest mere inches from mine. I stilled, war waging within me between desire and dread. His cigarette-and-rosemary scent flooded my senses, stoking the aching want in my middle.

"You're not like anyone I've ever met," I exhaled, trying to rid myself of the taste of him.

A drop-dead waiter that could spot an undiscovered Caravaggio. Who could see *me*, just as hidden and unexplored.

"Mm. What if that's a *bad* thing?" he dared, his head inclining. His long fingers reached for the cigarette I still clutched between mine. Skin brushed against the satin of my gloves, a subtle invitation.

Do you want to have a bit of fun?

Fates and Furies fuck it all, yes I did.

Before my better parts could win out, I laced my fingers between his, relishing the kiss of our palms together. I took one more brave step closer, our breaths mingling like the fragrant air blowing through the windows. My eyes snagged on his pink mouth. "I have a thing for bad boys."

A beat, as he leaned in. So close, I could see the light flecks of warm brown in his dark irises. Not just brown. *Caramel honey.* "Do you ever take your mask off?"

I blinked, the words tangling in my head. Here I was ogling his mouth, and he wanted to know about my *mask*? "This stupid thing? It's just for the party."

"You know what I mean." A warm chuckle rolled through him as something softened in his posture, broad shoulders relaxing. He removed the white mask from his own face, and my tongue went dry. Without the obstruction, his undeniable beauty struck me like a bat to the stomach. Strong, full brows framed his dark eyes in perfect contrast to the smooth skin stretched across high cheekbones. Classically handsome, like a Michelangelo, but with a ruggedness that offered a modern twist. He cleared his throat, and I diverted my eyes, realizing that not only had I failed to answer his question, I'd been shamelessly staring.

"I just mean…" he continued, a crack in his voice his first imperfection. It made him all the more alluring. "Everyone hides. Do you ever wish you could just be someone else for a night?"

At that, my gaze flicked back to his, something unlocking in me that I refused to name. Something I'd buried for centuries.

I *had* been someone else. I'd been hundreds of versions of the same original design, each replication fleeting and impermanent. I'd been a prince and a scholar, a businessman and a tailor. I'd helped small men climb to greatness and witnessed great men fall to ruin, all with a single touch of my littlest finger.

But I was an illusion. Smoke and shadows, less corporeal than one of Athene's concocted dreams. I was a trophy, passed between lives and ages, a decorative commemoration of other great men's success.

A lucky charm, worn around the neck of history's most prominent visionaries and innovators.

Without my gift, I was nothing. Empty. A gilded frame, hollow of any substance or worth.

"I'd settle for being myself for once," I replied, my voice just as vacant. Not that I knew *who* I was. I hadn't been certified authentic since that first life, and I never wanted to go back to that, either. Back to sitting in my eldest sister's shadow, back to trying to fill my father's massive footsteps, back to begging for scraps of my mother's affection…

I'd rather be a pretty trophy than a discarded son.

Fingers caressing my cheek tugged me back to the present before I could fully lose myself to the undertow of that thoughtline. My mask was off before I could protest. Another electric shiver ran down my spine as his gaze settled on mine.

"Just as I thought," he said, palm lingering against my cheek. His dark eyes roved over every inch of my exposed face, drinking in every shade of my coloring like *I* was the Caravaggio. "A masterpiece."

"Maybe just a replica." I leaned against the touch, knots twisting my stomach. This man saw me, maybe clearer than I did myself.

A pang of guilt made me straighten. Fates and fucking Furies, I'd been so wrapped up in myself, in the attention, I hadn't bothered with basic introductions. My smile was sheepish, my cheeks flushing. "Do you have a name?"

"Luca," he answered, rubbing his calloused thumb over my cheek. He leaned his forehead against mine, cigarette breath intoxicating. "Yours?"

"Mar—" I stammered, before remembering myself. Remembering my purpose.

Correntes didn't sneak off with random *male* waiters. The lie slipped easily from my tongue, my name another mask. "Mario."

When he pressed his lips to mine, all other thoughts died in my mind. No names, no histories, no responsibilities. Just the smoky taste of his mouth, the rough texture of his hands on my face. Just the spark of energy buzzing in my veins, the aching need squeezing my middle—

Just *Luca*. The only name I ever wanted to say again.

He withdrew—too *soon*—my chest heaving in labored breaths, my knees buckling beneath me. I shook off the heady euphoria clouding my thoughts, ignoring the irregular rhythm of my pounding heart.

"Well, *Mario*," he purred, the name a reverent prayer. He stepped away, the distance between us a chasm I would gladly drown in for just another taste of him. "I better get going before I lose my job. But thank you for letting me escape for a moment."

He turned to leave, and panic seized my chest. I grabbed his wrist, halting him.

No one turned their back on a Corrente.

And there was a hidden, heavy part of me that would throw the title away for just one more lingering moment in his presence.

"Will I—" I swallowed the uncharacteristic lump that lodged itself in my throat, my voice tight. "Will I see you again?"

He shifted out of my grip, and my disappointment sank heavy to my toes. But the corner of his mouth tugged upwards. "If we're lucky."

And then he walked through the door, leaving me and the Caravaggio lost and unnamed.

～

BALSHASAR / *SOMEWHERE, A LONG TIME AGO* / CARVING IN STONE

TANGLED HAIR AND THE DAMP SMELL OF FRESH HAY. Roving kisses—exploring the planes of his work-chiseled chest. Deep laughter and dirty backs, a summer spent in the haven of tall reeds and sunny skies. A season wasted away in the ecstasy of denial.

"Crops are dying, Balshasar," Xeres warned, the furrow between his brows deepening as his tilled-soil eyes got that far-away look. But I'd rub the spot away like Mama always washed stains—working at it until I could pretend it'd never been there at all.

Famine never lingered long. Abba would stop her. This too would pass.

Early fall passed too, the empty scratch of hunger harder to ignore as the harvest reaped little fruit. His family was starving along with mine. He'd gotten thinner, his ribs poking me whenever he laid his body onto mine. His kisses were just as famished—desperate and frenzied, but I didn't care. He could devour me whole if it meant just another day in his touch. Another taste.

Plague would be next. According to my father, they always followed Famine's footsteps. And with them came hacking lungs and withered wills. Fever-soaked brows despite the coming winter chill. My siblings and I would survive—we were woven of thicker threads.

But Xerxes might not.

Abba had not stopped his sister. Yet my faith in him remained. This too would pass.

I would make sure of it.

～

MARCELLO | *TUSCANY, PRESENT DAY* | ACRYLIC ON CANVAS.

REGRET SNARED MY EVERY THOUGHT as I stood in the empty hallway of my family home, just outside of the small chapel at the back of the estate. My father waited inside; kneeling in prayer as he did every evening, pious as he was persistent. Lorenzo Corrente was the perfect image of the modern Italian man; devoutly Catholic in personal practice, viciously cutthroat in business. A reputation he hadn't just crafted, but *earned,* through deed and delivery time and time again.

How I'd face him, knowing what I'd done–

A Corrente, sneaking around in the hallways with a mysterious commoner. *Kissing him*, no less, until I was weak in the knees. Weak of will. I'd been with men before–with curtains shut in secret rooms, discretionary agreements signed and dotted. But to be so out in the open with him, at a business function, no less...it had been a mistake. *I* was the mistake. The modern world was far more accepting of those attracted to the same sex, but the mostly Roman Catholic, traditional elite of the art world were not. Of my world. If the media ever found out, I'd be scandalized.

Or, much, *much* worse. If my *father* ever found out, I'd be disowned.

I shifted my weight, shoes squeaking on the tile floor. From behind the polished door, a sharp intake of breath silenced my thoughts. Then, a deep voice. "Marcello, is that you?"

I rubbed a hand over my face, as if I could wipe away my shame, before squaring my shoulders and opening the door. "Good evening, Father."

Lorenzo Corrente did not turn to look at me. He stayed kneeling in one of the three pews in front of the small marble altar, still dressed in his expensive blue suit from the day. The single lit candle warmed his brown-and-grey-curls to gold, casting his round frame in bronze. El Greco's *The Crucifixion* hung in front of him, my father praying to both his deities: God and art. "How was the gala?"

I took two long strides across the room, shuffling into the pew and kneeling at his side. Despite the generous cushion, the tuffet bit into my legs, rigid and unforgiving as the church itself. I signed myself with the cross. But I did not pray to the same Father, Son, and Holy Ghost as Lorenzo did. No, the Fates and Furies ruled me, a truth I could not escape no matter how devoted I was to the families I was born into.

"The gallery is dismal, but the building is worth something," I reported, dutiful as an altar boy. "There's a Caravaggio original tucked in the servant's rooms. Untitled."

"Lucky you." My father's head finally snapped in my direction. Light eyes plotted as they shimmered in the candlelight, a smile carving his face. "We'll have to purchase it when they go belly-up next week."

And they would go belly-up—my father would write the *Tuscan Times* before first light with his glaring review. Their doors would shut, and they'd turn to the only bidder they had available—

Him.

I always had luck on my side, but Lorenzo Corrente had something else. An ambition that made my own gifts quiver and quake. He reminded me of Cosimo that way—the de Medici patriarch just as efficient and calculating.

I had a lucky streak of reincarnating as the heir of powerful men. A trophy to mark their hard-won victories. A lucky charm.

I pretended to mutter a prayer to my father's God under my breath before standing to go. "If it's all right with you, I'm going to turn in."

"Marcello." My name was a command on his tongue. A weapon to be wielded. I stilled.

"Yes," I coughed, a kernel of my regret and fear lodged in my throat. Did he know what I'd done?

Father stood, those light eyes watching me with an intent that made my skin crawl. He clapped his hand on my shoulder, squeezing the tense muscle that connected my arm to my neck. "We have been invited to lunch tomorrow afternoon."

Relief untangled the knots in my chest. Nothing out of the ordinary, then. We went to business lunches twice a week, my father always proud to show me off to clients. "Where?"

A resigned sigh as he faced the altar again. "The Fiore estate."

My head snapped to face him, searching for signs of madness. I'd seen it before—great, powerful men succumbing to illnesses of the mind. The Fiores were a plague on this land, more effective in ruining things than my Zizi Resheph. They were new blood in the art world, which was worse than saying they were the antichrist in my father's Bible. Their installments and galleries popped up all over Tuscany and Venice. Each filled with 'modern art,' no sense or style, diminishing the landscape with cold, industrial tackiness.

Loud. Gaudy. Cocky. *Progressive.* The Fiores were everything we were not. Everything *Tuscany* was not.

Though I guessed the 14th century aristocracy said the same thing about the Renaissance.

"What the fuck do we have to go to that hovel for?" I snorted, still waiting for the punchline.

But my father's face held no trace of trickery or jest. Cold as stone, he stared up at *The Crucifixion* with steady reverence and unfeeling calculation.

"*Language,*" he warned, jerking his head to the ever-watching painting. "Carlo Fiore's son is back from the tacky American university, and the Fiores have invited all of the prominent families in the business to celebrate his return."

I rolled my eyes. I'd luckily never met the younger Fiore—Luigi or something not worth remembering— but I'd heard the stories circulating in some of the groups we both frequented. Leone had a reputation as a party boy with a crude sense of humor and terrible taste. "And why would we go? From what I've heard, his son is just as classless as Carlo."

"Why do you think the Fiores are the only other art dealers that beat us to the punch?" My father's voice edged with a calm violence I'd seen the Fury of War employ time and time again. Powerful men did not need to be loud to be dangerous. Lorenzo's tone barely tracked higher than a whisper. "They don't have more money than us. They certainly don't have better taste. And yet, at the last four auctions, they outbid us and secured under-the-table deals before we even knew what was going on. Why do you think that is, Marcello?"

My chest squeezed.

No mask could hide your failures, Balshasar.

The Fiores were succeeding because I was failing. My infallible gift, suddenly faulty. Because I wasn't *enough*.

I sounded small when I finally spoke–like the little boy I used to be. "Maybe they're lucky."

A chuckle escaped my father's chest, rumbling like an incoming storm. "No, dear boy. We are lucky. *You* are lucky. And you're going to use that gift to find out how the Fiores are robbing us of our God-given respect."

I straightened up. Shoved down all thoughts of doubt or dismay. Lifted my chin.

I was Marcello fucking Corrente. I did not fail.

Not anymore.

"Yes, Father."

THE FIORE ESTATE SCREAMED 'CHEAP VULGARITY.' As we drove up the long, winding driveway, lined with strange, asymmetrical sculptures made of junk metal, my distaste became a palpable ball in my throat.

The massive house had the same lifeless, metallic look to it– white concrete square structures, stacked on top of each other, with large blocks of windows everywhere. Modern design that lacked any character or originality. Only straight lines and sharp metallics, drenched in harsh lighting.

Carlo stood on the uniform gray steps, matching the mansion. He was not an ugly man—soft brown hair with a tasteful kiss of silver running through it, highlighting his sun-touched skin. A thin frame that spoke of lingering muscles from his youth. But he wore a black-and-white striped *Versace* suit that would've had Gianni rolling in his grave. It was like dressing the statue of David in an 'Amore Roma' t-shirt.

Lorenzo and I shared an eye roll before stepping out of our black *Alpha Romeo*.

"Welcome, friends." Carlo grabbed my father's shoulders, planting kisses on both of his cheeks. "*Buongiorno.*"

My father never wore his distaste on his face, but I knew the signs. The tightness in his jaw, the tension in his broad shoulders. But his smile was all warmth, a mask Lorenzo Corrente had perfected before he passed it on to me. "*Salve*, Carlo. You remember my son, yes?"

"Marcello, who could forget! Your face is always on the screen." Carlo threw his hands up before squeezing my face like I was a small child, hairy knuckles tickling my cheek. "Firenze's favorite pretty boy."

I matched my father's mask, squashing the rage squirming in my gut. "*Ciao, Signore.*"

He let go, and I straightened the sleeves of my plain black Armani sweater, my power humming in my middle. Power that had decided conflicts and felled empires. It didn't take kindly to coddling from fools.

The aggressive grumble of an engine stayed any other thoughts, drowning them out. I spun to the noise, produced by the clunky silver-and-orange design of a *Lamborghini Egoista*. Fates and Furies, it was the fugliest wannabe rocketship of a car I'd ever seen.

"Here he is, the man of the hour, late as always!" Carlo bellowed, elbowing my father in the ribs. "My son isn't as dutiful as yours,

Lorenzo. You'll have to share some advice on how you get yours to behave. Meet my boy, Luca."

The name flashed in my head too fast to process, interrupted as the car door swung upwards.

But instead of a man in a spacesuit, a tall figure stepped out. A simple black shirt hugged his sculpted chest, well-tailored jeans traveling the vast length of his legs. His honey-brown hair slicked back, accentuating the high planes of his perfect face.

He removed his simple sunglasses, and dark eyes with flecks of amber found mine.

Every muscle in my body coiled in response. My heart skipped a beat. Maybe two.

"You," I hissed before I could catch myself.

The waiter. *My* waiter.

Luca *Fiore.*

"Salve, Signore," he addressed my father with a small bow, gaze never leaving mine. A smirk curled his lips. *"Mario,* right?"

"Marcello, you *pazzo,*" Carlo chuckled, smacking his son upside the head.

"Ah, my apologies," Luca laughed as he rubbed the spot. "Marcello."

My legs shook as he said my name, the taunt a twisted knife in my stomach. Luca, who'd somehow seen me for who I was, who'd offered a beautiful oasis of respite in a desert of drudgery and pressure. Luca, who'd be dangerous and exciting and my own little secret, to be taken to this grave and the next.

Luca fucking *Fiore,* son of the most obnoxious art dealer in Italy. A rival, whose family I was destined to ruin.

Who could ruin me if he ever let word slip about what we'd done.

My heart pounded so loudly in my ears, I almost missed Carlo's casual suggestion. "Lorenzo, why don't you and I go discuss business inside with the others, and Luca can give Marcello the tour of the grounds. Young men should enjoy life while they are young, don't you agree?"

I swiveled to my father, barely masking my fraying panic. I had to run. Had to get away, to find the space to use my gift and right this wrong...

Lorenzo nodded, eyes narrowed. "Yes, go ahead, Marcello."

I swallowed hard, sweat coating my shaking palms. I had to get away, or to shut this down before it blew up in my face. "Father, perhaps it would be best if I joined you—"

A single word shot an arrow through any last protest I might have conjured. "Go."

I stilled, Lorenzo's light eyes flaring with warning. Another misstep would spell mutiny.

Art should be seen, not heard. Visible, but silent. Just as I'd always been, my curse in this lifetime and all those that came before.

I did my best to clear the worry from my tone, slipping my mask back in place. "Yes, Father."

Carlo led him inside, and the tension didn't eddy from my back until the door closed fully behind them. I exhaled, accepting the single sliver of luck as best I could. At least with my father in the house, I could have a word with Luca. Could make sure that if he spoke, it would be mutually assured destruction.

I spun on my heel, tilting my chin up, ready to do just that.

Luca had other plans.

He leaned against his obnoxious car, arms crossed so the carved muscles of his biceps strained against the tight tee. He was a study on the human form, even the edges of the dark snake tattoo winding itself around the limb.

Fates and Furies, I was so screwed.

He looked past me, watching the door our fathers walked through with a curious tint in his dark gaze. "Do you always listen to Papa's orders, little prince?"

I clenched my fists at my side, the only demonstration of my frustration. A Corrente did not display his emotions. I tilted my head to the side, matching his mocking smile. "Do you always pose as a waiter and lie to people?"

"What's in a name?" He shrugged, but the teasing in his tone evaporated, replaced with a smooth sincerity I hated even more. "I didn't lie. I gave you my real name. Unlike you, *Mario*."

"You knew who I was," I fired back, struggling to rein in the anger bubbling in my gut. I'd been many people in my lives, but I refused to play the fool. "I had no idea who you were. You pretended to *work* there. It's a lie by omission."

He pushed off the car, running a hand over his face. Like *he* was frustrated with *me*. "I *was* there for work. I had a tip-off about that Caravaggio." He towered over me again, his voice a low drawl. His jaw clenched, but gaze softened. "And everything else I said was the truth."

My cheeks warmed, but I crossed my arms, like that could protect my already-bruised heart. "Like wishing you could be someone else, hmm?"

"Yes," he said easily, the tension in his frame dissolving. His hand drifted towards mine–not close enough to touch–but the desire clear. The light flecks in his eyes shone even brighter in the warm sunlight of the afternoon. "I thought you'd understand that part."

I did. Better than I understood most things.

I wanted to be someone else. Not in name, no–I'd traded title and lineage time and time again. But the core of who I was–the tainted, worthless soul that failed–I wished I could change him. Fix him. Because no matter the lifetime, no matter the last name or location...

He still managed to remind me of all the things I didn't have. Of all the disasters I failed to stop.

My eldest sister's threadbare smile, as she tried to hold all the frayed strings of the family together. My brother Eris' sunken cheeks as the horror consumed him from inside out. Edana's anxiety, Talitha's avoidance, Athene's rage, all three of my youngest sisters lost to themselves. Caedmon's heart-shattering questions: *"When will Mama come back?"*

Because I wasn't there. Because I'd bargained with the wrong Fury.

No, not anymore. Now, I was more. I was better.

I tilted my chin, swallowing down the coal-hot anxiety burning my throat. "You thought wrong. I'm proud to be a Corrente."

Proud of any family that was willing to take me in after mine had cast me out. Any legacy I could elevate instead of destroy.

Luca bit his lip to fight a grin. But despite the mirth in his tone, those eyes saw. They knew. "Who's the liar now?"

"What do you want from me, hmm?" I grit my teeth, biting back venomous words I wanted to spew at him. How dare he strip me of my paint and hang me back up, exposed and worthless, as he kept all of his secrets tucked away behind those pretty lips? A humorless laugh expelled from my chest on a cool breath. "Why show me the fresco? To rub my nose in it?"

Luca blinked, wrenching back like I'd slapped him. Like I'd hurt him.

I'd meant to. I'd wanted him to feel just as bare and raw as I did.

But my gut did somersaults as guilt tried to upend me.

When Luca let loose a sigh, I did too, unaware that I'd been holding my breath. He twirled his cigarette between his fingers, the fidget the only marker that perhaps he was nervous, too.

"I didn't show you the fresco to hurt you, *Marcello.*" The honey-sweet gentleness with which he said my name did little to mask the bitter taste of my shame. He kicked the first concrete step to the house with the toe of his boot, the echo of another smile twisting his face. "Art is meant to be *shared.* I spent the last four years in New York, studying at Colombia, staying at the Met or the MOMA until they closed with my classmates, just enjoying it all. For all our fathers and the other dealers say they love the art itself, when was the last time anyone in this damned country *appreciated* it?"

His words pinged around my head like the clapper of a church bell, ringing out a melody just as sacred. I let myself imagine the scene for just a moment; Luca and I stretched along the sun-bleached steps of the Met with a cigarette dangling from his mouth, the blaring horns of garish yellow taxis mixing with the coo of pigeons as we discussed the classical styling and tragic context of Jaques Louis-David's the *Death of Socrates*. As the public took in the art for *pleasure*, not for profit.

It was a pretty picture, one I'd take out and look at for years to come.

But I was just a witness, not a painter. I had no brushes to turn daydreams into materiality.

I shrugged as I tucked the dream away. "My father always says it's a mistake to mix pleasure with business."

My father also would advise against kissing strange men at galas. Or talking to them at all, especially after finding out they were the son of his greatest rival.

But Fates damn me, I had no power over the tug that pulled at me every time our eyes met. I wanted to sit here and stare at him for as long as he'd let me, to appreciate every graceful line of his form, the expertly shaded contour of his face, the softly blended peach color of his mouth.

Art was meant to be witnessed, and he was a masterpiece.

I took a tentative step closer, the leather of my boot scuffing against his. He inhaled, breathing me in, pretty lips caressing his next words with the finesse of a master painter. "I prefer to savor things, *Marcello*. Don't you?"

My heartbeat pounded the song of war against my ribs. Something lightning hot burned within, a wanting I'd never known. A need I'd never acknowledged. I fucking wanted him, so badly that I was half-desperate to taste claim his mouth right here, right now. In the bright daylight, standing on the steps to his father's house, with everyone important in the art world waiting just beyond the threshold. Where my *father* waited, probably watching me from one of the too-large windows.

They were always watching.

But the walls I'd built through the centuries stood tall, unshakable as the pyramids. Wanting had no place in Marcello Corrente's universe.

'*Your heart has no place in this world, Balshasar.*'

I sheltered the useless organ behind ancient stone. I turned away, unwilling to witness the effect of my cruelty. "I don't waste my time on replicas."

BALSHASAR / *SOMEWHERE, A LONG TIME AGO* / INK ON PAPYRUS

THE TASTE OF LIGHTNING LUCK, POWERFUL AND CRACKLING. Stitched of my mother's sunshine and my father's darkness, fate held in my palms. It buzzed in my veins, ready to be unleashed. Ready to right the wrongs of the world.

Resheph came carrying the scythe of sickness, their one ill-green eye set on us all. But a little bit of luck could remedy the worst malady they could conjure. The bargain was struck; they could sip from luck's cup as long as they left my family untouched. My lover, too.

But Resheph did not come alone.

My luck had run out.

I did not see him coming. Blinded by selfish desire, by my lover's consuming tilled-soil stare. Blinded by my own inflated ego, by deals with Plague that drained my luck and dampened my senses. So wrapped up in myself, I forgot to be my mother's son. My father's heir.

Tyr did not pass quickly. He took his time driving his scythe through my mother's heart, through her mind. He waged his war quietly, whispering in her ear, planting the putrid seeds of doubt.

Abba had not stopped the Fury of War.

Neither did I.

～

MARCELLO | *ROME, PRESENT DAY* | WATERCOLOR ON CANVAS.

EVERYTHING THAT COULD GO WRONG, DID.

The Vittori Family auction was the pinnacle of the season. Everyone who mattered attended, making the trip to the capital no matter what else they had going on. Firenze was the homeland of art and classical beauty, but Roma was the center of commerce. And the Vittori auction could make or break entire fortunes.

Last year, we'd come out with *Raphael* and *DaVinci* originals, both thought to be lost pieces, for a fraction of what they were worth. Donna Vittori, the family head, had called me a "lucky little *bastardo*!" after I managed to win the bid on a technicality.

If only she knew.

But it seemed my luck had run out.

Sitting straight-backed next to my father in the third row of stiff wrought-iron chairs, sweat licked the back of my neck despite the chilled room. We were tucked between several of the other prominent families, all of us dressed in our finest, but there was a vicious edge to the atmosphere, one that scratched my skin. Lorenzo's white-knuckled grip wrinkled the fabric of his best trousers, his mouth pressed into a firm line.

Corrente men didn't betray their emotions outwardly, but I knew my father well enough to read him like a book.

Furious.

And it was my fault.

"Marcello, do something," he whispered as the auctioneer prattled off, his knife-sharp tone cutting through the din. "This is the fifth piece we've lost out on. Our investors need new blood."

Shame cracked through me, a single splinter in my glass facade. Our usual plan was failing. Every time a new piece came out, I called to the vast well of liquid luck running through my veins. But there was no answer today. No sense of value or premonitions of profits.

Just dry, hollow emptiness.

Fates-damned *normalcy*.

Tonight, my chances were just as good as everyone else's in the room. I'd make a blind guess or an educated risk, and my father would place a bid. But there were people better prepared and deals already struck that without my gift, I could not supersede.

Corrente's were not meant to live like everyone else. We were meant to be greater.

I hung my head, tuning out the grating rattle of the auctioneer's hurried speech. "I'm *trying*."

The admission escaped before I could recognize the blunder, the ugly phrase deprecating my worth in a single breath.

Try was not a word Corrente men used. It was a curse, a pitiful placation that had no place in our vernacular.

"There is no try, Marcello, there is only *do*." My father's jaw clenched tightly, his words burning like a brand across my skin. "And unless you plan on doing something, you can take your leave now. I'll finish this myself."

I blinked at him, that crack of shame fracturing further. I'd been at my father's side for every auction since I was fourteen, a whole decade of life spent as his right hand. My luck had earned him fame and fortune beyond imagination. Had defied logic and law for his sake. But now one bad night, one single blunder, and he was ready to dismiss me like a servant?

My fists clenched at my sides as I stood, swiftly exiting the main hall before the tears could spill onto the polished tile floors.

No, my father was right. I was useless, a too-proud egotistical prick that had little worth outside of my stolen gift.

I wove through the rows of attendees, barely choking down the hot emotion rising up my throat as I half-sprinted out of the cramped room. Murmurs reached my ears and the watchers whispered, but I couldn't hear them over my pounding heart.

A few rows back, Luca watched me, seated next to his own father. His brow knotted, like he was concerned—but the pity was worse. I was a fucking Corrente. Pity had no place in my world.

I tore my gaze from Luca before he could draw me in with his strange gravitational pull.

I managed to make it outside, the night air of old Rome wrapping around me in a too-tight embrace. Mopeds whizzed past the tall building, the sound of revelry echoing from down the street. Normally, it would be a comfort, the culture immersive, an escape from my own body. But tonight, everything was too tight, too close. Too loud. My mask, hiding away my flaws. The gaze of the world, a camera always snapping in my face. My father's disappointment. Luca's warm lure.

"Failing again, *Balshasar*?" A familiar voice taunted—too close. Too dark.

My blood ran cold, a chill creeping through me as dark and lonely as a winter storm.

My breath held, I spun to face my uncle.

I wasn't a short man, but I still had to tilt my face up to see him properly. He stood against the brick wall of the building, his amber skin blending with the russet shadows. Black stubble framed his square jaw before sweeping upwards into his hairline, his tightly coiled curls smooth. He wore a simple red suit, the pop of color a bright spot in the evening shade, but his black eyes devoured the light of the nearby streetlamp. They held the horrors of centuries of bloodshed, their endless abyss the keeper of a thousand lives lost to conquest's mighty scythe.

I tried—and failed—to keep the warble of fear from my voice. "Tyr."

"Frustrating, isn't it?" He pushed off the brick, a wicked smile carving his handsome face. The scent of clove wafted from him, demanding attention. "Without that power of yours, there is nothing you can do."

My throat went dry, a thousand quick quips dying in the desert of my tongue. I had no witty retort, no confident mask to wear.

The Fury of War had killed every last one with a single strike and a smile.

The way my luck faltered tonight, so eerily similar to the way it did that season so many lifetimes ago...

My mother's seaside stare, lifeless. My father's broken screams, echoing from the garden.

It had to be him. Had to be his trickery.

His fault.

"Is this *your* doing?" I breathed, knees locking underneath me.

But Tyr ignored the useless question, running his hands over the lapels of his blood-red suit. The streetlamp flickered as he took a step closer, that smile unwavering. "I'm surprised you didn't recognize him yourself, even after so many lifetimes apart."

A beat, but the words didn't click together, puzzle pieces strewn haphazardly across a table.

"What?"

"The Fiore boy?" Tyr raised an eyebrow, and my stomach dropped to my toes. He pressed closer—too close—a dark chuckle clawing its way out of his throat. "He's your *tether*. His soul a direct match for yours. Sometimes fate gets in the way, even for you."

The world spun in dizzying colors, my shoes fused to the cobblestone streets below. My gut knotted, bile squeezing up from its depths to burn my throat.

My tether.

My soulmate.

Xerxes.

No, it couldn't be. Not Xerxes. Not anymore.

"Luca?" I asked aloud, as if to remind myself of the difference. Warm hazel eyes, instead of deep brown. A wealthy family, not some poor starving farmboy. They couldn't be more different, lives that were separated by every law of time and space... "He can't be *him*, he's—"

Intriguing and taunting. Breathtaking and charged with that lightning hot energy. Too perfect to look away, too dangerous to fall for. Just like Xerxes was.

"Deliciously handsome, I must admit," Tyr supplied his own rationale with a cruel wink. "Harder to resist this time. Such a shame that he also saps your luck."

"Shut up." Rage filled my lungs with fire, ready to spew. But it was another mask, another mirage. My hands shook, the world threatening to give out below me. To swallow me into the cold, dark earth, into Tyr's inky pit of victims.

Luca was my fucking tether. My person. My soulmate.

My single weakness.

"Your family won't prosper while he lives," Tyr warned, resting his palm on my cheek, like a doting uncle, not the king of curses and cruelty. Like *family*, not the Fury of conquest. Dark eyes watered with crocodile tears. "You know this, *Balshasar*. Reputations can come undone with a single stray thread."

With quick fingers, he plucked a strand of my hair from my head. I winced at the brief pain, but Tyr did not coddle. He turned away, another family member ready to discard me.

And as he stalked off into the night, I unraveled.

I RAN THROUGH THE WINDING STREETS OF ROMA, not caring who saw. Who watched. Let them gawk and point, let them whisper and whine. The rumor mill kept the world turning.

I was Marcello Corrente. I answered to no one.

Not even the Fates, the tricky old witches. They could toy with my heartstrings all they wanted, could tie them in knots and tangle them up with Luca Fiore if they pleased. But I was luck incarnate. I was cunning and advantage made corporeal.

I would make my own fate.

My father would ask where I'd gone off to, even though he'd

dismissed me. But later, I'd craft my excuse. That was a problem for later.

In this moment, I had a single task.

My Zio Tyr was a vicious being. He'd have me kill Luca for pure sport, for his own sick amusement. But I'd been tricked by him too many times to trust him implicitly.

Still, I'd worked too hard to build the Corrente name to stop now. Tonight had been a serious blunder. Without new work, our investors would be out for blood, just as feral as Tyr himself. But without a bone to throw them, they'd pull out– a financial blow that would take a miracle to recover from.

Good thing I was made of miracles.

The cobblestone beneath my feet soon shifted to run down asphalt, the polished stone and stucco of the buildings dissolving into concrete slabs and worn wooden slats. Roma was the city of commerce, but it had its slums, too. A seedy underbelly that my father would rather die than frequent.

But with the rats and the ragged, sickness thrived in the dampest, darkest shadows of every city. And I needed a word with Plague.

It was time to strike another deal.

Their door was unmarked, a little hole-in-the-wall sandwiched between a boarded up nightclub and a run-down liquor store. Customers stumbled out from the latter, spilling onto the pot-holed street like knocked-over trash, bringing with them the scent of sour booze and regret.

I let them wobble up the alley before I slid into Resheph's shop.

I had to squint to adjust to the harsh fluorescent sheen of overhead tubes, the off-putting blue tinting the room in a lurid, sickly pale. On shelves, glass vials glowed with the same unnatural, garish tint, the poisons inside labeled as anything but.

High fructose-corn syrup. Aspartame. Red #3. Enriched Vegetable Oil.

With the dawn of the twenty-first century and chemistry, medicine had evolved, vaccines and antivirals a steep innovation that made sickness near obsolete.

But Plague had grown too. *Learned.* Mastered the art of slow sickness, of disguising carcinogens as sweet treats. Of turning food into toxins. Of letting corporations and their cheap 'additives' infect people worldwide.

They leaned against the counter across the small room, their mismatched eyes just as unsettling as the fluorescents. Golden blond curls framed their thin, structured face, their wide eyes and sharp jaw an androgynous mix that most painters would've killed for a chance to study. But their aura rang of ancient afflictions, a pretty flower too poisonous to touch.

I stood straighter, meeting their uneven gaze head on. "Hi there, Zizi Resheph."

"*Balshasar,*" they crooned, resting their cheek on a fist. "I've been expecting you."

I flattened my suit against my frame, my shoes clacking against the clean slate floor. Of the four Furies, Resheph was the most reasonable. They favored logic above emotion, and much like Lorenzo Corrente, they couldn't pass up a good deal when it presented itself.

I was about to hand them one on a silver platter.

"Please just call me Marcello," I said easily, the familiar mask slipping into place. Correntes spoke the language of business from the moment we were born. "I need a potion. Something that could keep someone down for a few days without killing them."

Resheph looked me over once, stare dragging with a chemical precision. Then, after a long breath. "Is this punishment? Do you want them to feel ill?"

Once, lifetimes ago, I'd asked Resheph for the opposite. For a respite, for protection. For my lover's safety amidst the storm.

But I'd been wrong then. Foolish. I'd handed over my greatest asset, all in favor of my foolish heart.

Your heart has no place in this world, Balshasar.

No, not anymore. The heart was built for breaking. I had no use for anything that fragile. Even if it beat wildly in my ribs, the mere thought of harming Luca as painful as carving the organ out of my chest.

I didn't need to harm him. Not like Tyr wanted me to.

But I couldn't let myself love him either. Couldn't get distracted by that soft smile. Those eyes that saw. That knew.

I shook my head. "No, just...something to keep him tucked in bed for a few days."

Resheph nodded, fiddling behind the counter to fill my order. No further questions, no prying glances, no emotion. Just business. Finally, they placed a small plastic bag of pea-sized white pills on the counter. "Let two dissolve in his drink, roll him on his side, and he'll be dead asleep for at least a weekend." Their eyes narrowed, green-and-blue glowing in the harsh truth of the flickering bulb-light. "But this will cost you, *Balshasar*."

I scoffed, unclipping the gold Rolex from my wrist and tossing it onto the counter. I had twelve more at home, and they weren't even near the top of my collection. "Put it on my tab, Zizi."

They tilted their head, a wheezing laugh escaping their lungs. "The price is not paid in coin, dear boy. You know this better than most."

They were right. Money came and went. Miracles were priceless.

"See you soon, Zizi," I said, purposely running my hand over the edge of the countertop, imbuing it with my gift. This far away from Luca, the luck sprang easily to my fingertips, the lightning skittering across the stone, charging the very surface with pure energy. "Good luck."

TWO THINGS LED me to the right flat—my luck, and a gaudy, exclusive edition sports car that was not hard to track down. Parked on Vita della Mattonaia in front of a tattoo parlor, it was hard to imagine that the tattoo artists and starving architecture students might have managed to snag such a limited edition ride.

Less of a castle than I imagined, the penthouse flat still took up the top two floors of the tall building, the exposed brick of the hall and dulled brass fixtures the only features "cheapening" the space.

But it was private, tucked away in the alleys behind the universities, the building hard to pick out from the other old dorms in the area. Here, Luca wasn't Carlo's son—the doorman didn't even know the Fiore name. Here, he could just be a twenty-something with a stupid car living in a nice flat in the most beautiful city in the world.

A part of me felt guilty for disrupting his little pocket of peace, my hesitation snagging on the ugly carpet in the hall for the first time. My resolve had been unwavering the entire hour-and-a-half train ride from Roma, the trip plenty of time for me to renege on my revenge plot.

No, not revenge. Restoration. Luca would be fine after a few days, and so would my family. It would all be right as rain. It was time to wipe off the film of chaos that Luca Fiore had dusted over my life with his first champagne-bubbled grin. Time to remember my purpose, my careful planning, as heir to the Corrente name. To rejuvenate my family's legacy before this lifetime ended up just like the first.

It still took all my might to knock.

I don't know what I expected at half three in the morning, but when he opened the door in a pair of low-cut sweatpants, his chest bare save for the tattoos—Latin passages of text— scrawled across his cut form, my mouth went entirely dry.

"*Marcello?*" He rubbed the lingering sleep from his eyes before narrowing them at me. "Are you all right?"

I swallowed hard, trying not to let my traitorous gaze dip below his chest. I was here to drug this man—not gape at him like a sculpture. I shoved my shaking hands in my pockets, clasping the small pill bag as a lifeline. "Can I—can I come in?"

Luca's full lips pursed before he stepped aside, ushering me into the room. "Yeah, sure."

My shoes scuffed against the deep hardwood as I shuffled through, running a hand through my unruly curls. A crackling fire in a gas chimney warmed the tasteful flat. A leather couch dominated the space, ornately carved cherry-oak end-tables on either side. Industrial bronze lamps added to the orange glow, their metallic structure a welcome contrast to the antique softness of the rest of the decor, lighting the oil painting that hung above the mantle–an artist even *I* didn't recognize–the image of a woman's smiling face bathing in sunlight dappled in a classical style.

My heartbeat battered my chest. This was not the tasteless bachelor pad I'd imagined. Not just some fuck-off space for Luca to crawl to after a long night partying with the university frats.

This was a *home*. *His* home. Lived in and loved.

I beat back the guilt clawing its way up my chest, focusing on the delicate grooves in the hardwood floor. "Sorry to trouble you so late."

Sorry for what I'm about to do.

Luca ran a tired hand over his face as he walked into the open concept towards the kitchen, leaning his forearms against the wide granite island. "I should probably ask how you found me, but honestly, I'm relieved you're here."

I gulped back my satisfied surprise, the part of me desperate for scraps of attention savoring that word; *relieved.*

Wanted.

I did my best to not let my reaction show on my face, but it was a failed effort as my brows flew up. "What? Why?"

He shrugged, the action emphasizing the strong muscles in his shoulders. "I was worried. When you walked out of the auction, and then your father–" He trailed off before he could leap off that cliff, perhaps sensing the way my gut clenched at the mention of Lorenzo. Honeycomb eyes melted to pools of warm amber. "Tell me what's going on, and maybe I can help."

A part of me surged to the surface, hot and molten and desperate to spill. To tell him everything—every demand my father made of me, every failure of my past that compelled me to obedience now. Again, here I was at the precipice of letting this man in, letting him *see*. It was madness that I hadn't realized who he was earlier.

Xerxes.

No. Not anymore.

Those that saw me got hurt. I'd never let anyone in like that again. I fixed the lapel of my jacket, still in my tux from the auction. Still in my Corrente costume. Still Marcello, not Balshasar. But the smile I wore didn't quite fit right. "It's nothing."

Luca tilted his head. "Then why are you here?"

The pillbag in my pocket practically burned.

"I wanted to see you." A lie and a truth. More truth than I was willing to admit, even to myself.

Luca sighed, the hint of a smile curving his lips. "You're not a very good liar, but I like your company." He pushed off the island, jerking his head to the leather couch before fiddling through the cabinets. He pulled two martini glasses from the shelf above the fridge, stretching his half-naked form to reach. "Have a seat, I'll get you a drink."

I shoved back the weakest parts of me, remembering myself. My Corrente name. I didn't come here to flirt and forget. I came here to make one thing in my Fates-damned lives right.

"Why don't you let me?" I sprang forward, snagging the glasses from his hands. This was my chance. A quick nightcap with some crushed up pills and I'd lay him on his lovely couch and get out before I lost my resolve. A solid plan, one maybe my sister Talitha could be proud of. She'd always been the cunning one.

Luca had other thoughts. He crossed his arms over his chest, covering the dark ink of his ribs. "You want to make the drinks in *my* house? You don't know where anything is."

I took a steadying breath, letting it gild my smile. I was Marcello Corrente. Luck bowed at my feet, and I would not back down.

"I'm resourceful." I shrugged, my voice dipping in seduction.

Another one of Talitha's tricks. Not that I needed to do much 'tricking' with my own desire motivating at least half of my actions. I set the glasses on the island, peering up from beneath my lashes. "It's the least I could do for barging in like this. I'm an excellent mixologist."

Luca's gaze drifted to my lips, heat flaring in my middle. He exhaled a heavy hum that vibrated through my bones. "Fine, suit yourself."

Without another word, he strode over to his couch and plopped down, kicking his feet up on the armrest to warm them by the fire, propping his head up on his hands. Facing away, thank the fucking Fates and Furies.

I made quick work on the cocktail, grabbing a grapefruit from his refrigerator and squeezing it into the martini glass before finishing it off with two shots of his top shelf gin and a splash of triple sec from his well-stocked liquor cabinet.

The two pills fizzed as they dissolved in the mixture, bubbling like the guilt in my gut. But as I stirred the white powder away, I shoved down the useless feeling, burying it beneath centuries of the same. Guilt had no place in Marcello Corrente's world, and neither did love. It didn't matter if Luca was my tether, or whatever other form of torture the Fates and Furies decided to taunt me with. He was just a man. And he was in my way.

I carried the drinks over carefully, making sure to set the right one on the coaster next to Luca.

Luca, who'd somehow managed to drift off in the time it took me to make two martinis.

His long eyelashes brushed against his cheek, the fireplace casting his bronze skin in deep amber. His dark hair stuck out in odd directions, the leather fabric of the seat sticking to his bare skin in a way that could not be comfortable. But still, his chest rose and fell in heavy breaths, the Latin tattoo undulating with him.

My eyes narrowed on the text, finally making out the words.

Tici ipsi dic vere.

To thine own self be true.

My own breath stuck in my chest, the air turned to molasses.

Art was meant to be witnessed, and Fates and Furies, this man was a masterpiece. The traitorous organ beneath my ribs threatened to burst, desperate to taste his parted lips. To *savor* him. To be true to my own desires for once, to live and enjoy...

I must have said something aloud, because his eyes fluttered open again, their warm hazel trapping me in their snare.

"Sorry, I nodded off." His smile ran me through as he sat up and grabbed the cocktail, lifting it in the air. "Cheers."

My voice hurried out just before the poison could stain his lips.

"Actually–that one is mine." I covered the rim with a hand, offering the other glass instead. "Sorry, less gin."

Relief flooded every inch of me when he let go without hesitation, trading his fate for a luckier lot. Still, those eyes narrowed, a different suspicion creeping over his previously unguarded expression. "Are you ready to tell me what's really going on?"

Yes. No. Maybe.

I wanted to. Wanted to blurt it all out.

You're my tether. My soulmate.

My weakness.

My father needs me.

Marcello Corrente had no weaknesses. But Balshasar...

My mother's lifeless stare.

I placed the poisoned martini on the table, discarding it with the last of my resolve. I could not harm him. Not in this life, or any of my lives before.

"I would if I knew." I fell onto the couch next to him, giving into the soft padding, wishing it would swallow me whole. My head fell back into the embrace of the leather, my eyes meeting the woman in the painting. Her joy was a mockery to my misery. "Who painted that? I don't recognize it."

"I did."

My jaw hit the floor. He was an *artist?*

I stared at the painting with newfound appreciation. The high contrast color palette, the sheer *technique* in the way the sun hit the woman's face...the emotion in her sparkling eyes. It wasn't just well executed...it was *evocative*. Demanding to be felt, not just seen.

"Who is she?"

Luca's weight shifted on the couch next to me. "My mother. She died a long time ago."

My gut clenched, a stabbing pain poking my softest parts.

My mother's seaside stare, lifeless. My father's broken screams, echoing from the garden.

All I had of my past–my *first* family–were memories of failure and heartache. The sour, bitter taste of tragedy. But Luca...Luca remembered his mother in vivid color. He honored her legacy in strokes of glorious sunlight to be displayed above a warm hearth.

For all my luck and good taste, I'd never *created* anything. Never learned a skill outside of steering fortune's favor my way, or furthering my family's endeavors instead of learning my own. For centuries, that was enough.

Now...

Do you want to have a bit of fun?

I turned to him, tears blurring my eyes, to find him already looking at me. "It's stunning."

"Yes you are," he said without missing a beat, his hand drifting closer to mine from where it rested on the couch. Like a magnet, drawn to me.

Like a tether.

"Luca–" I warned, fear pricking at the back of my throat like the first signs of sickness. Of plague. Tethers got hurt when they were tied to the son of a Fury. When Plague and War breathed down my neck, life after hideous life.

But Luca painted over my anxiety with wide brushstrokes, re-coloring it to suit his image. His *vision*. He took my hand, fingers fitting through mine like they belonged there.

Tici ipsi dic vere.

To thine own self be true.

"I wish I could go back to that night at the gala, you know. It keeps me up at night. I wish I would've told you who I was then so you'd trust me now. Wish I was brave enough to be myself. Wish I would've stayed with you a little longer in that room, maybe, too." His words were unhurried, the steady pace of a patient painter's hand. But his gaze burned, *brandished*, unrelenting in both heat and urgency. "Seen what would've happened if I didn't run away like Cinderella after just one kiss."

The silly organ ticked up its stride in my chest. "I wish we could go back, too."

A truth, so painful and potent it stung.

I wanted desperately to go back. Not just to our little moment together, but to that first life. To that summer in the barn. To that somewhere, sometime *before* I made my mistakes. I wished I hadn't run from him then. Or my family. I wished I'd been there, wish I hadn't relied on my fickle luck to save us.

Luca's hand tightened in mine, tethering me back to the present. To Marcello and Luca instead of Xerxes and Balshasar. "But then I think I'm lucky enough to have gotten that moment. To have met you, despite all the bullshit surrounding us."

I couldn't go back. Couldn't right the wrongs of the world before.

But I would not repeat Balshasar's mistakes.

Insecurity had no place in Marcello Corrente's world.

I didn't hesitate this time as I crashed into Luca, my mouth finding his. He stilled in surprise for a breath, but then he rose to meet my call, kissing me back like his life depended on it. Mine certainly did. My mouth parted, and he stole the breath straight from my lungs, greedily nipping at my lip as his tongue intruded. He pulled me from my seat to sit me across his lap, the *want* we shared evident through his thin gray sweatpants in a way that set every nerve in my body on fire.

My fingers tangled in his short hair, tugging him closer as my tongue explored and devoured. Gluttony had always been my brother Eris' vice, but with Luca, I was a starved man, famished for every scrap of him I could get. My hands trailed from his hair to his chest, every new texture of his skin a sensation to be savored.

Luca tore his mouth from mine, a growl rumbling through him. "Are you sure about this?" His stare pierced through me, seeing too much, too deep.

But I wanted him there. Wanted him to ravage my deepest, darkest, ugliest parts. Wanted him to know. To *see*.

"Certain." I shifted to straddle him, not breaking eye contact for once, my craving and conviction pressing against his. "Having second thoughts?"

War ravaged my emotions. I wanted him to say yes. Wanted him to shove me off of him, to send me packing. To punish me for my cruelty and my self-centered rage. To remind me I was not enough. That I didn't deserve this simple pleasure.

But when his smile lit his face again, the parts of me that longed to stay forever won out, their triumph ringing through my veins like a song.

"Not this time."

And with the victory hymn singing through my heart, I let him take me to bed.

BALSHASAR / *SOMEWHERE, A LONG TIME AGO* / SCULPTURE IN CLAY.

WINTER FROZE over the last cracks of my ravaged heart. But the stain of my failure was too stubborn to wash from the fabric of my being. It dyed every strand of me a blood red—the same red that soiled the earth the night my mother died.

"You can forget, but it does not change what you've done, child,"

Tyr laughed, his scythe still stuck between my ribs, in the empty spot my mother left.

My mother's seaside stare, lifeless. My father's broken screams, echoing from the garden. My eldest sister's threadbare smile as she tried to hold all the frayed strings of the family together. My brother Eris' sunken cheeks as the horror consumed him from inside out. Edana's anxiety, Talitha's avoidance, Athene's rage, all three of my youngest sisters lost to themselves. Caedmon's heart-shattering questions, *"Where is Mama? When will she come back?"*

Because I wasn't there. Because I'd let Tyr take my luck. Because I'd given it freely to the wrong Fury, all to protect a farm boy with nothing to his name. With nothing to offer, no reassurance of a future.

I didn't see Xerxes anymore. I'd never let myself indulge again. I didn't deserve it. He left for happier climes, taking his family and his summer-scented smile with him.

"Your heart has no place in this world, Balshasar," the Fury of War teased as he departed, my tattered family debris at his feet.

My heart was gone, buried with my mother. Lost with my lover.

My luck too, had passed.

∿

MARCELLO | *TUSCANY, PRESENT DAY* | Splatter on canvas.

I WOKE TO THE BLARING ALARM, the aggressive buzz yanking me from the nightmare I'd been trapped in.

My mother's seaside stare, lifeless. My father's broken screams, echoing from the garden. My eldest sister's threadbare smile as she tried to hold all the frayed strings of the family together. My brother Eris' sunken cheeks as the horror consumed him from inside out. Edana's anxiety, Talitha's avoidance, Athene's rage, all three of my youngest sisters lost to themselves.

Caedmon's heart-shattering questions, *"Where is Mama? When will she come back?"*

I blinked, blotting out the memories as I fumbled around the unfamiliar bedside table to silence the incessant noise...

No, not an alarm. Notifications. Hundreds. *Thousands.* Comments and tags pouring in from every social media platform I frequented. Text messages and emails, their themes all circling the uncomfortable mix of urgency and violent curiosity.

Are you okay?

Did you know?

Sorry to hear about your dad, man.

Check this out.

This is an outrage!

Then the article titles from my news app. All the same horrific line. My stomach dropped straight to hell.

Lorenzo Corrente Arrested on Embezzlement Charges at the Vittori Auction House.

I bolted straight up, not caring if I disturbed Luca at my side. His silk-soft sheets suddenly turned to sandpaper against my skin, everything too hot, too itchy, too close. Shaking fingers clicked the link to the first article, a video popping up on my phone.

A video of my father, his hands cuffed behind his back, dozens of reporters swarming him as the officer escorted him to the police car. A scowl on his face as they shoved microphones in his face. As the young male officer prattled off his privacy rights.

"You are under arrest for charges of embezzlement against the tax commissions of several regions. You are entitled to a lawyer, and to remain silent...."

"Where is my son?" Lorenzo snapped as they tried to shove him in the back of the car. *"Get me Marcello, he'll explain everything..."*

I shut the video off before the bile stirring in my gut ruined Luca's sheets.

"Marcello? Is everything alright?" His hand stroked my back, sleep thick in his deep voice. But I barely heard him, the joy of last night forgotten as my ears rang with my father's graveled voice instead.

Where is my son?

Not there. Not at his side, where I should've been. Not there to protect him. Off fucking the rival's son, tarnishing my name.

I should've known better. Tyr hadn't just shown up to taunt me—he'd been there to wage war.

Your family won't prosper while he lives. You know this, Balshasar. Reputations can come undone with a single stray thread.

It was a threat, not a warning.

Of course, I had no idea my father was embezzling funds. My luck should've been enough to keep us well in the green. But greed touched us all in different ways, trying to fill holes in our soul that could never be truly sated. And had I known, I could've used my luck to stop it.

No. I'd chosen to go to Resheph. I made a deal with the wrong Fury *again*.

The price is not paid in coin, dear boy. You know this better than most.

Another night spent with my tether instead of protecting my kin. Another price too heavy to pay, my pride blinding me from the truth.

Lifetime after lifetime, nothing changed. I was still the same broken, self-centered boy that abandoned my family in their time of need.

"Marcello—" Luca's concern cut through the spiral of self-loathing, wrenching me back to my body with aggressive force. Too much, too *close*.

I was worried. When you walked out of the auction, and then your father—

"Did you know?" I spun to face him, leaping from the bed, my legs wobbling beneath me.

Luca's eyes widened, a frown creasing the corners of his mouth. "You didn't? I thought that's why you came, I—"

"I have to go," I cut him off, scrambling to pick up my clothes from the floor, tugging my pants on clumsily over my fear-leadened legs. As I dressed again, I shut out all the sweat-soaked, lust-filled memories from the night before, my clothes a suit of armor against the onslaught. Every touch, every kiss— I'd given more of myself to him than I'd ever given anyone.

Given more of my luck, too.

And now I was drained of it, the lightning in my veins slumbering like a storm rolling out, the satisfied calm *after* the only thing left. It wasn't enough to save my father.

I wasn't enough.

"Marcello wait, let me help you." Luca snagged my suit jacket from the ground before I did, concern glimmering in his gaze. "I thought you knew, but we can fix this together. My family has contacts, and I'll drive you to the police station..."

"No one can help me." I snatched the jacket from his grip as I shut down the last of my emotions. I wouldn't give him any more. I couldn't. I watched as my words struck him, the molten amber of his eyes hardened into impenetrable stone. Eyes that saw through my bullshit. Eyes that judged me for the piece of crap I was. I swallowed the lump in my throat, turning away before he could discover my most fragile parts. "Goodbye, Xerxes."

"What? Marcello—"

I fled through the door before he could finish his sentence, out into his living room, into the poorly carpeted hallway, and down the stairs. I didn't care that we were on the top floor. My dead legs couldn't feel anything anyway, just the panic that surged through every fiber of my useless body.

Numb fingers swiped open my still buzzing phone, hastily dialing the number as I stumbled down, floor after horrible floor. At least I knew the digits by heart, though I'd never called before. I'd forced Edana to give it to me a few years back, pretending to need it for 'official sin business', though I hadn't mustered the courage to hit the call button.

Today, I had no other choice.

I finally pressed the green phone symbol, the shrill ringing on the other end matching the screaming inside my head.

Your heart has no place in this world, Balshasar.

The price is not paid in coin.

Get me Marcello.

"Come on, pick up," I panted to myself on the fourth ring, nearly tripping as I finally found the bottom floor.

The fifth ring clicked short as I stepped through the threshold into the morning air.

"Hello?" The deep voice answered, *younger* than I'd last heard it, but filled with the same ancient sadness that somehow still resonated through the speakers of my smartphone.

Tears ached to spill from their beds, the little boy in me rising to the surface.

"I need you to take it all away," I cried, just a child begging his father to make it better.

Not Lorenzo.

Thanatos.

I couldn't do this anymore. Couldn't bear the weight on my shoulders, the power in my veins. All too much, too close, too bright.

I needed it to stop. Needed Abba to make it all better, to put an end to the Furies' cruelty. An end to my *shame.*

A beat passed, my breath held, until my father finally spoke again, my name a whispered prayer. "*Bal*–Marcello?"

The last dam holding back the tidal wave fractured and caved, the torrent of emotions bringing me to my knees. I crashed into the uneven sidewalk, the cobblestone biting through the expensive material of my trousers. Sobs wracked through me, words a hiccupped mess as I begged Death for a respite. "Take it. All my feelings. I can't live like this. I can't fall in love with him *and* protect my family. I can't keep the guilt and failure with me anymore...I'm not strong enough."

"I'm sorry," Thanatos answered, my father's tone cracked with the piteous emotion. "But no."

Despair stole the air from my lungs, leaving me breathless and battered.

"Why? I've never bothered you, never asked you for anything in all of these lives." I curled into a ball on the ground, the rage deflating me as I spat my poisonous truths through the phone. Passersby whispered, but I didn't care. Let them all see. Let them pick at my exposed, bleeding heart. I wouldn't need it much longer. It was a relic of ages past, just like I was. My voice sounded far away as it echoed back at me through the speaker. "It's not like you need me around anyway. I'm just a broken, cocky, imperfect piece of shit that the rest of you would rather forget."

"Oh Fates and Furies, Balshasar..." Thanatos chuckled, but the sound held no humor. Only a knowing that sobered my sobs, a sadness that matched my own. "I never needed you to be perfect. I just needed you to be happy. And I know I ruined that for you, so I kept my distance. But you've always been more than enough."

Another beat, as I processed. As the words sank into my skin, into my soul.

Enough.

All I'd ever wanted was to be enough. To make my family–my father–proud enough.

To be enough to make my mother stay, enough to keep her out of Tyr's reach. Enough to lead my siblings towards the light, to fight back the Fates and Furies on their behalf.

But now, I'd *had* enough. Enough of the games, the lies, the masks. Enough of cutting out my own heart as a sacrifice to legacies I'd never live long enough to see.

Enough love to make me *want*.

"What am I supposed to do now?" I whispered, half to my father still on the other line, half to myself. I'd had enough, and I had no clue what that meant next. "I'm out of luck, I can't *fix* it."

A long pause on the line, so long I thought he might have hung up if not for the lack of a beep. An infinite moment, as the Fury of Death took a deep breath. As my father considered. Then, "You don't need to do or fix anything, Marcello. Just go *be* happy. You've earned it."

"But what about Lorenzo—"

Death cut me off, a command and an answer. "You don't need to shrink yourself to make space for your family anymore. It's time." A breath again, then my Abba added, "I love you."

When the line went dead, so did the last fearful parts of me.

Pride had no place in Marcello Corrente's world. Neither did Balshasar. Nor his mistakes. His burdens.

It was time I finally laid him to rest.

Lorenzo Corrente had the power to turn even the barest, least fashionable jail cell in all of Italy into a grand meeting room with his presence alone. Even under the flickering fluorescent lights, his posture remained ramrod straight as he sat against the lonely bench, the bars around him just as rigid. The damp smell of mildew and regret slammed into me as I entered the tiny space, the officer's keys jingling as he unlocked my father's cage.

He looked up as my shoes echoed across the concrete slab flooring, light eyes already narrowed in impatience. "You're late, Marcello."

My fingernails pinched into my palms as I donned my mask for the last time. The dutiful son finishing his final deal. "I'm sorry, Father. It took me time to get things sorted."

My father groaned as he stood, cracking his neck and rolling out his shoulders. He strode through the door without a look back, straightening the cuffs of his wrinkled dress shirt. "I take it this is all cleared up now?"

"For now." I pursed my lips as I followed down the hallway to the main office of the station. This would be the hardest part, but I'd anticipated his attitude, as I had been all my life. I cleared my throat of any lingering insecurity. "I paid your bail."

My father halted in his tracks, tension running down his proud spine. "The prosecution hasn't been paid off?"

"Not this time." I stuffed my hands in my pockets, but kept my chin high. I was Marcello Corrente, and shame had no place in my world. I ushered my father into the office, gesturing to the tall man sitting there. "But I managed to work a little magic. This is Cesario Ricci. He'll be taking on your case."

Cesario stood and dipped his head in deference, the lawyer straightening his lopsided tie. He wasn't the sharpest-looking man I'd ever seen, his tweed suit horrendous and his wrinkled shirt a travesty, but his reputation spoke for him instead. They called him *Lo Squalo*—the shark. He flashed a jagged smile. "It's a pleasure to meet you, sir. Your son speaks very fondly of you."

Lorenzo's face turned beet red, the fondness far from mutual as he shot daggers at me, the perfect replica of Hodler's *The Angry Man*.

"A lawyer?" he seethed, and I fought a wince. "Marcello, what is the meaning of all of this? Surely you have some other ideas in that head of yours."

I sighed, fighting back the parts of me that wanted to fall at his feet and beg for forgiveness. That wanted to linger a little longer in his shadow, his lucky charm and favored son. But I'd planned for this. Exhaustion crept along my back, the last day spent making calls and fielding press and laying plans catching up with me. I shrugged, letting loose a weary smile. "This was all I could afford. I had to sell the *El Greco* back to the church."

The untaxed sons-of-bitches were the only patrons that could buy it without recourse from the government, and I needed cash on hand.

Lorenzo scoffed, waving me off like I was a gnat buzzing around his head. "Then contact my accountant. We'll see to it the rest is all paid."

I squared my shoulders, the lightning in my veins crackling and begging to be used. It'd been a full day since I'd seen Luca, so there was plenty of the potent power to go around. It would be as easy as breathing—a single touch on my father's cheek, and his problems would be solved. If I wished it, I could change fate to my liking.

But I was done with simple fixes for powerful men who didn't deserve it. Tired of putting my family name before my own.

Lorenzo Corrente did not own the world, not anymore. Nor did he own me.

"Your accounts are all frozen, Papa," I said gently, the blow softened by the last remnants of the son I used to be. Then, stronger, "Lorenzo, it's over. Do whatever Cesario says, and maybe you'll make it out of this without significant jail time."

Cesario nodded, the shark ready to devour this case. Fates and Furies, I paid him well enough—and in advance. The church's cash was as good as gold. A lawyer's loyalty could be bought.

Mine couldn't. Not anymore.

I turned to go, but the growl that escaped my father's throat stayed my hand on the doorknob.

"Where the hell do you think you're going, boy?" Lorenzo ground out, his emotion betrayed by his tone, composure falling away. Gone was the king of deals, the impassive, refined man I'd grown up desperate to impress. Corrente men did not let emotion rule them, but perhaps Lorenzo had forgotten his own sage advice.

I shook my head, hiding my own war of feelings behind the scraps of my mask. The guilt and relief, the rage and giddy excitement—he would get none of it. None of *me.* Not anymore. "I can't stay. I'm sorry, but it's time to go."

Lorenzo waggled a finger in my face, his silver-and-brown curls sticking out in disarray. "You are *lucky* I'm a patient man. I'll give you one more chance to fix this *right*, or I'll disown you."

I met my father's gaze. Let him see, for a brief moment, the resolve in my own. The confidence I'd learned from *him.*

And the love I'd learned from my first father.

"Lorenzo, you have nothing to take from me," I whispered before turning the knob, stepping out into the next chapter. "It's time I made my own luck."

∼

MARCELLO | *MANHATTAN, PRESENT DAY* | OIL ON
CANVAS.

THE YELLOW SPLOTCH of color pooled around my feet as I took in the
vast space, Van Gogh's *Starry Night* projected around me in vivid
hues.

I'd seen the real thing half a dozen times—it was only a few blocks
up, stored at the Museum of Modern Art. Since moving to New York,
I spent half my time between there and the Met. As the newest
curator on both boards, it was part of the job. I'd even purchased
several of Van Gogh's other paintings, touching them with my own
two hands...

But nothing compared to this. The immersive experience cast the
whole world in Vincent's extraordinary brushstrokes, in his marigold
memories and cerulean emotion. People wandered around the space,
stars in their eyes matching the plotted celestial spots on the walls.

Art was not meant to be kept and curated. Not meant to be stored
and sold.

Art was meant to be witnessed. Experienced.

Shared.

Tears bit the corners of my eyes, but a smile stretched my
cheeks.

A hand slipped into mine, calloused palm sending tingles of
static electricity through me. Luca smirked, honey eyes tracking the
stains across my cheeks. A soft laugh tumbled from his perfect lips,
his free thumb scrubbing away the moisture. "Whoa, there, it's just a
replica."

I squeezed his hand tighter, a tether to this life. To this reality,
bright and free of the dark clouds of my past. "It's real to me."

My partner leaned in, pressing his mouth to mine in a soft kiss. I
savored the moment, the cigarette and coffee taste of him. Here, in
the middle of the room, with dozens of others milling about.

No one watched. No one cared. I was still Marcello Corrente, but that meant nothing here. Here, I was just another body, another witness to the true experience. Another young man in love, taking in art, following my own whims and wants.

Luca broke away, stealing my breath with him.

"Do you wanna go have some fun?" Hazel eyes glimmered with mischief. Eyes that saw my many facets, every life and secret and story. "There is a pride parade tomorrow in the village. We could go buy slutty outfits in SoHo and make a day of it."

I imagined the scene as vividly as any painting in my collection. Luca's broad chest and sinful tattoos on display in some ridiculous, tacky outfit, both of us baking in the heat that rose from the asphalt streets, glitter and glamor dancing around us in rainbow streaks.

I tugged his hand, a smile breaking my stoicism. Denial had no place in Marcello Corrente's world—not anymore. "Let's go shopping now."

Luca laughed, the sound like bright splatter on a canvas. "Do you think we'll make it on time for the dinner reservations?"

A dormant spark tickled through my veins. "If we get lucky."

Forget Me Not

Cass Maren

CHAPTER 7
FORGET ME NOT
CASS MAREN

PART I: THE SILVER TETHER | *LONDON, PRESENT DAY*

Winter was full of dangerous reminders. Lingering whispers blanketed the city in broken promises and fleeting dreams. Ghosts of the past.

Most nights I dreamt in memories. The taste of salt, the crashing of waves. The delicate whisper of my name off my mother's lips. *Mnemosyne*. Soaked in joy and triumph, the stolen memories lived inside me as if they were my own, woven into the very recesses of my being.

Their sorrow was mine too. The memories of grief and pain that I'd plucked from others for my own keeping. Memories I bore as punishment for the sins of my past lives.

That place by the sea haunted me most. Nights of restless sleep taunted by the shadow of that first life, always out of reach. A solitary golden thread brushing my fingertips before being ripped back to the living hell of my reality. I'd once been able to taste the difference between the salty seaside of my memories and those of my mother. My father. Now the line that separated one from the other was nothing more than a blur.

I'd known joy once. Now all I had left was the ghost of it, the harrowing reminder of what I could no longer obtain. I spent days and nights piecing together moments, agonizing over those whispered reminders of places and people. Chasing golden threads. Wanting something always out of reach. The wanting never quelled the emptiness inside.

The curse of a good dream was that you never wanted it to end. Memories were largely the same. Ending too soon, always leaving me greedy for more. It would have been too easy to stay wrapped up in bed. Wrapped up in the past, the mistakes, the promises I'd broken. Bound to an endless cycle of misery and remembrance.

But reality beckoned me, and like the obedient daughter I was, I heeded her call.

In winter, London woke before the sun. An infallible routine was the only answer to the relentless temptation of oblivion. Candlelight danced across the walls of my Shoreditch flat. A small lump of a cat occupied the pillows I carefully straightened as I made my bed. Calliope, sweet in temperament but steadfast in her resolve, showed interest neither in moving nor in the fact that I had yet to finish making my bed. Cal's golden feline eyes dared me to move her myself, a challenge I knew better than to accept. Instead, I brushed my fingers over her soft black coat, and she rewarded me with the loud thrum of a contented purr.

Of all the wonders of the modern world, a hot shower was my favorite luxury. I let the heat envelope me, near-scalding water streaming over my pale flesh until the memories of my dreams melted away.

Promise me, my mother's voice echoed in my mind. *Promise me you'll look after them.*

I turned the dial, steam slithering towards the ceiling as I shoved the memory to the back of my mind. I stood there until the only thing left behind was a pulsing ache somewhere between pain and pleasure.

The stark contrast of the brisk cold outside my flat stung my cheeks on my short commute to the nearest tube station. Morning winter mist kissed my eyelashes as I sipped coffee from my thermos and slid a copy of The Guardian under my arm. The steady patter of my heels on the pavement blended into the bustle of cars and buses whizzing by. The busyness of bodies shuffling through the streets drowned out the whispers.

I savored the silence.

The sun rose, streams of light glistening over slick cobblestone and asphalt. I'd been known for my steady gait, the ease with which I glided across silt and snow without so much as a bobble in my step. I'd mastered such confidence with centuries of practice. A carefully crafted lie.

But one whiff of cedar and leather nearly brought me to my knees. The familiar scent flooded my nostrils, and my ankle gave out. My thermos crashed to the ground, my neatly folded newspaper now splayed out onto the wet pavement. I reached desperately for the steady arm of a passerby. My heart pounded inside my chest, clawing against flesh and bone.

"All right there?" asked the man attached to the arm I clung to.

It wasn't *his* voice, not really. And yet the aching familiarity of the tone, the cadence, stoked the flame of the depleted embers deep inside my bones. My fingers latched to his tweed trench, my knees betraying my confident stature. I steadied myself, my eyes slowly raking over the stranger before me.

No, not a stranger.

Promise me? he whispered in my mind.

"Stephen," I couldn't help but whisper, a strangled pull from a memory long past.

The warmth in his brown eyes pierced through my soul to the place where he'd known me before. Where we'd once belonged to each other. His thick brows creased, eyes widening as his arm slid under my back, pulling me back to my feet. A nervous laugh pulsed from his lungs, his breath visible in the crisp morning air. "Sorry, no. *Daniel*, last I checked."

I shook off the temporary paralysis, pushing Stephen's smile to the back of my mind and quickly forcing one of my own. "Yes, of course. Sorry, you just...remind me of someone."

The wobble in my knees calmed, but beneath the shell of my composure, my heart threatened to erupt with a lifetime of yearning I'd caged away since...

Promise me?

"My apologies to your Stephen, then, if you mistook me for him," Daniel replied, a lighthearted chuckle as he ran his gloved fingers through his thick black curls.

Self-deprecating humor. Stephen's go-to defense mechanism. He'd always been charming but painfully unaware of it. Time slowed to a crawl, garbled words tangled at the back of my tongue, and the corners of his lips curled upwards in the same way I'd memorized a lifetime ago.

The inevitability of this moment hung thick in the winter morning air, and I could barely muster the words to speak. I glanced down at the space between us, a thin silver string lodged somewhere beneath my ribcage hanging slack for the first time in decades, peeking out from beneath my coat and tied somewhere beneath his.

It was *him*.

I willed him to recognize me, to see my soul hidden beneath my unfamiliar features of this new life. To find me again like we'd promised before. But as his grip loosened around me, my hope dissipated into morning mist.

"So sorry to be rude," said Daniel, that smile still smothered over his dark features. "But I'm actually running a bit late for work. First day and all. I hate to make a bad impression. But you're all right?"

"Yes," I answered quickly, straightening my blouse. "Just clumsier than usual. Thanks for breaking my fall."

Stupid joke, but he laughed. That hearty warm laugh that permeated my soul in an instant.

Tears sprang to my eyes. I looked away, wiping them on the sleeve of my coat, and when I turned back, he was walking in the opposite direction.

The tether between us stretched with each step. I looked over my shoulder, hoping to find his gaze, but he'd already disappeared into the crowd of grey coats. The busyness of bodies. My stomach sank.

Some ghosts were inescapable.

I DECIDED to skip the tube, hoping the long walk would sober the shaking in my fingers, but when I arrived at the *Athenaeum*, my veins still buzzed from the encounter. Cedar and leather lingered. Flashes of Stephen fought their way to the surface.

Calloused fingers wrapped around worn leatherbound books. Sunlight kissing the corners of his upturned lips as he slept. A catalog of every moment we'd spent together bursting at the hinges of the cage I'd locked it in.

Suffocating and small, the walls of my office closed in on me. I pressed my forehead against the door as I shut it, hitting it gently to erase the embarrassment of my interaction with Daniel.

"You're late."

My hand jolted to my chest, a violent gasp escaping from my lungs.

A pair of pale eyes accompanied a stern expression from the woman leaning against my desk, arms crossed over her chest.

Penella, one of my three keepers. The three meddling Fates whom I'd been bound to after my first life were once punishment for my sins. Now they were...something else entirely.

"You're never late," she added, one brow raised.

So much for infallible routines.

"I ran into an old friend," was all I could say, because Penn could smell bullshit from a mile away. I pointed to the book in her hands. "What have you got there?"

A flimsy distraction.

Still, her brow arched as she eyed my coat and the wrinkles in my pleated trousers. She pulled a thick leather-bound tome from beneath her arms and slid it across my desk, sending my neatly stowed to-do list and pens scattering. My fingers twitched at the disorder.

I stood over it, flipping through the pages filled with pristine looped lettering in an ancient tongue.

"Adeeba finished penning this one this morning," Penn said. "Danoma will be in with its owner soon. It'll need tending to."

Tending to. She meant it needed my *special touch.* Memories pulled from a mortal life, woven into the spine of the book for safe-keeping. The Fates had found my peculiar gift so intriguing that they'd scattered my siblings across the globe, thrust into their next lives, but I was trapped at their side. Forced to always remember. I'd begged for death, and instead I became their apprentice.

My fingers grazed over the book's spine, an entire life assembled into one volume. I'd seen my books once, neatly settled on the shelves of Adeeba's office behind lock and key. Volume after volume locked in this place both in and out of time. The *Athenaeum* was nowhere and everywhere all at once, the place *between.* Out in the world I could be Naomi Laurent and, if I was lucky, pretend I wasn't haunted by centuries of pain. Here I had nothing but the agony of remembering.

My siblings had all moved on with time. Adeeba often said time healed all wounds, but for me it became my misfortune. Not time itself, but the constant reminder of it. Hurtling through the unknown with the weight of my misdeeds and broken promises threaded beneath my skin. Memories I'd stolen to comfort my wandering soul. Comfort or penance, I couldn't always tell the difference. Instead I mindlessly consumed every image, every memory belonging to each of them. My siblings, my mother, even my father.

Death.

That's where the memories began. Shrouded in death.

Somewhere on the pages of the ancient tome that was my first life, Adeeba's delicate handwriting detailed those memories as well. Paraphrasing the life I'd had somewhere laced in seafoam and salt. But no memory was as clear as my own.

Thana, the gods had called me. Daughter of Death. But to my mother, I was simply...*Mnemosyne*.

I'd been born a sin against nature. The first abomination to the gods. But not the last.

Promise me, my mother's memory whispered. *Promise me you'll look after them.*

My parents' love transcended space and time, defying the laws of nature. My father, a Fury, an Angel of Death, had risked everything for the love of one woman. One *mortal* woman. Even the fates of his own children. I couldn't blame him; not entirely, anyways. I'd seen what the universe could do to keep them apart, the lengths to which they would go to untether two souls bound by fate.

But I never truly understood that decision until Stephen. I bore the curse of my sins from my first life, for my defiance in the faces of Fate and Fury. Every life since the beginning, I'd lived by their rules, burdened by the misery of my siblings. Burdened by unkept promises. I'd watched their lives end in tragedy and pain, again and again, indifferent to my own. If they would suffer, so must I. But it wasn't until Stephen was ripped from me that I truly knew my father's pain. Understood the unbridled willingness to accept damnation in order to reverse the past.

Whatever the cost.

~

PART II: WAR MAKES MONSTERS OF US ALL | *LONDON, SUMMER 1944*

RINGING FILLED MY EARS.

Another night of bombings tore through my city, and my uncle's laughter echoed within each wave of destruction. Cruel and cunning, Tyr had always been the perfect vessel of the gods' wrath. It was no wonder why my sister, Athene, found in him a place to channel her anger. Her own lust for vengeance.

I'd seen centuries of war, watching the fury of my father's siblings pour across the land. Humanity dangled by delicate threads, and the capricious gods were easily swayed, easily angered. I was living proof of that; each of Death's children were. My father too, who once did the gods' bidding, now walked through life as a permanent reminder of what it meant to anger those who controlled our fates. *The Pale Rider*, reduced to nothing more than a mere plaything of the gods.

The Fates would say War was swifter than Plague or Famine. But my uncle was patient in his games. So when I sent the man I loved to war in the year 1940, Tyr made me live every excruciating moment of it.

Stephen's letters stopped a week before the missiles that summer. I'd have been worried if they hadn't stopped before. We'd weathered four years of madness; I could survive a few weeks. War was nasty business and though I was not made for fighting at the fronts with a gun in my hand, I fought back the memories entwined in mortals' dreams when war came to haunt them upon their return. The Fates warned me not to meddle, but I couldn't bear the agony on the soldiers' faces when they returned home.

Outside of the constraints of time and space, the Fates had the luxury of indifference. But time had yet to saddle me with such apathy. For centuries, souls suffered around me, and I refused to stand by and watch.

Somehow the apartment in Shoreditch stood, though two streets over missiles tore through my neighbors' homes. Muffled cries reverberated against my eardrums. But I ran, my scuffed leather boots carrying me through the rubble-lined streets. My knees stung, scraped and bloody as I tripped over brick and stone. My lungs burned, ash and smoke poisoning each heaving breath.

War was not quick. War took his time.

I rushed to a fallen woman's side, crouching next to her as she sobbed, clutching blood-drenched linens to her chest. I frantically searched for the bleeding wound, but as I pulled back the saturated linen, I only found a child.

Shrieks of loss twisted at my heart, salt stinging my eyes as my vision blurred.

"Please!" the woman bellowed, the words drowned out by the ringing in my head. Her lips formed words through blood-stained teeth, I felt her desperation rising in my chest.

An older woman gripped the mother's shoulders with withered hands. Her features contorted with anguish, but she did not cry. She consoled. She whispered with lips pressed against the sobbing mother's ears.

"Mama," the woman wailed, voice scratching and hoarse, tapering off into a whisper. "My baby...she's...."

Mama, please, my young desperate voice rang. *Please don't do this.*

Promise me, Mnemosyne, my mother's voice replied. *Promise me you'll look after them.*

My throat tightened, a lump lodging itself somewhere in the raw and aching throat that stifled an imminent sob. With shaking hands, I reached out. The woman's fingers clutched the swaddling, a rigid, death-like grip against the tarnished linen. I slid the gloves from my hands, pressing my fingers over the bruised and battered flesh of her gnarled fingers.

And I stole it.

The memory of her child's lifeless eyes. The memory of painful cries of the child who lay limp in her arms. The memory of the letter sitting on the nightstand with news her husband was never coming home. All of it, gone.

"Look now," I whispered, closing the child's eyes with the soft graze of my fingertips. "See how she sleeps?"

I pressed my hand to the woman's cheek, not to take but this time to give. A reminder, *a whisper of a memory of her daughter's even breaths, the light of the hearth flickering off of her tawny cheeks. A soft lullaby filling the room.*

The woman's desperate sobs faded, replaced by a faint smile in the corner of her bruised lips. She stroked her daughter's hair, humming the familiar lullaby as she pulled the baby close. Eventually I'd have to take more, the temporary bliss only enough to soothe the woman's broken heart briefly before the cold ache of reality reared its ugly head once again. But not yet. I would not take more until she'd had one last moment to hold her child without the pain that would come after.

My father would have left nothing. Just a shell of a woman who once loved. A shell like the man he was now. Nothing more. Even death would have been better than nothingness, I'd told him once. But he'd long abandoned that courtesy when my mother's life disappeared from behind her eyes.

"Mnemosyne," a warm voice came.

Adeeba's tender touch pressed against my shoulder.

Of course. Wherever there was death, the Fates were sure to follow. I shook my head.

"Not yet," I said, my voice firm. "She needs more time with the child. Tell Danoma she can wait."

Adeeba's gaze fell from mine. "I'm not here for the child."

My brows furrowed. No, she wouldn't be. Adeeba rarely left the *Athenaeum*. She had Penn and Danoma to do her bidding. Today, something was different. Of all my keepers, Adeeba was the most composed. She never faltered. Never looked at me the way she did in that moment. Not since the beginning. Though she did not beg, a quiet urgency flashed in her eyes.

My heart sank into my gut.

I fumbled desperately with the buttons of my coat, eyes raking over the silver tether fastened neatly beneath my ribcage. So different than the golden threads of my siblings, of the half-god, half-mortal lives we were cursed too. The silver thread represented something else entirely. A tether from one soul to another.

Mine flickered, the dim light pulsing with every beat of my racing heart.

"No." The garbled words left my throat with a wretched gasp. "It is not his time."

Adeeba squeezed my shoulder. "I am so sorry, child."

I jerked away from her grasp, shaking my head.

"No." I said again, this time leaping to my feet.

And I ran as fast as my feet would carry me.

I'D STOLEN Stpehen's book from Adeeba's collection the first day I met him. My cheeks were wind-chapped and pink, my scarf damp with melted snow. The scent of leather and cedar sparked my senses even then. He was the kind of person whose absence was felt the moment he left the room. A flame extinguished. And I was completely drawn to that flame.

The story was incomplete, but I devoured every page. The eldest son of a large family. An officer in the British army. He'd grown up by the sea. He worked hard, and had never been in love. That infectious laugh of his wasn't simply for show. He loved life, completely infatuated with living every moment to the fullest.

And my name. *Naomi Adelman*, there in neatly-written black ink. *His wife, Naomi.*

I had lived countless lives and never considered what it would be like to be loved. I'd given love freely, even when it was not wanted. In truth I was most desperate not to love, but to *be* loved.

And Stephen was love like I'd never known. Like the very thought of him ripped the breath from my lungs. Before this, all I'd known was the whisper of my name off my mother's lips, the absent smile of my youngest brother, the proud sparkle in my father's eyes. But that was before. All I'd known until Stephen was darkness. Darkness and regrets and broken promises. Endless memories of every mistake I'd made.

But with Stephen there was happiness. For eight years and seventy-five days, I knew joy and warmth amongst the suffering my uncle had wrought upon my life.

I should have known it was too good to last.

My old rooms in the *Athenaeum* sat nestled in a tower atop a long set of winding steps. I fumbled with the lock on the wardrobe in the corner of the room. I shoved open the doors, combing through dozens of copies of books I'd hidden away. *Balshasar, Erisichthon, Edana, Athene, Talitha, Caedmon.* I paused as I combed through the books of my siblings' first lives. There at the end. *Stephen Lawrence.*

I'd read every page of his life. I knew though we'd never have children, our lives would be whole and content. I knew our arguments would be few and our love-making plentiful. I knew that I'd go before him in this life and he would never love again. He'd die an old man, in his sleep, with a smile on his lips and head filled with dreams.

I *knew* this was not his time.

But as my fingers flipped through each page, they came to an abrupt halt just halfway through the once-full pages.

14 June, 1944

He sits in a medical tent in Normandy, France, suffering from a gunshot wound. The camps do not have the sufficient staff, and he sends them to care for more critically wounded soldiers from his unit. He barely feels the pain as others scream out for their mothers, for wives they'll likely never see again. Stephen lies quietly, his hand pressed to the letter he has yet to send beneath the uniform jacket soaked in blood. He'll ask someone to send it for him; he doesn't like to keep his wife waiting. He's cold, shivering in the cot as he pulls the picture from his jacket pocket and smiles. He whispers, "Naomi" before his eyes grow heavy. On his lips, a smile remains, and he fades into the darkness. Thus ends the life of Stephen Alexander Lawrence II.

Again and again I read the words, so cold, so short.

"No," I whispered. "This isn't how it ends."

"You aren't supposed to have that."

Adeeba's words were soft. She didn't scold me, but still the anger rose in my veins as I spun to face her.

"This *isn't* how it ends!" I shouted. "He dies as an old man, at peace and in his sleep. Not over there in one of Tyr's bloody wars!"

Adeeba's eyes widened. I hadn't screamed at her since the beginning, since my mother's lifeless body lay in my father's arms. Since I ripped the memories from their grasp as they pulled her soul away.

Knees shaking, I gripped the brass frame of my childhood bed. I pressed the book to my chest, holding the remnants of Stephen's life against the place where my heart ripped into shreds. Tears spilled over dust-stained cheeks.

"It *is* the end, Mnemosyne," Penn said from the doorway. "I am sorry. But it is done."

"It cannot be done!" I pleaded, turning back to Adeeba. "You told me what was written *must* come to pass! You *told* me that what is done cannot be undone! He was supposed to live!"

"The revision was not my decision," insisted Adeeba, stepping closer. I shoved her hand away.

"Whose decision was it?! What did he do to deserve this? He was good!"

Adeeba pressed her hands to my cheeks. This time, I did not push them away. She pressed her forehead to mine. "*You* are good, my child. We do not choose our fates, not even me. I simply record the will of the gods."

"Who?" I asked again, my hands encircling her wrists. "Who changed it?"

Adeeba's gaze fell from mine. It was the only answer I needed.

"Mnemosyne," a third voice interrupted.

Danoma entered the room, long dark hair curled and pinned. Always beautiful, but for the first time since I'd be exiled to this place, she didn't smile. No playful smirk on her lips, no twinkle of challenge in her eyes. She grabbed my hand.

"Come," she said. "Before it is too late."

The book slipped from my grasp, falling with a loud thump to the stone floor. Danoma's plum heels echoed off stone walls as she led me down the dim corridors. At the end of the hall, an imposing red door called to me.

My steps slowed and then halted as I stared up at the intricately carved wood.

I'd never been allowed in this wing of the *Athenaeum*, never allowed to see what secrets the Fates kept locked away.

"What's in there?"

Danoma's smile returned. Tender and warm like Adeeba's.

"It is where they come...the souls...after," she explained. "Your father used to bring them here, before. But as *Death* no longer abides the will of the gods, the task has fallen to me."

A beat. A hard and deliberate thump beneath the silent cavern of my chest leapt to life. I reached for the doorknob. Penn's hand closed over mine.

"You mustn't ever come here without us," said Penn from behind me. "This isn't like the books you stole, Mnemosyne. You must promise."

Promise me, Mnemosyne, came my mother's desperate whisper.

All I could do was nod. I would have agreed to anything in that moment. What was one more broken promise?

Danoma pressed her fingers to the red paint. "It appears as the place they loved most. It brings them comfort to be somewhere familiar."

The door swung open to reveal my Shoreditch flat. The scent of sugared cakes and balsam filled the air, the crackling pop of a fire at the hearth. A sob escaped my lungs when I saw him sitting in his chair. He stood, his long legs crossing the room in a few mere steps as he lifted me from the ground and into his arms.

"My love," he breathed against my hair.

I couldn't form words. Not one single word as he held me there. My fingers dug into his coat and inhaled that familiar cedar scent. He lowered me slowly, letting my soiled boots touch the rug his mother had bought us when we moved last spring.

"I'm so sorry," I managed between strangled cries.

He pulled my face from his shoulder, pressing his thumbs beneath my eyes and wiping the tears. They were quickly replaced by more.

"When you told me of this place, I had no idea." Stephen motioned to the room around them. Everything exactly as I remembered at Christmas. The last time I'd seen him.

"This wasn't supposed to happen," I said. "You were supposed to..."

"Mnemosyne," Adeeba warned.

These secrets weren't meant for mortals. Stephen already knew more than he was meant to.

"It doesn't matter now," said Stephen. "I am just glad you are here so I can be with you." His calloused hands laced between mine. "So I can feel you one last time."

I shook my head. This couldn't be the last time. No – wouldn't.

"This is a mistake," I whispered. "I wanted more time."

Stephen pulled me against him. I gazed up into his warm eyes, endless pools of dark brown wonder. "I would not trade anything for the time I had with you. Every moment with you, Naomi, has been pure joy."

"You and I...this..." I motioned to the silver tether that hung between us. "I have waited centuries for you. How can I say goodbye now?"

A heavy sigh poured from his lungs, and he pressed his forehead down to mine. "It is not goodbye, my love. My soul will always find yours. I could never forget you."

But you will, I wanted to scream. I glanced at the teapot in Penn's hands as she watched from the corner of our living room. One sip, and every memory of this life would dissipate into nothing. Our tether would be severed, and he would be readied for his next life. Whenever that would be.

Like we'd never happened. How could a love like ours simply be erased into nothing? Our love belonged in the stars, written for all eternity. Not a footnote of fate.

"It is time," Adeeba's voice came.

My eyes widened, jolting to Stephen's face. I was cursed with memories, and yet I searched his face with a ferocious hunger that devoured every detail as if I might forget him the moment he was ripped from me. The crook in his thick brows, the scar on his chin, the hidden smile in the corner of his lips.

I pressed mine to his, the taste of salt on my tongue as he deepened our kiss. His hands tangled in my hair, pulling the already tangled mass of chestnut curls around his fingers. There was no place for time in that moment. I had no recollection of where or when, only that he and I existed there as one.

Danoma cleared her throat. I could have killed her had I known how.

"I love you," I gasped against his lips.

"And I you, always."

"I will find you."

That smile. "You promise?" he asked.

"I promise."

I hoped it sounded like a comforting lie, that my aunts would not recognize the determined ache in my voice. The same defiant rage that had flowed through my veins the night they'd taken my mother.

Penn poured the liquid into a teacup from the set on the mantle. His favorite cup with the chip in the handle. His eyes never left mine as he sipped, every memory draining from his eyes. And my hand never left his, letting each of those memories flood into me where they would stay until I could fix this.

Until I could find him again.

My eyes darted to the floor as Danoma pulled Stephen away, ushering him towards the door. I didn't want to see him look at me as a stranger, as if we'd never met. When we were alone, Adeeba stepped towards me, pulling a pair of gold scissors from her coat pocket. My hand jerked to the tether at my abdomen.

"No." It came out as a strangled sob as I dropped to my knees. "Aunt, please."

"I'm sorry, child. It must be done."

"But how..." I gasped for air. "How will I find him without it?"

I looked to Penn. I'd seen her tether souls countless times.

"That's not how it works, Mnemosyne," she answered. "Just like what Adeeba writes on those pages, it is not our decision. I do not choose who is tethered. You do not choose."

But we belong together, my soul cried.

"In this life, yes," Penn replied to my internal plea. "But maybe not the next. It is up to the gods."

The gods. It was *because* of them that he died.

"Then why tether us at all?" I demanded. "Why allow such joy if it was to be so callously ripped away?"

Penn's eyes fell.

Because that was the point. Because the gods did not want me to have joy. None of my family.

And I knew one god who relished in our misery most.

<small>THERE WAS</small> a lounge in the *Athenaeum* where Penn kept her favorite whiskey. She didn't like to share, but she couldn't deny the gods their spoils.

I found Tyr sitting next to the fire, a cigarette hanging lazily between his fingers and a tall pour of whiskey in the crystal glass against his lips. The air shifted when I stepped through the door, still and patient as if the *Athenaeum* held its breath.

The leather armchair creaked as he shifted, the smugness permeating from my uncle's vicious smile.

"Gods, you look awful, *Thana.*"

I hated that name.

I crossed the room and swung my arm back but before I could release it to wipe the smirk from his lips he was on his feet, hand around my wrist.

"Tsk tsk, niece, play nice."

"How could you?" I ground out from my clenched teeth. "He was an innocent."

"What does innocence have to do with it?" he asked, a wrinkle between his brows. "If the gods cared for innocence, then we wouldn't be here."

"He was supposed to live!"

"Yes, a mistake it seems. Sneaky Adeeba. She'll have to answer for that little oversight. Did you truly think the gods would allow you such peace after your great insult?"

"I bear my sins again and again. I have spent centuries enduring the misery you and the other Furies have wrought. When will it be enough?"

"When you relinquish what you stole," he hissed. "It was your greed that cursed you. Your reluctance to abide the gods' will. When you sink to your knees and beg for forgiveness before the authority that allows you to breathe, then perhaps it will be enough."

Promise me, Mnemosyne, my mother whispered in the back of my mind. *Salt and wind brushed against my face as Tyr stood over my mother's lifeless body. Taunting eyes and that vicious smirk.* My father's fury rushed through my veins, but tears spilled down my cheeks.

"I took what did not belong to them. What *they* stole from *me.*"

Another laugh, another sickening jeer. "You are weak, *Thana.* Just like your father. To love a mortal is a god's greatest sin. Have you still not learned that? Had you been more like your sister, Athene, perhaps your man would still—"

I cut his words off with my hand to his throat. I'd never known anger like this. Never felt the rising heat of pure wrath that had belonged to my sister until now. I slammed Tyr against the bookshelf.

He was taller, stronger. He'd never expect such rage from me. Not from *Thana*. Death's daughter was weak like her father, he'd said it himself. Quick to tears, not to anger.

But in time he'd forgotten what *Death* could do. I had not.

I remembered everything.

"Stay away from my family," I hissed in a voice I didn't recognize. "Stay away from Athene, or I promise you I will spend every minute of my eternity dedicated to your misery."

Surprise turned to amusement, and his silver eyes burned bright.

"Do you think it wise to threaten me, *Mnemosyne*?" My true name off of his lips stoked the fire within me. "You think you suffer now? Wait until you see what hell I will unleash upon you."

I squeezed harder—not for the pain, but to find what my mind so desperately searched for. I could feel every single golden thread of the Fury's life within my grasp. Every moment in time, every cruel and calculating move he'd ever made. Every life he'd ended, every family he'd torn apart, every society he'd brought to ruin.

And the mortal he'd loved.

My quivering lips quirked at the corners.

"There," I gasped, my lungs strained. "I did not think it was possible for someone like you to love."

"I..." he stuttered, eyes wide as I pressed the thread harder, my sharp nails digging into the golden string that tied this memory to the cage where he'd hidden it.

"Leave Athene alone, or I will take this memory from you this very instant. It would be a shame. He is *exquisite*."

For the first time, I saw fear flash behind my uncle's eyes.

"Then again, as you said. To love a mortal is a god's greatest sin. Perhaps relieving you of this memory is for the best."

I dug my nail into the thread again, and his hand flew to my wrist.

"Don't!"

"Leave them alone," I instructed again, my chin high, voice steady. "Swear it."

Athene didn't need my protection. None of them did. Still the weight of my promise to my mother hung heavy across my shoulders.

"I swear," he grumbled, defeated.

My hands shook as I released him, backing away as the fury inside of me dissolved into nothingness. I waited for the ache of Stephen's loss to return, but I was left only with a flood of numbness.

This was better, I thought. Better than the pain and the tears. Better than the rage and the anger. I had always believed it was too simple, too lazy to take everything away when you could at least have the good. But as Stephen's smile burned into my mind, I thought for a moment perhaps the good memories were just as terrible. Maybe my father had been right about that after all.

"You really are like him," Tyr whispered, adjusting the collar of his suit jacket, straightening his tie. "My brother was once someone to be feared. I saw him in your eyes just now. You could be a master of death with my help. No longer mastered *by* it."

He held his hand out in front of me, and I narrowed my eyes.

"I would rather live this cursed life forever."

Tyr scoffed. He tilted his head in a curt nod as he walked towards the door.

"Well, *Thana*, you just might get your wish."

～

PART III: THE TIES THAT BIND | *LONDON, PRESENT DAY*

Daniel. It sounded strange on my tongue, but I didn't care what he was called so long as it was him. I scoured the *Athenaeum* for his book, but the Fates must have known I'd look for it eventually, because it was nowhere to be found. I'd have to learn what I could the old-fashioned way.

The spotty wi-fi in my flat slowed my search. I would normally just use the computer back in my office, but the last thing I wanted was Penn or Danoma breathing down my back. I scrolled eagerly down the page of "Daniels" on the endless stream of social media profiles across the screen of my laptop. The bitter taste of disappointment lingered on the back of my throat.

None of them were *him*. None of them were *mine*.

Things were easier before. Long ago, when people rarely left their villages. It would have been easy enough to ask about a new face. Now I lived in a city with millions of faces. One of those faces belonged to Stephen. No, *Daniel*.

I conjured the memory of our encounter. *Slick streets and morning rain. Dark eyes and gloved hands. That same smile that had haunted me every night. But something else existed behind that smile. Wide eyes...a spark of familiarity, perhaps?*

I couldn't be sure.

I pulled the book from my bedside table, flipping through the pages. Wedged between love poems, a weathered photograph peeked out. My fingertips grazed over our faces. My simple wedding gown. Stephen's uniform, neatly pressed. It was the last picture I had left, the only one I'd kept from my last life. I'd clung to the physical memento as if the perfect recollection of our time together didn't fill me every moment of every day. Memories were clearer. The honey-sweet taste of our happiness achingly real. But the photograph was proof. Tangible and real.

Calliope nudged my foot, a persistent *meow* to remind me she hadn't been fed in the last twelve minutes.

"Not now, Cal," I muttered, squinting my eyes back at the profile photos splayed out on the screen in front of me.

No one familiar popped up. I don't know what I expected. Not everyone used social media. I'd never been particularly fond of it, but created an account for the sole purpose of keeping track of my siblings in our most recent lives. Most people overshared, too many pictures, long-winded rants, or – the worst of it – mind-numbingly dull videos I'd never fully understood.

Now the world was oversaturated in content, making Daniel a needle in a haystack.

I pinched the bridge of my nose.

Just my luck.

A soft *ding* of a notification pulled my attention to my mobile. An email from the curator of a new art gallery in the Shoreditch area. I'd met Iseul in New York last spring. One of my latest attempts to disconnect from the world for a few weeks. The experiment had been an utter failure. I could never disconnect from the memories. Not for long.

Naomi, the email read. *Thought of you when I saw this collection and wondered if you'd be interested. I remembered your exquisite taste, and I think this artist is going to be something special. I'll reserve a ticket at the door. Hope you can make it. x Iseul*

My eyes darted to my closet.

A strappy silk piece hung delicately on the back of the door. Waiting. Wanting.

But Daniel was waiting for me too. Somewhere, amongst a sea of selfies, his brown eyes beckoned me. Taunted me to find him.

And I'd promised Stephen I would.

I glanced at the email again.

Perhaps it would be my lucky night after all.

❧

I ARRIVED an hour after the gallery opened. There was no use in arriving early when the person you were looking for was known to be fashionably late. I checked my coat, my exposed skin welcoming the warmth of the artificial heat as I stepped through the door. Champagne-colored silk hung from thin straps over my shoulders. A low dip in the dress exposed the milk-white flesh of my back. The will-call attendant stumbled over her words as she handed me my ticket, eyes wide, mouth agape. I flashed a polite smile, blood red lips raised at the corners.

It was not the same as love, but I appreciated the admiration nonetheless. I spent most nights alone with only the ghost of my past lives as company. I was desperate for something real, like the hidden photograph on my bedside table.

At the center of the room, a large painting pulled at my attention. I pulled a flute of champagne to my lips, memorizing every detailed brushstroke. Bubbles fizzed over my tongue, diluting the agony permeating from the image splayed out across the canvas. Two figures, tangled in thin strokes of red—a thread. Bound like the silver tether that tugged beneath my bones. The sharp curves of their bodies as they clung to one another was an all-too-familiar pain.

Whispers filled the room, prying my gaze from the painting.

Strangers stared, expressions of wonder as their greedy eyes took their fill. But not at me. Every eye in the room was trained on *him*.

"Mnemosyne. Timeless as ever," a warm voice purred from behind me, inviting as fine Italian wine.

I spun around, taking in the dark, discerning eyes that had evaded me for centuries.

"We'll call him Balshasar," my mother's voice hummed over the crashing waves. "You're a big sister now, Mnemosyne. You must always look out for your brother."

Another broken promise.

Truth be told, I'd tried everything I could to keep it. To watch over my brother, Death's second-born. But my first life had been a series of missteps. Choices and sacrifices to save my family, and in return, I'd only brought them pain. I didn't blame him for wanting nothing to do with me.

Waves crashed and the stars danced. Balshasar's small fingers tangled with mine as he stared up at the sky and laughed. "Tell me another story, Mimi!" Balshasar begged. "One with a happy ending."

Now he stood before me as Marcello Corrente, a faint hint of a smile on his lips and lifetimes of unspoken words in his eyes. At his side, a man brimming with confidence grinned. Their fingers locked together, a silver tether hanging between them.

"Marcello," I whispered, my voice strained.

He cleared his throat, shifting his feet and straightening his back. He was the picture of elegance, but beneath the leather Bontonis and Armani suit, I saw the spark of my brother's apprehension.

My heart sank. Still strangers, after all this time.

"You like the painting?" he asked, eyes darting up at the piece behind me. "I had it commissioned. The artist is up and coming. I discovered him on the streets of *Firenze*."

The man at Marcello's side quirked his brow.

"*We* discovered him. He wouldn't have caught your eye if I hadn't suggested that little detour."

A laugh poured from my brother's throat. A sound that had lived solely in my memory for centuries.

"Luca is always taking credit for my good eye."

"And Marcello is always taking credit for sheer luck."

My lips curved into a smile.

"Some things never change," I whispered.

"We all change, Mnemosyne." The amusement in his voice faded. "It's just you that hasn't."

"Marcello," Luca muttered under his breath.

My hand flew up at the same time as my brother's.

"It's okay. Let him finish," I urged.

Marcello sighed. "I don't want to drudge up the past. That's your specialty." His words lanced the shattered remnants of my heart. "We've all made mistakes. But it's time to move on."

Coming here was a mistake. A desperate whim I had no right to indulge. I stood there before Marcello's gaze, his eyes searching mine, and I hoped he couldn't see the anguish buried beneath my smile.

"I just–" My voice broke. "I wanted to protect the family. All of you."

His eyes softened. "You don't have to protect us anymore." He turned to Luca. "I've found my happy ending."

Happy ending. Panic rose in my chest. It couldn't end like this. On the tips of my fingers, energy pulsed. Remnants of a moment I'd clung to since the beginning. Tentatively, I reached up, placing my palm against my brother's cheek. He flinched at the touch, eyes widening. I swallowed the heavy lump in my throat.

A breath of summer air kissed my cheeks. Seafoam danced across my feet as they slowly sank in layers of wet sand. Balshasar popped out from beneath the water, dodging incoming waves as laughter filled the air.

"Mimi, come in!" my brother shouted, begging me to heed the ocean's call.

My feet sat frozen in place, my gut churning as the waves crested and fell, bursting into foam across the shore. It looked deep. Too deep. What if I–

"Don't be scared! I'll protect you," Balshasar promised.

I took a deep breath. Legs shaking, I swallowed my salt-stained doubts, and compelled myself forward. The waist-deep water chilled my bones, stealing my breath as I walked slowly out to meet him. Wave upon wave chased me, daring me to go further. Again Balshasar bellowed my nickname, urging me to find him.

Another wave, far too large to escape, swallowed me whole. I panicked, my heart racing as I flipped and turned, tangled inside the tumultuous wave. I reached out, clawing for the surface. A hand wrapped around mine, pulling me up until I tasted air in my lungs.

Fear contorted my features, my heart racing against my ribcage.

But as Balshasar met me with a toothy smile, tranquil bliss flooded my veins.

Marcello's eyes danced, his fingers sliding over mine where they rested on his cheek. The finality of an unspoken goodbye lingered between us. Words died on the tip of my tongue, superfluous in that moment. With a soft smile and the whisper of a memory long-passed, I turned to leave.

"Mnemosyne," he said quickly.

I glanced over my shoulder. He shifted again, but the composed mask did not return. Instead, the rawness of my brother's emotions illuminated his features.

"I have a gift for you too," he said, nodding towards the wall across the room.

My eyes followed, snagging on a large painting of a woman compiled of seafoam and stars. But it wasn't the painting that caught my eye, nor the immediate kindredness that flooded my veins at her likeness.

Instead, my eyes were glued to the figure standing in front of it and the silver tether taut between us. Breath ripped from my lungs. I propelled my shaking legs forward. Like that day at the sea, my ankles wobbled. Halfway across the room, I glanced back at Marcello. He didn't speak, but raised his glass of champagne in a silent toast.

Don't be scared, Mimi.

I nodded, raising my glass as well, before I spun back towards the painting and stepped forward. Ready for the plunge.

The patter of my heels paused at his side. Knees quivering, I inhaled the familiar cedar and leather scent that pooled around him. His gaze lingered over the painting, leaning in as if inspecting the woman beneath every brushstroke. Marcello's name sat on a placard next to the canvas, beneath the artist's and the date of commission.

Memories of Salt & Stars

An ache in my throat returned.

"There's something familiar about her," came Daniel's voice as he studied the figure.

"Oh?" I asked, facing him. "You know her?"

"No, it's not that. Like a feeling or..." He turned to face me. "A dream." A long pause. "Oh...it's you."

Remember me.

"Brick Lane! That's right." The fakeness clawed at my pride. "You're—"

"Not Stephen," he reminded.

A pang in the pit of my stomach. *Not* Stephen.

"Of course. It was—" I paused for effect. As if his name hadn't preoccupied my last seven days of obsession. "Daniel," I spoke, the word still foreign on my tongue.

"Yes, Daniel Ansari," he added.

Ansari. It would shorten my search later.

"I noticed you're standing on your own. A drastic improvement over our last encounter."

Still charming. Stephen was in there somewhere. I would find him.

"Yes, I've managed well enough. I hope you made it to your new job on time?"

"Yes, thanks! First day at the University. I didn't want to be late to the lecture."

"You're a faculty at the University?" I asked. Stephen never went to university, although he thought about enrolling after the war.

Daniel nodded. "I'm in the art department." I shifted, straining to focus as yet another difference between Daniel and Stephen sprang to the surface. "In fact, I dragged some of my students to the gala." He craned his neck around, eyes darting across the room for familiar faces. "They're around here somewhere. Probably consuming more free champagne than art."

"Do you know the artist?" I asked.

"No, but I saw the collection was commissioned by Marcello Corrente. His collections have always been the envy of every fine art historian around. But recently he's been branching out. Sharing more with us *mere* mortals. I count myself lucky to even get a glimpse of it."

I swallowed a chuckle. If he only knew. I pointed to the painted figure.

"So, you said she felt like dream?"

Remember me.

His grin widened, white teeth exposed. He combed his fingers through the curls of his dark hair.

"It's strange. All of these pieces are almost connected, like pieces of memories splayed out across a canvas. But this one…it's hard to explain dreams. When I look up at her, I recognize that look."

"The sorrow?" I asked, a pang in my chest as I gazed over her seafoam tears, trailing her face.

"Sorrow?" he asked, then shook his head. "No, I think it's more like…longing. A deep and profound want."

My breath caught in my lungs.

Centuries of want filled my memories. The empty cavern in my chest.

"What do you think she longs for?" I asked, staring up at her.

What did *I* long for? Stephen? My mother?

"Peace," he said. "Look at the arch there in her shoulders. It's like she carries the weight of the world with her but refuses to give in."

"Maybe her work isn't done. Maybe the world needs her."

Daniel shrugged, sipping his champagne. A wide smile spread over his face. Not Stephen's smile, but a nice smile all the same. "Maybe the world can fuck off."

If it were only that easy.

"Dr. Ansari," a loud young voice interrupted. Daniel pivoted towards who I could only presume was one of his students standing across the room, waving. "The others and I had some questions about the assignment."

Several guests turned, their eyes narrowing on the student. Daniel pressed his fingers to his lips, shaking his head.

"Can't take them anywhere," joked Daniel. He spun back around. "Oh…wait. I didn't catch your name earlier."

I reached out, offering my hand. He fumbled with his glass,

swapping it to his left hand and wiping the condensation from his hand to his blazer before gripping mine. His fingers wrapped around my hand, his grip firm but lacking the rough calluses of his previous life.

"Naomi Laurent."

Remember me.

"*Naomi*," came the breathy sigh in my memory. *Tangled limbs wrapped neatly by the fire. Balsam filled the air as the flickering flames illuminated the nearly decorated tree in the corner of the room. Leave could be revoked at any time, even at Christmas. Time wasted perfecting crimson bows and popcorn garlands no longer commanded my attention. Not nearly as much as naked flesh and whispered promises.*

Glass shattered. At my feet, the remnants of Daniel's champagne flute scattered across the marble floor. He stumbled back, eyes wide as our hands separated. I knelt down, slowly grabbing the glass stem. A hush settled over the crowd, all eyes analyzing the pair of idiots who'd ruined the *vibe*.

Daniel sunk down to his knees, cursing under his breath as glass pierced his palms.

"Careful!" I hissed, reaching out for his hand but he flinched, pulling it away.

Our eyes met again, this time his dark eyes filled with fear. He stepped backward, and my stomach lurched as the tether stretched.

A staff member rushed over, ushering us away from the jagged shards and sweeping up the remains of Daniel's party foul. Another staff member insisted on inspecting Daniel's hand, but again he pulled it away.

"I'm fine," he said, a resigned sigh following his lie. "I guess I'm the clumsy one now."

I offered a laugh. Forced. Something not right about it, but I swallowed the doubt and rose to my feet.

A phone buzzed somewhere beneath his blazer. Two, then three times before he reached for it, the agitation in his brows softening as he glanced down at the screen.

"Hello, love."

Two simple words, and yet it might as well have been a punch to the gut. The wind knocked from my lungs. I forgot how to breathe. All sound dissolved away as a quirk in his lips appeared, that small smile I recognized better than anyone. But this one wasn't for me.

Daniel gazed at his watch.

"Shouldn't be but another hour. I had about twelve students show up and we're just getting into the meat of things," he said. "What do you say I pick up a bottle of that wine you like on my way home?" A warm laugh. "Yes and the cake. I promise."

I will find you. I promise.

Daniel held his hand up over the receiver. "Sorry, I should get going. Nice chatting with you."

A *lie*. The polite courtesy of the words left a cold void in my chest, and I slid my fingers over my gut as the silver thread twisted and tangled deep inside of me. With each step, agony dug her clutches into me. The gods were truly cruel.

"Naughty Mnemosyne," came an amused purr at my back.

Over my shoulder, Danoma parted the crowd. Dripping in emerald silk, she demanded every gaze in the room. Everyone followed the sensual sway of her hips as she approached me. Dark, elegant curls hung neatly over her collarbone and down her back.

She tapped her cane against the marble floor, a rhythmic thrumming that matched the cadence of her stilettos. Her black polished fingers brushed lazily over the glass bauble at the top. Her eyes drifted to Daniel's retreating form, then back to me. With an arch in her brow and the shake of her head, she let out a sigh.

"You weren't supposed to find him again. I should have known you'd manage somehow. You've always been the resourceful one."

I straightened, facing her with my heart pounding.

Her gaze locked with the silver thread hanging from my abdomen. Her smile faded, grip tightening around the glass bauble, and her jaw clenched.

"*What* have you done?"

~

PART IV: L'ENFANT SANS MÈRE DU HAVRE | *LE HAVRE, 1999*

SUMMER AFTERNOONS soaked the streets of Le Havre. Thunder bellowed from heavy clouds and tangled in the howling gusts, the gods taunting me.

The church lobby sat empty, aside from Sœur Dubeau. She lowered her glasses, casting a disapproving scowl in my direction. I ignored her, scribbling my notes down in the weathered notebook in my lap. The tapping of her sensible black oxfords distracted my thoughts, muddled the images I fought to conjure.

Being a child was the worst part of the reincarnation.

The body, the thoughts and memories coming back in unpredictable spurts. The loss.

My mind shifted to *Maman* and *Papa*. I let out a long, broken breath.

Nous t'aimons, Nadine.

Another city by the sea. Another mother with salt-stained lips and a smile more radiant than sunshine.

Another family lost. I told myself I wouldn't get attached to the people who brought my new form into this world. But the Laurents were kind parents. Loving and warm, and the gods could not abide that.

Not for me.

Promise me, Mnemosyne. The voice crashed through my mind, memories lurching to the surface as *Maman's* features slipped into a pair of seafoam and sage eyes that haunted my dreams. Tears sprang to my eyes, blurring my vision.

Alone, again. I wasn't foolish enough to long for peace. Peace was for daughters who kept their promises, for sisters who protected their siblings from vengeful gods. Peace, as it seemed, was for everyone but me.

I glanced down at the notebook on my lap, tracing my fingers around the scribbled names of my siblings. Had they found peace?

I thought of Caedmon...no, not Caedmon anymore. *Cardan.* He was the youngest, the one our mother had protected most. I thought I was protecting him too. I'd stolen from each of them, hoping in doing so I could keep my promise to our mother. But at what cost? Here I was centuries of lives later, still separated by my sins. Still desperately alone.

The heavy wood door creaked, a figure pushing it open as she peered around the corner. Water dribbled onto the marble floors as she folded her umbrella. Sœur Dubeau's incessant tapping ceased. Her posture straightened and she snapped her fingers at me to straighten as well. Once again, the obedient daughter abided her demands.

The figure peeled back the hood of her elegant raincoat. It had been years, but Adeeba hadn't aged a day. A warm, maternal smile turned up the corners of her lips as she spotted me in the corner. She'd worn that same smile the day we'd met.

"*Bonjour, Madame,*" Dubeau said, her demeanor shifting to the ever attentive and kind headmistress of the orphanage that she most certainly wasn't. "*Comment puis-je vous aider?*"

"Good afternoon. We spoke on the phone yesterday. My sister came earlier this week to fill out paperwork regarding Nadine Laurent. I was told I could come today to collect her."

"*Ah oui,*" Dubeau replied, her amusement fading. "*Viens ici, Nadine,*" she commanded.

I slammed the notebook shut, letting out a heavy breath as my small legs carried me across the lobby.

"Why you would want her, I do not know. She is a most peculiar child," the woman whispered in her best English.

Adeeba's soft grin never faltered.

"My sisters and I are peculiar as well. We think she will be the perfect fit with our family."

Once outside on the sidewalk, we stood in silence, huddled

beneath Adeeba's umbrella and waiting for cars to pass. It was twelve blocks to the *Athenaeum* in this city. I'd counted every day since the memories came back. Most times it was dread in the pit of my stomach, knowing they'd come for me. A start to the same cycle from which I could never escape. But this time felt different.

Rain pattered heavily over the umbrella. I tilted my head upwards, gazing at the woman I'd known for centuries, and something swirled in the pit of my stomach. I'd been a young woman when the gods cursed me to live amongst the Fates. Do their bidding. I'd been resentful, angry. And not just in the first life. Many lives. Many lives filled to the brim with bitter contempt between us.

And yet in every life, Adeeba waited for me. Always ready to take me to the *Athenaeum*. Always there to take me *home*.

I'd never called it home before. It had always been my cage. But memories told a different story. In my last life I'd died an old woman. Weak with age and filled with regrets. I never recovered after Stephen. Years of searching and hoping, trying to correct my past sins, only making them worse.

My weathered hands slipped into Adeeba's. A light squeeze. A kiss brushed across my forehead. Penn's reluctant smile. A whiff of Danoma's perfume.

They were always with me at the end. When no one else was.

A soft sigh poured from my lungs.

"We've missed you too, Mnemosyne."

Tears stung my eyes again. Her hand squeezed mine.

"Penn will never admit it, but she's been lonely with only us for company."

"You mean she's tired of having to do my work?"

Adeeba's laugh filled the air. She stroked my hair, her fingers twisting in the raven ringlets that cascaded down my back. She pulled a ribbon from her jacket pocket. My heart swelled, ready to burst.

My mother's light humming filled my ears. Sea salt sprayed the hem of my dress as she tied a ribbon at the end of my braid and placed it over my shoulder. *"I am thankful for you, my sweet Mnemosyne. I pray you will always know my love."*

My mother's voice echoed as I stared down at the tattered bit of ribbon. Adeeba pulled my hair back, tying it into a delicate bow.

My small hand squeezed the Fate's.

"I've missed you too," I whispered.

MY HEAVY EYELIDS drooped late into the night after we returned to the *Athenaeum*. I sat at the door listening for the Aunts' laughter before slipping out into the empty halls. Cold marble stung my bare feet as I tiptoed through the corridors. My small feet maneuvered easily in and out of rooms and solitary hallways until I came to that same familiar door.

It looked bigger from my height, more formidable than before. I pressed my hand to the handle, a warning pulsing from the cold metal against my flesh. I had no idea what awaited me this time, only that it wasn't Stephen. I looked down at my enclosed hand, spreading my fingers to reveal a glowing silver thread.

Something so pure that could bind two souls together was not of this world, that much I knew. It had taken me most of my previous life, and countless glasses of whiskey, to convince Penn to tell me where she'd learned how to make a tether. Through multiple realms and multiple doors of the *Athenaeum*, I finally tracked down a magi tailor, like Penn, who could fabricate something so precious.

Selennia, a land teeming with magic. Real magic. It was both familiar and strange, a place I'd never been but I knew like the back of my hand. I'd scoured my mother's memories, the ones I clung to, replayed again and again as if there was something written in that first life that would be the answer to it all. Through her eyes, everything glittered. Every blissful moment of love she felt for my father and my siblings. I'd lived them all.

A young woman stood beneath an aching willow tree. She pressed her hands to a young man, his sullen eyes burned bright with joy and love.

Death smiled.

And between them, a silver tether draped over their hands by an elderly magi woman.

I stared down at my own tether, imbued with every memory I'd stolen from Stephen the night he'd walked through the gate.

Every moment with you has been pure joy, he'd said, but that wasn't true. Together we were happy, but every life had its moments. Hard times. Heartache and pain. My fingers closed over the thread in my hand. He would know none of it in this life, I swore. Only the good.

I reached for the ornate door's handle, wrapping my small fingers around it—and paused.

Penn's warning clawed at the back of my mind. *You must never come here without us.* From somewhere beneath the door, the heavenly scent of balsam filled my nostrils. *Mnemosyne, you must promise.*

I turned the knob.

Some promises were worth breaking.

PART V: IT FEELS LIKE A LIE | *LONDON, PRESENT DAY*

Danoma's pacing echoed through the *Athenaeum's* courtyard. Stone pillars at the center of the library, tangled with vines and flowers always in bloom. Moonlight leaked through, glittering across the glass bauble of her cane. Her dark knuckles paled as her grip tightened around it, her piercing gaze washing over me.

"How did you do this?" she said, motioning to the tether at my abdomen but then quickly held up her hand. "Actually, no. Don't tell me. I don't want to know."

Her disappointment washed over me. I'd been many things in many lives. A disappointment to many, to myself. But I'd never gotten used to the ache in the pit of my stomach. Another promise broken. But this one had been worth it, hadn't it?

"Aunt, please, I can explain."

Her eyes widened, and her stilettos came to an abrupt halt.

"*Explain*? Mnemosyne, what you have done has no excuse. You have tampered with fate. Not even Adeeba can protect you if the gods were to find out."

"*If?*" I asked.

"Just because they *can* see all doesn't mean they wish to." Danoma stepped close, peering down at the silver thread as she pulled back my coat. "You have to get rid of this. Right now, before it's too late."

I clutched my coat to my chest, fingers trembling.

"No," my feeble voice fought. "Do not take this from me. I beg of you. I've never once asked for anything."

"This is not just *anything*, Mnemosyne. This is a man's *life*!"

"But he is not just *any* man. Just because they all mean nothing to you doesn't mean they aren't important!"

Danoma's eyes narrowed.

"You think any of us chose to be here? That your family is the only one who has suffered?"

She wasn't wrong. I had seen suffering, a world of it in every century, every civilization drenched in agony. I had always assumed the Fates were part of that plan. The tools of the gods, alongside Famine, War, and Plague.

"Our sins brought us here too," she whispered, hearing my thoughts. "We 'do the gods' bidding' because that is our curse to bear. I've known loss you could never fathom. So please don't stand there preaching to me how unfairly you have been treated. You chose to stay like this. You're not a martyr, Mnemosyne. You're a coward."

I swallowed the lump in my throat.

"Danoma, I—"

She held up her hand, clearing her throat.

"No. This is about *that*." She pointed again to the tether. "You think that man is the same one you left behind in 1944?"

Hello, love. Again the words slammed at the back of my mind. Words for someone else. Words that should have been mine. My eyes slammed shut as I forced the memory from my mind.

"He's a shell of Stephen. Don't let your greed blind you. Even you can see that. Daniel has a life, one that you have stolen by meddling in things you do not understand."

Truth spilled out through Danoma's words, but that visceral need returned to me, the wound feral and fresh as if Tyr stood before me ripping Stephen away once again. I'd waited decades for him. How could I let him go without a fight?

"Please. Just give me more time."

Danoma stared at me, her head shaking slowly.

"Fix your mess, Mnemosyne. Before it's too late."

I WAITED for the answers in the bottom of my glass, hoping the third gin and tonic would succeed where the previous two had failed. I cursed the gods for binding me to the Fates, wishing instead for the fog of a mortal brain that could cloud the pulsing images of my previous lives. Each one littered with mistakes.

Instead I sat at the pub, stone cold sober and forced to relive Danoma's words over and over.

Daniel has a life.

How could he have a life when it wasn't with me? Hadn't he asked me to find him again? Hadn't I promised?

Some promises are worth breaking, my mind taunted, and I slammed the glass down on the counter of the bar.

"It won't get you drunk, but whiskey is the far superior drink," a bored voice said from beside me.

I tensed, gazing over my stiff shoulder to find Penn lighting a cigarette in a three-piece tweed suit, her legs crossed and eyebrow arched.

"Lovely," I scoffed. "Are you here to scold me too?"

"Yes," she admitted, directing the bartender towards the bottle of amber liquid on the top shelf. "But I have to say, I'm also a bit impressed. I spent most of my first life learning to create a tether. I didn't think you'd ever find another magi who could."

"I had to show the magi a memory of it because she was convinced it wasn't possible."

Something akin to pride swept over Penn's features.

"Ah, your mother's."

I nodded.

Windswept hair and eyes of sea and sage. A vow spoken in soft, giddy whispers. A smile on Death's face. A bond that would last lifetimes.

"That was the first tether I ever made," Penn mused, sipping her whiskey.

My eyes widened.

"But you..." words failed me. I'd seen the memory a thousand times...the elderly magi by the sea.

"Your mother saw me differently. Just as you do. Just like your siblings."

"But you work for the gods."

"And by making that tether I broke a vow. You're not the only one trying to atone for their sins."

Penn never broke the rules.

"Some are worth breaking." Her words taunted me. My words.

I'd broken my promise to Penn, to Danoma, to Adeeba. And here I was, the consequences laid bare before me. *Daniel has a life.*

"I didn't know," I whispered. "When I sought out his soul. When I attached the tether. I thought it would be like before. That we'd find each other again. What did I do wrong?"

Penn shook her head, taking a long drag from her cigarette and tapping the ashes into the crystal tray on the bartop.

"Who says you did it wrong?"

"He doesn't remember me."

"Because they aren't his memories," she whispered. "You gave him a life that wasn't his. To him, it's like...a dream." My brows furrowed. Penn let out a heavy sigh. "You didn't know Stephen before you'd met him, did you?"

"I think I'd have remembered."

"He had another life, another tether. Someone who wasn't you." A stab to my chest. "You sense the difference, don't you?"

"Was she..." the words turned to ash in my mouth. My sister's envy flooding my veins. "Was she meant to be his tether?"

Penn shook her head, signaling the bartender with a casual flick of her fingers.

"He wasn't meant to have a tether in this life. I don't always bind souls, it would take far too much time." She paused, eyes trained on the bartender as he slid a glass of her favorite whiskey in front of me. "If I'm being honest, I didn't tether him out of respect for you. I had a feeling you might find him again. I didn't want to cause you more pain."

I pulled the glass tentatively to my lips, allowing the sharp bite of spices and vanilla to drown out the shame.

"You knew I'd find him?"

"You are Death's daughter, even if you don't share the same affinity for good liquor. Erisichthon has that going for him, at least."

Another sip stung the back of my throat.

"Maybe you're right." I scoffed. "The others have all moved on. It's just the two of us left. Maybe that's how it's meant to be. I deserve to suffer for what I did to them. They all might have moved on sooner if I'd never meddled in their lives."

Stolen memories.

"Haven't you suffered enough?" asked Penn.

I gazed up at her, the question I'd asked Tyr long ago. I'd meant it then, my family had been through enough. But had I? None of us were innocent, perhaps me least of all.

I would rather live this cursed life forever, I'd told my uncle once. Maybe this was me getting that wish.

"Was it worth it?"

My eyes snapped up to Penn.

"Was what worth it?"

"That day, when you stole your mother's memories. Her soul was gone...why did you take them?"

Death and his bride sat together on the ridge overlooking the sea as the sky bled into reds, purples and pinks. The sun dipped low, the last whisper of twilight kissing the horizon. This was the place. This was where she wanted to start their family. By the sea and beneath the stars. Where the world could forget about them. Where they could be happy.

My mother's memory sprang tears from my eyes. The salty pools spilled down my cheeks. My heart ached for her, for that place by the sea. For the sound of her voice that felt forever out of reach.

"Mnemosyne," the woman whispered with a wide grin. She brushed her fingers over my eyes, small and dainty. I fit so delicately in the crook of her arm as she rocked me. Her sweet voice sang in a soft melody I could barely remember.

"I didn't want her to be forgotten." I wiped my eyes, smearing mascara across my cheeks. "She loved us so much, and when they came for her..." I paused, my eyes connecting with Penn's. "When *you* came for her, I couldn't let it all be for nothing. The life she lived was precious, and the gods wanted to erase her from existence."

Penn smothered the cigarette in the pile of ashes and set it aside. She slid her hand over my wrist.

A flash of a woman with dark skin and red paint over her eyelids grinned back at me. Grey curls peeked out from jet black hair. She pressed her hands to my face and smiled.

"That's my mother," Penn said. "I don't have your gifts, Mnemosyne, but I can see my mother's face every time I close my eyes. People live on in the memories of others. You don't need her memories to keep her spirit alive. She is alive in you, in your brothers and sisters. Each of you carries the flame of her within you. Here."

Penn placed her hand over her chest. She'd never been particularly sentimental but her words opened the floodgates in my heart as I clung desperately to my mother's memories. The images of each of us growing, taking our first steps, laughing together as a family. In her memories we were together. In her memories we were happy. It was all I had left of us.

Penn squeezed my arm.

"You have clung to the others and this cursed life for so long. But you don't have to bear that pain any longer. You were ready in your last life. Before Stephen. We wanted you to have a chance at love before you left. We had no idea–" Penn trailed off, clearing her throat.

"Stephen was–"

"A gift, Mnemosyne. The gods were displeased with us, but we wanted that for you. For you to find peace. It was a burden we were willing to bear. I had no idea Tyr would interfere."

My shoulders sank, a weight I'd carried for centuries bearing down on me. For centuries the gods had cursed me to live without the love I so desperately sought. Alone, without family. Penn had tethered Stephen's soul to mine. Adeeba had written us a beautiful life. Danoma ensured we had the chance to say goodbye.

This whole time I'd lived under the bitter assumption that he'd been stolen from me. But he'd been a gift I should have never had. He'd only been mine for a mere moment. Because of the Fates.

Nearly everything about Daniel had been wrong from the beginning. I'd been blinded by crooked smiles and cedar and leather. Blinded by the man I once loved. Greedy for a past that was now set in stone. Daniel had a life, and I'd ripped that from him.

On a selfish whim.

"Daniel deserves to be free," I whispered. "I have to give him his life back."

"Do you want us to be there?" Penn asked.

I shook my head. Danoma was right; this was my mess. I needed to do this alone.

"But when it's time to sever the–" My stomach plummeted at the reminder. "Will you be there? All of you?"

"Of course. We'll always be there for you. When you're ready."

SOMEWHERE BENEATH MY RIBS, the tether slackened.

I waited by the Thames, my breath dispersing out into the night air as I stood beneath the streetlamps. Snow dusted my hair and scarf. Soft and delicate snowflakes that melted as soon as they hit the stone walking path. I rubbed my gloved hands together, staring up at the grey sky and wishing for stars.

Cold, damp fields of grass pricked against my skin. Stephen pointed up towards the sky, and I let him tell me the names of every constellation I already knew. Beaming, he told me he'd read about them in a library book. Studied the stars and their stories. I couldn't tell him then that the stories I'd grown up with were different. That when I was a child, they had different names. It didn't matter. What difference did the name make when they still had the same effect?

Dread poured from my lungs as the tether's pressure disappeared. I turned, and Daniel stood beneath a bare tree, tangled branches silhouetted against the light of the street lamp.

"Naomi," he whispered.

A lump grew in my throat.

"Daniel," I replied.

He stepped closer, his brows creased. I offered a small smile, a poor consultation to the confusion brimming in his eyes.

"We have to stop meeting like this." A joke, a warm chuckle from him that accompanied the nervous fingers that sifted through his hair.

"I come here most nights. It's the only place in London that reminds me of home."

It wasn't entirely true. Home was the crash of waves and the sting of salt against my eyes. Home was a place I'd never been able to find no matter how many of my mother's memories I scoured.

But the river was Stephen. *The steady stream of water. Walking beneath dimly lit street lanterns and a light mist of rain.* Stephen was home when I'd had nothing left.

Daniel stood across from me, leaning against the stone railing. His eyes searched mine like they'd have the answers he couldn't bear to ask for.

"I've dreamt of this place," he said. "The same but different. You know how dreams can be." I nodded. More than anyone. "To be honest, I've dreamt of this place for years."

"The Thames?" I asked.

He shook his head.

"No. Well, yes, the Thames, but everything else here. Places I've never even been to. Streets that no longer look the same. It's like I'm dreaming of someone else's life. Maybe that sounds insane. I don't know. Have you ever had a dream so vivid that when you wake up there's a brief moment where you forget what's real?"

I swallowed. The agony hung heavy in his words.

"My dreams are complicated," I replied. "I spend more time wishing my dreams were real. When things were better. Happier."

"It only seems happier," he said.

I looked up, narrowing my eyes.

"What do you mean?"

"I have this dream sometimes, like I'm someone else and I live this life, this beautiful life with someone I love. And it's perfect. But when I wake up, something always strikes me."

My pulse raced.

"What?" The feeble word fell from my lips.

Daniel's gaze fell. "It feels like a lie."

A lump in my throat grew as I fought back the tears that stung my eyes.

"A lie?" I barely managed, lips quivering.

"No life could be that perfect. But in these dreams I'm always smiling. Always laughing. I can't imagine a life without hardships and pain."

"Sometimes the pain is too much," I attempted. An excuse. A lie I'd told myself over and over. "Don't you ever wish it would disappear?"

A genuine smile slid over his features as he shook his head.

"Sure. sometimes. But without the pain, how would I know how much joy there is in the happiest moments? Pain makes us human. The human experience is the true beauty of life. There is nothing more human than to suffer and to overcome that suffering."

My chest tightened, the tether between us strained. I placed my hand over my abdomen, but the ache persisted.

"What if we don't know how to overcome it?" I breathed, my voice knotted in a strangled sob.

"We don't always have to do that alone."

For centuries, I had been alone. Desperately searching for the family I'd left behind in my first life. I couldn't move on knowing they were out there, just alone as me. But as I stood there, consumed by Daniel's words, I recognized a truth I'd kept hidden deep inside of me.

A candle flickered in the small room. Three figures stood around the brass-framed bed. One of the women placed a bouquet of fresh flowers in the vase next to me. The other stood over me, stroking my white hair. I could barely muster a smile, and a youthful hand grasped my wrinkled fingers.

Not alone.

Adeeba, Penn, Danoma. Always waiting, always there at the end. Every time.

The tether stretched.

Daniel stepped back, checking his phone with his lips upturned at the corners.

Hello, love, he'd said before. His brown eyes lit up. A flash of Stephen appeared for the briefest moment. He had someone waiting for him. Someone who loved him just as much as I'd loved him a lifetime ago.

Daniel deserves to be free.

I closed the distance between us, my legs slow, heavy. I reached out, pulling the glove from my fingers and encircled his wrist with my bare hand. His eyes darted up, brows creased.

I opened my mouth to speak, to explain the sudden familiarity of my touch, but nothing came. What was I supposed to say to the man I loved? I'd promised I would find him in this life. Promised we'd be together. And yet here we stood on two separate paths. Daniel and Naomi.

No—Naomi was dead. I'd been too blind to let her be at peace. Naomi had lived her life.

It was time for Daniel to live his.

I sucked in a breath, swallowing the harrowing wail that accompanied the breaking of my heart as I searched for the threads in his mind. Pulling delicately at each familiar sliver of us that I'd delicately woven into his soul years ago.

The subtle brush of his fingers against mine as we walked along the Thames. The slow dance in the empty streets to the sound of rain pattering against cobblestone. The laughter pouring from his lungs as he carried me up three flights of stairs the time I'd sprained my ankle. The scent of sugar cookies and balsam. Our first kiss. Our last.

Every single memory spun itself around my shattered soul until all that was left was the strange indifference of a man who barely knew me at all.

And for the first time in centuries, I breathed the weight of the world out into the night air.

∿

PART VI: MAY WE MEET AGAIN | *SEASIDE BEHAVIORAL HOSPITAL, PRESENT DAY*

I summoned Death on a sunny winter day.

He waited patiently on a park bench outside the hospital where he worked. The overgrown garden sat forgotten, brown and lifeless from winter's lethal kiss. Fitting. Death surrounded by death.

The last time I'd seen him, he'd begged me to wipe away the memories haunting him. Visions of my mother. He'd never asked before, content in his own self-loathing. Something I'd once admonished him for, yet somehow—despite centuries of running in the opposite direction—I'd become just like him in the end.

Tyr had been right about one thing.

Now, something had changed. Dark circles hung under his eyes, his pale cheeks sunken in, but he didn't look quite as broken as before.

"Not sleeping again?" I asked.

He tilted his head, sullen eyes peering up at me with an unexpected softness. Relief? Perhaps I'd changed my mind, he might have wondered. Perhaps I was here to fix things.

I'd never been fond of his way of fixing. Not that my way had been much better. I'd learned that the hard way.

For a brief moment as I stared down at his broken eyes, temptation jolted at the tips of my fingers. If I took the misery from him, would he finally find peace?

"I've been reading too much," he replied, attempting a lopsided grin.

Adeeba mentioned she'd seen him in the *Athenaeum*. Scouring shelves. An unhealthy obsession that rivaled my own.

I sat down next to him. The old bench creaked under our weight, and we both let out a soft, nervous laugh.

"I guess it's got its limits. Only one sulking immortal per bench."

Joking was awkward. We'd never been particularly good at it. Too much tension, resentment. I'd harbored it for so long, I hardly remembered what it had been like before all of this.

Death stared down at the infant and smiled. Precious and delicate and small. She had her mother's heart-shaped mouth, but her eyes were dark, infinite pools that mirrored his own. "Thana is no name for something so sweet," he whispered, pressing his lips to my forehead.

"I'd be lying if I said I wasn't surprised to see you."

"I was just hoping for some company."

"Well, I'm afraid I'm not the best at the moment."

"At least you won't be alone," I offered.

We sat in silence. Birds chirping from the barren trees overhead. People passed and I watched each of them, the threads of their mortal lives hanging in the balance of this fickle world we lived in. An elderly man hugging a child. A woman cradling her son as they cried. Lives crashing and colliding around us as if we were of little consequence at all.

I'd been blind to it before, always thinking my significance was more than it was. That I'd somehow been responsible for it all. But the world would go on without me. People would continue to laugh and cry and there would be balance. I only hoped somewhere there would still be a fond memory of me from time to time.

As pathetic as it sounded, the fear of being forgotten weighed heavily on me. The end was so close, and yet a piece of me still clung to this world. As I looked at my father, suffocating under the weight of his own sins, I now suspected why.

He turned his head, his eyes gazing through me as if I was a child once again. His brows creased. "Something's different."

"I was going to say the same about you. It's been a while since I've seen...what is it? Hope?"

A smirk. "You could call it that."

I dropped my gaze to my hands, wringing the hem of my blouse. I reached out for his hand, for a whisper of comfort I'd long since abandoned.

"I'm leaving soon, Abba."

His back straightened. The fog cleared from his weary eyes.

"Can I see you again? Our meetings are always too short, and now that the others have moved on..." He paused, eyes dancing over mine. Realization slunk his shoulders. "Wait...when you say you're leaving?"

I nodded. "It's time."

A cascade of emotions flooded his features.

"But Mimi, you're so young."

I let out a soft laugh. "I'm thousands of years old. I've lived so many lives. And I'm tired."

He sat processing my words for a long moment, eyes searching as if there was something he might be able to say that would stop me. I could stay, wait for him to work out the mess that was his existence. Wait for him to finally find peace. But it would do no good. He didn't need me anymore. I had to trust that whatever that shift was would bring him down the path on his own, as it had led me.

"I've found peace, or something like it," I told him. "I've forgiven myself. I hope one day you can forgive yourself too. *She* would want that."

Tears sprang to his eyes, his lips quivering. He leaned forward, hiding his face in his hands, and I brushed my fingers over his back.

A woman stood by the sea, laughing as seafoam kissed the hem of her linen dress. The icy breath of wind rushed over her pink cheeks and she glanced over her shoulder. "Come, my love," she called, her arms waving in large sweeping motions as a figure smirked from the rocks nearby.

"Are you mad?!" he shouted. "It's freezing."

The woman rushed towards him, gripping his hands and pulling him to his feet. "Scared you'll catch your Death?" she teased.

A deep, resounding chuckle poured from his lungs. He followed her, his dark curls tangled from the wind. He hissed as the cold water rushed over his feet. The woman beamed, stroking the large roundness of her belly. "Are you happy, my love?" she asked.

The man gazed back at his wife and smiled. "Yes."

My father gasped as I pulled my hand away.

I shuddered, the rush of the memory leaving my mind as it buried itself somewhere within my father's. The pang in my chest grew at the loss of it. My fingers trembled, hot tears pooling in my eyes.

But the void was not pain. It was freedom. A broken sigh of relief clawed itself from my lungs.

"That belongs to you now." My voice quivered. "It's the last one I had. I saved it for you."

His swollen eyes met mine as I rose to leave. He grasped my hand.

"Mimi, wait," he sobbed. "Do you still...believe in happy endings?"

I leaned down, kissing his cheek.

"Someone has to."

THE RED DOOR at the end of the hall beckoned. Energy pulsed from the crimson paint, brimming with expectation. As if it had been waiting for me all this time. The last time, its imposing warning sought to repel me at all costs. But I was no longer trespassing in this sacred place. Now it welcomed me like an old friend.

Still, my heart pounded, waiting to discover what awaited me when I stepped through that door. Perhaps I wasn't as brave as I thought.

"You are braver than most, Naomi," Adeeba whispered into my ear.

I squeezed her hand. "Mnemosyne," I replied.

Naomi was laid to rest with her memories tucked neatly in the book on Adeeba's shelf. Gone was the life I'd lived in her shoes. All that was left was Mnemosyne.

"Go on then, we don't have all day," Danoma chirped, but without her usual bite. Fondness dripped from her laugh and glowing smile.

I reached for the doorknob, twisting the brass mechanism and pushing the door open. Light flooded the room. Tall windows stretched from floor to ceiling, and outside the sea danced, crashing against jagged rocks. I inhaled the faint saltiness trickling in.

"I don't know this place," I said, searching the cottage room for a shred of familiarity.

"The room is never wrong," Danoma answered, ushering me towards the chair by the windows.

I sat down, gazing out at the cloudless sky, gulls gliding with outstretched wings on the wind. Adeeba sat across from me, Penn to my right. Danoma leaned dramatically against the window frame, her ruby lips upturned at the sides.

"How long can I stay here?" I asked, my heart in my throat.

"As long as you want," Adeeba replied. "It's a beautiful day. We could just sit here for a while."

A nervous chuckle tumbled out of me. "If I don't do this now, I'm scared I'll never do it."

I was ready, or I wanted to be. Still a sense of dread hung over me, something so heavy I could barely muster a smile.

"You can let go," Penn said from next to me. "I know you've given back all of the good, but it's time to let go of the bad as well."

The bad?

Not *my* bad, I realized. I'd spent months intricately weaving all of the memories I'd hoarded into my mother's book. Into my siblings' books. Stephen's. Each book now sat neatly in its place entombed with the memories of the lives I'd stolen. But there was still something left. Threads still waiting to be unraveled from their tangled cages beneath my bones.

A lifeless child in her mother's arms. A soldier's screams as he called out for his fallen friend in the night. Loss after loss. Misery beyond misery. I'd taken these memories to ease the pain of others. Never before had I considered the pain it had brought to me.

Penn extended her hand, palm facing up with an offering to take that burden from me. With a hesitant touch, memories poured out of me, rushing to the surface from each of their forgotten caverns. With each pull, my shoulders slumped further, a weight removed. New threads stitched themselves together in the void buried beneath my ribcage, tattered pieces of a heart that shattered too many times finally made whole.

The stars burst into flames, fluttering across the sky in wild plumes of color. A childish giggle left my lips, my small arms curling around Adeeba's neck. Penn's eyes glittered, eyeing the flittering flames dancing in the night. Danoma's curls bounced as she spun in circles, the tulle of her dress reaching out to every corner of our tiny rooftop perch. Adeeba's steady heartbeat thrummed against my ear where I rested my head on her chest.

I welcomed the flood of euphoria pulsing through my veins.

My eyes refocused, the shaking in my hands subsiding.

Penn reached across the coffee table, sliding a teacup in front of me. I stared down at it, the clear steaming liquid. Unassuming and simple.

"Why did they want me to be with you?" I'd never had the courage to ask before. "I could have ended up alone in every life, but the three of you were always there. Why?"

Penn glanced to Adeeba and Adeeba to Danoma. The three sisters smiled.

"They thought you'd end up like us, in that *Athenaeum* forever. They didn't think you'd ever be strong enough to let go, surrounded by so much death," Adeeba answered.

"They were sorely mistaken," Penn added, her white teeth splayed.

"We didn't want you to make the same mistakes we did," said Danoma. "And while we couldn't interfere with your fate, we knew what you needed most. And it was a blessing to each of us to be able to give that to you."

I was desperate to be loved, I'd thought once. And here I'd had it all along. These three women. My aunts...my *mothers*.

"What will happen?" I managed through a strangled sob. "When I go?"

"We don't know," Adeeba answered.

My brows creased. "But you know everything."

"Not yet. Whatever happens in your next life, Mnemosyne, will be entirely new."

My next life. This wouldn't be like before. Every life I carried the burden of memory with me, but now there was nothing left to take. Who would I be without Mnemosyne?

"Whoever you want," Danoma answered.

"Will I see you again?" The words tumbled out of me with the desperation of a small child. Centuries together suddenly didn't seem like enough.

Adeeba's soft hands curled around mine. Danoma's palms pressed down on my shoulders. Even Penn reached over, her hand on my knee.

"We certainly hope so," Adeeba answered.

"May you only know peace, Mnemosyne," Danoma whispered. "And may our souls one day meet again."

I reached for the teacup, soothed by the scent of lemon and honey. I sipped, savoring the taste as the warm liquid poured over my tongue.

It tasted like home.

           ~

PART VII: FORGET ME NOT | *CEANN DÙNAID, GALLAIBH, 25 YEARS LATER*

THERE IS COMFORT in the unfamiliar.

I'd never been to this particular seaside village and yet I climbed the towering path up the bluffs like my legs had walked the path a thousand times before. Standing at the top of the hill, I gazed out over the sea, chest heaving. My calves would punish me later, but the view was worth it. Tumultuous waves crashed against the rocky cliffs of the peninsula. I stood surrounded by a vastness of blue-grey, gusts of wind twisting my braids like wild dancing threads.

I didn't even care that I was completely lost.

The clouds rumbled overhead, dark, ominous skies pouring in from offshore. A light drizzle of rain kissed my windswept cheeks. My eyes fluttered shut, highland mist sprinkling my lashes. Brisk summertime rains and salty seaside air.

Yes, this place would do nicely.

At the base of the path, a quaint shop stood, smoke rising from the stone chimney. I pushed the door open, looking like a tourist with my crumpled map under my arm. A bell over the door jingled, alerting the woman at the counter to my arrival. She glanced up from her copy of *Macbeth*, fair eyes beneath half-moon glasses. A kind smile spread across her face.

"Welcome." The softness of her voice filled me with an immediate warmth. "Can I help you, love?"

"I was just doing a bit of exploring and got caught in a bit of a summer storm," I explained.

"New to the area?" the woman asked, eyes trailing down towards the map. "Or just visiting?"

I placed the wet, crumpled map on the counter with a small chuckle.

"A bit of both. My mum used to spend summers in Scotland as a kid. I've never really been north of Glasgow, and so I thought I'd be a little adventurous. I rented out a house in the area to stay in while I work on my book."

A genuine curiosity filled the woman's widened eyes. Most people nodded politely when I mentioned my work, an air of judgment lingering after several follow up questions revealed, no – it in fact was not *just a hobby* "Ah! A writer?! How lovely. I've always considered myself a bit of a writer as well. My name is Addie."

"I'm Nora," I replied, then pulled my phone from my pocket. "You don't happen to know where '*Seas the Day*' Cottage is, do you?" I asked, pulling up the photo the owner had sent.

The woman glanced down at my phone, pulling it towards her face as she squinted, and her smile widened.

"Oh aye! I know it well. My youngest sister Dan mentioned she was letting it out for the summer. She's actually out running a quick errand and should be back any minute if you'd like to wait a while? We can put the kettle on for you."

"Or a nip of whiskey," a second voice said, looking out from the storeroom behind the front desk. A tall woman with sharp features reached up and grabbed a bottle of whiskey from the shelf.

"Oh, the tea will be fine, thanks. I've never been overly fond of whiskey."

The woman shrugged, a small smirk on her lips. "Suit yourself."

"Ignore her. My sister looks for any excuse to break out the good stuff. Just the water then, Penn?"

The woman gave a curt nod before disappearing once again into the back room. Light clatter filled the silence as I pulled my hood down. Shivering, I walked over to the fireplace. I reached towards the flame, letting the toasty warmth rush over my frozen fingertips. Shelves spanned the walls, filled with books and various oddities. Over the fireplace hung a painting of an elegant young woman. Her brown eyes peered down at me, beckoning me to look closer.

Something tugged beneath my chest, that same tug I'd felt when Mum had suggested I travel a bit to get my head out of the cloud of writer's block. The same tug I'd felt the entire drive up from Glasgow. Like I knew this place before I'd ever really seen it. The woman stared down at me with a secret of a smile in the corner of her lips.

"Lovely isn't she?" Addie asked, standing at my side.

"She is," I whispered, eyes glued to the portrait. "Do you know her?"

"A long time ago, she was very dear to us. She loved the sea."

A kindred spirit.

Penn appeared again in her oversized knitted jumper, three eclectic mugs balanced precariously in her hands. She held one out, and I welcomed the heat against my palms. Steam rose from the cup, a delicate warning of what would likely burn my tongue if I rushed.

"So what brings you all the way to Caithness? The cottage is lovely, but of all the places to stay..." Penn trailed off, glancing up at the portrait as well as she sipped her tea. The smokey-honey scent emitting from her mug hinted hers was spiked with something stronger than sugar and cream.

"I wanted somewhere I could escape for a while. Focus and fall in love with my writing again. I saw the cottage online and something about it felt so...I don't know. Is it silly to say fate?"

The two sisters chuckled.

"Fate can be funny like that," Addie replied. "It's a small village, but you'll be no' lacking for company. The people love getting to know newcomers."

"Fair warning," Penn said, dryly.

"Oh I don't mind."

I liked meeting new people. The word had always called to me in a way I'd never been able to properly articulate. University in Boston had been a temporary cure. But nowhere had ever brought me such peace quite like view at the top of the hill, the warmth of the fire against my palms. The comforting eyes of the woman in the portrait above me. This was the first time I'd ever connected to a place so deeply. This place at the end of the world.

The bell over the door chimed again, and my head spun to see a woman with pristine curls falling down her back. She wore vibrant green trousers with perfectly pressed pleats, stilettos tapping across the wooden floorboards as she crossed the room. Her gloved fingers curled around her cane, a glass bauble at the top. She pulled her sunglasses down the tip of her nose, gazing at me with a knowing smile.

"Well, well, well, Sisters. Who do we have here?"

"Dan, meet Nora. She's letting out the cottage," Addie introduced. "Nora, meet our younger sister Dan."

Dan pulled off the leather gloves and reached out her hand. I stared down at her polished fingernails, grinning as I took her hand in mine. She gazed up at the portrait above the fireplace, then back at me, white teeth exposed as her smile widened.

"Welcome home."

Home. I'd been searching for the meaning of that word for so long I wasn't sure if it truly existed. Could wanderers have homes? Now, standing here before three peculiar sisters in this place at the edge of the world, I thought – perhaps – maybe they could.

And for the first time since I could remember, that insistent tug beneath my ribs slackened.

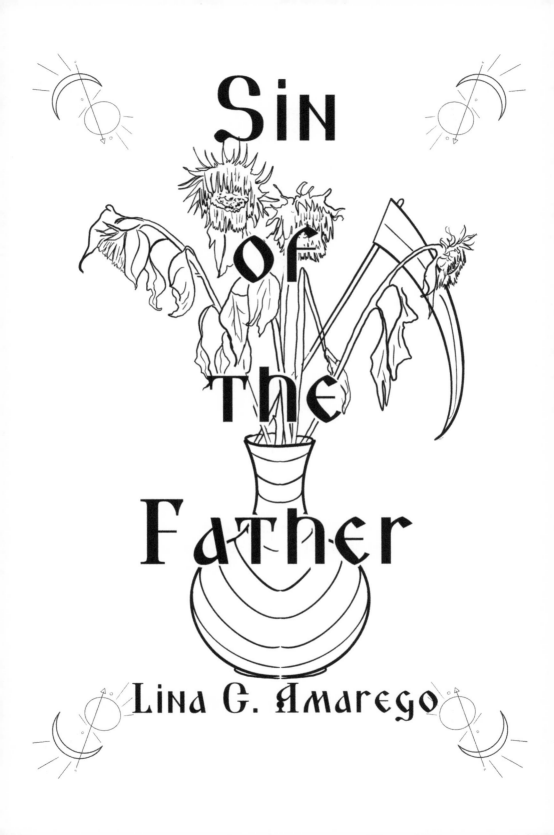

CHAPTER 8

SIN OF THE FATHER

LINA C. AMAREGO

I. SHOCK

O f all the side effects of living, grief was the most nefarious. Across the lifetimes I'd lived, no wound could ever cut as deeply, no malady could rot and ruin a person like misery did. I'd seen it cleave through families and fell empires with indiscriminate viciousness.

My footsteps cried with loneliness as they echoed across the polished linoleum floor. My tall, pale reflection was my only company as it stared up at me from the tile's face: black, unruly curls and dark empty eyes the perfect picture of the Angel of Death. The fluorescent lights flickered like falling stars, discordant with the lifeless white of the long halls. But there were no wishes left to make, not tonight. Wishes didn't come true in a place like Seaside Behavioral Health Hospital. Not that many of the occupants had much left to wish for.

Despair had the distinct taste of acid and ash.

I made my way to the last room in the east wing, as I had many times over my last five years of employment here. As always, I could taste the bitter sorrow the second I walked through the front doors, the pungent ash burning my tongue the closer I got. The night staff milled about, unaffected, tired eyes focused on their routine tasks. No one spared a glance in my direction. No one cared, especially not during the witching hour.

I cared. An unforgivable flaw.

It hadn't been this bad in years. Lifetimes, maybe.

There was a stint in the Dark Ages where the rot and ruin were suffocating, my siblings carving their paths, every home drenched in the vicious scent. But despite all the technology and supposed triumphs of the modern age, things were beginning to mirror the plague.

Cycles could not be broken, after all. Fates and Furies damn us.

I tugged at the collar of my sweater, a soft black cotton-blend that did nothing to soothe me as I finally made my way to my office.

Mrs. Pelora already stretched across the brown leather couch, aged form sinking into the softness. She didn't bother to sit up or adjust her rumpled hospital gown as I entered, taking my favored armchair across from her. In here, the taste was overwhelming, like swallowing down freshly burned coal.

A night nurse stood bored at her side, eyelids drooping as she stifled a yawn. Still, I managed a kind smile. "You can go now."

The woman nodded, exiting the room without a second glance back at the withered old lady she was sworn to watch.

No one cared, especially when the patients were this close to the edge.

I trained my smile on the woman. "Good evening, Elain."

"No it isn't, doc." Eyes darted to me, bloodshot and puffy.

No, it wasn't, a truth we both could taste—bittersweet like burnt sugar.

Of all the afflictions known to man, heartbreak was the harshest.

"I got a call from the nurses. Said you refused to eat again," I sighed. She looked away, ignoring my accusation. A part of her already belonged to the great beyond, and I knew there was very little I could do to coax her back to the land of the living. "Is that the plan, Elain? Suicide by starvation? I wonder what Winston would think."

Her head whipped back to me with lighting speed, thin lips flattening into a grim line. For a moment, the acidic, chemical scent of rage filled the air, washing away everything in its path like bleach.

Good. Play a little longer, dear. Don't give in quite yet.

"Winston can't think. He's dead," Elain snapped, sitting straight for a moment, her breath labored. She crashed again back into the couch. Her chest sank as she folded her arms, an outward reflection of the hollow, jagged hole in her heart. Tears lined bloodshot eyes. "I just want to be with my husband again."

Of all the hurts I'd ever witnessed, depression was the deadliest.

I swallowed the fresh smokiness coating my tongue, her grief potent as the debris after a forest fire. It had ravaged every part of her, leaving not even a seed to plant and regrow.

"Grief is a cruel companion, and I won't tell you how to mourn." I kept my voice low; the small comfort as effective as a Band-Aid on a bullet wound. It did nothing to stop the hemorrhaging sorrow pouring from every inch of her. "But it is my job to keep you safe. What do you need to stay safe, hmm? Let's make a plan."

A shuddering sob, buried beneath mountains of ash. "I need to stop feeling this."

I sat further back in my chair, wishing I could sink through it. I knew the second I stepped into Seaside that it would be like this. There was nothing even *I* could do, no pill to offer or intervention left to try that would soothe the frayed, singed edges of this woman's tattered, burned soul.

And yet, I cared. Too much. A dangerous, foolish disorder of my own.

I hated this part, merciful as it was.

"Let's explore that idea." I leaned forward, letting the ashy, smoky scent envelop me as I inched closer. "Say I could do that for you. Could take all of your sadness and grief away. Would that make you happy?"

A final test, to see what could be salvaged. One last hopeful, hapless shot in the dark.

The old woman wrang her frail, grooved hands together, as if trying to summon the last taste of happiness or joy from the cracked, lifeless desert.

"I don't care about happy. I just don't want to hurt anymore." Dark eyes met mine, thousands of memories sifting through their windows. Rose and citrus mixed in the air, with notes of vanilla and honey. Happiness and excitement, comfort and love. Mnemosyne would have a very full book to bind for this woman. But the ash over-powered all as she spoke, dusting it all in a dark veil. "I've had enough of it all. Enough joy—seeing my son born, my granddaughter. Enough love—Winston gave me more of that than I could ever hope to return. But I have had more than my share of sorrow, and I'm tired. Why can't any of you let an old woman die in peace?"

Her words struck me like breaking glass, tiny shards somehow cutting deep.

Of all the Furies known to the universes, despondency was the most unforgivable.

I always knew when they passed my stubborn Athene, when they stopped bargaining and begging and crying for sweet Mnemosyne to change their fate....then there was no going back.

She'd arrived at the final, forgotten sin's door, ready for respite.

I took her skeletal hands in mine, surprised at their comfortable warmth. "I can't let you die in pain."

She jerked back. "You doctors are all the same, worried about saving lives without understanding what makes a life worth living."

It stung, like lemon juice in an open cut. But she was right. I'd lived enough lives to know the harsh, hateful truth.

Of all the emotions one could experience, love was the most villainous. It coaxed people closer, making them believe life had purpose and meaning. Letting them tie their lives together into inseparable, unbreakable threads.

And when love was lost, when the knots were cut... It took everything else away with it, leaving only the vacant, vicious void of grief behind.

"I said I can't let you die in *pain*." I reached out, wiping an errant tear from her sunken cheek. "Not that I would save your life."

Not that there was anything else left to save. Only the mercy of a peaceful, emotionless end.

"Take it all away, please." A desperate, final plea as she grabbed my hands.

I squeezed gently, bracing myself as the floodgates opened between us. Sadness crashed into me like a tidal wave, drowning out all else. But I kept my kind smile intact, struggling to keep my head above water as I took in every last drop.

I waited until there was nothing left, until all that waited in her eyes was that endless, vacant nothingness.

She was alive, yes. Breathing. Blinking. Heart beating.

But I'd taken her pain, her sorrow. Everything. She'd be little more than a vegetable, a soulless husk without the will for words.

"Rest in peace, Elain."

~

BEFORE

ACID AND ASH, *choking me from the inside. Sea-and-sage-colored eyes staring into nothingness—eyes that once sparkled like sea-glass in sunlight. A pool of blood dampened the dry, cracked earth, a sacrifice to gods forsaken.*

A clammy hand clasped to my chest—hands that were once warm as fresh-baked bread—too cold, too stiff. My voice broke like cracking thunder, too harsh, too loud. "Why, why did you do this? Chara, please."

A hoarse whisper– her voice once a sweet melody. "Let me rest, Thanatos."

A defiant plea. "No, don't leave, I can't do this without you."

A dull smile carved her blanched face. "The pain, it's too much. I did not want to live long enough to resent you." Tears streaked the image of the River Styx across her cheeks, death breathing down her neck already. "I can't take it. Can't watch my children suffer. Death will take it all away."

"Chara," A desperate prayer, one last declaration of love and hope–

Silence. Stillness.

Sorrow.

~

II. DEPRESSION

Elain Pelora died two days after I took her grief. With nothing left to fuel it, her body gave in to the call of the great beyond.

I'd never been fond of funerals, as I imagined not many mortals were. But, across lifetimes and customs, some had certainly been interesting. The familiar scent of despair was always palpable, the choking, burning ash. But mortals had a tendency to surprise me, now and again. Rose and coffee; joy and triumph that none would ever admit. It hid behind their masks of sadness, secrets taken to the grave. Fresh pine and spoiled milk; relief and regret, as caretakers stepped down from their duties, or as daughters mourned the plans they wished they had made.

Throughout the centuries and worlds, the Vikings did it best. I lived among them for two lifetimes, both as a Völva– a healer and a seer. But death had never been a punishment for them. The burning pyres they lit were the only contributors to the ashy scent; instead, their emotions all smelled of sweet wine and fresh-cut flowers. Of celebration.

Today's funeral was far from that. A testament to how well-loved Elian was, the gathered masses all reeked of the overpowering sadness. The room was covered in some of the most gorgeous floral arrangements I'd ever seen—sunflowers and tulips, a riotous smear of springtime colors against the sea of black suits and frocks—and yet not a single note of their fragrance reached me through the ashen scent. I'd even doused my black suit in my strongest cologne, hoping the sandalwood and bergamot could drown out the burnt odor. But even Mr. Tom Ford was no match.

"We are gathered here today to grieve the loss of Elain Pelora, beloved wife, treasured mother and grandmother..." A balding, round-bellied pastor droned from his pulpit, and a fresh wave of cedar and cilantro washed the room as boredom sanded down the sharp edge of sorrow.

I stifled a yawn. I had seen many kinds of prayer and mourning and lived enough lives to see the rise and fall of empires. Both on earth, and in the realms beyond. The Mayans, the Greeks, the Romans and Celts...the Magi of Selennia and the artists of Antica. People always put their faith in kings and prophets and gods...in the end, they all died alone.

At least Elain hadn't died in pain. Long-term suffering was a curse of the living.

Much like the congregation now, stiff pews biting into their backs, the endless croaking of Father What's-his-fart accosting their ears...

Their suffering would make a generous sacrifice to their dead friend.

I folded my hands and closed my eyes, tuning out the old man's miserable voice. From my seat in the back, no one would notice one dozing stranger, even as tall as I was. Perhaps it would look like I was deep in prayer...

A shift in the scent caught my attention first, rose and tea-leaves, love and interest. My eyes fluttered open, my own intrigue stirred.

A sharp inhale of breath rocked me, a dirge of long-forgotten feelings ringing through my ears. Fury and disbelief, curiosity and something I would not name...

I'd never seen her before; the wild, tightly wound curls spilling over her shoulders like a wicked waterfall over rigid stone, the amber skin casting her athletic frame in bronze. But her eyes—the distinct shade of sea and sage, an undecided blend of green and blue—

I'd know those eyes anywhere. Knew them in the very pits of my blackened soul.

Her throat bobbed as she took the pulpit, a pale-knuckled grasp on either side of the stained wood. "My grandmother was a beacon in my life, the most radiant woman most of us had ever known."

The rest of her words became a blur as the sadness slammed into me like an anvil. Ash and acid, bitter and burnt. Blistering. How it hadn't suffocated me the second I walked in, I didn't know. Had she held it in all this time?

A raucous ringing in my ears deafened me, heart thudding like a freight train in my mortal chest. I clenched my jaw, focusing all my will on the meager scent of my cologne.

Her eulogy was not long, and it was not sad. Shoulders in the rows in front of me shook with gentle laughter, their humor misting the air like bubble-gum. Then, long sighs were let loose, carrying with them tinges of ginger and seawater, respect and longing.

But nothing came close to the overpowering, all-consuming scent of her grief. Masked behind that brilliant, bright smile. Simmering behind that sea-and-sage stare.

It took all of my strength—all the self-control amassed through thousands of lifetimes and bodies—not to stand and leave. I could have. *Should* have. No one would pay any mind to the stranger excusing himself from the back row. No one cared.

I cared. A character defect, for sure.

It hadn't been this bad in years. Lifetimes, maybe. Her sorrow made her grandmother's seem like a light appetizer before the main course.

The speech ended, and the sickening scent leashed itself as she stepped down, disappearing without any lingering whiff. I breathed deeply, lungs aching for relief from the asphyxiating smell. Final rites moved quickly, and I stood to leave as soon as the off-key choir's final notes echoed through the hollow hall.

I quietly pushed open the wood door, slinking through like a shadow.

"How did you know my grandmother?"

Her arms crossed against her chest as I nearly slammed into her, stumbling to right myself before I accidentally fell down the flight of stone steps. She barely came up to my chest, my gangly height staggering next to her. Her stance rumpled the fabric of the bright yellow dress she wore, like the sunshine ready to expel any gathered darkness. Even sullen Carden would've done cartwheels in the street to see this shade, and Balshasar would've commissioned artists to capture the hue. Somehow, I hadn't noticed that earlier—a splash of rebellious color against the sea of black. A celebration amidst the mourning.

She might have liked a Viking funeral.

"I'm sorry, I—" Eloquence failed, her teal gaze turning my tongue into a stammering fool. I hadn't even seen her slip out, a rare oversight on my part, especially considering her starkly contrasted outfit. I braced myself, holding my breath, waiting for the harsh assault of that taste again...

But nothing came. Only a kind, gentle smile on her generous mouth. "I don't recognize you. But I could see the pain on your face through the whole service. How did you know her?"

Pain born not of my sorrow for Elain, but of *hers*. I tugged at my tie and ran a hand through my unkempt dark curls, clearing my throat of the last of my incompetence. "Your grandmother was a patient of mine. I'm—"

"You're Dr. Ashton," she finished for me, flashing another one of those sunshine grins my way.

I stared down at the enigma of a woman, fighting back the flurry of curiosity aching in my chest. I could've just excused myself then and walked out. I should've.

"Tristan," I said instead, extending a handshake. "Your name?"

"I'm Hope." Slender fingers clasped around mine, warm like fresh-poured coffee. A chill ran up my spine. "She talked about you quite a bit. Thank you for being there for her...when I couldn't."

Of all the words in the world, hope was the most haunting one. It lingered long after it should, a guest overstaying its welcome in this wretched place.

The irony was not lost on me, but her name rang a bell. Hope, Elain's only granddaughter—an orphan, now, if I recalled correctly. The old woman always spoke fondly of her 'little sunbeam,' who had taken over their flower shop a few years back. I now saw how fitting the nickname was.

But still, despite the warmth and light of her exterior, I could sense it, lingering beneath. The aftertaste of that unending, unspeakable pain.

I only realized I was still shaking her hand when she tore hers away, tilting her head to the side, raking an appraising look over me. "Do you come to all your patients' funerals?"

I stuffed my hands in my pockets before they could make a further fool out of me. "Only the ones that die."

"Why?" she asked.

I blinked twice, surprise stirring from the buried depths of my core. In all my lifetimes, through all the funerals I'd attended and officiated, I thought I'd seen and heard it all.

No one ever asked me why I did it. No one cared.

I cared. An unspeakable tragedy.

And that's *why*, despite all my defenses. Why I sat through dirge after dirge, through every mangled sermon and tear-soaked eulogy.

I cared because I knew the mortals I'd saved could not any longer.

Her expectant gaze still demanded an answer. But I simply shrugged, managing a kind smile that sheltered the truth. "Good place to pick up new clients."

The corner of her mouth curled upwards. "You're pretty funny."

"I've never been accused as such in my life." Lives, really. Humor had never been my forte. Even Edana couldn't stoke a passion for comedy from my dry, cracked heart, despite my many visitations to her delightful coffee shop.

Hope opened her mouth to respond, but the doors behind us cracked, the first sobbing mourner exiting the church.

"Hope, dear! Oh, I'm so sorry for your loss." A stubby woman with a lopsided black bonnet crushed Hope into a hug, planting her sniffling face in her mess of curls. "But look how tall you've gotten!"

"Thank you, Auntie Bea," the girl laughed, the sound like bubbling champagne.

And with that, I remembered where I was. *Who* I was.

The Angel of Death did not make friends at funerals.

I didn't deserve them.

I turned and fled down the steps before I stayed long enough to forget again.

∾

BEFORE

SAGE AND SEA-SALT, *soothing the rough burn in my belly. Hair the color of coal swayed in the breeze that carried her bird-song laugh. She stared at me through thick lashes, an invitation for a Fury to lay down his scythe.*

A silk-smooth palm stroking my face—a face that was once harsh and cruel, too dark, too lost. Her voice lilted like a lark, too sweet, too pure. "Why don't you stay with me? Thanatos, please."

A hesitant answer—once a cold command. "I can't, Chara."

A radiant smile. "Says who?"

A simple hope stabbed my long-lost heart. "The gods will be angry. My siblings need me..." Worry knotted itself in my ribs, but life still cleaved its way through the barren rivers of my veins. "But I can't leave you, either. I love you too much to let you go."

"Thanatos." A breathless devotion, our first riotous pronouncement of fidelity and family as her lips claimed mine—

Triumph. Terror.
Tragedy.

III. DENIAL

WEEKS PASSED IN A HAZE of stale dissociation. My work was rarely better than mundane, the musty scent of monotony a constant in Seaside Behavioral. There had been several instances over the last few years that I thought of inviting Caedmon or Edana to help breathe *some* life into the drab institute. But there was usually comfort in routine. A clear set of expectations that led to little surprise.

But now, the tedium was maddening. Whenever unoccupied–which was often–my mind wandered down long forgotten halls I'd much rather leave unvisited. Some led to Hope, the memory of her sunshine yellow dress and tilted smile so clear, I thought perhaps Mnemosyne was testing my willpower, tugging at strings to see how sturdy they were. The daydreams were so palpable, it took all my strength not to beg Eris to devour them straight from my mind. Though it had been centuries since a mortal had surprised me so thoroughly, it made sense that I would struggle to shake her lingering effect. A few dozen lives ago, there had been another woman from a different world called Selennia, during its first age, that had a similar sway over me. But it was later discovered she was just an incredibly talented Psyche Magi that was very good at manipulating my dreams to her liking.

Others–darker, older corridors, dusty with disuse and dread–led back to the start, a beginning I thought I'd buried lifetimes ago. To memories of a different set of sage eyes, to a deeper, endless sorrow.

I fought the unwanted advances of my subconscious by throwing myself into my work, taking day and night shifts as often as Human Resources would allow. Not that there was much going on in either shift–places like this kept all their patients as stable as possible, which was synonymous with unsatisfied. Numbness was the only medicine for many of the residents.

Not that I blamed them. Cycles could not be broken, after all. Happiness was a dangerous weapon even in the right hands.

It was a Tuesday afternoon shift–no different than any other–when change came for me. I felt her before I saw her. Felt the familiar sting of ash coat my throat, smelled the subtle hint of spiced curiosity. Though it could've been any visitor, I knew in a deep, dangerous part of me that it was her. Her scent wafted through the open doorway of my office moments before she sauntered through.

Today, her wild curls were schooled in a tight knot at the top of her head, emphasizing the high planes of her face. A checkered shirt and ripped denim jeans were cinched by a light blue apron–reading *Pelora's Petals*–tied around her slim waist. The color complimented her deep skin like the sky against warm earth, a perfect contrast of opposites. She knocked twice on the ajar door, despite me already staring directly at her.

I shifted in my leather chair, fighting back the uncomfortable whirlwind of my own surprise that dared me to make foolish choices. I offered a practiced, professional smile, one that fit the unchanging dullness of the hospital. "I'm not taking on any new patients."

"Good, because I'm not crazy." She grinned, sticking her hands to her wide hips. A wave of bubble-gum flavored giggles fizzed from her mouth. "How about lunch, Doc?"

Of all the agents the Fates employed, change was the most unfavorable. It doused this girl in chaos, unpredictable and unprecedented. And the fool I was, I took the bait. "For what?"

The ash and acid drowned out any other flavors for another long beat, Hope's hands fisted in the oversized pockets of her apron. "I have questions about my grandma." She gnawed at her lower lip, eyes glassy with tears that refused to fall. "She...she was all I had left, and the last few days...she wasn't herself. I want to know what changed, and I was hoping you could clarify."

"That's a violation of her confidentiality rights," I sighed, scooping my satchel from its perch on my couch and standing, readying to leave. The presence of her grief overwhelmed the tiny space, discomfort sticking my sweater to my back in a sheen of fresh sweat.

I cared about this woman, whether or not I consented to it, as I did for most mortals. A fatal misstep on my part. But I knew the answers she sought only ended in more sadness and the kind of unseen wounds that frequented this establishment.

But she guarded the doorway before I could brush past her, a formidable barrier made of sunlight and sincerity. She looked up at me with *those* eyes, the cinnamon taste of her determination biting my tongue. "She's dead, Doc. I just want some closure."

Fates and Furies damn me. I could've brushed past and never looked back, which was well within my professional right. I should've.

Instead, I tossed the strap of my leather bag over my shoulder and nodded once, gesturing into the linoleum hallway. "I know a place."

IT WOULD BE a lie to say I chose Seaside Behavioral for its epic view of the Atlantic and fantastic pay rates. In fact, it was one of the least prestigious establishments on the New England coast, a blemish to the psychiatric community as a whole.

But it was close to *Deja Brew*, the coffee shop Edana and her partner owned. Even without my dear daughter's help, it would've had the best cup of joe in any and every universe. The added bonus of her presence managed to soothe and inspire even my tattered edges.

I was a regular now, a position that took lots of time and trust to earn. Eddie had never held a grudge against me like most of the others did—her sweet disposition welcoming even when I hadn't deserved it. Still, I felt the need to make my amends first, and after several instances where her gifts invoked the wrong type of passion in some unsavory clientele, I'd been more than happy to intervene and take away the emotions that fueled their fury. Since then, our relationship had gotten far more comfortable, an easy, quiet bond that gave sweet respite from my dark loneliness. But I rarely—and by rarely, I meant *never*—brought guests personally. Of course I'd recommended the place to every colleague and former patient I came across, but my visits were often only accompanied by a good book and an ocean-side view.

Now, Hope sat across from me at the small oak-faced table, the warm lighting casting her skin in a sunset glow. She stared out the window, the gray ocean lapping the rocky shore.

Holding the tray in one hand, Edana's eyes darted between Hope and I so forcefully, the action swished the long, dark ponytail atop her head. Her cloyingly sweet curiosity mixed with her typical, sour anxiety assaulted my senses, drowning out even the potent smell of fresh-brewed coffee steaming from our mugs. I cleared my throat.

"One black coffee with no extras." She winked at me, placing the unadorned ceramic cup in front of me first before carefully setting a towering drink in front of Hope. "And a peppermint swirl cappuccino with extra whipped cream. Enjoy."

"Thanks, Wit," I raised a brow at her, using her chosen name. It fit this version of her—short and perky like a shot of espresso. Luckily, another customer walked through the door, bringing the taste of salted hunger and caramel desire with him.

Wit skittered away to greet him, her slouchy white shirt hanging untucked from the back of her black slacks, giving her a tail.

Hope smiled as she watched her, a small chuckle as she shamelessly licked the overflowing whipped cream from the side of her cup. She looked back to me, a mustache of white on her upper lip. "A friend of yours?"

I fought the urge to reach out and wipe the stain with my thumb, instead handing her a small square napkin.

"Distant family, actually." I stretched the truth. *A daughter from my first life* would surely get me committed to Seaside myself. I took a deep sip of my own drink, letting the bold roast ground me back to my purpose. Hope needed closure, not a picture of my family tree or tortured past. "So, tell me more about what you want to know. Death tends to leave lots of unhealed wounds."

I would know, having formerly held the title.

She spooned a scoop of whipped cream in her mouth, licking the metal clean before speaking. "This isn't my first loss...my mom died in childbirth, and my dad died of cancer last year. Then Grandpa and Grandma..."

Her tone was bright, but the bitter ash overtook the coffee. I watched as the memories danced behind her blue-green stare.

"It must be difficult." I swallowed down the lump of discomfort in my throat with another deep drag of my drink. I donned my most soothing tone, one I saved for Seaside. "Perhaps you should seek therapy to help you cope with the grief."

She shook her head violently, a few curls flying free from their bound prison. Another full smile crinkled her eyes. "No thanks. I'm holding onto it as long as I can."

"What? Why?"

She shrugged, staring out at the sea again. It kissed the shore gently, the cloud-cover painting the scene in dull gray. Still, Hope watched as if it had all the colors of a Van Gogh. After another long moment, she spoke, her voice an ocean away. "It's all I have left of the people I love. A reminder of how happy they made me, and how full they used to make my heart."

Of all the ailments I'd studied, none were more elusive than grief. Its many stages made it hard to catch, buried in denial and wrath, covered by bargaining. I knew all too well how easy it was to sheathe mine deeply. But Hope wore hers on her sleeve, a badge to honor her dead.

A bitter tinge of pity worked its way up from the pit of my stomach. "I wouldn't wish that pain on anyone."

At that, she trained the full intensity of her gaze on me, hands clasping her mug tightly. "My grandma didn't feel pain at the end. I saw her two days before, and you could tell. She felt nothing. She couldn't even fake it." Her full lips pulled into a soured grimace. "Did you give her something? To help numb it all?"

Nothing given, but something *taken.*

An errant pang of guilt rattled my chest. I hated this part, merciful as it was. There were always side effects to treatment. Many of the mortals I'd helped had family who'd sought answers, who hid their mourning behind hypervigilance. Sometimes, they needed something–*someone*–to blame. And I was often a willing sacrifice to the pyre of their condemnation to help ease their ache.

I could've told Hope a honeyed lie, that I'd given Elain a stronger dose to help her move on. That her grandmother hadn't been on the brink of giving up, that I was the cold, clinical doctor that pushed her over the edge.

I could've. I should've.

"No, I didn't give her anything outside of her normal medication," I finally answered instead, unwilling to stoke her scorn or contempt for reasons I didn't dare explore. "But perhaps she chose to let it all go."

For the first time since knowing her, Hope's sunlit mask fell, revealing the cloudy chasm of sorrow beneath, as gray and hopeless as the sea outside. The smell consumed the small cafe, a greedy ghost that devoured all in its path. "No, my grandma was a fighter. She wouldn't have given up..."

Her lower lip wobbled as she trailed off, stormy tears springing to her eyes. On an instinct long forgotten, I grabbed her hand, offering a life raft against the choppy waves. "I hope you continue to remember her that way. It's a testament to the person she was, not the shell grief made her." She could hate or blame me, but I would not let her blame Elain. I would not let the memory of her surrogate mother be a dark strand woven into her book. I lowered my voice, my thumb rubbing the back of her hand in circular strokes. "But not everyone is as strong as you are. There is no shame in surrender. Sometimes, it's the only mercy we can give ourselves."

Hope blinked twice at me, mask slipping back into place. Slowly, she pulled her hand away, sheltering it beneath the table. "Is that your professional opinion, or a personal anecdote?"

Again, the reality of who and *where* I was slammed back into me. I was a doctor, and Hope was a patient's relative. I could observe and treat the afflictions of the heart, but I did not have a place in anyone's.

The Angel of Death did not comfort friends over a cup of coffee.

Even if he could, he didn't have any.

"Both." I quickly downed the last of my drink before standing, pulling my wallet out and tossing a twenty on the table. I gave her one last smile—professional and polite. Clinical and calculated. "I need to get back to work. Enjoy the coffee. This place has a healing atmosphere to it."

I didn't bother saying goodbye to Wit before leaving. Maybe she could give Hope what I couldn't.

BEFORE

SAFFRON AND ROTTEN FRUIT, *worry mounting as her pacing sped up. Hair tangled and knotted, sleepless bruises beneath her eyes the color of nightshade. The chorus of children's playful screams echoing through the open window—an omen of the horror to come.*

A fist pressed to her sunken stomach–once round with life–too empty, too thin. Her voice quivered like the last flower standing against the first winter winds. "They are coming for me, Thanatos."

A harsh dismissal–once a kind comfort. "Chara, enough. We'll be fine."

A frenzied cry. "First the crops dying, now the blight in the village—they are already here!"

A pang of dread twisted my hollow gut. "This is just the cycle of things, Chara." Denial tasted like piss on my lips, hope still pounding in every heartbeat clanging against my brittle ribs. "Things will turn around, and the children aren't purely mortal. We are strong enough to survive this."

"Thanatos." A helpless whisper, the first fracture in the foundation between us—

Confusion. Chaos.

Calamity.

∼

IV. BARGAINING

THERE WAS NO RETURNING to work in my current state of unraveling, memories and daydreams flashing behind my eyes every time I bothered to blink. *Sage-and-sea eyes, cracked earth and gathering clouds.* As I aimlessly wandered, the taste of my own bitterness and hurt coated my tongue in an unquenchable ash, pungent no matter how many times I swallowed it back, no matter what liquid I poured down my throat.

It hadn't been this bad in nearly a century; my control over my own emotions usually ironclad. But something about that girl had picked the lock, the first criminal feelings freeing themselves from their cages.

The last time I let myself feel, the last time Death resurrected from the box I'd buried him in...

The 1920s and 30s. Two decades of complete mayhem and madness. A plague—Spanish influenza, Resheph's doing—ravaging the population with a simple virus. Erra, also content to stir trouble, sent the Dust Bowl, sweeping away everything in her path, famine breaking across the continent. The Great Depression framed by two

World Wars, Tyr truly staking his claim on this earth, the king of war doing what he did best.

Mortals could not handle my memories. The world had descended into darkness, and it was my fault. Without me in control, there was no counter to my siblings' ambition. No shield against the Fates' cruel plans.

No, I could not let myself slip again. If I could not hold back the dark horseman inside of me, I needed to find someone who would.

I shot her a quick text, the location of a nearby bar I'd heard some of the night nurses rave about, tilting my own meandering path towards it.

I knew she'd beat me there—a benefit of working in the Library of Souls. She sat straight-backed on a barstool, her deep brown hair smoothed into a perfect bun at the nape of her neck. Her pleated, rose-colored pants, slim black turtleneck, and expensive tweed trench belonged in an English boarding school with Cardan, not in this dive. Her classic gin and tonic sat untouched on the counter in front of her, her manicured nails tapping restlessly against the highball.

She turned her head the second I walked into the low-lit room, the smell of the patrons' musty shame and citrus lust a sickening mixture that made me cough. But even here, the ash was inescapable. She waved me over, but her dark eyes narrowed with concern.

As always, my eldest saw too much. I ran my hand through my errant curls, suddenly very aware of how scraggly I'd let my normally trimmed beard get in the last week.

"You look terrible," she said by way of greeting, her heart-shaped mouth pulled into a tight frown as I plopped onto the stool next to her.

"Thank you?" I chuckled, smoothing out my rumpled sweater, heat rising to my cheeks. "You almost sounded like Athene there."

Dark eyes lightened—the same shade as mine, even in this life— a twinge of a smile pulling at her lips. Mnemosyne always had a soft spot for her younger siblings, even if she didn't pull her punches with me. "I'll take that as a compliment. Now what did you ask me here for?"

Straight to the point, efficient as always. I sighed, unable to put off the inevitable any longer. Every moment I wasted, the worse it would get.

I met her gaze head on, ready to sacrifice the last pieces of pain— of *her*—I had left. "Take my memories."

Mnemosyne blinked, face falling to an unreadable mask. "What?"

"I've never asked, because I saw them as my penance—" I kept my voice low, but I struggled to mask the quiver that shook my breath— "But they are making me weak. I was a Fury once. That is my role. My heart—the memories of her—they cloud my judgment, and we all know how dangerous that is."

Lips pursed to pity, those all-seeing eyes raking over every inch of my face.

"Flashbacks again?" she asked, and I nodded. She exhaled sharply, the scent of concern and guilt stirring in an uncomfortable cocktail. "What brought them on?"

Acid-and-ash.

Sea-and-sage.

"She has her eyes, Mimi." Her nickname slipped through the cracks of my resolve along with the admission, the sting of tears burning my tired eyes. Her eyes blew wide—it had been millennia since I used the endearment, a long-forgotten fatherly affection.

Of all the wounds I'd carried with me, ones of the heart were the hardest to heal. For me, and for the family that bore my sins. There was no medicine or tincture to soothe the blistering ache, no drug to soften the sharp edges. The only salvation was to forget. To let go.

Mnemosyne—no, Naomi now—covered my shaking hand with gentle fingers, stilling the tremors. But the acid and ash—mixed with the spice of pity—still enveloped her like a cloud of perfume. "I can't take them from you."

"I–" I swallowed the protest, shoving the disappointment that rocked through my center down where I kept the rest of my traitorous emotions. She'd already been through so much; I would not make my suffering hers. *Again.* I painted on a see-through smile. "You've gotten wiser."

Naomi took a small sip of her drink, blush coloring her pale cheeks. She lifted a hand, flagging down the burly bartender without a word, her authority natural. "He'll need a whiskey, neat–top shelf."

The attendant nodded once, reaching for the amber liquid on the wall. He poured me a generous two-knuckles worth, winking at Naomi before hurrying to the next customer.

I clinked the glass against hers and tossed it back, the contents burning my throat and settling uncomfortably in my stomach. I coughed, the warm buzz already creeping through my veins. "I see we are resorting to the old fashioned way of forgetting."

"It's simple, but effective. But really, I worry about you." Naomi offered a strained smile, but concern still clung to her scent. "I don't want you to be the only one left behind."

Her throat bobbed once before she straightened her porcelain mask once more, her control impeccable as always. She pushed her drink away, slipping off the stool in a swift motion, righting her coat, readying to go.

I grabbed her wrist, the claws of loneliness sinking painfully into my sides. "Can't you stay for a drink?"

"Maybe another night." She shook her head, patting my slumped shoulder. "The library doesn't wait."

No, the Fates she worked for waited for no one. Their agenda superseded all, unaffected by the wake of pain they left behind. Undeterred by the woes of the mortals they were meant to guard.

"Take care of yourself, Mimi," I muttered as she walked away, her sharp kitten heels clicking against the scratched hardwood. I shrugged, taking her unfinished drink and tossing it back, trying not to make a face as the citrus bubbles burned down my gullet.

I rarely drank–I'd seen enough of alcohol's long-term effects throughout my lives to avoid the stuff. It had a similar power to mine—numbing the senses, drowning and diluting feelings. But it was not a mercy. It was a harsh, demanding master, one that required a steep price in return for its services. Good lives ruined, families fractured, anguish amplified instead of resolved.

But one night of forgetting couldn't hurt. Maybe even the Angel of Death deserved a night off to recoup and relax.

I flagged down the bartender again—and again—letting the whiskey wash away the acid and ash sloshing in my stomach. Letting the memories slip away with my fine motor skills, the anger numbed with my articulation.

Six or seven glasses in, I was finally starting to feel...nothing. The numbing agent left behind only a pleasant spinning sensation.

Until a now-familiar face slipped into Naomi's empty seat, sage-and-sea stirring the sorrow in my chest once more.

Except this time, I hadn't smelled or felt her coming at all. Her scent gave nothing of her emotion, the only hint at her inner life those big eyes staring at me.

"Are you stalking me now?" Hope leaned against the bar, lips quirked to the side. She crossed her legs, her tight jeans emphasizing their shapeliness, her petal-pink blouse falling dangerously low on her shoulders.

My personal vice, here to taunt my already-tortured soul.

Fates and Furies damn me.

I snorted, staring into my empty glass, wishing it full again. Slurred words slipped past my loosened lips before I could snatch them back. "No. The fucking Fates just have a very cruel sense of humor."

"You're drunk." An astute observation. She giggled, tossing her well-coiffed curls, further revealing the bare bronze skin of her shoulder. Were shoulders always that enticing? I blinked hard, trying to focus on the words tumbling—too fast—from her pretty lips. "I didn't think psychiatrists did that. Aren't you supposed to be the sane one?"

"They'd need to rewrite all their books to describe how messed up my head is." I shrugged, pushing back from the bar. I did not have the patience to be played with by the Fates tonight–or the self-control to stop thinking with my dick. I armored the last strands of my sensibility together to slide off my stool, to head out and put this siren far behind me–

The room spun–or maybe I did–colors and lights blurring in a kaleidoscope.

Shit.

"Whoa, there–" Slim but strong arms caught me, steadying me before I hit the ground. I dwarfed her, but Hope held firm as she studied me, that stupid grin still plastered on her face, pretty eyes sparkling in the dingy bar's fluorescents. "Listen, my place is around the corner. Why don't you come with me and we can sober you up a bit."

I snorted, eyes trained on her mouth. "Is that a line to get me to come home with you?"

"Oh wow, you *are* insane." Her laugh glittered like starlight–or maybe I was seeing stars. She swatted my chest playfully before grabbing my arm and throwing it over her bare shoulders. I shuddered at the contact, her soft skin just underneath my fingertips. Wrapping her arm low around my waist, she led me towards the door. "Let's go, you lush. You need some fresh air."

I should've walked away, should've sat my ass back at the bar and called a cab. I could've.

I didn't.

The night air slammed into me as we stepped outside, the refreshing chill cooling my liquor-warmed face.

"You smell like a liquor cabinet," Hope grumbled as we stumbled down the uneven sidewalk, dodging other patrons of the establishments lined on the block.

I sniffed, confirming her complaint–but noting something else.

Or more acutely, its absence.

No ash. No acid. No decay and ruin, no sorrow and grief stinking up the air around her.

Just fresh tulips and warm vanilla, floral and sweet and delicious. Just the perfume of a woman who worked in a flower shop and loved sweet coffee and smiled like sunlight...

"Were you on a date?" I blurted out, something else festering with the whiskey in my gut, a primal tug that made me want to lean a little closer to my makeshift crutch.

We slowed, Hope's tone tentative. "No. It was my friend's birthday."

At that, a nervous burst of emotion misted between us, the taste of spice and something fruity–desire and affection.

For her friend, I assumed. "Huh. That's why you taste like choco-late-covered strawberries and cinnamon buns right now."

I must have said it aloud, which undoubtedly made me sound like a pervert. Clearly a dangerous misstep by a drunken fool, because she stopped us both short, nearly tossing me to the pavement.

"Excuse me?" She unraveled from under my arm, sticking her fists to her hips. Still, a smile tugged at her mouth. "I want whatever you're on."

Great, now she thought I was a pervert *and* an addict.

I rubbed an exhausted hand over my too-tight, too-warm face. I would have words one day with whatever devious soul created liquor.

"It's a primordial gift granted by the cosmos–" I explained before snapping my mouth shut, realizing the double-blunder.

Fates and fucking Furies.

Our gazes met as I waited for her to run screaming or punch me in the face.

Instead, she inhaled, and *laughed.*

"And I thought you said you weren't funny," she huffed in between heaving chuckles, wiping a stray tear from the corner of her eye. The delicious scent grew, tinged with candied humor and the bubble-gum sound of her obnoxious, adorable laugh. "You're fucking with me."

"No, I'm serious all the time," I chuckled back, her laughter infectious as the plague. The world spun as the air grew thin, but I didn't care. "I would never fuck with you."

"Are you saying I'm unfuckable? Jeez, you psych-heads are picky," she fired back, quick as a whip, her viral malady of giggles intensifying. "I guess Freud would say I don't look enough like your mother."

And I laughed. *Hard.*

Not a fake one, not for pleasantries or politeness. A real, unadulterated, boisterous *guffaw*. It clawed its way out of me, breaking free from its fetters and dancing through the chilly air on the back of my breath. Fueled by strawberries and silliness, by desire and drunken fumbles. By something I hadn't felt in millennia.

"I have no comment for confidentiality purposes." My shoulders shook as I gasped out the words, and she stuck her tongue out at me like we were five-year-olds on a playground. "But if you looked like my mother, we would have a real problem."

Considering my 'mother' was technically a primordial vat of darkness and chaos, of course. At least, in my original life. In this one, she was just some poor teenager named Susan from Minnesota who left me on the steps of a local firehouse with a note that said 'Teen mom, sorry. Love, Susan'.

"Sorry, I know this is unprofessional," she snorted hard, a fresh round of laughter taking us both like consumption. "I'll stop teasing—I'm sure the sexy, aloof psychiatrist vibes are really hard to maintain."

At that, the laughter blew out like a candle without oxygen. Something else crawled out of my gut, following the path the humor took, working its way to my malleable, whiskey-freed lips. "You think I'm sexy?"

"I think you're drunk." She stopped laughing too. But she didn't stop looking at me with those eyes. Sage and sea. Sass and sincerity.

Maybe she was blessed by the cosmos too. A creature of chaos and *sunlight* instead of darkness. Of easy laughter and flowery joy. Like the extra scoop of a sundae, or like finding a twenty in the pocket of your favorite sweater. Like starlight against the night sky. The small, untaintable moments of pleasure in a world fraught with pain.

"I think you're the most alluring, radiant creature in the twelve known universes."

Eyes blew wide, the lemony scent of shock bursting forth.

Fates and Furies, that one was out loud, too. I clapped my hand over my mouth, as if somehow, that would put the words back.

The Angel of Death didn't have crushes.

But Hope grinned wide and tucked herself against my side again, sliding beneath my arm. She was so small, but sturdy. Heat radiated through my skin despite the nightly chill.

"I think you're really, *really* drunk," she said sweetly, her breath warm and fragrant and so close. She pointed to an apartment complex two buildings down, its brick face staring at us. "That's my place up there. Let's go before you say something and I have to commit you to your own hospital."

Tension dissolved from my frame, and I let her lead me.

Somewhere between the street and the stairwell, my facilities started shutting down, the adrenaline and desire beaten back by whiskey's mighty sword. The world swayed in a dizzying blur, each step requiring the full labor of focus just to get my footing solid. We climbed for what felt like eternity, the most winding walk-up in all my lives, a true task of suffering designed by the cruel Fates.

Finally, I practically crawled to her door as she fumbled for her keys, opening the door to the dark apartment.

I didn't wait for her to turn the lights on as I shuffled first into the hallway that opened up to a small living room, my legs and my stomach fighting for which would give first.

"Let's go, couch is this way." Her hands grabbed my shoulders and pushed me in the right direction, my savior leading me to her sofa. I fell into it without further command, toppling like the tower of Babel.

The pillowy furniture must have also been enchanted, because the second I touched it, my limbs sank deep into its warm embrace, the spinning finally halting. My eyes fluttered.

She crossed her arms, her silhouette the only thing I could make out in the dark room, before pressing a quiet kiss to my cheek. "Rest well, Doc."

And though it was near-black, though I was drunk and stupid and half asleep...I imagined her perfect blue-green stare watching me as my own eyes closed. "G'night, Chara."

BEFORE

ROSEBUDS AND SUNFLOWER FIELDS, *her voice a soothing lullaby. Six little heads, focused on her and bobbing along, six smiles with the brightness of sunlight. The song of their laughter joined in Chara's tale, a perfect harmony of family found and finished.*

A babe pressed to her breast—eyes closed in sleep—too small, too precious. His breathing steady, a rhythmic percussion adding to the symphony of the morning. "Meet your new brother, my cherubs. This is Caedmon."

A high pitched snort—a burst of color. "He's kind of ugly, Mama."

A light prod to Eris's side from Balshasar. "You looked like that as a baby, too."

A blanket of warmth spread across my face with my smile. "Enough bickering, all of you, and say hello to your brother." *Pride straightened my spine, emboldened by the love pouring sweet heat into my veins.* "You're all perfect, even if you were once ugly little poopers."

"Thanatos." *A gentle warning from my wife, a melody against the chorus of shoulder-shaking laughter from the little ones.*

Fury. Fate.

Forgiveness.

~

V. TESTING

SHAME SMELLED like thinly-veiled garbage. Like someone had tried to spray the scent away, only to add to the odor.

Mingling with strong coffee, the potent smell roused me from my nightmare-drenched sleep. Perhaps I'd have to pay a visit to Eris soon...see if he had an appetite for any of my haunting dreams. I squinted against the light pouring through the open window, lighting the unfamiliar surroundings and adding to the pounding headache hammering against my skull.

I surveyed the living room, trying to gather my senses. A warm brown coffee table sporting a bouquet of sunflowers sat directly opposite the soft blue couch I laid across, and a soft, woven blanket covered my feet. I sat up, vision spinning, my stomach rising and falling again like I was jumping on a trampoline.

Hanging plants and chaotic bookshelves decorated much of the exposed brick walls, long green branches and haphazardly stacked pages both waving in the breeze of the cracked window, the floral-patterned curtains nearly transparent with the early morning light.

My shame stank up the room despite the flowers and ferns, only adding to my nausea. Fates and Furies damn me, what had I done?

"Good morning, sunshine." The reminder skipped into the room, wearing a pale pink pair of sweatpants that defined her shapely hips and a tight, midriff sports top that hugged her muscles and exposed the flat planes of her stomach. Her curls were tamed in a tight braid, a light sheen of sweat the only stain on her bronze brow. She smiled as she settled into the whimsical yellow chair across from the couch, placing the cardboard tray of coffees she carried–marked with *Deja Brew's* logo–on the table between us.

Fates and Furies, had she already worked out and gotten coffee this morning? My eyes darted to the tiny wooden clock on the wall—its hands marked just before nine in the morning.

I had no idea what I must have looked like right now, but given the taste of bile and alcohol still mixing on my tongue, and the sour, sweat-soaked smell of my sweater, I had a good guess.

"I'm so unbelievably sorry." I hung my throbbing head in my hands, covering my face as if it did anything to hide my shame.

"Don't sweat it," Hope laughed, sliding one of the paper coffee cups my way. "We've all been there. It makes you human."

Funny, since I felt entirely weak and *mortal* right now, my throat dry and my head swirling.

I peeked through my pale fingers, noting my name scribbled on the side of the cup with a winky-face that had to be from Wit. Another wave of shame made me want to vomit.

Instead, I picked up the gesture—gratitude settling my stomach—and took a deep sip. The warm, bitter liquid slid down my throat easier than I expected, a wash of calm coating my nerves. I'd have to thank Wit for that later. Now, my eyes settled on the too-perky saint in front of me, who only stared with amusement, not a hint of judgment clouding the sage and sea.

"Thank you." I lifted my cup. "For the coffee and the couch."

She shrugged, taking the last drag of her own, the smell of peppermint and chocolate wafting my way as it met her lips. "That place really has the best coffee."

I nodded. Hopefully, while last night resulted in nothing but a harsh hangover and enough embarrassment to last me several life-times, Wit had at least earned a new regular.

I stood, ignoring the protest of my sore back and cracking knees. I was only thirty-five in this body, but I felt ancient. I ran a hand over my hair and straightened my sweater, hating the way the material bunched and rumpled from a night's sleep. "I should get moving. I've taken up too much of your kindness already."

Hope didn't budge from her seat to see me out—she just crossed her legs and cocked her head to the side, curiosity churning in the air.

"Who is Chara?"

I sat before my legs could buckle beneath me.

A different pain thundered in my head, unrelated to the hangover. A much deeper, festering nausea rocked my frame. The name was a punch to the gut, hearing it out loud after so many years, so many lives–

"I–" I gaped, words escaping my fried brain, only one remaining. *Chara.*

"You said her name last night," Hope watched me with those eyes–*her* eyes–a softness to her voice. Then, a snort, one that cleared the tension pressurizing the air around me. "Among some other delicious blackmail, might I add. Something about twelve universes…"

Fates and Furies.

"Chara is my wife." I cut her off to save the embarrassment, surprised at myself for saying her name without wincing. Still, my chest squeezed tightly, ash chasing the coffee taste. "*Was*, I should say."

Hope blinked, but didn't reveal any further surprise despite the spiced tea-blend of curiosity I could taste from her. "Divorce?"

In a way, yes. If divorce meant abandonment. If it meant separation, complete and final.

If it meant drinking a whole vial of nightshade and taking your own life to leave your husband and seven children alone, leave them to fight the impending trouble all on their own…

"She died." I gave the easy explanation, the only one I could push through the choking, burning acid and ash. "A long time ago."

Hope stared again. For a too-long moment, she said nothing.

I bunkered down, ready for the 'sorry', for the inevitable condolence that would make my stomach turn. It was the same in every life, every universe. Piss-flavored pity for the widower. For the forgotten sin.

"Never goes away, does it?" she said instead, that heart-stopping smile spreading like the sunshine filling the room. "The pain."

At this point, the shock shouldn't have surprised me. Not with her. This creature of chaos and goodness. This full-bloomed flower of a woman that always brought a dash of color to the gray world around her.

Cycles could not be broken, but Hope did not subscribe to them.

And despite the soul deep ache that still wrung my chest like a dishrag, despite the bottomless chasm of guilt and grief I'd stuffed beneath layer after layer of ash...

I smiled back. "No, it doesn't go away."

The admission dredged up more of that unending hurt for both of us—I could taste it in the air, her sorrow and mine, both mangled and mingling.

"I never met my mom. She died having me, but she wrote me a letter. Like she knew what was going to happen to her." She shook her head, salty tears kissing her cheeks. But the smile never wavered, even as her voice did. "She told me she loved me, of course. But she also said that pain was the point. It hurts to remind us we are alive, and that we have been loved. I didn't get it until later, obviously... when Dad was sick and angry. Then with Gram and Gramps..."

Hope trailed off, ash dousing her colorful frame in gray.

"You've had more than your share," I acknowledged, for her and I both. I'd lived lifetimes beyond lifetimes, and yet somehow, our pain mirrored each others', equal offerings on Fate's cruel scales.

Hope shook her head, a curl popping out of the braid. "Because I've been loved more than most ever get to be. I see it as a gift."

And then, the ash was marred by something greater.

Rosebuds and sunflowers. Fresh as spring and as warm as summer. Love and...

Fates and Furies damn me.

For once in my many lifetimes, I was inclined to agree with her. This effervescent enigma of a creature, more energizing than the warm coffee in my hand, had woken something I'd long forgotten.

Hope, her namesake.

Hope that maybe... I didn't have to be completely alone. That maybe, I could give myself permission to let someone in instead of shutting it all out.

Hope that even the most incurable souls could heal, even just a little.

"I have to get going, but–" I stood again, renewed by that tiny spark she gave me. Fishing in my back pocket, I handed her a crumpled business card. "But if you ever need someone to talk to about the pain, give me a call."

She took it and crossed her arms, suspicion salting her narrowed stare. "I told you, I don't need a therapist."

And despite my lifetimes of learning, despite the tingling worry tugging at the back of my brain...

I let myself care again. A defiant choice.

"How about a friend, then?" I shoved my hands in my front pockets, rocking back and forth on my heels as the vulnerability scraped uncomfortably beneath my skin. "A sexy, aloof psychologist friend, maybe..."

Her hearty laugh soothed something deep. She stood, punching my arm as she passed me. "Touché, Freud. Come on, I'll show you out."

Something else–unrelated to the hangover–fluttered in my middle as I let her lead me to the door. I vaguely remembered stumbling in the night before, unable to appreciate the wall of mismatched picture frames lining the thin corridor. I trailed over them as we passed, pictures of Hope and Elain in many, a handful of photos of a slew of late-twenty-something girls I assumed had to be her friends...

One caught my eye and held it.

And my stomach slid to my toes.

A man, with Hope's bronze skin and wild curls. His arm wrapped around a short woman's frame...

A woman with blue-green eyes and long black hair that rolled in waves away from her olive complexion. A woman whose smile captured the whole sun, whose tender fingers had once held the world.

Chara.

Not an imitation, but a perfect replication. Her twin in every aspect, down to the tiny birthmark on her left cheek.

"Where did you get this photo?" The breath blew out of me without my command as I snatched the frame off the nail it hung on.

No question, it was her. No doubt that the Fates had not yet tired of fucking with me. Chara had been alive. Alive and *here*.

Fates and fucking *Furies*.

Hope stared over my shoulder, a gentleness to her tone as she pointed to the photo. "Oh, that's my parents. When they first met."

Here and happy and healthy and married to another man... starting and *leaving* another family...

"She's your mother?" I stuttered the stupid question, heartbeat screaming in my ears, too many scents marring my senses...

"Yeah...is everything okay?" Hope stepped back, narrowing those eyes that saw too much.

Chara's eyes.

Chara's *daughter*.

"Fine." I brushed past her, tucking a different photo into my pocket before opening the door with the last resolve my trembling hand could muster. "Thanks again for everything."

Of all the Furies, Death had once been the most frightening. And he rose again from his grave within me, ready to have a word with the Fates that would not let him rest.

~

VI. ANGER

THE FATES HAD MANY NAMES throughout cultures and timelines. The Celts' triple-faced goddess; the Mother, Maiden, and Crone. The Greeks called them The Moirai, the Norse called them the Norns. Shakespeare named them the Weird Sisters after a chance encounter, or so Cardan said, as had many other poets and writers throughout the ages. I was pretty sure they'd even had something to do with the original Blue Man Group, but I couldn't be sure.

But no matter what form they took, Adeeba, Pennella, and Danoma had a taste for trickery and trouble that ought to have made them Furies. The witches sat in their bloody library, life after life, weaving fate and fucking over the rest of the world for fun.

It was their job—given to them from powers outside and above the universes known and unknown. The Authority. But I knew them well enough to know how they delighted in it—each book of life written to their taste, each story threaded to match their visions. They were authors with a taste for angst, each of us just characters in their scheme.

And after centuries—*millennia*—I'd had enough. They'd finally cut one string too painfully close to the quick.

It had been ages since I'd called on my dark gift, but stepping into the power felt like donning an old pair of worn boots and finding they still fit. It rumbled deep in my chest, a swirling storm darkening the skyway. I'd once been their ally, a coworker, dragging the souls of the dead and damned to their infinite red door, readying them for reincarnation.

Not anymore.

The local library was meager at best, sagging shelves often undusted, books frequently tattered and torn. A teenager with dark hair and a Nirvana t-shirt manned the front desk as I entered, flipping through his phone, the woody, stale taste of his disinterest mirroring the environment. He didn't even look up as I stormed in, careening for the stacks at the very back of the place.

My power shifted in my middle as the stacks did, unkempt metal shelves dissolving into craftsman mahogany, the stained carpet beneath my shoes transforming to black and white checkered marble. Each book on the towering stacks sang with energy as I entered the Library of Souls.

The three witches sat together at the front desk, unfazed by my arrival. To the naked eye, they could be triplets: their otherworldly forms both ageless and ancient; their deep set eyes pure white and pupilless, endless expanses of white that held the secrets of the universe; their golden hair made of the same gauzy, metallic material they wove from. Mortals saw them not as they were, but as what they wanted them to be; projections of the imagination, of their innermost desires or fears. But I'd always seen them clearly. Not even Fate could hide from Death, after all.

But despite their near-identical appearance, they were easily distinguished by their personalities. Pennella stirred a cup of tea with a silver spoon, reading a book, her severe features holding no emotion. She didn't bother to lift her head, the slick bun at the top pointed at me. At her side, Adeeba scratched in a different tome, bright eyes utterly focused, her bone structure sharp beneath her skin like she'd barely taken time to eat or breathe these days. But her golden mane hung in a long, loose braid, giving her a soft elegance that counteracted her sunken cheeks. And with her feet up on the desk, Danoma, as always, idly tended to her weaving, humming an off-beat tune as she set to ruin her sisters' quiet. She tossed her perfectly curled hair over her shoulder, a wry smile carving her features as she said, "My my, Thanatos, you look cross. I almost mistook you for Tyr."

I slammed my hands on the desk, my dark gift taking over as my voice rumbled low in my chest. "How long have you been toying with me?"

At that, the sisters all lifted their heads, Adeeba flattening me with a slow blink and a too-kind smile. "I have no time for toys, Thanatos. What troubles you?"

Bile rose to my throat with my rage, as the smell of her sincerity accosted me. The worst part about her kindness was it wasn't at all faked. This creature had always believed herself a mother to humanity, a generous benefactor keeping the balance. I was not my brother, not a maker of war, but I was a Fury, and I wouldn't be blinded by her well-intended atrocities.

I stole the book from beneath her quill, tucking it under my arm and demanding her full attention. "Did you write this particular joke at my expense, Adeeba, or was Danoma meddling outside of her business again?"

Penella let loose an exasperated sigh, shutting her own reading and training her unseeing gaze on me. "You're going to need to start making sense if you want us to help you."

The memory-keeper had always been the least pleasant of the three, and by definition, the least odious to me. At least she didn't pretend to be a saint in sinner's clothes. She just met everyone and everything with the same no-nonsense severity. But now, her apathy grated against my every nerve.

I straightened up, addressing her with the same unfeeling glare. "Chara's been reincarnating."

"Yes," she deadpanned before reopening her book and thumbing to her spot. "Now that we've cleared that up, may I return to my book?"

"Easy, Penn." Adeeba laid a gentle hand on her sister's arm before pointing that sickeningly sweet smile at me again. "I'm sorry, Thanatos. I imagine this must be a shock for you."

My heart threatened to burst in my chest, an odd reminder that I had one at all. Pain laced my voice with a vulnerability I detested. "How could you not tell me?"

"It was not our secret to tell as it was not your duty to know," Danoma piped in, setting her golden threads down as she leaned forward, resting her chin in her hand, a curious look blazing at me. "But now that you found out on your own, everything is in order!"

"We could not tell you. It was part of the curse handed to her."

Adeeba frowned, sadness swimming in her endless, milky gaze. Her voice was soft as a lullaby, but it rattled me to my core. "She was to always reincarnate with you and the children, but she may never get too close to any of you. She could only watch from afar. And if she ever tried to start her own family again, she would suffer a gruesome death and the cycle would begin again."

A flash of pain shot through me, but was gone as soon as it came. We'd all suffered our curses, and while I never wished any harm to Chara, there was no arguing she in part deserved it.

But Hope did not.

The death-spell in my veins swirled again, ready to be unleashed. If I had any power over the Fates, I would've ended them millennia ago. But even if I couldn't harm them, perhaps I could frighten them. I let the smallest sliver of my power go, the darkness shaking the room as it sucked the heat from the air. "Did one of my siblings put you all up to this? Is Tyr trying to get to me?" A humorless laugh fell from my lips. "Because it worked. But how dare you all bring her daughter into this, to use her–"

At that, the weaver's brow knotted together, her head tilted. "Your daughters all have gold threads, we can't interfere–"

"Not *my* daughters. Chara's daughter with another man," I spat the words, each one coated thoroughly in the burning, ashy taste of my sorrow. My betrayal. The room shook again, nearby books tumbling from their shelves. "Hope Pelora."

Pennella's lifeless expression shifted ever so slightly, a frown tugging her mouth into the first tell of her distress. "Chara cannot have children. It's her penance."

I expelled a huff of breath, tugging the photo I'd stored in my pocket out and placing it upright on the desk in front of them. Hope's sunshine smile looked back up at us, her white teeth a beacon in the dark room. And in the background behind her, a larger copy of the same photo that I'd found in her apartment nestled itself between two pots of teeming plants.

Chara, watching over Hope, the resemblance clear as day.

"You're telling me this isn't her?" I scoffed at the Fates, pointing to both women in the photo in case they couldn't actually see with those horrid eyes of theirs. "Hope Pelora is not some pawn in your scheme to make my life miserable. I will leave her alone if that's what it takes. But you will not harm her to get to me."

Adeeba stood from the desk, covering her mouth as she stared at the photo like it had just bitten her. "Hope Pelora is dead. Her book is only a page long–an infant that died with her mother in birth. This must be incorrect somehow."

Danoma nodded along, though her usual smirk fell. She shut her eyes, the tang of magic scenting the air. "And I can't locate her thread. She is no longer with the living."

At that, my heart threatened to stop all together.

Hope could not be dead. A world without her was meaningless. I would not let it happen.

Not again.

"That's impossible. I just saw her this morning," I stammered, my pulse deafening as I grasped for answers. "Elain–her grand-mother, she crossed over recently. Surely she mentioned her."

"Elain, I remember her," Penella interjected, and a small spark of something I didn't dare name rocketed through me again. "She drank the tea and I saw her memories... But there was no mention of a granddaughter. Her dead son, but..."

"This is not a game!" I roared, and the entire library rumbled with it, crashes of books making the witches wince. But I didn't care. Not for them. Only for her.

For Chara's daughter.

"We are not playing." Adeeba's sweet voice was edged with a note of power, and though I could not taste the Fate's emotions, I didn't need to. She'd hit her limit with my tantrum.

I took a steadying breath, letting it ground me back to my body, my power sliding within my control once more.

"Look." I pointed to the photo again, at the tangible evidence of the woman who had swept into my life and flipped it upside down.

Who had given the Fury of Death a reason to smile after millennia of sorrow. Who had seen me for *who* I was, not *what* I was, who had helped me see myself again. "She is an adult now, late twenties, and she's kind in the most genuine way and runs her grandmother's flower shop and laughs like a hyena, and I just slept on her couch. She has to be in Elain's book, or Chara's...check Chara's most recent book."

The three Fates exchanged a loaded glance before nodding once in unison. Adeeba floated to the nearest bookstacks, the shapeless black dress she wore sweeping across the tiled floor. With a shaky hand, she grabbed an emerald green hardback from the middle shelf, opening it to the very last page.

The color rushed from her cheeks as her eyes shot to her sisters, who rushed to her side without a word.

"This is impossible," Adeeba whispered as she pointed to text on the back page. "I didn't write this. I have no clue how it got there."

The other two Fates inhaled a sharp gasp. The wrinkles in Penn's brow deepened. "She shouldn't be alive."

"Some destinies are beyond understanding." Danoma stared over her sisters' shoulder at the page, and then to me. I stepped closer, my limbs quaking beneath me like a newborn fawn. I couldn't taste it, but concern and wonder were painted in broad strokes across their features as all three Fates eyed me warily.

"She's a miracle." Adeeba breathed, looking down at the page one last time. "But we did not do this, Thanatos. Her fate must serve a greater purpose than even we are privy to understand."

I scanned her face with every gift I had, natural and learned. Not a trace of dishonesty or trickery. The Fates had not concocted this plan.

If anything, they were victims too. The higher order the universe had made had plans for us all. For all the credit I gave Fate, Balshasar had taught me well enough that a bit of luck and free will could change any destiny.

Slowly, like I might chomp her arm off, Adeeba handed me the book, allowing me to see the ink carefully etched onto the last page. In Adeeba's familiar, strict handwriting, black ink told the horrible story of Chara's most recent end.

But then beneath it, a single line written in gold, the typeface bold and glittering against the creme-colored page.

And despite all Fates and Furies, defying all curses and odds, the little girl she mothered lived. Hope.

"Why did she have to be hers?" Tears blurred the page as they sprung to my eyes, stinging and soothing all at once. "Chara's. Why did she have to be *her* daughter? Just to torment me?"

Or to save me, from the curse we'd placed on each other. From the millennia alone, left behind in Chara's wake, just as she had been.

Adeeba stepped closer, white eyes seeing everything as the ghost of her famous smile lifted the corners of her mouth. "We've done you many disservices over the centuries. I think perhaps we owe you a favor."

"These are the books of every life Chara has lived since the first." Danoma gestured to the rest of the shelf they stood in front of, hundreds of spines in a rainbow of colors all carved with the same curved mark on them.

My stomach knotted as I took them in, each novel a gateway to my reliving my past pain. Each book a doorway to the answers that might free me from it.

Pennella cleared her throat, tucking her hands behind her. "Most of them are rather short. But you may stay and read as long as you'd like."

And then the Fates left me alone to read and mourn and grieve until my tears ran dryer than the pages of each and every worn book in the Library of Souls.

∿

BEFORE

Sage and sea, *color unchanged throughout the lifetimes. A memory of what was lost. A woman, consumed by her own grief, again and again. The call of her blade a battle cry, begging her to end it all.*

A child in the distance—always out of reach—too lonely, too cold. Her heart aching, begging for the torment to end after all this time. "I just want to be with my babies."

A woman with a cane, severe features drawn. "They aren't yours anymore, Chara."

A gasp of pain through her limbs. "I can't bear it alone. I need him."

A sad sigh from the keeper of memory. "You should have held on tighter the first time." Her words cleaved through the woman's resolve, sadness scenting the air for miles. "There is a lesson to be learned."

"Thanatos." A final prayer to the god of Death as the sharp end of the blade kissed her skin, blood watering the dry earth.

A cycle ends. Another repeats.

Silver hair and wrinkled skin, *the mark of a life long lived. A woman, withering away in a lonely rocking chair, again and again. Another life sentence served for the mistakes of the past, her only company the quiet woods.*

A wolf's howl in the distance—another lonely soul ripped from its pack— too piercing, too quiet. Her bones aching next to the crackling hearth, ready for the end to greet her again. "I'm ready to go now."

A woman with a cup of tea, sighing as she misted into the one-roomed cabin. "You don't have to be completely alone, Chara."

A slow, shuddering breath. "I deserve it after what I've done. How selfish I've been."

A playful frown from the weaver of fate. "You could do so much good. " Her words enveloped the woman as the fragrant scent of her tea invited a forgotten feeling. "There are others that could use your love."

"Thanatos." A final goodbye to the man she loved long ago as she took a sip of the weaver's tea, her memories slipping away with her life.

A cycle ends. Another repeats.

~

TEAR-STAINED CHEEKS AND TINY COFFINS, the mark of little lives stamped out. A woman, with sunken cheeks and an empty womb, again and again. Another payment to the cruel god of death, who cursed all she touched and loved.

A single rose laid on a grave–a body that never knew the sting of breath–too small, too sudden. Her soul aching to join her unborn babe in the great beyond. "This is not their curse to bear. This is cruelty."

A woman with a worn book, offering a soothing hand. "The cosmos are neither cruel nor kind, Chara."

A heaving, hoarse sob. "There has to be another way. I have to fix this."

A sad smile from the writer of life. "All cycles can be broken." Her words stoked a forsaken fire in her breast, fanning the flames of determination. "It's time to try again."

"Thanatos." A final threat to the Fury who'd stolen from her once again as she said goodbye to her resting babe.

A cycle ends. Another repeats.

~

GLOWING SKIN AND SWOLLEN BELLY, the hint of a life yet to begin. A woman, learning to hope, again and again. Another defiant stand against the tides of fate, a sacrifice and a wish.

A baby's cry down the corridor–a different child meeting its mother–too precious, too painful. The woman's body aching in the hospital bed as it neared the end and the beginning. "We're almost there, Hope. Just a little longer."

A man with dark skin next to her, worry on his brow. "I don't under-

stand what that letter was about. The doctors said you and the baby will both be fine. C-sections now are extremely safe."

A quiet, knowing smile. "Just promise me you'll give it to her no matter what."

A gentle squeeze from his warm hand. "You'll tell her yourself. " He whispered quietly to her belly, a bittersweet sadness gripping the woman's heart, "Mommy and I can't wait to meet you."

"Thanatos." The woman cried in pain as life drained from her limbs, drowned out by the blaring flatline of the machine, one final act as new life carved from her middle.

And despite all Fates and Furies, defying all curses and odds, the little girl torn from her womb lived.

Happiness. Heartache.

Hope.

～

VII. ACCEPTANCE

OF ALL THE DIAGNOSES I dealt with, depression was still the hardest to treat. Modern medicine was a godsend, sertraline and fluoxetine the new deities I worshiped. But still, not even careful chemistry could convince a soul to live when it so keenly welcomed the escape of Death's dark embrace.

But death was only a temporary escape. It came and passed just as quickly as the seasons, and even when the body perished, the soul lived on. Sometimes, it still carried that sadness with it, beyond the grave and into the next life.

It had taken me weeks to read through Chara's lives. Weeks of drowning in my own depression as I read about the sadness that burdened her, the guilt. The black and white pages were the only witness to my suffering as I read over and over again the pain of my first love's every life. Weeks of sleepless, hopeless nights. Weeks of wishing I could end it all, weeks of not wanting any of it to stop.

After Mimi left, offering me the last piece of Chara's life—her love for me—I realized the truth.

Death was temporary. Love could be eternal.

So I did what a Fury did best. I went back to work.

Not all cycles could be broken, after all.

In my dusty office in Seaside Behavioral, the scent of Spencer Ganes' sorrow suffocated me. I struggled to retain my mask, not wanting to upset the young man with my discomfort. Only nineteen, and already, he'd faced so much trauma and abuse from foster parent after foster parent, it was easy to see why he'd been so consumed by the heaviness of his own pain. But I had a sinking feeling this was not his first cursed life either. The taste of his agony was ancient, and I suspected he'd been suffering long before he walked into this office.

He stretched across the worn brown leather of the couch, his dark hair falling in front of his eyes as he sat with his wraith-like arms crossed.

I sighed back into my own seat, tugging at the light blue collar of my short-sleeved button up. It was getting warm already, and the smell certainly didn't help. But I put on my best smile anyway. "Tell me, Spencer—what good would killing yourself do?"

Spencer rolled his eyes, huffing a breath that sent his fringe flying out of his face. The bruises under his eyes spoke volumes, and the acid and ash only permeated deeper into my lungs. "Listen, Dr. Ashton, you're a good guy, but you don't get it. What's the point of living if there's no one to give a shit about you?"

I sighed. No one cared about orphaned whelps with enough trauma to tranquilize an elephant.

"But I care, Spencer." A character fault, no doubt, but one I took pride in all the same.

Spencer snorted, the slight odor of ammonia annoyance accompanying the sound. "They pay you to say that."

I cracked a grin and winked at him. "Please, not nearly enough."

At that, citrus amusement gathered at the back of my tongue, mixing with the overwhelming ash. Good. Of all the short-term remedies I'd tried, humor was the easiest to digest.

Running with it, I leaned forward, breathing him in deeply. "Mr. Ganes, do you believe in fate or free will?"

Golden brown eyes flicked to me, narrowed in equal parts scrutiny and curiosity. "I dunno, what kind of question is that?"

"Humor me." I shrugged, letting the bouquet of his emotions envelop me.

Spencer sat up ever so slightly, the worn leather couch groaning as he shifted his weight. After a long pause, he answered, gaze darkening in the shoddy lamplight of the office. "Fate, I guess. None of us have any control."

Sorrow won out again in the room, ash coating everything in a thick layer of debris. But Spencer had yet to land on the final sin's doorstep.

"So, if you believe in fate, how do you know life won't get better?" My grin widened like I was the damned Cheshire cat. "Who's to say that the Fates don't have a lovely person for you down the line who will make up for all the love you've lost?"

Spencer shot me a look of betrayal that cut through the stagnancy, my trickery bringing his rage to the surface once more. "I've changed my mind."

I sat back, folding my arms to mirror his stance. "Free will, then?"

"Yeah." His voice rose, anger souring the room. "There is no grand plan, just people making shitty choices. And you can't trust people."

I nodded, giving him a moment to cool down before I perched a brow. "Would you like to know what I think?"

Another snort. "You'll tell me anyway."

"I'm predictable," I chuckled before I leaned closer, meeting his gaze. Golden eyes shone back, so full of potential, it hurt to feel his misery this close. He was so young, too young to have suffered as he did. But that also meant there was so much life left to live. So much to hope for, if I could only show him how. I kept my voice low, the small comfort just enough to manage the harshest of the pain. "I believe life is a balance of both. Sometimes, Fate hands you a shitty hand, or people hurt you for no good reason. But there is one thing you always have control over, and that's how you react. Suicide is a pretty bold action of free will. To escape, to end it all. But so is surviving. So is living every day, and believing that the choices you make matter, despite it all."

Something twinkled in his eyes as they welled with tears, that sorrow spilling over as I tapped into the soul-deep wound. He'd been hurt. So unbelievably damaged.

But he could heal.

"It's just so fucking hard." His throat worked hard as he swallowed. "I want it all to go away."

My heart ached for him, my power surging in my veins. It wanted to answer his call, to offer the respite of oblivion. But there was no mercy in pure apathy. It only lobotomized the soul, taking away the good with the bad.

"Nothing can erase it all entirely." I reached out, placing my hand on his knee. At my touch, my power reached out to consume—but this time, only a morsel. Just enough to take the edge off, like any good antidepressant would. His shoulders relaxed ever so slightly as I continued, the ash in my mouth abating. "But some things help. I've seen you hanging out in the art therapy department. Why don't you go and draw your feelings about free will and fate before our next session? Perhaps a little creative inspiration can turn that pain into something beautiful."

Skin a little clearer and eyes a little brighter, the boy nodded. "I think I'd like that."

He stood to go, the taste of determination enough to douse me in pure joy. He was not yet healed, but healing. A journey, not just a destination.

"Knock knock," Hope said as Spencer swung open the door, her arms full of a gorgeous bouquet of tulips and peonies to break up the monotony of the dull room. But it was her beauty, as always, that truly brightened every space she greeted. Today, she wore another yellow sundress—new, by the looks of it—that could rival the sunshine itself.

"Come in." I smiled, unable to help myself. In the year since we met, the sheer force of her presence never got old, never failing to fill me with wonder and awe. "We were just wrapping up."

Spencer's eye blew wide as he took in the ray of sunshine incarnate, blush coloring his pale cheeks. "Can I draw her instead for my assignment?"

Hope laughed, rosewater and champagne clearing the air. She took the slightly wilted flowers from the vase on my desk and handed them to Spencer before she tucked the fresh bouquet into the container. "No, but you can practice still-life on these old flowers."

And even though she was handing him drooping flowers, the young man took them in his hand with a grin wider than the Sahara desert. He jerked his chin at me before scurrying out of the room. "See you tomorrow, Dr. A."

"He looks better." Hope's gaze trailed after him before the sea-and-sage refocused on me. "So do you."

I ran a self-conscious hand through my dark trimmed curls, heat filling my cheeks. Fates and Furies, I'd had hundreds of thousands of haircuts in my lifetimes. I had no business blushing like a schoolboy. But then again, in so many ways, this life was my first. First without carrying the burden of my sins with me, first that I let myself wish and dream. I gave her a shy grin. "Shall we? The usual?"

Coffee at the *Deja Brew*, our daily afternoon retreat. It'd become a ritual in the last few months, a simple, harmless pleasure I indulged in.

It was a risk, to let myself care. To enjoy her company, her friendship, her affection. To sip and savor a cup of dark roast coffee when loss was the only guarantee this life afforded. Hope wasn't supposed to exist at all, a bold defiance to the cosmos, born of a mother's infallible love and sacrifice. There was no telling when the universe would demand its repayment, would steal her from me and end the light and love she was made from. Or, no guarantee that my siblings wouldn't get to her first, would try and fulfill their vengeance on Chara, the human woman who dared to love a Fury, by demanding Hope's life instead.

No foreseeing the standard trials and tribulations of human existence, either. The many illnesses that could ravage a person, as cancer had her father, or any number of accidents and tragedies that only the Fates could predict.

It was a risk to love her, knowing I would one day lose her.

But I did all the same. Because if I had learned anything from reading Chara's many lives, it was that somehow, that was the point. Even if I lost her, the love wouldn't die.

Her touch brought me back to the moment as her palm grazed the stubble of my cheek, a wicked grin tugging at her full lips. "It's like you can read my mind, professor."

"You're my favorite book." I leaned in and pressed a gentle kiss on her cheek, savoring the feel of her soft skin against my lips. If I one day had to lose her, I would love her with every part of me in the meantime.

"That one was cheesy even for you." Hope scrunched her nose as she pulled back, but the only taste on my tongue was the candied humor and fresh happiness that followed her wherever she went. "But I love it. And you. Tell me again how I'm 'the most alluring, radiant creature in the twelve known universes?'"

I tucked her to my side, her wild curls tickling my neck as we headed out for coffee. No matter what Fate threw in our paths, I'd stay right here, her protector or confidant or whatever else she needed of me. Her guardian angel or her escape. "You're the most incredible, tantalizing, heart-stopping beast in the entire cosmos."

Love tasted of rosewater and sunshine. Of sea and sage, of flowers in full bloom and coffee mixed with cinnamon.

And of all the cures discovered, love was the most universal.

Acknowledgments

FROM LINA C. AMAREGO

As a small, independent author, the task of writing and publishing a novel can be an isolating road, but the process of creating and curating this anthology was far from lonely, thanks to the incredible collaborative efforts of many wonderful colleagues.

To my co-authors, Cassidy, Cass, C.M., Maddie, L.E, and Kayla; thank you for your time, your energy, and most of all, your *talent*. The collective creativity of this group was awe inspiring, and I am honored to have written beside such massively accomplished, gifted creators. Thank you for letting me fall in love with all of your characters, for dealing with my endless questions in the group chat, and for the positive insight you each brought to the project. It would be physically impossible for me to be more proud of the story we've told, and I am eternally grateful that I got to make it with all of you.

To our co-author and editor, Cassidy Clarke; Thank you for being the final weaver of this tale. For polishing it to a standard we can all be proud of, and to going above and beyond to add your expertise and attention to detail to this project.

To our proofreader, Renee Dugan: thank you for lending us your all-seeing eyes, your wisdom, and your mastery over this artform. It was an honor to leave our fate in your capable hands.

To our cover artists & 99Designs contest winners, Jesh Art Studio and Betelgeuse; thank you for giving this tome its stunning faces. Your creativity and professionalism were both second to none.

To Stacey Willis, our creative consultant for pride; thank you for your innovative take on an old classic, your imaginative approach to the work, and for navigating time-zones with us to lend your voice to the story.

To Kathryn at Sapphire Ink Press; thank you for fearlessly leading our release & promotional activities. You made the daunting task of marketing manageable, and your confidence and support were essential to this release.

To my husband, AJ; thank you for talking me through the burnout. For encouraging me to tell the story even when it hurt. For being by my side with an iced-coffee and a treat when I needed it most. For that ramen date that sparked the first 'what-if' conversation, and for pushing me to turn it into a 'when'. I love you more every day.

And to our readers and fellow writers who relate to our sinful crew; the cycle-breakers, the magic-makers, the earth-shakers. The brave souls fighting to heal and change the narrative of generational trauma. The weary wounded still learning to love the darker parts of themselves. We see you. We accept you. We are you. Thank you.

FROM CASSIDY CLARKE

To my mom, who always wonders why my characters have mommy issues no matter which book I'm writing, even when EVERY OTHER CHARACTER HAS DADDY ISSUES: I'm not doing it on purpose. I promise I love you and you're doing great. XOXO.

And to anyone who loves a little slower, a little safer. It's okay to wait for it. Some people will leave before you're ready, but the right ones won't. It's all right if your heart takes its time.

FROM CASS MAREN

I never know how to properly thank someone for giving me the opportunities to be unapologetically myself. "Thank you" feels too simple, but sometimes it's the best we can do. Sharing my craft has always been tricky. I am equally passionate about sharing my ideas and terrified that they will be laughed at. It makes for an interesting state of mind as a writer, but I have been lucky to be surrounded by people who have constantly supported me and encouraged me to pursue my love for storytelling.

I could thank a thousand people for the nitty-gritty details that went into creating this short story, but I want to take this opportunity to thank, above all, the listeners in my life. The people who listen to the sudden influx of a new idea, the rambling chaos that ensues once my mind begins to connect the pieces like I'm that meme of Charlie from *It's Always Sunny in Philadelphia* erratically explaining ideas tied together with bits of red thread.

To my husband, who is endlessly supportive of my weirdness and creativity, who sits for hours listening to the ideas as I try to explain an entire plot whilst still remaining spoiler-free.

To my mom, who listened to every story I ever told since I could speak in full sentences and for helping me work through the writer's block moments that plague me.

To my dad, who listened even when he didn't fully understand what I was talking about (I'm not known for being concise), but always made an effort to connect with my interests and get excited about stories with me. To my best friend, who is endlessly patient and listens as I describe in painstaking detail the lore behind my stories and for always reminding me that "no, Cass...it is not, in fact, trash" when I put something out into the world. And to my soul sister from Michigan who reads all of my writing and listens to every word as I pour my soul out on the page.

Thank you to the women of this anthology for standing together to put this out into the world, for sharing your brilliance with me, and sharing our names on the page together. I am honored to have been on this journey with you.

And lastly, thank you to Lina for always listening and helping me grow as a writer, and a human. I'm forever thankful.

FROM C.M. MCCANN

I just want to thank Lina for giving me the opportunity to write this story. It had been a long time since I had written due to having a very time-consuming baby, and this project gave me the chance to break into that again. Finding the time to get pen to paper sometimes felt like pulling teeth, but it was absolutely worth it. So, Lina, thank you from the bottom of my heart for taking a chance on me and putting up with my mom-brain. My story wouldn't be the same without you.

FROM MADDIE JENSEN

To Lei & Tracey, for supporting me through all of my whirlwind ideas, listening to me stress over my plots and whether my writing and characters are good enough. You both have an endless stream of patience, thank you.

To Tessa, who has always been there when I have doubts with my storyline, and whose friendship and writing knowledge I am constantly thankful for. You are never afraid to tell me if something doesn't work, or if something needs changing, and I could not have come this far without your insight and encouragement.

To my fellow writers in this anthology, I am in awe of your talent and dedication. I am especially thankful to Cass, who has been there for years supporting me with my current project specifically, and to Lina, who had enough faith in me to include me in this amazing anthology. I cannot thank you all enough for your support.

FROM L.E. REINER

I cannot express the depth of gratitude I feel to not only the publishers of this incredible project, but to Lina Amarego herself. When I submitted for the sin of Sloth, I did not have high hopes of being selected. I feel I am one of the lucky few writers out there who do not suffer from imposter syndrome, though my outlook is rooted in practicality. I was one of the more *small-time* authors submitting to be a part of something big, and I feared that my lack of social media presence and following might impact the decision to bring me on board.

But Lina is a true creative, a dreamer and passionate artist who not only sees potential in a story, but the writer as well. As a thanks to her and my co-authors, I worked tirelessly to not only produce the best representation of the sin of Sloth for this project, but to boost my social media presence and following in order to contribute in a similar manner that Lina has contributed to my writing career. I can say in all confidence, the work produced for this project, with the help and guidance of Lina and my co-authors, is one of my favorite stories I've had the pleasure of writing.

FROM KAYLA WHITTLE

Writing is both incredibly isolating and very community oriented work, and I feel incredibly lucky for the support, advice, friendship, and love I've received throughout my career so far. Without these people, my words never would have made it to the page, let alone publication.

Thank you to Emily, for always reading what I send to you even if I don't tell you that I've actually sent anything so you never know what's in your inbox. For always supporting me, celebrating with me, and helping me become a better version of myself. I love you, beech!

To my family, for never second-guessing my decision to drop the Education major and dedicate myself fully to English & Creative Writing. You've always encouraged me and supported me, helping me to grow into the person I am today. Thank you.

Thank you to The Cool Hats Club, Sabrina, Samantha, Hailey, Cassidy, Sylvia, and everyone else who has taken the time to read, critique, and better my writing. Thank you for helping me tell my stories, and I appreciate each of you more than you will ever know!

The Pentagon and Marvel Movie Squad: I'll forever cherish your friendship and am lucky to have all of you in my life.

My fellow anthology writers, incredibly talented individuals who took so much time to help me develop my character and story! I cannot wait to follow along with each of your careers and am excited for your future projects!

Thank you to Lina, for this wonderful opportunity and her encouragement and support in bringing more representation and diversity to the publishing world. Thank you for seeing the potential in Wit, and your enthusiastic reaction to my original thought of *what if the reincarnation of Lust was ace?* was so validating and wonderful.

Thank you to every reader who decides to pick up this book. I hope your passions guide you well.

ABOUT THE AUTHORS

LINA C. AMAREGO

Growing up on the east coast in small-town New Jersey, Lina spent her early days playing pretend and making up stories for her friends and family. Little did they know, that pastime would soon turn into a lifelong passion for storytelling in all of its forms. While she's a couple's therapist by profession, she's a writer at heart. When she's not scribbling ideas about fictional worlds into the margins of her notebooks, Lina spends her time reading anything she can get her hands on, driving her husband crazy with her wild daydreams, and snuggling her adorable pups.

Lina founded Silver Wheel Press in 2020 as a publishing label for her own debut NA Fantasy novel, Daughter of the Deep (an Indie-Brag recipient), first in the Children of Lyr Series. However, in 2021 the project expanded to include other authors, creating a hybrid publishing group designed to uplift and inspire independent storytellers. Silver Wheel Press remains dedicated to supporting quality stories told with authenticity, creativity, and just enough fantasy to keep the daydreams alive. You can find her on Instagram @Lina_Amarego_Writes or www.silverwheelpress.com.

CASSIDY CLARKE

Cassidy Clarke is a proud Michigander, free-lance editor, and NA author who subsists on chicken tenders, ketchup, and fantasy books. She recently graduated with her BA in Creative Writing, which has allowed her to pursue her passion for storytelling and helping others make their books the absolute best they can be. *THE SALTWATER HEIR* is her debut novel, a high fantasy love letter to the lost princess daydreams of her childhood and an attempt to put her experience growing up with three younger siblings to good use. She spends her days writing like she's running out of time, binging Critical Role on Youtube and GBBO on Netflix, and baking the world's best chocolate chip cookies.

CASS MAREN

Cass Maren is a U.S. author of fantasy adventures steeped in rich world-building. Her depth of imagination and extensive studies of history and lore, mix realism and the ethereal into her immersive fantasy worlds.

Born and raised in the sweltering wilds of Florida, Cass has been sharing her love of storytelling since she could hold a pencil. She shares her passion for life and adventure with her husband, Nick and their two pups. When not writing, she channels her creativity into photography, design and painfully curated aesthetics.

Writing is her lifeblood, and she feels most at home with a blank page, a rainy day, and cup of hot tea. Her greatest wish is to share her stories with the world, in hopes that they can bring as much joy to someone as they bring to her.

C.M. MCCANN

C.M. McCann is a US based YA Fantasy author with a love for creating. Whether through dance, or words, or even candles, telling stories is her passion. From a young age, she's lived within the worlds of others, and it wasn't long before she started to spin her own.

When not writing, you can find her at home with one of her ever-rotating hobbies, or spending time with her small family. Of Fate & Fury is her first publication.

MADDIE JENSEN

Maddie is an author from Sydney, Australia. She has been reading and writing from a very young age, and is particularly invested in complex characters, healthy relationships, and well-written female protagonists. She's the oldest of three siblings and the owner of two very cute bunnies called Kenobi and Kylo. She has a Bachelor of Arts in Journalism, though she works in administration. *Blood of Queens* is her debut novel, though she has been featured in several anthologies since 2018.

L.E. REINER

L.E. Reiner is a gothic romance/high fantasy author who started her writing career in the film industry. After graduating with a BFA in filmmaking and working in Los Angeles as a screenwriter, L.E. decided to follow her passion of writing novels. She is an award-winning screenwriter and filmmaker and is currently writing book three of four in her high fantasy series—Divine Beings.

As a child, her mother used to read her stories by Edgar Allen Poe, which ignited her passion for gothic horror and romance. This carried over into her filmmaking career with the production of the short film, Annabel: A Story of Possession, and television pilot, The Town of Monroeville. Her gothic romance novels include, debut novel, The House of Mad, and (upcoming) The Garden of Wilted Roses.

KAYLA WHITTLE

Kayla Whittle works as an acquisitions editor at a medical publisher. She has previously had stories published in *Luna Station Quarterly* and *The Colored Lens*. She also has stories in the anthologies *Beyond the Veil* by Ghost Orchid Press, *Exquisite Poison* by Phantom House Press, and *Eros & Thanatos* by Quill & Crow Publishing House. One of her stories has also been featured on Flash Fiction Podcast.

Most often she can be found on Instagram @caughtbetweenthepages or on Twitter @kaylawhitwrites. When not writing, she's usually busy reading or planning her next Disney vacation. She currently resides in New Jersey.

Ingram Content Group UK Ltd.
Milton Keynes UK
UKHW040640190323
418778UK00019B/265/J

9 781734 826586